*continued . . .*

*published by Signet

# Black Star

★

ROBERT
GANDT

A SIGNET BOOK

SIGNET
Published by New American Library, a division of
Penguin Group (USA) Inc., 375 Hudson Street,
New York, New York 10014, U.S.A.
Penguin Books Ltd, 80 Strand,
London WC2R 0RL, England
Penguin Books Australia Ltd, 250 Camberwell Road,
Camberwell, Victoria 3124, Australia
Penguin Books Canada Ltd, 10 Alcorn Avenue,
Toronto, Ontario, Canada M4V 3B2
Penguin Books (N.Z.) Ltd, Cnr Rosedale and Airborne Roads,
Albany, Auckland 1310, New Zealand

Penguin Books Ltd, Registered Offices:
80 Strand, London WC2R 0RL, England

First published by Signet, an imprint of New American Library,
a division of Penguin Group (USA) Inc.

First Printing, November 2003
10 9 8 7 6 5 4 3 2 1

For Brad Gandt,
fellow flyer, adventurer, super son

## ACKNOWLEDGMENTS

I have learned not to be surprised when my literary conjectures come close to the truth. While the Black Star stealth jet is entirely a product of the author's imagination, much of the associated technology either is under development or has been hypothesized by observers of the aerospace business.

The support team that nudged the first two Brick Maxwell novels to publication has again worked its magic. A salute and thanks go to fellow conspirator and fighter pilot Lieutenant Commander Allen "Zoomie" Baker, for his help with technical and literary matters. Another round of thanks to my editor, Doug Grad, whose enthusiasm for military fiction makes him a great partner. To my literary agent, Alice Martell, of the Martell Agency, a big hug and thanks again.

A special salute to the real-life heroes in the cockpits and on the flight decks and in the field who are confronting our nation's enemies.

"The guy you don't see will kill you."
*Brigadier General Robin Olds, USAF*

"In war nothing is impossible, provided you use audacity."
*General George S. Patton, USA*

"Nothing is true in tactics."
*Commander Randy Cunningham, USN*

# CHAPTER ONE

# DYNASTY ONE

*South China Sea*
*1515, Wednesday, 10 September*

*Something isn't right.*

The thought kept buzzing like a gnat in Captain Laura Quimby's head. Again she peered into the monochrome green display.

Nothing. The sky was still empty. No one out there except Dynasty One and the shooters flying cover for him.

Quimby removed her glasses and tossed them onto the console. She was getting a bad feeling about this. Something didn't compute.

"He's transmitting again," said First Lieutenant Pete Clegg, the Raven sitting at the console next to her. "Same guy, south coast of Hainan."

"What are the linguists getting on him?"

"It sounds like ground-controlled intercept stuff. Like he's vectoring an airborne client."

*Intercept*? The thought sent a rush of uneasiness through Quimby. "What client? What are we missing? Do you see anything out there?"

Clegg stared at his own display and shook his head.

"Nothing in Dynasty's threat sector. A couple of bogeys over Hainan—looks like Flankers out of Lingshui. Too far away to be a factor."

Quimby nodded. She was seeing the same thing. Flankers were Russian-built SU-27 fighters. They were fast and dangerous, but this pair was out of range. There were no radar targets in the South China Sea except the four Navy shooters from the _Reagan_, and the jetliner—Dynasty One—carrying Li Hou-sheng, the President of the Republic of China.

On Quimby's display they looked like symbols in a computer game, little yellow triangles all pointed northwest toward Taiwan. The four F/A-18E Super Hornets were in a wide combat spread above and on either side of the Airbus A-300.

Nothing else. No intruders, no uninvited guests.

She tilted back in her high padded stool and gazed around the red-lighted cabin. Pete Clegg and First Lieutenant Matt Ricchi, her two fellow Ravens—electronic-warfare officers—were hunched over their consoles. All thirty crew members of the RC-135 Rivet Joint reconnaissance jet—Ravens, linguists, mission coordinators, air intelligence analysts—were preoccupied with tracking Dynasty One.

Another wave of uncertainty descended upon Laura Quimby. How many surveillance missions had she flown along the coast of China? Thirty-some, and they had all been predictable, routine. Sometimes the Chinese liked to put fighters up just to let you know they could tag you when they wanted to. They might make a couple of head fakes with their Flankers, or even with the old F-7 fighters, variants of the Russian MiG-21 Fishbed. It was a game they played, nothing more.

Or so it had been until this morning at 1115 hours.

That was the moment when Li Hou-sheng took the podium at the Southeast Asian Nations conference in Kuala Lumpur and delivered a shock to all of Asia. Henceforth, he declared to the delegates, Taiwan was a free and sovereign country. Reunification with the communist government of mainland China was no longer a consideration.

Li's announcement had the approximate effect, Quimby decided, of sticking a lighted cigar up a bull's ass. Anyone with a memory knew that Beijing would never accept the notion that Taiwan was anything but an unruly province of mainland China. Despite their differences, Taiwan would always be a part of the People's Republic of China. If necessary, the PRC would use force to ensure that.

The United States, which had long urged both sides to work toward a peaceful reunification, was caught in the middle. To discourage any overt action against Li's jet, the USS *Ronald Reagan*, deployed in the South China Sea, was ordered to supply fighter escort for Dynasty One during its flight back to Taipei. For four hundred miles, the route paralleled the Chinese coastline. When the jet was within fighter range of Taiwan, ROC F-16s would take over and escort the Airbus the rest of the way into Taipei.

"Did you see that?" asked Clegg.

"Did I see what?"

"A contact. Zero-four-zero from Dynasty One, about seventy miles."

Quimby slid her glasses back onto her nose and peered into her display. She didn't see anything. Spurious traces were nothing unusual for these sensors. The scanners on the RC-135 were so sensitive, crews liked to say, they could detect birds crapping on a power line.

Clegg was new, still on his first deployment to Kadena. As the senior Raven, Quimby was the tactical coordinator on this mission. It was her job to sort out the spurious stuff from the real.

"Did you get an electronic ID?"

"No. One sweep, very faint, and it was gone."

"Sun spots. You get that sometimes in late afternoon."

Clegg looked dubious. "Think we ought to alert the shooters?"

Quimby thought for a second. Everyone was jumpy enough. No sense in transmitting alerts if you didn't have data.

"No. Not unless we have a valid target."

"Deep Throat, this is Runner One-one. What's the picture?"

"No change, Runner," came the voice of the controller in the RC-135. "Picture still clear. You guys are alone out there."

From the cockpit of his F/A-18E Super Hornet, Commander Brick Maxwell acknowledged. It was the third time in the past twenty minutes he had checked. From his perch at 35,000 feet, he could make out the dark shadow of the Vietnamese coastline. A patchwork of puffy cumulus lay between his flight of four Hornets and the gray surface of the South China Sea.

Nearly a mile below, silhouetted against the clouds, was the slim, swept-wing shape of a jetliner.

Picture still clear. A dry run. Maybe the Chinese fighters really were staying on the ground.

"Runner One-one," said the controller on the discrete UHF frequency. "Do you still have a visual on Dynasty One?

"Affirmative," answered Maxwell. "Nine o'clock low, three miles."

"That's your guy. He'll switch to Manila Control now, maintaining flight level three-five-oh."

It was a pain in the butt, flying fighter cover for an airplane with whom you weren't talking. The Airbus had only commercial VHF—very high frequency—radios. Though the Hornets were equipped with VHF in addition to the standard military UHF—the ultrahigh frequency band—they were deliberately not communicating with the Airbus. Without question, the Chinese were eavesdropping today on the VHF band.

Watching the jetliner carve through the afternoon sky toward Taiwan, Maxwell wondered how Li's declaration would play out. Would China try to take Taiwan by force, as it had long threatened?

*God help us*, he thought. Another war. And the worst kind—a Hatfield–McCoy feud between people of the same blood—who hated each other's guts. Each equipped with enough high-tech weapons to obliterate the other.

The USS *Reagan* was in the line of fire from both sides.

The thought made Maxwell uneasy. He kept his eye on the Airbus as it continued along the airway northward. Another five hundred miles, then the Taiwanese F-16s would show up to escort Dynasty One the rest of the way. He'd be off the hook.

Li Hou-sheng wasn't much of a drinker. Seldom did he take more than a sip of wine at dinner or a glass of champagne on a special occasion.

Today was such an occasion. He turned to the others in the forward cabin of the jetliner and raised his glass. "To Taiwan," he said in a hearty voice. "To the sovereign Republic of China."

The others—three cabinet ministers, the Vice Premier, a dozen members of the legislative Yuan, and Madame Li, his wife of eighteen years—all raised their glasses, but not with enthusiasm. In muted voices they repeated, "To the sovereign Republic of China."

Li could see the uneasiness in the legislators' faces. They looked like witnesses to an execution. He had deliberately kept them uninformed about his plan to declare Taiwan's independence at the SEA conference. Now they were indignant, angry, frightened.

In particular, Li could feel the antagonism of George Tseng, the former leader of the opposition Kuomintang party. Tseng had gone through the motions of toasting, but he quickly set his glass aside. Now he was giving Li a baleful look. His champagne was untouched.

Tseng was a problem, Li reflected. It had been a mistake naming him to the post of Vice Premier—the second most important job in the Yuan, Taiwan's legislative body. After the bitterly close election, Li wanted to demonstrate that he was reaching out to all the factions in Taiwan—even quarrelsome opposition members like Tseng.

Now Tseng was one of Li's most virulent critics. It was Tseng and the Premier, Franklin Huang, who led the noisy pro-Beijing faction—those who wanted to negotiate Taiwan's return to the stewardship of mainland China.

Tseng was glowering at him. "You have destroyed Taiwan," he said.

A hush fell over the cabin. Li felt the eyes of the others on him. Be calm, he told himself. It was critical that the others not be infected with Tseng's negativism. "As usual, Tseng, you miss the point. Taiwan has always been a free country. I have simply made it official."

"China will never permit Taiwan to claim independence. It means war."

"You sound like a mouthpiece for Beijing. We've been hearing that same threat for fifty years."

"It is no longer a threat. After what you've done, China will take Taiwan by force."

Li shook his head, smiling. "I know it's difficult for you, but you should try not to be hysterical. The communists are incompetent, but they're not crazy. They realize that Taiwan has a powerful defense force, and that we have an even more powerful ally."

Tseng scoffed. "The Americans? Are you so naive as to

think the United States will alienate its favored trading partner—the People's Republic of China—over little Taiwan?"

Li nodded, liking the way this was going. In a concilia-
tory voice he said, "Tell me, what do you think the American response to today's declaration will be?"

"They will abandon us. At this very minute we are in danger of attack. The Americans have washed their hands of
us."

"Very interesting," said Li. It was the moment he had
been waiting for. He tossed down the remainder of his
champagne, then strolled over to the nearest cabin window.
With one hand he slid open the plastic shade over the window. Sunlight streamed into the cabin.

He motioned to Tseng. "Look up there. Tell me what you
see."

Wearing a sour expression, Tseng went to the window. He
peered outside, squinting against the intense sunlight.

Then he saw it. He jumped back from the window as if
he'd been zapped with a cattle prod. "Fighters! There are
fighters out there. We are being attacked by—"

"Super Hornets," said Li. "From the USS *Reagan.*
They're not attacking, they're protecting us. Now what is
this drivel you're telling us, Tseng? Do you still think the
Americans have abandoned us?"

The massive shape of the three-engine U.S. Air Force
KC-10 tanker filled Maxwell's windshield. He eased the
throttles back a notch, letting the Hornet slip backward, dis-
engaging the refueling probe from the drogue.

As he slid to a high perch off the tanker's left wing, his
wingman, B.J. Johnson, nestled herself into position on the
drogue.

Still on station with Dynasty One was Maxwell's second
section, Pearly Gates and Flash Gordon, who had already re-
fueled from the tanker. This would be their last in-flight re-

fueling session before they turned the escort duty over to the F-16s.

Maxwell watched Johnson's Hornet plug in to the KC-10, slurping up fuel like a horse at a spring. Tanking was a fact of life for a Hornet pilot. Even with the larger tanks and longer range of the new F/A-18 Super Hornet, the jet still required in-flight refueling in order to reach an objective and return. Plugging in to the tanker was as critical a skill as landing aboard a carrier.

When Johnson was topped off, she slid back from the tanker and joined Maxwell's left wing. The two jets climbed away from the KC-10 and turned back toward the Airbus, twenty miles away. In the distance he could see the slick profiles of Gates's and Gordon's Hornets, still on station, two thousand feet above the jetliner.

Three hundred more miles, then they'd pick up the ROC F-16s. They would turn back to the south, pay one more visit to the tanker, then they'd land aboard the *Reagan*. End of mission.

Still, Maxwell couldn't get over this nagging feeling. Where were the Chinese fighters? Even before the inflammatory announcement by the Taiwanese President, the Chinese had been willing to send up jets just for the hell of it. Now that they had a reason to be hostile, they were staying low.

It didn't make sense.

With that thought, Maxwell's eyes went again to the Airbus. The A-300 was a wide-body, twin-engine jet, cruising just above a puffy cloud layer at .82 Mach. It would make a nice fat, vulnerable target for—

*What was that?* Behind the Airbus, a mile or so in trail. Something—a glimmer, a shadow against the clouds, a reflection.

It was gone.

Maxwell strained his eyes, peering intently at the empty

sky. Nothing. He went to his MFD—multifunction display—checking radar and infrared returns. Still nothing.

He was getting jumpy. He'd be glad when they were finished babysitting this airliner and returned to the steel deck of the *Reagan*. He was beginning to imagine—

*Something else.* Something odd down there.

No, he wasn't imagining.

A black puff, like a spurt of exhaust, spat from the Airbus's right engine.

Maxwell felt the hair stand up on the back of his neck. The A-300's engine nacelle seemed to expand in size, swelling like a balloon. In the next instant, a sphere of orange flame appeared around the engine, then engulfed the entire wing.

As if in slow motion, the long tapered wing folded back, then cleaved through the tail surfaces of the Airbus. Sheared aluminum fluttered like confetti in the wake of the dismembered jet.

Maxwell stared in disbelief. The Airbus was rolling to the right, its nose slipping downward, spewing a trail of flame and smoke and debris. The big jet was descending in a corkscrew path toward the sea.

The voice of the Rivet Joint controller burst through the earphones in his helmet. "Runner One-one, answer up. This is Deep Throat. We just lost the squawk on Dynasty One, and he's not talking to us. Have you got a visual on him?"

Maxwell's eyes were still fixed on the jetliner. It was breaking up, shedding large pieces as it tumbled toward the ocean. He shook his head, still unable to believe what he was seeing.

"Runner One-one, do you copy Deep Throat? What's going on out there?"

Maxwell keyed the mike button on the throttle. "Dynasty One just blew up. He's going into the water."

Several seconds passed. The controller's voice was

strained. "Maybe we didn't copy right, Runner. Sounded like you said—"

"Something happened. His number two engine blew up and took the wing off."

"Are you engaged?" The controller was asking the obvious. *Are hostile aircraft involved?*

Maxwell had already swung the nose of his Hornet toward the empty sky where the Airbus had been. He glanced at the MFD, then waited for several sweeps of the radar. Still nothing. "Negative. Runner One-one, clean. Runner One-three, do you have a picture?"

"One-three's clean," answered Pearly Gates.

"One-two's clean," called B.J. Johnson.

"One-four's clean," dittoed Flash Gordon.

All clean. No one painting a bogey in their midst.

"Anyone got a visual?"

Nothing. No bogeys. The sky was empty.

"Shit," said the controller, her voice cracking. "What happened?"

Maxwell's eyes were still sweeping the sky. Four miles below, he could see Dynasty One plunging toward the South China Sea.

He told the truth. "I don't know."

# CHAPTER TWO

# OPENING SHOTS

*Taipei, Taiwan*
*1640, Wednesday, 10 September*

"Thank you, Mr. President. Yes, we will take your suggestion under advisement."

Charlotte Soong hung up the phone and turned to the assembled members of her cabinet. *Her cabinet.* The immensity of the new role still caused her to have palpitations. Until an hour and a half ago, she had been Vice President of the Republic of China, which, in the politics of Taiwan, meant almost nothing. Now she was the head of state. As never before in her life, she needed to display strength.

"The President of the United States sends his condolences," she said to the group, which included the three senior officers of Taiwan's military forces. "He joins us in mourning the death of President Li and his party."

"Never mind his condolences," said Franklin Huang, the Premier and head of the legislative Yuan. "What does he counsel you to do?"

Charlotte Soong tilted her chin and gazed at Huang. In the weeks since the election of Li and his running mate, Charlotte Soong, Franklin Huang had made no secret of his contempt for her. He was vocal in his opinion that a woman should have no role in Taiwan's affairs of state.

"He urges restraint," she said. "He says there is no credible evidence that the People's Republic had any involvement in President Li's death."

"Does he offer an explanation of why one of our newest airliners should suddenly blow up while it was flying near the Chinese coast? Beneath the eyes of the American fighter pilots who were supposed to protect it? Does he think it was an act of God?"

At this, several ministers, including Leung Tsi-chien, Minister of Defense, gave a derisive chuckle. Leung was another who had criticized Charlotte Soong's nomination as Vice President.

An uneasy silence fell over the ministers. She could feel the tension in the room. Huang was busy scribbling on his notepad. Next to him, Leung was whispering something in the ear of Ma Wang, the crotchety old Foreign Minister. Ma was one of the few remaining officials in Taiwan who had been born in mainland China.

*They're up to something*, she told herself. Leung and Huang were schemers with a history of plotting coups in the government. *What are they up to?*

In the next minute she knew. Huang lowered his notepad and stepped forward. He glanced at Leung, who nodded.

Huang cleared his throat. "Mrs. Soong, we have—"

"Mind your manners, Premier Huang. You will address me as 'Madame President.'"

Huang blinked as if he'd been slapped. "Um, yes, if you insist. In fact, that is the subject we wish to discuss."

"You are taking much too long to do it. Please get to the point."

Huang blinked again, then glanced over to Leung.

Leung took over. "Madame President, in this moment of crisis, it is the consensus of the cabinet that you should give consideration to . . . ah, yielding the authority of your office."

Charlotte Soong kept her face expressionless. She was right. They were up to no good. "Make yourself clear, Minister Leung. What are you suggesting? That I resign from the office of President?"

"It is well known that you were chosen by Li Hou-sheng to be his Vice President because you are a woman, and the widow of a popular statesman."

She nodded. That much was true. Her popularity had soared in the two years since Kenneth Soong, her husband and the minority party leader, was assassinated. That Beijing ordered the murder she had no doubt, but the killers were never apprehended. She had continued her husband's cause, writing articles, making public appearances on behalf of the party he founded, and eventually running for office.

She focused on Leung. "Li Hou-sheng chose me as his successor knowing that I was qualified to be the head of state."

"You were chosen in order to ensure his election. There was never any thought that you would succeed him."

"Never any thought by you, you mean." She peered around the room, pausing to look each of the ministers in the eye. "Let me remind you, I am the only constitutionally elected official in this room. Each of you is an appointee who serves at my pleasure." She fixed her eyes again on Leung. "Leung Tsi-chien, your post as Minister of Defense is the most critical position in my cabinet. If I do not have your full loyalty, I must insist on your immediate resignation."

Leung's eyes flashed, and he stepped forward. "Resignation? This is preposterous. You have no right to—"

"Your opportunity to resign has passed. You may consider yourself dismissed. You will leave the cabinet room immediately."

Leung's chest puffed out, but before he could protest he saw Colonel Tsu, the President's chief of security, moving toward him from across the room. The unsmiling colonel wore an automatic pistol at his hip.

Leung knew he was defeated. He turned to fire a final menacing scowl at Charlotte Soong. "You have made a severe mistake. I promise you, you will regret this action." As Tsu seized his elbow, he wheeled and stormed out of the cabinet room.

She waited until he was gone. She turned her gaze on Franklin Huang. "And you, Premier Huang? Must I ask for a resignation from you?"

Huang was a famous bully in Taiwanese politics. He had been a formidable adversary of her husband. Appointing him as Taiwan's Premier had been Li's idea. It was supposed to be a gesture of reconciliation with the opposing political faction. It had been a serious mistake.

Now she would have to deal with him.

Huang met her gaze. She could see that he was weighing his options. After a moment, he shook his head. "No, Madame President. You have made your position clear."

She looked around the table. "Any others? Speak now, or your opportunity will have passed."

The cabinet members exchanged uncertain glances. Finally, old Ma Wang, senior of the ministers, spoke up. "Madame President, you must understand our concerns. Most of us believe that an act of war has been perpetrated on us."

"And so do I, Minister Ma."

Ma peered at her curiously. "But an act of war against Taiwan should not go unanswered."

"You are quite correct. It should not."

Ma's eyes narrowed. "Perhaps you can enlighten us, Madame President."

Charlotte Soong nodded to one of the uniformed officers,

General Wu Hsin-chieh, who was the air force Chief of Staff and the senior military officer of Taiwan. The general stepped around the conference table and pulled down a wall-length map at the end of the room. The map covered Taiwan, the Taiwan Strait, and the coast of mainland China.

With a long pointer, the General tapped an area on the mainland. "Here," he said, then tapped three more places, "here, here, and here, according to our latest reconnaissance, the PLA is assembling an amphibious assault force of at least eighty thousand troops."

At this, a buzz of excited conversation erupted among the ministers. It was their worst nightmare. "Amphibious force?" said Ma Wang. "That can mean only one thing. They intend to invade us."

General Wu nodded.

"But we must do something."

The General didn't reply. He nodded to Charlotte Soong, who stepped in front of the map and faced the ministers. "You are correct again, Minister. We must do something. And so we shall."

*USS* Ronald Reagan

Darkness was settling over the South China Sea.

Maxwell rolled his Hornet wings-level in the groove. In the dwindling light, the gray mass of the USS *Reagan* filled his windshield. At the port edge of the deck, he could see the Fresnel lens—the optical glide slope indicator. The yellow "ball" was between the green datum lights on the lens, indicating that Maxwell's Hornet was on a precise descent path to the deck.

"Hornet ball, five-point-four."

"Roger, ball."

The contract was made. Maxwell was reporting to the LSO—landing signal officer—that he had a visual reference on the ball, and that his remaining fuel was 5,400 pounds. With his terse reply, the LSO acknowledged that he was controlling the Hornet in the groove.

Maxwell knew the voice—Lieutenant Commander Big Mac MacFarquhar, the air wing LSO. As the senior LSO aboard the *Reagan*, Big Mac had the job of supervising all the squadron LSOs.

"A *lii—ittle powerrrrr*," called Big Mac in his soothing LSO voice. Maxwell nudged the throttles forward, adding a tiny increment of thrust.

The Hornet swept over the ramp. Maxwell kept his eyes fixed on the ball, fine-tuning his control movements, keeping the ball in the center of the lens. The Hornet slammed down on the deck. Maxwell felt himself rammed forward into the harness straps as the tailhook engaged an arresting wire.

A good pass. Not perfect, but he knew he'd snagged the three wire. Of the four arresting wires strung across the carrier's landing deck, number three was the target. It was called a *tweener* pass—somewhere in between a fair and an OK landing grade. The fact that he had snagged the three wire would weigh in his favor as the LSOs assigned his grade.

Following the yellow-shirts' lighted wands, he taxied the Hornet to the starboard forward deck. Behind him in rapid succession the other members of his flight—B.J. Johnson, Pearly Gates, Flash Gordon—landed and exited the wires.

He was still climbing out of the cockpit when he saw Bullet Alexander, his squadron executive officer. He was wearing the standard-issue float-coat survival vest and the Mickey Mouse cranial protector that was required equipment on the flight deck.

"Let me guess," said Maxwell, stepping down onto the steel deck. "CAG told you to get us down to the intel office for debriefing." *CAG* was an extinct title that stood for *Com-*

*mander, Air Group.* In the Navy's tradition of retaining anti-
quated terms, it still applied to the Air Wing Commander.

Alexander kept a straight face. "Not exactly. What he said
was—and I'm quoting verbatim here—'Tell those pecker-
heads to get their sorry asses down here on the double.'"

Maxwell shrugged. No surprise. The world was waiting
to hear why the President of Taiwan, while enjoying the protection of fighters from the *Reagan*'s air wing, now resided
at the bottom of the South China Sea. Phones would be ring-
ing at every military base from the USS *Reagan* to the White
House.

He waited for his other three pilots to climb down from
their jets. Wearing grim expressions, the pilots of his flight
joined him. B.J. Johnson, who was the only woman pilot in
the Roadrunner squadron, looked like she was going to a funeral.

With Maxwell in the lead, they descended the ladder to
the O-3 level, then followed the long passageway to the intel
office. No one spoke. Each pilot was alone with his
thoughts. Gone was the usual jubilation, the wisecracking,
the adrenaline rush of trapping back aboard a carrier at sea.

Gates broke the silence. "Are they gonna court-martial
us?"

Maxwell looked over his shoulder. "What for?"

"We were supposed to get the Taiwanese President home
in one piece. We blew it."

B.J. Johnson whirled on Gates. "What do you mean? Our
job was to intercept bogeys." She jabbed a finger at Gates.
"Did you tag a bogey?"

"No."

"Nobody else did either. The goddamn Airbus just exploded. You saw it. It wasn't our fault." She turned to
Maxwell, her voice cracking. "Isn't that right, Skipper?"

Maxwell nodded. He could see the frustration and anger
in all their faces. He gave B.J. a nudge on down the pas-

sageway. "That's right. But don't be surprised if nobody believes us."

*Taiwan Strait*

Commander Lei Fu-Sheng, captain of the Taiwanese frigate *Kai Yang*, watched in stunned fascination as the Harpoon missiles leaped from their launchers. He had never witnessed an actual firing of the Harpoons, and he was unprepared for the spectacle. He could see the plume of fire from each missile as it arced into the darkness. Against the black void of the Taiwan Strait, they looked like fire-tailed comets from hell.

The RGM-84L Harpoon missile had been delivered by the United States to the Taiwanese navy as an antiship weapon. It hadn't taken long for clever Taiwanese engineers to conclude that their newly acquired maritime weapon could be reconfigured with different warheads and guidance software and made to behave like a land-attack Tomahawk cruise missile—a critical weapon that had been denied them by their American patrons. In its new role, the Harpoon could be directed against any coastal target, land or sea.

Including amphibious assault-force depots.

As the first salvo of Harpoons flashed into the night, Commander Lei caught a flicker of light off to port. It was several miles distant, barely distinguishable in the inky blackness, but he knew it was the *Kai Yang*'s sister ship, *Han Yang*, firing her own complement of Harpoons. Taiwan possessed a total of four Cheng Kung–class guided missile frigates—all former U.S. Navy destroyers of the Perry class—and each was now on station in the Taiwan Strait, firing missiles at Chinese amphibious force depots.

"Battery one reports all missiles fired, Captain," said the fire control officer over his sound-powered speaker. "Standing by battery two."

Peering into the blackness, Lei tried to imagine the low-flying Harpoons skimming the sea toward the mainland. Retrofitted with GPS—global positioning system—guidance units, the surface-skimming Harpoons were autonomous weapons, requiring no further input from their owners. But they were subsonic missiles, nearly fifteen feet in length, vulnerable to intercept by radar-guided surface-to-air missiles as well as conventional antiaircraft batteries. When matched against the instruments of sophisticated warfare, the Harpoon was a primitive weapon. Tonight's success hinged on surprise—and the Air Force's ability to take out the air defense sites.

Lei barked a command into his sound-powered telephone. "Fire battery two."

Three seconds later, another blaze of light, this one from the aft quad launcher. A salvo of four more Harpoons, one after the other, leaped from the tubes.

Lei kept his eyes on the orange plumes until each missile had vanished in the murk. The *Kai Yang*'s primary mission was completed. The Harpoons were away. They would find their way to the targets—or be destroyed en route.

Commander Lei still could not overcome his astonishment. Taiwan attacking China! In the scramble to gather his crew, arm his ship, and rush the *Kai Yang* to sea, Lei had not taken the time to reflect on the gravity of the situation. Now, with his missiles soaring toward their targets on the mainland, he felt himself filled with a mixture of awe and fear.

Fourteen years. That was how long he had been an officer in the Taiwanese navy, and for his entire career he had prepared for this moment. In every hypothetical battle scenario, he had fought the People's Liberation Navy for control of the Taiwan Strait. In each instance, it was assumed that the PLA navy would strike first.

Now this. A preemptive strike by Taiwan. *Why?*

Staring into the black void, Lei tried to make sense of the

situation. The President's plane had gone down. That much he knew. Was China responsible? Probably.

*So who ordered the strike?*

Taiwan's politicians, at least those in the current ruling party, were known for their exaggerated sense of caution. Although Madame Soong, the Vice President, was the acting head of state, Lei could not imagine her giving such an order. Lei had met her once, during the inaugural ceremonies, and though she seemed attractive and bright enough for a woman, it was inconceivable that she could function as Commander-in-Chief. It had to be one of the cabinet ministers. Leung? Or perhaps Wu Hsin-chieh, the air force Chief of Staff.

*God help us*, thought Lei.

In the darkness over the strait, he could barely discern the outline of the lead destroyer escort, on a parallel course a thousand meters to starboard. His second escort was in trail, displaced another thousand meters to port and out of view. Except for the two hand-me-down escort vessels, the *Kai Yang* was on her own in a sea filled with PLA navy warships. The Taiwan Strait would soon become a killing field.

As if tuned to Lei's thoughts, the officer of the deck, a young lieutenant, broke the silence. "*Han Yang* reports a sonar contact, Captain."

Lei's attention snapped back to the bridge. *Han Yang*, the *Kai Yang*'s missile-firing sister ship, was on station five kilometers southeast. "Get the range and bearing," he said to the officer of the deck. "Be quick about it."

"They say it's a momentary contact. Possibly spurious."

Lei shook his head. There was no such thing as a spurious contact. Not tonight. They were all real as far as he was concerned. "Keep the channel open. Tell them we want the contact data."

Lei silently cursed the obsolete command and control system that was common to *Kai Yang* and *Han Yang*, as well as

most of the frigates in the Taiwanese navy. Every modern
navy in the world, including the PLA navy, possessed real-
time data-linked exchange of information between units.
Every navy except Taiwan's. It was another item of super-
sophisticated equipment the United States chose to withhold
from them. It meant that whatever *Han Yang*'s captain was
seeing on his sonar displays would have to be relayed by
radio to *Kai Yang*.

The seconds ticked past as Lei waited for details. He
paced his narrow bridge, staring into the darkness. *What
kind of contact was it?* His own sonar operators weren't
picking up any returns. *A submarine?* China had four new
Russian-built Project 877 Kilo-class submarines as well as
half a dozen indigenous Ming-class boats. The Kilo class,
with their diesel-electric drives and anechoic tile coating,
were the stealthiest and most difficult to hunt of all undersea
vessels. They were even quieter than the newer Xia-class
nuclear attack submarines. The Kilo class emitted almost no
acoustical signature.

*Don't let it be a Kilo*, thought Lei. Not yet. They had just
begun to fight.

He glanced at the luminous face of his watch. His Harpoon missiles were five minutes from their targets. Only
thirty kilometers. What an irony it would be if *Kai Yang*
were sunk before its own missiles had reached their targets.

"Active contact," the OOD reported. "*Han Yang* reports a
target—definitely a submarine—zero-three-zero degrees,
four thousand meters."

Lei felt a cold chill run through him. That put the contact
between *Han Yang* and *Kai Yang*. His own sonar array was
still showing nothing.

It had to be a Kilo. If it were a noisy Ming class, they
would have identified it already. *Whom was he tracking*?

In the next minute, he knew. To the southwest, an orange
glow lit the blackened sea. For several seconds, Lei could

see the line of the horizon as a pulse of flame boiled into the sky. In the glow of the fireball, he saw a familiar silhouette.

*Han Yang.* In its death pyre, the guided-missile frigate was tearing itself apart. As its ordnance magazines exploded, flaming debris pierced the sky like roman candles.

Stunned, Lei stared at the blazing spectacle. Within seconds, *Han Yang*'s bow separated from the hull and slipped from view into the churning sea. Her destroyer escorts were racing like greyhounds to the location of the original contact.

"Sonar contact, Captain. Two-two-zero, five thousand meters."

Lei's attention went to the repeater display at his own console. Yes, there it was. He could see it winking yellow in the green screen. That distinctive seven-bladed propeller signature identified it as a Kilo class.

It had just torpedoed the *Han Yang.*

"Deploy decoys," Lei ordered. "Commence acoustical jamming."

"Aye, sir."

The sonar decoys were designed to simulate the signatures of *Kai Yang* and her escorts. If the submarine put more torpedoes in the water, they might be fooled into tracking the decoys.

Or they might not. Lei had never placed much faith in defensive devices like decoys and acoustical jammers. The best way to deal with a killer submarine was to engage him. Put him on the defensive. Then kill him.

"Ready torpedo tubes."

"Aye, Captain. Torpedoes loaded and ready."


*USS* Ronald Reagan

It was going worse than Boyce expected. He gnawed on his cigar, keeping his silence while he watched the debriefing of the Hornet pilots.

"What happened to the Airbus?" asked the Battle Group Commander, a rear admiral named Jack Hightree.

Brick Maxwell answered. "I don't know, Admiral."

For several seconds, a silence fell over the flag conference space. Along one side of the long steel table sat the other three pilots, Gates, Gordon, and Johnson, all looking like prisoners on death row. Next to the Admiral was the flag intelligence officer, an owlish-faced commander named Harvey Wentz.

Boyce could see the strain of the long mission in Maxwell's face. His eyes were red-rimmed, the lines of the oxygen mask still etched on his face.

Captain Red Boyce was the *Reagan*'s Air Wing Commander. He remembered how he had stuck his neck out several months ago, picking Maxwell to be the skipper of the VFA-36 Roadrunners over half a dozen more experienced candidates. He knew that Maxwell was regarded by many in the air wing to be a carpetbagger—a former test pilot and astronaut who hadn't paid his dues.

As it turned out, he'd been right about Maxwell. Since taking command of the Roadrunners, he had distinguished himself by shooting down three MiGs and leading two successful alpha strikes against Middle Eastern targets.

Maxwell was the kind of officer who knew how to follow orders—but knew how to call an audible change when they got in the way of the mission. He was the officer Boyce tapped for the most delicate jobs.

Like escorting Dynasty One.

"I don't get it, Commander Maxwell," said Wentz, the intelligence officer. "You were there watching the jetliner go down, and you say you don't know what happened?"

"That's exactly what I said. I saw the right engine explode. I can't explain what caused that to happen."

"Didn't you see anything suspicious, a visual or electronic return in the vicinity?"

He paused for a moment, remembering. "Yes, I thought I saw something—but it was so momentary I couldn't be sure it was real."

Wentz looked like a hound sniffing the air. "Oh? What was it?"

"Something in my peripheral view. Just a flicker, maybe a reflection on the canopy. When I looked again it was gone."

"Why didn't you report it?" Wentz's voice had an accusatory edge to it.

"There was no time. A couple of seconds later, the Airbus blew up. The four of us did a sweep of the sector. There was nothing out there. Nothing visual, nothing on the radar. The Rivet Joint confirmed it."

Wentz scribbled on his legal pad. "Let me get this straight, Commander. You're saying you think something out there—some spurious target you lost contact with—may have shot down the Airbus?"

"What the hell is this?" Maxwell snapped. "A debriefing or an inquisition?"

"You said you saw something, but you failed to report it."

Maxwell was leaning forward in his chair, nearly close enough to seize Wentz's windpipe. Boyce gave him a kick under the table. "Knock it off," he said to Wentz. "Everybody chill out for a moment. Brick and his flight just finished a tough mission and we're all a little uptight."

From the end of the table, Admiral Hightree said, "This may save us a lot of trouble." He slid a two-inch-thick document across the table. Its cover bore the title "Uncontained Fan Jet Failures."

A fan jet was a high bypass engine that developed most of its thrust through the "fan," the huge front stage compressor. It was the type of power plant used on all modern jetliners.

Hightree said, "This just came in from Defense Intel. It's a study NASA put together a couple of years ago. The airline industry has had sixteen of these failures in the past decade. Most of the time when one of these big fan jets comes apart it does some damage but the jet lands okay. But in a worst-case scenario, if the shrapnel happened to rip through a fuel tank in the wing or some other vital part . . ."

"Kabloom," said Boyce.

Hightree nodded. "Once in a blue moon an airplane blows up for no good reason. Like TWA 800 in 1996. Sometimes it's an internal failure, sometimes a freak accident. Sometimes we never know."

For several seconds, no one spoke. The thick document lay on the table between them like a lab specimen.

"So that's the company line?" said Maxwell. "They're going to say Dynasty One just blew up?"

Hightree shrugged. "It's plausible."

Boyce looked at Maxwell. "You were there. Do you believe it?"

"No."

"Then I don't either." Boyce removed his cigar and looked around the room. "It had to be the ChiComs. I can't explain how, but I know in my gut the little bastards did it."

"With what, CAG?" said Pearly Gates. He and B.J. Johnson and Flash Gordon sat in a row on one side of the table. "Some kind of stealth fighter? A no-see-um missile?"

Boyce shook his head. "If we were talking about a Western country, or Russia or Israel, I'd say it was possible. China, no way. With the exception of the SU-27s they got from Russia, their homegrown fighters couldn't beat the Albanian air force."

"Maybe they've gotten technology from Russia we don't know about."

At this, Wentz came out of his funk. "That's been checked out with NSA and CIA, and they're quite certain the Russians don't have such a thing. Even if they did, we feel sure they wouldn't pass it to the Chinese."

Admiral Hightree spoke up. "The fact is, it doesn't matter what you believe. International politics will determine what happened. The United States wants to head off a war between China and Taiwan, and if it means signing off on a cockamamy accident theory, that's what they're going to do."

"What about the Taiwanese?" asked Maxwell. "Do they buy the accident theory?"

"They have no choice," said the Admiral. "Taiwan can't attack China without the support of the United States. China won't attack Taiwan as long as the United States supports Taiwan. Like it or not, we're caught in the—"

The red telephone on the bulkhead—the direct line from CIC, the Combat Information Center—was jangling.

The Admiral snatched up the phone. As he listened to the voice from CIC, his brow seemed to lower over his eyes. "Hell, yes! Send the order. Tell group ops I'm on my way to the bridge."

Even before Hightree could hang up, the voice of the bosun's mate was booming over the public address. "General Quarters! General Quarters! All hands man your battle stations. This is not a drill."

Hightree headed for the door, grabbing his float coat from the rack on the bulkhead.

"What's going on, Admiral?" asked Boyce.

"Get to your stations," said Hightree, opening the door. "Disregard everything I said about heading off a war. Missiles are launching from both sides of the strait."

"Are we in it?"

"We'll know in a few minutes. We've got bogeys inbound, seventy miles."

# CHAPTER THREE

# DREAMLAND

*Groom Lake, Nevada*
*1945, Wednesday, 10 September*

As he felt the brakes release on the 737, Dr. Raymond Lutz punched the timer on his wrist chronometer. It was something he always did for no reason except that he was an engineer and he was obsessive about such things. He wanted to know how long it took the jetliner to lift off the runway at Groom Lake.

As usual, the cabin was dark. The unmarked jet was showing no anticollision strobes, no navigation lights, no illumination outside the cockpit. The crew didn't even use the taxi lights.

Through the cabin window Lutz could make out the dim runway edge markers, which he knew were directional, visible only if you were aligned with the runway. As far as the world was concerned, this five-mile-long piece of concrete in the wilderness of Nevada didn't exist.

He watched the darkened landscape blur past the window. In the clear desert night, he could make out the silhouette of the high terrain to the west. It had once been a favorite place for snoopers until the Air Force took possession of all the high ground around the base.

The nose of the 737 rotated upward from the runway. Lutz hit the button on his timer.

"How long?" asked the man across the aisle. Lutz recognized the voice. It was Feingold, another physicist. He worked in the RAM—radar absorbent material—lab opposite Lutz's unit in the big hangar.

"Twenty-eight seconds."

Feingold chuckled. "It's the same every time, give or take a couple seconds. Isn't that interesting?"

Not especially, thought Lutz. He made a show of turning his back to the window. If he let Feingold engage him in conversation, he'd invite himself to come along to the casino, go to some shows, be his new best friend. Feingold was a jerk.

It was Friday evening, and the unmarked Boeing jet was nearly full. Back at Groom Lake, four more jetliners were lined up, waiting to depart from the five-mile-long runway, taking their passengers on the short flight back to McCarran Field in Las Vegas.

The dark hollow of the research complex dropped away from Lutz's view. The barren mountains of Nevada sprawled out beneath the night sky. He was glad to get out of the place. He was sick to death of algorithms and electrochromatic technology and jerk-face engineers like Feingold.

A sharp pain in his abdomen brought his thoughts back to the cabin of the Boeing. He shifted in his seat, rubbing his stomach with his hand.

"Want a Pepcid?" Feingold again. He was holding out a little foil package of pills. "I get that acid reflux thing sometimes myself."

"No, thanks."

"Always work for me."

Lutz turned back to the window and forced himself to ignore the discomfort in his gut. Fuck Feingold and his pills. From experience he knew how long it would take the object to transit his intestinal tract. An hour. Two at the most. It was a disgusting way to transport data, but it was efficient. He'd gotten used to it.

He hadn't planned a drop this weekend. At the morning conference of the Calypso Blue project managers, they were briefed on the incident over the Taiwan Strait. Someone had already postulated how the Taiwanese President's airplane had been downed.

That meant danger for Raymond Lutz.

Now they wanted the Calypso Blue team to come up with electronic countermeasures. For the rest of the day Lutz's team ran computer-based algorithms, searching for a technological miracle that would penetrate electrochromatic cloaking.

Lutz hated the whole process. It was the classic irrationality of war. You use your best intellect developing a bulletproof technology. When you succeed, you then waste the same intellect to defeat it. The sum of your work came to zero.

Which was why he had opted out of the game. All those high-sounding virtues—patriotism, duty, loyalty—were meaningless to him. Had his country returned his loyalty when he served as a military officer? Had they recognized his obvious brilliance by admitting him into their precious astronaut corps?

The recollection of how they treated him caused Lutz to clench his jaw muscles in anger. He owed them nothing. In fact, quite the opposite, his own government owed him an immeasurable amount, and now he was collecting.

Today had been productive, at least for Lutz. Some of the formulae his team at Groom Lake had come up with contained the seeds of potent electronic countermeasures. They were close to developing a tool that might unmask the electrochromatic process.

When he collected the results of the day's work from his eight engineers and mathematicians, he compiled them, compressed the data into a file, then copied it to a digital storage chip the size of a cashew nut. When he was finished, there was no trace of the process except the master file, which he encrypted and moved to the team's top-secret optical filing unit.

The memory chip took a different route.

Lutz waited until the last minute before he logged out of his workspace. Long ago he had learned about the concealed video camera and the two audio bugs that someone—presumably the FBI—had planted. He also presumed that such devices were planted in the workspace of every technician at the facility.

For the benefit of the single-view video, he made a show of compiling the data and storing it in the optical unit. What the camera couldn't see was the loader card that contained the chip. At the same time the data went into the optical unit, it transferred onto the chip.

In the men's room, which he knew was also video monitored, he washed his hands, brushed his teeth, and swallowed his daily glucosamine tablets—one of which was the microchip wrapped in a soft, insoluble green gel.

No publications, hardware, software, or personal data devices were allowed to leave the ultrasecret labs at the research facility. The Groom Lake facility possessed the most sophisticated security equipment outside the White House and the CIA headquarters. There were retinal identification devices, ultrasound scanners, and metal detectors so sensitive they could read the iron content in a subject's blood.

Lutz passed through them all. After he'd used his coded ID card to sign out with the last security agent, he walked across the unlit ramp and boarded the first of the five 737s.

Now his gut felt like he'd swallowed a tin can. The 737 was on the downwind leg of its approach to McCarran.

"Look at those lights," said Feingold. "Did you know Las Vegas burns more kilowatts than the rest of Nevada combined?"

"No," said Lutz. Nor did he give a damn. The 737 was flying through some low-altitude turbulence, bumping around like a truck on a desert road. He wanted to land, get rid of the goddamned chip.

He winced as the jet thumped down on the runway. When the flight attendant opened the main cabin door, Lutz was the first to deplane.

Feingold was behind him. "Hey, Ray, whaddya say we go have a drink and check out the—"

He didn't wait. Before Feingold could catch up, he was in a taxi and on his way downtown.

*USS* Ronald Reagan

After three hours at General Quarters, the *Reagan*'s captain gave the order to stand down. The inbound bogeys— SU-27 Flankers from bases in mainland China—had given the *Reagan* battle group a wide berth. While pummeling each other with missiles, both sides—China and Taiwan— were keeping a respectful distance from U.S. warships.

Maxwell was feeling the fatigue of the long mission, then the strain of the debriefing. He left the ready room and made his way to his stateroom. After he'd popped open a warm Coke, he flopped into the steel chair at his desk and powered up the Compaq notebook. Half a minute later he was logged on to the Athena net, the ship's satellite connection to the World Wide Web.

Something about the Mail Waiting icon bothered him. The way it was flashing. He had a feeling it was not good news.

*Date: 10 September*
*From: Claire.Phillips@MBS.com*
*To: SMaxwell.VFA36@USSRonaldReagan.Navy.mil*
*Subj: Unexpected dilemma*

*My dearest Sam—*
    *This is the hardest letter I have ever written. I'm*

*supposed to be a journalist who makes her living by communicating in plain English. I've agonized for three hours over this one. No matter how I say it, it doesn't come out right.*

*Something has happened. Our life—the one you and I were planning together—has changed. Here's the story. No spin, no flourishes.*

*When you and I resumed our romance last year in Dubai, I was about to be divorced from my husband, Christopher Tyrwhitt, from whom I had been separated for a year and a half. As you know, a few weeks before the divorce was to become final, I heard from Chris's boss in Sydney that Chris had been killed while on assignment in Baghdad. According to the official story from the Iraqi foreign ministry, he was shot by army guards while he was trespassing in a prohibited area. World Wide News, Chris's agency, was unable to determine the real circumstances, but the story seemed plausible, knowing Chris. No body, no funeral. I was informed that my late husband was buried in Iraq. End of story.*

*Enter Sam Maxwell. And a new life.*

*Until now. Life is stranger than fiction, Sam. One afternoon last week a man appeared in the door of my Washington office. He looked familiar, though thinner and grayer than I remembered, but when he spoke I knew instantly who it was. My husband had returned from the dead.*

*He was, quite literally, full of holes. He had been shot three times. The details of his "death" and disappearance are quite sensitive, but the U.S. government made some very complicated exchanges in order to free him from Iraq.*

*Now the hard part. I am badly disoriented. Do I love you? Yes, deeply. But I am still the wife of Chris*

*Tyrwhitt. I realize that I was wrong in some of my
judgments about him. He is not the scoundrel I
thought him to be (or at least as much of a
scoundrel). His actions in Iraq, though he is not at
liberty to discuss them in detail, were more honorable
and noble than I would have dreamed.*

*Chris is making no demands. He says that we can
proceed with the divorce if that is my wish. He also
insists that he loves me, has always loved me, and
wants to remain married. I believe him.*

*Please give me some time and space to work this
out, Sam. I no longer know up from down. What I feel
for you is real and true, but a part of me is still in
love with a ghost. I don't know if it is real or not.*

*Please understand.*

*With love,*
*Claire*

For a solid five minutes he sat motionless, staring at the
screen. The pixels on the display winked back at him like
stars in a galaxy.

*That's all they are*, he thought. *Pixels. Bytes. Microscopic
pulses of energy.* How could something so inconsequential
have the power to cause him this much pain?

He kept waiting for the anger to spew out, like steam from
a cauldron. Nothing came. There was only a deadness inside
him. He felt more alone than ever before in his life.

Claire. She had entered his life when they were both young,
still careless with their hearts. For reasons neither understood,
they went different ways, he to the space shuttle and a new
life and love; she to a career as a broadcast journalist and marriage to a dashing reporter named Chris Tyrwhitt.

Years later, when they found each other again, it seemed
like a storybook romance. He was a widower, his astronaut

wife lost in a training accident. Claire was divorcing her wastrel husband. They were more in love than ever before. It seemed too good to be true.

And so it was.

She was right about one thing, he thought. Life *was* stranger than fiction. And a hell of a lot more cruel.

For another five minutes he sat at the computer, trying to compose his jumbled thoughts. In tiny increments, the anger began to come, rising in a slow simmer. His hands returned to the keyboard. Slowly, without looking up or taking his fingers from the keys, he typed a reply.

*Date: 10 September*
*From: SMaxwell.VFA36@USSRonaldReagan.Navy.mil*
*To: Claire.Phillips@MBS.com*
*Subj: Re: Unexpected dilemma*

*Dear Mrs. Tyrwhitt—*
   *I am very sorry to hear about your problem. I am even more sorry to hear that the reappearance of your husband presents a dilemma. It can only mean that our relationship was based on shakier ground than I thought. As you know, that's one of those things I'm not good at—figuring out relationships. Especially ours.*
   *You say you need time and space to work it out. Not a problem. You may have all the time and space you need.*
   *Please have a happy life.*

*As always,*
*Sam*

For a minute he stared at the message while a vat of dark emotions stirred inside him. The screen swam in his vision, pixels and lines running together in a blurry amalgam.

He slid the mouse pointer on the screen to the SEND button.

*Don't* said a voice inside him. He knew he was angry, bitter, jealous. Filled with irrational thoughts. Not a good time to send a message to the girl you love.

*To hell with it. It's over. Finito. Send it.*

His finger went to the left-click button on the mouse—

A rap on the stateroom door.

He hesitated, his hand on the mouse. Finally he rose and swung the door open.

The wide bulk of Commander Bullet Alexander filled the doorway. "Sorry to bother you, Skipper. CAG wants us in the air wing office ASAP."

Alexander had come by his call sign naturally. He was a handsome, burly-shouldered African-American man with a shaved skull that approximated the shape of a .45 caliber round. He had come aboard a month ago as Maxwell's new executive officer.

"Give me a second."

He returned to his desk. The mouse arrow still covered the SEND button on the message screen. He saw Alexander watching him from the doorway.

His hand hovered over the mouse key. He didn't have to reply to the message. He could let it molder there in the In folder while he considered. Nothing had to be done now.

Abruptly he reached down and slapped the SEND button.

Snatching his hat off the hook on the bulkhead, he stormed out of the room. He closed the door behind him with a vicious slam.

"Something the matter, Brick?"

"No." Maxwell gave him a ferocious look. "Why the hell do you think something's the matter?"

"Oh, no reason." Alexander kept his eyes straight ahead. "What's her name?"

# CHAPTER FOUR

# POSTER BOY

*Las Vegas, Nevada*
*2155, Wednesday, 10 September*

*Bleep, bleep, bleep, bleep.*

To Raymond Lutz, the incessant twittering of the half-acre of electronic slot machines sounded like music. It was natural that he would choose Caesar's Palace to do his business. He loved it here—the glittering lights, the electronic sound effects, the underlying current of greed and hedonism.

He followed his usual pattern. First, a drink. Lutz didn't particularly like liquor, but it had a calming effect on him. That was something he needed at the moment.

His eyes scanned the floor while he sipped the Scotch and water. Same crowd as always. Hicks from the Midwest, hopeful idiots blowing their vacation stash, guys with gold chains and pinkie rings impressing flashy girlfriends. Hookers, hustlers, junkies, bimbos.

A good place to get lost.

He cruised the floor until he saw a blackjack table that looked promising. The female dealer, a cute redhead, seemed friendly enough. Only two other players sat at the table. He took a seat at the end.

Lutz was a disciplined player, adhering to the rigid system of odds and probabilities that he had developed on his computer. After two hours of small-stakes play, he was nearly eight hundred dollars ahead. Not a big profit, but better than average. His system worked in small increments, not big hauls.

Time for the next phase.

He strolled down to the rows of slots, pausing to hit a five-dollar machine for a dozen losing passes. He moved on, picking up another Scotch at the small corner bar. His nerves were kicking up again. He needed calming.

In the third row of dollar slots he came to the machine he was looking for. A chain-smoking woman who looked like she just left a trailer park was shoving her last chip into the machine.

Another loser.

"Goddamn thing," she muttered, giving the machine a slap. "They're rigged. Every damn one of them." She walked away, still cursing.

Lutz took her place. This one was ripe.

He made a stack of one-dollar chips and began feeding them into the machine. Every half dozen or so passes he would get a few chips back. Finally, when his stack of chips was nearly gone, the row of oranges in the machine jiggled into alignment. Lights flashed and a warbling sound emanated from the machine. A pile of chips clattered into the tray.

Jackpot.

Or something close to it. Maybe fifty chips filled the tray. Lutz didn't bother counting them. It amounted to slightly less than he had already stuffed into the machine. What the hell, that was Vegas.

He rose and removed the chips, stuffing them into each

side pocket of his sport coat. He took one last swipe of the tray with his hand, then made his way down to the big bar at the far end where a woman country singer was just cranking up.

Not until he had settled onto a stool and was into his next drink did he allow himself to think about the chip. The microchip that he had smuggled from the laboratory. The one he had enclosed between the two halves of a casino dollar chip.

He was relaxed now. The booze was kicking in, and the drop was done. Lutz felt like laughing out loud.

Actually, it *was* very funny. A joke that he would never share. To think that the secrets of Groom Lake made their way, via his intestinal tract, to the tray of a slot machine where they were retrieved by a courier.

And delivered to China.

The adrenaline rush from the drop was beginning to kick in. He felt excited, exhilarated, and, as usual, horny. It was time for the next phase of the evening.

He looked around, then caught the eye of the blonde in the leather skirt sitting down the bar. He knew her. She was a hooker, but a very special one. She smiled at him, and Lutz nodded a greeting. He picked up his drink and moved down the bar.

*Frigate* Kai Yang, *Taiwan Strait*

"Do we search for survivors, Captain?" asked Lieutenant Yao-ming, the officer of the deck.

Commander Lei Fu-sheng peered through the darkness toward the eastern horizon. Fifteen kilometers away, it was still glowing orange where the *Han Yang* had exploded.

"No. Let her destroyer escort sweep the area." In truth, he doubted that they would find anyone alive. When the *Han Yang* took the torpedo amidships, a secondary explosion—it had to be an ordnance magazine—had split the frigate apart like a firecracker in a shoebox.

Lei wanted this submarine. The Chinese boat commander was proving himself to be extraordinarily bold. Immediately after killing the *Han Yang*, he had turned and targeted Lei's own frigate, the *Kai Yang*. Lei had been forced to go to flank speed, deploy his decoys, and emit maximum acoustical jamming.

He steered a course that would take them, he hoped, directly over the killer sub.

"Sonar contact again, Captain. Zero-four-zero, five thousand meters, contact fading. It's definitely a Kilo."

Lei nodded. Even with the obsolete sonar equipment that had been delivered with the former U.S. Navy Knox-class frigate, the sonar man could distinguish that unique seven-blade propeller signature.

*A Kilo class*—which explained why the contact was fading again. The newer indigenous Ming-class boats were also quiet, and they carried greater firepower, including a battery of antiship and land-attack missiles. But for pure murderous undetectability, nothing could touch a Kilo. The PLA navy possessed at least four of them.

One was out there now, trying to kill them.

As if responding to Lei's thoughts, the sonar man yelled, "Torpedo in the water!" His voice had risen an octave. "Forty-five hundred meters, tracking two-two-zero."

*Damn*, thought Lei. The Kilo skipper was trigger-happy. Lei leaned over the green-lighted repeater display at his console. He could see the torpedo, a wiggly yellow symbol, moving at about forty knots.

Targeting the *Kai Yang*.

But the Kilo skipper had given away his big advantage. The *Kai Yang*'s combat information computer could calculate a new fix on the submarine based on the launch point of the torpedo.

"Decoys, noisemakers," said Lei. "Now! Get the NIXIE deployed." NIXIE was a noisemaking device that streamed a hundred yards behind the frigate. It made noises intended to attract the torpedo.

"Decoys are out, Captain. NIXIE is streaming. Acoustic jamming has commenced."

"Hard to port, two-eight-zero degrees. Flank speed."

The wiggly yellow symbol was tracking straight toward them. Lei guessed that the torpedo would not go to active tracking—using its own guidance sonar—until it had closed to within two thousand meters.

That suited his purposes. "Do you have a lock on the Kilo?"

"Yes, sir, bearing zero-three-zero, forty-five hundred meters."

Lei peered into his display. "Is this firing solution still valid?"

The fire control officer looked up in surprise. "Yes, sir, but the enemy torpedo—"

"Come starboard, three-five-zero degrees." That would give them a good sixty degrees from the incoming torpedo. Still within the firing solution envelope.

As the bow swung back toward the enemy sub, Lei gave the command: "Fire tubes one and two."

"Aye, sir." The officer turned to his console and punched the keys, one after the other. "Tubes one and two, fire."

Two dull *whumps*, a second apart, rumbled up through the steel decks. The Mark 46 torpedoes were out of their tubes, beginning their own private search for the killer submarine.

"Incoming, now zero-three-five, one thousand yards." The sonar man's voice rose to a new level. "Active homing. The torpedo is homing."

Lei watched the yellow symbol on his display begin a curving pursuit path toward its quarry.

"Hard starboard, zero-three-zero," he commanded. He

saw the face of the helmsman blanch as he received the order. They were turning *into* the approaching torpedo.

Lei studied the advancing yellow symbol in the display. Everything depended on his skill—and the *Kai Yang*'s agility. Despite her age and obsolescence, the *Kai Yang* was a nimble warship. She could slice through the water with almost the same agility as the destroyer escorts.

For the next ten seconds, it seemed as if no one on the bridge of the *Kai Yang* breathed. The frigate was heeling hard to port, still in a maximum-rate turn. Lei steadied himself with one hand on the brass handrail, leaning against the tilt of the deck.

It was all a matter of timing now, making the incoming torpedo overshoot its pursuit curve. The torpedo was racing toward the *Kai Yang* at over forty knots, turning, matching the arcing course of the frigate, coming closer . . .

It missed the stern of the *Kai Yang* by twenty meters. Lei tensed himself, waiting for the proximity detonation.

No detonation.

A cheer went up on the bridge. Lei took a deep breath, then returned his attention to his pair of Mark 46 torpedoes. They were running in trail, both arcing to the right, picking up the bearing of the Kilo's last contact.

Lei tried to put himself in the shoes of the Kilo skipper. *What would you do? What would you be thinking?* The Kilo captain would know that his torpedo had missed. Perhaps he expected it and was prepared to fire another. Or else he knew he had overplayed his hand by taking a shot at a frigate. Would he go silent?

Lei knew. This sub commander was a risk taker. *He'll shoot again if he gets the chance. Don't give it to him.*

"Command active guidance. Snake search mode."

"Aye, Captain." The fire control officer initiated the torpedoes' active sonar guidance systems.

In snake search mode, the torpedoes would follow a serpentine course, probing the sea with their own active sonars. Lei knew he was activating the torpedoes' onboard seeking units dangerously early. It meant that the Mark 46s became autonomous predators in search of a target—*any* target, friend or foe.

It was a risk he had to take. If the Kilo skipper was thinking about another shot, he had to be discouraged, threatened into remaining passive.

"Contact fading on the Kilo," called out the sonar man.

Lei nodded. The *Kai Yang*'s ancient sonar equipment was losing the target. But he could see in the display that the Mark 46s were tracking. Still pinging. Still tracking *something*.

*Hurry*, urged Lei. *Find him*. The Kilo was out there somewhere in the black water, waiting, watching with his own passive sonar.

Then he saw it. The first Mark 46. Deviating from its undulating path. Veering off at a thirty degree angle to the right.

"Lock on," called out the sonar man. Lei could see by the young man's face that he was hearing the frantic pinging of the torpedo's guidance unit.

The second torpedo veered to the right, following the course of the first.

Lei held his breath again, counting the seconds. *Three . . . four . . . five . . .*

"Torpedo impact!" yelled the sonar man. His voice had a triumphal ring. "Second torpedo impact!"

The fire control officer looked over at Lei and raised his fist. "We got the bastard."

Lei turned to peer out into the darkness ahead of *Kai Yang*. There was nothing to see except whitecaps against a field of blackness. No horizon, no stars, no sign of life. Somewhere in the invisible depths, sixty men were experiencing violent death.

Lei felt no compassion for them. These were the same men who killed the crew of the *Han Yang*. Who would have killed *Kai Yang* if he had given them the chance.

The officer of the deck nudged Lei's arm. "Shall we take station and search for survivors, Captain?"

"No, Lieutenant, we will not. To hell with them."

*Chouzhou Air Base, People's Republic of China*

Colonel Zhang Yu made a show of ignoring the explosions outside. As the yellow lights of his bunker flickered, he lit a Golden Orchid cigarette. He sat back in his padded chair and exhaled a stream of smoke.

Another warhead impacted the concrete fortification of his bunker. Zhang forced himself not to wince. At this moment, it was critical that he reveal no sign of anxiety to the officers and technicians inside his headquarters.

What an irony, he reflected. In all their years of preparing for a war with Taiwan, it was assumed that *China* would strike Taiwan. Now this. *Taiwan* was attacking China.

Unbelievable. The mouse biting the cat.

The first weapons to strike the mainland were the HARMs—High Speed Antiradiation Missiles—launched by the initial wave of Taiwanese F-16s. These were the radar-hunting missiles that locked on to the energy-emitting radars of the Chinese air defense network.

There was no shortage of targets. Along the entire south China coast, GCI—ground-controlled intercept—sites were probing the sky over the Taiwan Strait. For the permanently situated sites, there was no escape even though the control officers abruptly shut down the emitters when they realized the sites were targeted by incoming missiles.

Colonel Zhang knew the Taiwanese had long ago designated the air defense command post for a first strike. Without the command hub, the air defense sites along the China coast would be shooting in the dark.

Listening to the explosions outside, Zhang marveled again at the turn of events. *Why did they launch a preemptive attack?* It did not fit their behavior pattern. Despite all their bluster about independence and sovereignty, Taiwanese politicians always conducted themselves with restraint. Why had they suddenly taken such an audacious course?

In a flash of insight, it came to him. *The woman.* Soong, the successor to the office of President. Because first her husband was assassinated, and then her patron, the troublesome Li Hou-sheng, she was behaving like a woman. Which was to say, irrational.

She had started a war.

So be it, thought Zhang, listening to the sounds of warfare outside. Taiwan had sealed its own fate. China would finish the war.

He turned to the captain who manned the communications console. "How many S-300 units still in action?" The S-300 was the new Russian-supplied surface-to-air missile with both low- and high-altitude capability.

The captain shook his head. "None of the stationary units are responding, Colonel. All the mobile units report that they are deploying. None are yet functioning."

Zhang nodded. It was bad news, but he wasn't surprised. The first targets in any air attack were the air defense sites. Without doubt, the coordinates of every fixed air defense site on the coast had been locked in to the guidance systems of the antiradiation missiles.

The mobile units were another matter. Not until they actually emitted radar signals, tracking incoming targets, could they be located by the Taiwanese fighters. It became a cat-and-mouse game, the air defense radars emitting only long enough to get SAMs—surface-to-air missiles—into the sky and locked on to targets. Then they would shut down and revert to jamming and decoying to thwart the incoming HARMs.

Zhang could see the tension in the other personnel in the command bunker—the captain at the communications console and the half dozen enlisted technicians. With each fresh explosion, they grew closer to panic. It was vital that they not lose their nerve now.

In truth, he wasn't unduly worried. His fortified shelter here at Chouzhou was in no danger from the Taiwanese bombs and missiles. It was unfortunate that the Taiwanese had seized the opportunity to strike first. But it was only a matter of hours before the battle would have begun anyway.

The air defense network would take some damage, but Zhang had no doubt the datalink and voice communications channels would remain open. They would recover. By morning, with the light of day to help him, he would be clearing the sky of Taiwanese fighters.


*USS* Ronald Reagan

Cmdr. Craze Manson caught Maxwell in the back of the ready room.

"Skipper, we need to talk."

Maxwell braced himself for trouble. Craze Manson never needed to talk unless he was up to something. "About?"

"The XO. I may be out of line, but this guy's got a serious credibility problem in this squadron. You know what I mean. Nobody is comfortable having him here."

He knew where Manson was going with this. Everyone knew that Craze Manson carried a massive chip on his shoulder. Newly promoted to commander, he made no secret of the fact that he had expected to be the next XO—executive officer—the number two job. In practice, the XO slot was the last stop before taking over command of the squadron.

Maxwell and CAG Boyce had agreed that Craze Manson was a bad choice. Instead, Bullet Alexander, who was just completing a tour with the Blue Angels, got the nod to be the Roadrunners' new XO.

"I must be missing something," said Maxwell. "Bullet's got a solid reputation."

"On the showboat circuit, maybe. Not out here in the fleet."

Maxwell nodded. A tour with the Blues, everyone knew, gave you name recognition and could be a career booster. In the opinion of many in the fleet, it had more to do with show business than it did the Navy.

"What are you saying, Craze? That Bullet can't carry his weight?"

"Look at his record. The guy's never flown a combat mission. He's been a poster boy for most of his career—the Blue Angels and the cocktail circuit. With all the qualified people in the zone, how did we get someone like that as our prospective skipper?"

For a while Maxwell didn't reply. It was true that Alexander had a classic case of bad timing. He missed Desert Storm because he was in postgraduate school. He was on shore duty during the Bosnia and Kosovo operations. He missed Afghanistan while he was assigned to the Blues.

But Maxwell and Boyce had agreed that Alexander was the right officer to be the new XO. Neither wanted the quarrelsome Manson as second-in-command of the Roadrunners. Or any other squadron.

He said, "Bullet's got more Hornet time than anyone here, including you or me."

"What kind of time? None in combat. He's got fewer traps on the boat than most first-tour pilots. He's a damn carpetbagger."

Maxwell had to smile. *Carpetbagger*. It was the same label Manson had applied to *him* when he was new to the squadron. He'd come back to the fleet after a long tour as a test pilot and then an astronaut. He was a carpetbagger too.

And a poster boy.

They had stopped calling him that after his three MiGs and the strikes in Iraq and Yemen. No more poster boy.

He had to admit that some of what Manson said was true. Alexander *was* a little short in real-world experience. Flying the air show circuit with the Blue Angels was not the same as serving in the fleet. It was tough to lead a squadron into combat when you hadn't been there yourself.

But he had chosen Alexander over other more qualified candidates because he sensed that Bullet had something special. An inner steel, a strength of character. He was a warrior.

He hoped he was right.

He could tell by Manson's hard expression that he wasn't buying it. Which was not surprising. Between the two existed a mutual dislike that went back to Maxwell's first months in the squadron. It came to a peak one day when Manson had walked out of a department-head meeting called by Maxwell, when he was the newly appointed XO. It was a critical moment. Manson had challenged his credibility.

He followed Manson outside the meeting room. Without warning, he seized his shirt collar and rapped Manson's head against the bulkhead. Before Manson could recover from his disbelief, he did it again.

By the third bang against the hard steel bulkhead, Manson had gotten the picture. Though his eyes were glazed, he was seeing Maxwell in a new light.

Since that day, an uneasy truce simmered between the two men.

"Look, Craze, if I didn't think Bullet was a solid player, I wouldn't have taken him on as XO. How about doing me and the squadron a big favor. Reserve judgment on him. Give the guy a break, okay?"

Manson's expression didn't change. "I take it that you are rejecting my opinion in this matter?"

"Take it any way you want. That's the way it is."

With exaggerated stiffness, Manson drew himself up to attention. "Will that be all, sir?"

"I sure as hell hope so."

A dark shadow passed over Manson's face. He turned on his heel and strode out of the ready room.

Maxwell shook his head. There was some kind of rule that every squadron had to have one asshole like Craze Manson. It was part of the integral structure of the military. Manson was a perpetually disgruntled officer who had climbed as far as he would go in the Navy's pyramidal system. It was unlikely that he would ever command a squadron of his own, and he would make life miserable for anyone who passed him on the way up.

Maxwell watched the door slam behind Manson. *Damn.* He had enough to think about—losing the President of Taiwan, a possible war, running a squadron—without worrying what Manson was up to. Maybe he should warn Bullet that someone was gunning for him.

No. If Bullet was going to take command someday, he had to deal with problems in his own way.

And then he had a thought that made him smile. Maybe it was time someone slammed Manson into a bulkhead again.

# CHAPTER FIVE

# CATFISH

*Taiwan Strait*
*0645, Thursday, 11 September*

"Razor One, this is Fat Boy. Bandits airborne off Longyan, thirty miles from the coastline, climbing out of twenty-five thousand." The voice of the Taiwanese controller in the E-2C cracked as he called out the targets.

"Razor One, roger," said the F-16 flight leader.

Razor was the collective call sign of the flight of four F-16As flying CAP—combat air patrol—on the southern edge of the battle area. Their station was midway between the southwest end of Taiwan and the Chinese mainland.

Twenty seconds ticked past. The flight leader was becoming impatient with the controller. He wanted some hard information. "Bogey dope," he called. How many bandits were out there? What bearing? Where the hell were they going?

"Fat Boy has a single group, heavy, thirty east of Alpha, heading east, climbing. Range one-twenty."

"Razor," acknowledged Major Catfish Bass, the flight leader. The bandits were coming his way, still a hundred twenty miles out. *Heavy* meant the controller was seeing multiple contacts within the group. That figured, thought Bass.

He checked his own situational display, trying to project the bandits' flight path. A hundred twenty miles was still too far out to commit. The trick was to draw them out over water, away from their SA-10 surface-to-air coverage. Into the killing zone.

Bass glanced over each shoulder. Perched on his left wing in a close combat spread was Lt. Wei-ling Ma, his wingman. Abeam his right wing was the second element, led by Capt. Jian Tsin, and his wingman, Lt. Choi Lum.

All young and eager, new to the F-16 Viper. Only Jian had more than a hundred hours in the Viper. None had never seen combat.

Bass was a United States Air Force exchange officer assigned to the Taiwanese air force. An instructor pilot from the F-16 replacement training unit at Luke AFB, outside of Phoenix, he had racked up over fifteen-hundred hours in the Viper, including a combat tour in Southwest Asia. Bass's job was to provide tactical training to pilots of the Taiwanese air force.

For a second an image floated across Bass's mind. He could visualize the apoplectic rage his boss—a two-star at Fifth Air Force HQ in Yokota—would have when he learned that Bass was flying combat missions against the PRC. The old man would have a shit fit.

He shoved the image from his mind. Screw it. It would take a team of lawyers a week to decipher his orders. They were written in such typical Air Force mumbo jumbo that they could be interpreted half a dozen ways. By his own loose interpretation, they did not exactly rule out operational missions. Then again, maybe they did. At the moment, he didn't want to think about it.

"Fat Boy has the group feet wet, heading east. Range eighty."

Eighty miles, coming this way. By the time they merged, the fight would be well outside the range of the deadly SA-10s.

"Razor. Turning nose hot."

Razor flight wheeled around and pointed their noses at the threat. Four radars scanned the blue sky ahead. They would soon be in detection range.

Bass saw them in his scope. "Razor One, contact, single group, bearing one-zero-zero for eighty miles, hot." *Hot* meant that the bandits were heading toward them.

"Fat Boy confirms. Those are your bandits. Razor One is cleared hot."

"Razor copies. Razor flight, knockers up, tapes on." It was the signal to his flight to flip their master armament switches from SAFE to ARM, then turn on the HUD video cameras mounted in the cockpit of each Viper.

Bass made another visual check on his flight. Wei was where he was supposed to be—abeam his left wing in combat spread. Jian's element was still correctly positioned off to the right.

So far, so good. His guys were hanging in there.

Early in his exchange assignment, Bass had run into the caste system of the Taiwanese air force, where tactical proficiency was less valued than political connection. Bass made it his business to identify the young fighter pilots with the greatest potential, regardless of their rank and connection.

These three—Wei-ling, Jian, and Choi—were his hand-picked students. For weeks he had drilled them in the complex discipline of four-ship tactics. They were eager and aggressive, almost worshipful in the way they emulated Bass's jargon and body language.

Bass's radar was showing a gaggle of at least four, maybe six fighters, clustered together at 25,000 feet. Forty miles and closing. His left thumb pushed the mike button, "Razor, gate." He gave the signal for afterburners. The four F-16s accelerated to supersonic speed.

Bass squinted at the horizon. He knew he'd see a firing solution in his multifunction display long before he could visually acquire the communist fighters, but he wanted a mental picture of how the fight would flow. Judging by their speed and altitude, the bandits were probably Chinese F-7s, homegrown variants of the Russian MiG-21 Fishbed. They were fast but obsolete. They might even be hauling iron bombs to a target on Taiwan.

So much the better. These gomers were toast.

The night before, Bass had stood on the blackened tarmac of the fighter base, his stomach churning, and watched his young pupils launch on the first wave of attacks against the mainland. Much as he wanted to go with them, he knew better. He couldn't risk having the Chinese capture an American pilot in the act of bombing them. If the communists didn't kill him, Major General Buckner would do it for them.

The initial attacks had gone well. The F-16–launched HARM missiles had succeeded in shutting down the Chinese coastal air-defense sites. Behind the HARM shooters, the F-16 and Mirage 2000 strikers had smashed their mainland targets—air defense complexes, the fighter bases at Fuzhou and Longxi, the supply depots and the port facilities at Xiamen and Mawei.

In all, sixty-three F-16s and forty-five Mirage 2000s participated in the attack. Two Vipers and three Mirages had not returned. That was an amazingly good ratio, considering the grim prestrike threat appraisals. They would have suffered a much higher loss rate if China had not been caught flat-footed.

*Well,* thought Bass, *kiss that advantage good-bye.* Taiwan's lean little air force was outnumbered three to one. Their best hope was their qualitative advantage. In addition to the new F-16s, the Taiwanese had sixty-some French-built Mirage 2000s, plus a hundred older Northrop F-5s. Overall, they were superior to anything the Chinese could put in the air—with the exception of the Russian-built SU-27 Flankers.

As in every air war, it depended on the guys in the cockpits.

As the dawn approached, Bass had reached a decision. He could no longer keep himself out of the fight. He assigned himself to lead a CAP—combat air patrol—over the strait. At least he wouldn't be hanging his unauthorized American butt out over the forbidden Chinese mainland. Really, he told himself, it wasn't much different from a regular training mission over the strait.

Yeah, right. Try running that one by the General.

The voice of the controller in the Hawkeye broke through his thoughts. "Fat Boy has bandits flanking north."

That meant the Fishbeds had taken a thirty degree or so turn to the north. Setting themselves up for the fight. Bass was sure they were getting ground-controlled intercept commands. The strait between China and Taiwan had become an electronic shooting gallery.

"Razor flight, check right forty." He would answer the bandits' flanking maneuver with an offset intercept.

As he brought the nose of his F-16 forty degrees right, he saw each of his other fighters moving with him, adjusting their positions to maintain a line abreast formation. Bass wanted to head off the oncoming Fishbeds, stay in front of them, keep them from getting around his wall of Vipers. At the right moment, he would turn in to them, bracket them, kill them with AIM-120 missiles.

With his right thumb, he slid the armament selector to AMRAAM. The AIM-120—called AMRAAM for Advanced Medium Range Air to Air Missile—was the great equalizer. The most modern missile in the U.S. inventory, it was one of the items withheld from the Taiwanese until just a few weeks ago. With a range of over thirty-five miles, the AMRAAM could kill from a greater distance than anything the Chinese possessed. Or so Catfish Bass fervently hoped.

Again he checked his scope. Range twenty-five. Six of them, still in a cluster. No, make that two flights of three, stacked in a vertical split of two thousand feet.

Like fat geese waiting to be killed.

"Razor, bracket," he ordered, banking his Viper hard to the left. Wei-ling matched the turn, and they rolled out forty-five degrees off their original heading. Jian's element rolled hard to right, also offsetting by forty-five degrees.

Now the flight of Vipers was split, heading ninety degrees apart. The maneuver would put the Vipers on either side of the Fishbeds.

Almost in range. Bass's plan was to target, shoot, and shoot again. Take out as many as he could before they merged. He had no intention of getting into a turning fight.

"Fat Boy shows the bandits maneuvering."

The Chinese fighters were waking up to the bracket attack. Two Fishbeds were angling toward him. Another pair was turning in to Razor Three's element. The center two were in a steep dive, running for the deck.

Range twenty-two miles.

"Razor One and Two will take the south group," Bass called. "Razor Three, target the north group. Razor Four, strip and take the center group diving for the deck. Fat Boy, watch for spitters."

The Fishbeds would be armed with AA-11 Archer missiles, he figured. The Archer was an infrared-guided, heat-seeking missile. It was a vicious close-in weapon, but it also had a head-on range of seven miles. The trick was to shoot before they came into IR range.

Approaching fifteen miles, Bass had two clear targets in the southern group of bandits. *Shoot them both.* He squeezed the trigger. The missile roared away from his jet like a giant bottle rocket. He could see the fire from its motor as it streaked toward the target.

"Razor One, Fox Three," he called, signaling the launch of an AMRAAM.

He stepped the target designator over to the second Fishbed and squeezed the trigger again. Another AMRAAM roared off the rail.

"Razor Three, Fox Three," he heard Jian call, announcing his own shot. A second later, Jian called a second missile away. Another target.

"Razor Two, Fox Three," called Wei. Then he took a second shot.

Six missiles in the air. *Shit hot,* thought Bass. That should give the gomers something to think about.

"Range ten miles," called Fat Boy. "Throttles." A reminder to pull their throttles out of afterburner and minimize hot IR emissions. Deny the enemy heat-seekers a target.

Bass squinted into his HUD. In the target designator box he saw the speck of the first Fishbed. As he watched, the speck erupted into a ball of bright yellow-orange fire. It looked like a cherry bomb going off in the distance. *Splash one Fishbed.*

To the left he saw a second speck, morphing into the delta-winged shape of an F-7 Fishbed. It had somehow evaded his second missile.

But not Wei-ling's. As Bass watched, the Fishbed burst into a yellow-orange fireball.

*Splash two.*

Both fireballs were plunging toward the sea below. "Thank you, God," Bass muttered in his oxygen mask. *And thank you, Uncle Sam, for the AMRAAMs.*

Bass looked over to his right. How was Jian doing? He was about to key the mike when he saw. Two more yellow-orange fireballs. Two black smoke trails.

Jian yelled on the radio, "Razor Three killed two rats, northern group!"

Bass grinned in spite of himself. *Rats?* They'd work on Jian's radio discipline in the debrief.

Now he was worried about Choi, Razor Four. He was supposed to be targeting the—

"Razor Four, Fox Two," called Choi, a triumphant ring in his voice. He had just taken a Sidewinder shot. "Trail bandit muzza fugga, middle group."

Bass winced at the mangled profanity. *Muzza fugga?*

"Fox Two, lead bandit, splash *two* muzza fugga rats." Choi had fired a second Sidewinder.

Bass had to shake his head. Yeah, radio discipline was clearly going to hell, but he might cut them some slack. Instead of shooting his precious AMRAAMs, Choi had closed to Sidewinder range. And killed two muzza fugga Fishbeds.

It was a good time to exit the fight. "Razor flight, reset," he called. "Bug east."

Bass reefed the nose of his F-16 around to a heading of 090. A feeling of elation swept over him. He felt like roaring and thumping his chest. *Six kills!* He and his student fighter pilots had just cut a swath through the PLA air force.

He saw Wei-ling rolling out in position on the right. Somewhere to the north, on the left side, was Jian. Below and behind them was Choi. They would regroup a little bit farther east, closer to the Taiwanese coastline—

*What was that?*

He glanced again at Wei-ling, a mile off his right wing. Something, a kind of shimmering blur, just behind Wei-ling's F-16.

And then it vanished.

He was still staring at the F-16 when it exploded.

Wei-ling's fighter was gone. In its place was a roiling orange fireball.

*What the hell happened?* Wei-ling had been vaporized.

There had been no radar warning, no contacts. The only thing that could have done that was a—

He reacted by instinct—a nine-G break turn toward the tumbling wreckage of Wei-ling's Viper. *Pull!* That was where the threat had to be. Rolling away from it would only expose his hot tailpipe.

He rolled inverted and pulled hard for the deck. At the same time, he hit the flare dispenser, spewing another trail of IR-decoying flares. He couldn't see it but he knew it was back there. A missile with his name on it.

His mind was sending urgent subliminal messages. *Pull hard. Maximum Gs, throw the missile off your tail. It's your only chance.*

In his gut he knew it wouldn't work. Whatever had killed Wei-ling already had the drop on him. His only hope was to avoid taking a hit straight up the tailpipe. His F-16 was already on the G-limiter. He had no idea where the enemy was, or even what kind of fighter had engaged him. All he could do was pray.

When the explosion came from behind, he knew what happened. He *had* outturned the missile. Almost. The warhead had missed but come close enough to detonate the proximity fuse.

The airframe had a new vibration to it. It felt like pieces were coming off the tail. He pulled the throttle back, then tried nudging the nose of the F-16 up. The jet responded, coming almost to level flight.

He felt a *thunk* that rattled the airframe. Now the F-16 was no longer responding to his inputs with the stick. When the red FIRE light illuminated on his panel, he knew he had run out of options.

Major Catfish Bass muttered a silent prayer and reached for the ejection handle.

*USS* Ronald Reagan

*Ratta-tatta-tatta-tatta.*

Maxwell kept the rhythm going, working the punching bag with both gloves, rotating each fist in a steady tempo. *Ratta-tatta-tatta-tatta.*

He was in the fitness room, just off the hangar deck on the port side. He'd been at it for ten minutes, working up a sweat, when he became aware of someone standing behind him. In his peripheral vision he saw Bullet Alexander.

"Pretty impressive, Skipper. Didn't know you were a boxer."

"Ex-boxer." He kept working the bag, keeping up the tempo. "Golden gloves, then intercollegiate when I was at Rensselaer."

"Me, I never liked getting slapped around like that. I liked football because they gave you a face guard. If you wanted to rough somebody up, you just steamrolled him on the scrimmage line."

Maxwell kept his eyes on the bag, concentrating on the rhythm. He knew Alexander. He hadn't come down to the fitness room to talk about college sports. "What's on your mind, Bullet?"

"Oh, just thought you could use some advice."

"About?"

"Women."

Maxwell missed a beat with the gloves. "What?"

"Yeah. With all due respect, Brick, it's obvious that you don't know jack shit about them."

Maxwell gave the bag one final whack. He turned to peer at Alexander. "What the hell are you talking about?"

"Look at you, hammering at that bag like it was Bin Laden's skull because you're all torn up over some chick."

"Did it ever occur to you that there just might be *something* in this squadron that isn't any of your business?"

Alexander just smiled. "Actually, no. As your executive officer, I'm supposed to watch out for you. That's why I'm here."

"To advise me about women? What the hell makes you an expert on the subject?"

"Experience. Two wives, and a significant number of near misses in between. I've got battle scars to prove it."

Maxwell looked around the room. They were alone except for a young petty officer working the Nautilus gear. "You're not going to stop pestering me until you've said your piece. Get it over with. What is it about women that I'm missing?"

"Good. Now listen up. The first thing you have to understand about women is that you won't *ever* understand them. Period. End of story. Give up. They are weird creatures who don't behave like men, and we keep making ourselves crazy because we don't accept that."

"So, assuming I'm listening to your uninvited counsel, what should I be doing?"

"Quit taking it out on yourself. Or that punching bag. I gather that your girl—what's her name? Claire? She dumped you, right?"

Maxwell kept his face expressionless. "That's personal."

"She sent you a Dear John, right? By e-mail, probably. That's the way they do it these days."

"Something like that."

"That's life, Boss. My message to you is this. It's not something you gotta understand, or blame yourself for, or beat up a bag over. It's like a bad cat shot or a gomer getting lucky with a SAM. Shit happens. You accept it."

Maxwell knew in his gut that Bullet was making sense, but he could still feel the anger bubbling up in him. The urge was there. He wanted to pound the living shit out of something—the punching bag, a terrorist, an enemy fighter pilot.

Claire Phillips's husband.

He gave the bag one more vicious haymaker, then turned away from it.

"Okay, counselor, you said your piece. Let's get back to work. We've still got a squadron to run."

*Taiwan Strait*

*You've done it now, Bass. They're going to hang you by the balls.*

The thought played like a dirge in his mind as he descended toward the sea. It occurred to him that he would have been better off dead, blown to pieces like Wei-ling, who never knew what hit him.

In the distance he could see the wakes of vessels running across the surface. His chute had deployed automatically somewhere around ten thousand feet. That meant everyone in a twenty mile radius could see him floating down like a goddamn circus tent. Who were the good guys and who were the bad? They were all dark shapes on a gray sea.

A wave of dread passed over him. The PLA navy had enough boats and ships in the strait to make a floating bridge to Taiwan. Had they picked up electronic intel reports that two F-16s were down?

Bass had an unwavering fear of the open sea and of drowning, which had been a major factor in choosing the Air Force over the Navy or Marines. Water sucked, and he wanted nothing to do with it. At least he had some hang time before getting his feet wet.

He had gone through an ejection once before. But that was over dry land. He'd been nailed by an SA-3 that popped through an undercast in Iraq. In the confusion that followed—the Iraqis had been as surprised as he that they'd scored a hit—he was snatched out of Indian country by an Air Force helo.

Bass suspected that this occasion would be different. This

was not bumbling, incompetent Iraq. China was a global superpower with the largest military force in Asia. And he was supposedly a noncombatant who had just destroyed two of their aircraft. Would they try him as a war criminal or a spy?

The nearness of the sea below triggered another wave of fear. He tried to remember the drill after you went into the water. Would the chute release automatically? Didn't it have some kind of saltwater-activated gadgets? Was he supposed to inflate the flotation unit before he hit the water? What about the raft?

He fumbled for the handles of the flotation unit, found them, and gave them a yank. Both lobes of the unit inflated around his waist. Then he remembered the seat kit and life raft. God, yes, the raft! He found the release handle and—

*Sploosh!* He hadn't seen the slick, opaque surface of the sea rushing up at him. It felt like hitting concrete. He was deep under the surface, the water ramming into his nose and head cavities like hot lava.

Bass tried to resist the panic that was overcoming him. He couldn't breathe. *Why wasn't the flotation unit working?* He was supposed to float on the surface, not sink like a goddamn boat anchor.

Something was restraining him. He couldn't move his legs, couldn't see, couldn't kick to the surface. Couldn't breathe. *I'm drowning.* The realization came from deep inside him like a voice from his darkest dreams. *Drowning.* It was the worst thing that could happen. It was why he joined the Air Force instead of the fucking Navy—

He popped to the surface.

Air. Blessed air. He coughed, gasped, swallowed a quart of seawater, went into a fit of coughing, gasping for air. Around him was the canopy of the parachute, the shroud lines entangling him like a serpent.

Coughing, choking, trying to suck in a lungful of the

blessed air. As he coughed, regurgitating seawater, he became aware of something else.

A noise. A whop-whopping sound, like the blades of—

A helicopter.

*Oh, flaming god-awful motherfrigging shit. They're here already.* Maybe he should have drowned. Better than being tortured and used by the ChiComs.

He realized that he couldn't see. Had he been blinded by the impact? Something hurt like hell.

His helmet, his oxygen mask. The impact with the water had snatched his helmet over his forehead. The oxygen mask was up around his eyes, obscuring his vision, clamping around his face like a vise.

He unfastened the fitting, and the mask dropped free. The pain eased around his face and, as in a widening tunnel, his vision began to return.

The whopping noise was coming from directly overhead. He saw someone drop from a sling into the water. Bass tried to decide whether he should resist, make them kill him, or just surrender.

The dark figure in the water was wearing a wet suit. As the man reached for him, Bass threw a punch. Make the bastard take him by force.

The man easily deflected the punch. He seized Bass's arm. "Just calm down, bubba." The voice had a deep Texas twang. "We ain't got time to fight. We have to get your silly ass out of here."

# CHAPTER SIX

# DELIVERANCE

*Taiwan Strait*
*0745, Thursday, 11 September*

"The name is Swan. Parachute rigger, second class, but that ain't my real job. I'm an aircrewman, and my specialty is yanking people like you out of the drink. You're lucky I was on deck today, cause I'm the best damn sling man in the business."

Bass nodded. "I'm cold."

Another crewman produced towels, and a wool blanket that looked like a relic from the Korean War. It smelled like an old horse, but Bass didn't care.

"Sir, I need your name, rank, and some ID if you have it."

He unzipped a front flight-suit pocket and retrieved his combat wallet. Inside was currency from every country in that part of the world, including China—all soaking wet. He handed over his laminated U.S. Air Force ID card.

"Wow!" said the petty officer, Swan, looking at Bass's ID card. "A real live Air Force major. Who woulda thought we'd find a guy like you out here. I'll have to give this to the aircraft commander, but I'll get it back to you, promise."

Bass nodded. He didn't feel like talking.

Swan stepped through a door in the front of the helicopter. In five minutes he was back. He returned Bass's ID card.

"You'd just be flatass amazed," Swan went on, "how many guys don't know how to get out of their equipment. Sometimes we get there and all we find is a perfectly good raft floating in the water. Pilot got himself all snaggled up in the shroud lines and sank. Or else he forgot to buckle his float units together and he wound up face down in the water." Swan had a good chuckle over this.

He went on for another twenty minutes or so while the helicopter clattered low over the surface of the strait. Bass had no idea where they were going. He knew the Americans had him. He also knew he was in violation of at least four articles of the UCMJ—the Uniform Code of Military Justice. He needed to conjure up a good story, but his brain was still numb from nearly drowning. Whenever he tried to talk, he went into another spasm of coughing and vomiting seawater.

He felt the big helicopter climb and slow to a hover. Through the cabin window he could see the gray mass of a ship. One hell of a big ship. Had to be an aircraft carrier.

The wheels of the helicopter clunked down on the deck. The whopping of the unloaded blades took on a quiet whooshing sound.

Someone opened the main cabin door, and a din of turbine noise flooded the cabin. A figure wearing a float vest and a cranial protector appeared in the open door.

"Major Bass?" he yelled over the din outside. "Welcome to the USS *Ronald Reagan*. I'm the ship's XO. If you'll follow me, one of our flight surgeons will have a look at you. Then some other gentlemen would like to have a little chat."

Bass shook hands with Petty Officer Swan, then followed the man in the cranial helmet across the deck and through a door in the island superstructure. They climbed down a stairwell that looked for all the world like a ladder.

"Careful on the ladder. It's a little steep."

Bass felt wobbly. He climbed down carefully, first one, then two more ladders. He followed his escort through an oval-shaped doorway, then tripped on the raised metal ledge jutting up from the floor.

The man turned and helped him to his feet. "You'll have to watch out going through these hatches. The knee-knockers are hell on your shins. Especially when the deck's moving."

It was all gibberish to Bass. Hatches? Knee-knockers? He could sense blood oozing from his shin. From invisible loudspeakers came whistles and bells and announcements in some variant of English.

He noticed the smell—a mixture of gunmetal, oil, sweat, and something like paint. It was everywhere. Hanging from the ceiling were miles of wires and cables. Deep inside the metal maze, they came to the ship's sick bay. A white-jacketed flight surgeon and two medical corpsmen were waiting.

After a quick exam, the doctor declared him to be okay. Nothing broken, a few contusions from the high-speed ejection, and a lot of ingested salt water, which would soon be gone if he kept puking his guts out. The worst damage was the laceration on his shin.

The corpsman gave him dry khakis and new boots to replace his dripping flight gear. Then he was back in the passageway, following the same man who greeted him in the helicopter. His name was Walsh, Bass learned, and he wore the eagles of a Navy captain. On the back of his vest was his title: BIG XO. The men were accompanied by two unsmiling marines in battle dress uniforms.

Bass had not barfed for over five minutes. He was feeling good enough to resume worrying. *Why the hell am I being escorted by an O-6? Why the marine guard?*

After more turns and one ascent of a steel ladder, they

came to a door marked FLAG INTEL; AUTHORIZED PERSONNEL ONLY.

Walsh didn't bother knocking. He opened the door, ushered Bass into the room, then departed.

Bass blinked, taking in the scene. The glare of the harsh artificial light stung his eyes.

There were five of them, peering at him like owls. One was a civilian, wearing chinos, a polo shirt, and tortoiseshell glasses. Three were dressed in khakis and flight jackets—the faded-leather things with patches and rat-fur collars that the Navy favored. One more reason to choose the Air Force.

An older man with gray hair stood at the head of a steel conference table. He wore a black pullover sweater over his khakis with—*oh shit*—two stars on the epaulets.

"I want a lawyer," said Bass.

"What the hell for?" said a Navy captain with wispy red hair. "You wanna sue somebody?"

"I, uh, might be in a little trouble."

"Really? How come?"

"I wasn't supposed to be doing—"

"We've already figured out what you were doing. I just got off the SatPhone with a General Buckner at Yokota. I believe you know him?"

Bass felt like hurling again. "Uh, may I ask what he had to say?"

The captain, whose leather name tag identified him as Red Boyce, exchanged glances with the Admiral. The Admiral nodded.

"He said to tell you that you might as well get a job with the Navy or Marines or the Girl Scouts—he didn't give a damn—because he'd see to it you weren't allowed to shovel shit in the United States Air Force."

"The general has a temper."

"So I gather. He'll get over it when he hears about the two F-7s you shot down."

"It was two for two. I lost my wingman and my own jet in the fight."

"Yes, we know. That's what we want to talk to you about."

*Taipei, Taiwan*

*Be strong,* Charlotte Soong told herself. *Do not allow them to intimidate you.*

She forced herself to take long, deliberate strides as she entered the cabinet room. She wore a traditional flowered, high-collared Chinese silk dress. *Make them respect you.*

Not so many years ago, she had been regarded as a great beauty in Taipei society. Now that she had reached nearly fifty, Charlotte knew that her ample figure and stately carriage could still draw an appreciative gaze. Over her arm she carried the flowered umbrella, a talisman from the days of her marriage. The umbrella had become such a fixture that Taiwan's political satirists invariably depicted her with it in their cartoons.

The ministers rose to their feet. She stood for a moment at the head of the long rosewood table. She gave them a peremptory look and said, "Seats, gentlemen."

She spread her papers on the table before her. The first order of business was to receive reports about the effects of the war on the country.

"Madame President," said Ma Wang, the Foreign Minister. "Our citizens remain in good spirits, but it is not clear how long that will continue. As the missile attacks from the mainland destroy more public buildings, it will erode their morale."

She nodded. The Taiwanese were hardy people. For decades they had been braced for such a war with China. Now that it was here, and going reasonably well, they were proud and defiant. But she wondered how long they would support her while the Chinese missiles continued to rain down on them.

Premier Franklin Huang spoke up from the end of the long table. His voice was accusatory, as usual. "Why are the wonderful Patriot missiles we received from our so-called American friends not stopping the Chinese weapons? Were we not led to believe that the Patriots would protect us?"

Charlotte expected this. Instead of answering, she nodded to General Wu Hsin-chieh.

"The Patriot air defense batteries are performing well," said the General. "They are countering over half the incoming missiles from the mainland. That is a far better statistic than Israel experienced with Iraqi Scuds during the Gulf War."

"This is not Israel," said Huang. "And China can deliver more destruction than Iraq ever dreamed of. Why are we engaged in this senseless war?"

"We are engaged in a war of survival," said Charlotte. "We have no choice except to win. Unless you believe that we should allow ourselves to be invaded by the PLA and made a vassal province of China. Is that your choice, Premier Huang?"

It was best to get it over, she decided. If Huang swayed the other ministers to follow him, they would find a way to depose her. She had to deal with Huang.

"We do not have to fight," he said. "China has no interest in invading us. They want a peaceful relationship with Taiwan."

"Is it a peaceful relationship to murder our President? To mount an eighty thousand–man invasion force?"

"We have no evidence that they were responsible for the President's death. The invasion force was merely a contingency. It was not their intention to go to war."

"How is it you have such an understanding of China's intentions, Franklin?"

For the first time, Huang blinked. "I am a statesman. It is my responsibility to know such things."

"Do you communicate directly with Beijing, Premier Huang?"

Huang blinked again, no longer sure of himself. "In my official capacity as Premier, I have occasion to—"

"To talk with the enemy." She leaned forward over the table, pressing the attack. "Is that what you do, Premier Huang? What do you reveal to them about us?"

It was working. The other ministers were spellbound, watching the confrontation. "Of course I have official exchanges with the People's Republic," he said. "Nothing of a sensitive nature is discussed. It is all a matter of record. You may read the transcripts for yourself."

She nodded. Actually, it was no surprise that Huang or any other official communicated with China. It was not illegal. Modern wireless communication made it possible for any citizen of Taiwan to speak with anyone on the mainland. But it served the purpose of putting Huang on the defensive.

The crisis had passed, at least for the moment. Charlotte moved the discussions to the military situation. General Wu delivered an assessment, including attrition of aircraft and warships. Although air superiority had been achieved early in the conflict, the loss of F-16s was becoming a worrisome matter.

Ma Wang spoke up. "I don't understand. Why are we losing so many fighters over the strait now? Are the PLA pilots gaining some advantage over us?"

Wu hesitated and glanced at Charlotte Soong. He waited for a signal. She gave him an imperceptible head shake. *Don't tell them.*

Ma had come close to the truth. The PLA *did* possess an advantage over Taiwan's air force. An unexpected advantage. An invisible weapon—some kind of stealth craft—was decimating their fighter forces. It had been her intention to inform the cabinet about the terrifying airplane. If it weren't destroyed, Taiwan would lose the war.

But Charlotte Soong was a woman who trusted her intuition. Something was telling her to keep her silence. Technically, she was in violation of the constitution. Such information was supposed to be shared with her cabinet. But there was something about Huang. A feeling that still dwelled in her stomach after her clash with him.

*Whom can you trust?* She didn't know. *Is Huang a leak?* Maybe, maybe not. *It is too dangerous to take the chance of compromising the operation.*

General Wu understood her decision. "It is a matter of combat tactics," she heard him tell the ministers. "In order to eliminate China's ability to mount an invasion force, it was necessary to expose our fighters to heavy enemy defenses. Now that has been accomplished, and we will restrict our losses while we maintain air superiority."

Not a great answer, Charlotte thought, but good enough. Whether or not they believed it, the ministers had no choice but to accept it. Old Ma, ever the pragmatic politician, just shrugged. At the end of the table, Huang lapsed into a silent sulk. The other ministers were busy taking notes, whispering among themselves.

Charlotte concluded the business of the cabinet. It had gone as well as she could have expected. Her leadership had been tested, and she was still in office. If the secret war plan succeeded, they would applaud her decision to maintain silence. If it failed, it wouldn't matter. Taiwan would be finished.

She gathered her papers and rose. The ministers scrambled to their feet. The meeting was over.


*USS* Ronald Reagan

He should have figured it out, Bass thought. It was some kind of board of inquiry. Something the Navy did when they snatched Air Force exchange pilots out of the drink.

The civilian had to be a spook. The glasses, the haircut— CIA, NSA, something like that. He didn't have a name tag.

The two-star was in charge of a bunch of ships, including the big one they were on.

The red-haired captain seemed to be running the meeting. The other two were Navy commanders. One was obviously an intel officer. He looked like every other intel officer Bass had ever seen—same accusing eyes, same shitty attitude.

The other officer, whose name tag read BRICK MAXWELL, was a tall, athletic-looking guy with a brown mustache. He had a set of penetrating blue eyes and wore a bemused grin on his face. He had the body language of a fighter pilot. Bass wondered what he flew and if he was any good.

The captain pulled out a well-chewed cigar. He stuck it in his mouth and peered at Bass. "I'm Captain Boyce, the Air Wing Commander. The *Reagan* is your new home, at least until we can figure out what to do with you. Admiral Hightree here commands the battle group, and this is Mr. Ashby. He's on loan to us from the NSA."

*Bingo,* thought Bass. *A spook.*

"Commander Wentz here is the flag intelligence officer. The other officer is Commander Maxwell, who commands one of my Hornet squadrons."

*Bingo again.*

"Everything we discuss here is classified top secret, need-to-know only," said Boyce. "Do you understand?"

"Sir, I have a top secret clearance."

Wentz said, "We already know your security clearance. The subject matter here happens to be several levels above your clearance limit."

Bass nodded. *Above top secret?*

"This falls into special category intelligence—SPECAT—meaning highly restricted and compartmentalized. You've been cleared at this level only for as long as it takes us to debrief you."

Bass nodded again.

Wentz's eyes bored into Bass. "This subject matter is so

sensitive that its declassification review date is twenty years from now. Any disclosure or unauthorized discussion will result in trial by court-martial and lengthy incarceration. If you have no questions, sign this declaration of intent and understanding." He shoved a clipboard across the table.

Bass picked it up and began signing the papers. Typical intel puke, he thought. They were all jerks.

They took seats around the conference table. The intel officer punched the start button on a tape recorder in the center of the table.

Boyce unwrapped a fresh cigar. "Your wingman," he said. "What happened to him?"

Bass had to think for a second, reconstructing the image he had seen behind Wei-ling's jet just before the explosion. It still seemed like a bad dream.

He told them what he saw.

When he finished, Boyce and Maxwell looked at each other. Maxwell was nodding his head. "This 'glimmer' you call it. How far behind your wingman's jet was it?"

"A mile, maybe. It lasted just a second, then I saw Wei-ling's jet blow."

"Any RWR alert?"

"No. Nothing."

"Did your wingman report being spiked?"

"I don't think so. I had just checked his six, looking for any threat, and that's when I saw the . . . glimmer."

Everyone at the table leaned forward. "Describe it," said Boyce.

"Sort of a shimmering, miragelike distortion. I just saw it for a second, out of my peripheral vision. I thought it was an aircraft at first. It might have been the heat from Wei-ling's afterburner."

Boyce looked at Maxwell and nodded. "Did you see anything impact his jet?"

"No. It just blew."

"What was your reaction?"

"Get out of Dodge. A gut move—I figured I was next. Nine-G-limiter pull for the deck. It was the right move because the missile—whatever it was—missed a direct hit. I must have taken shrapnel in the tail when the prox fuse went."

For a moment, Boyce and Maxwell were both silent. Maxwell seemed deep in thought, focused on some faraway object.

Boyce was on his feet. "Goddamnit, it had to be a fighter—a Flanker or another Fishbed. He sneaked into the fight and nobody saw him."

"Why didn't their Hawkeye pick him up?" asked Maxwell.

"They missed him. Maybe he entered low, then came straight up."

Maxwell shook his head. "Not against the E-2 radar. It's optimized for overwater ops. Besides, with that many fighter radars covering the sector, I'd give spitters a near-zero probability."

Boyce looked exasperated. "Okay, what then? *Something* got behind the F-16s without being detected and took them both out. I'd bet my ass and a box of Cohibas it's the same something that flamed Dynasty One."

A silence fell over the group.

Finally, Maxwell said, "It's pretty obvious, isn't it?"

Boyce stared. "Maybe. You care to elaborate?"

Maxwell started to speak, then he looked at Bass. Boyce just shrugged. "Him? He's not going anywhere. His boss said to keep him until hell freezes over or the war is finished, whichever takes longer. Plus he just signed his life away. We own this little mercenary."

Bass forced a smile. Navy guys. It must come from living on boats. No booze, no women. It gave them a warped sense of humor.

# CHAPTER SEVEN

# THE WEDGE

*USS* Ronald Reagan
*Taiwan Strait*
*1015, Thursday, 11 September*

"A what?" Boyce shoved the cigar back in his mouth and stared at Maxwell.

"Stealth fighter," said Maxwell.

"You mean, like the F-117? Low radar signature, low observability?"

"Never mind low," offered Catfish Bass. "How about *zero*? If it was another fighter that hosed us, the thing was invisible. Not just to radar, but to the naked eye." Bass was starting to relax now that he wasn't going to jail. At least not immediately.

Boyce snorted. "We went through that already. There ain't no such animal." He kept staring at Maxwell. "Isn't that right, Commander Maxwell?"

Maxwell had seen that look before. When Boyce was on to something, he was like a bloodhound sniffing the wind.

"Stealth technology has come a long way since the F-117," said Maxwell, choosing his words carefully. "There might be a new generation."

"Might be, you say. Would it be anything you might know about?"

While Maxwell hesitated, still weighing how much to say, Ashby, the civilian, spoke up for the first time. "Commander Maxwell is right. There *is* a new generation of stealth aircraft." He tossed a manila folder onto the table. "There's the record, the part that's not included in his personnel file. When Maxwell was a test pilot, he was assigned for a year to the research facility at Groom Lake in Nevada. The place called Dreamland. He worked on a secret project codenamed Black Star."

At this, Maxwell cleared his throat. "Excuse me, Mr. Ashby, but that is not—"

"It's cleared," said Ashby. He held up the folder, showing the TOP SECRET stencil on the cover. "This matter is now the highest priority. SecDef has given the go-ahead to use all the tools we have to find out what the Chinese are using against us. Your knowledge of Black Star is one of the tools."

"Well, I'll be damned," said Boyce. "You're telling me that Brick here *knows* about such an airplane?"

"Not only knows about it. He flew it."

Maxwell felt Boyce staring at him. Boyce was shaking his head. "There's no end to the things you haven't told me."

"I wasn't supposed to tell you. Or anyone else. It was a black project."

Boyce aimed his cigar like a baton. "Another of your little side jobs when you were a space cadet. Now that we know, maybe this would be a good time for you to enlighten us about this thing called Black Star."

Maxwell glanced over at Ashby, who gave him a nod. He tilted back in his steel chair and twirled a pen in his hand, remembering. He let his thoughts roll back nearly five years, back to the Nevada high desert. To the place they called Dreamland.

\*    \*    \*

It looked like a wedge. A wedge on wheels.

That had been his first impression, standing there in the fluorescent light of Hangar 501 at Groom Lake. *A wedge with an attitude*. The Black Star didn't have the classical, pointy-nosed sleekness of a traditional fighter. Shimmering in the artificial light, the dark-skinned aircraft looked like an apparition. All angles and facets and blurred fixtures.

He had to whistle in amazement. It wasn't what he'd expected. Viewed from overhead, the airplane looked like a reversed kite, with an extended triangular frontal area, and a shallower, delta-shaped aft section. Oddest of all, it had no tail, no vertical stabilizer surface. Computer-commanded spoilers in the aft section of each wing gave the jet directional control.

"It's aerodynamically unstable," the project director informed him. "The only thing that keeps it from self-destructing in flight is the fly-by-wire flight control system."

Maxwell was one of three test pilots on the Black Star. One was Joe Hynes, an Air Force lieutenant colonel and veteran test pilot from the Edwards research facility in California. The other was Frank Eaker, a contract civilian who had earned his credentials on the F-117. Maxwell himself had just completed the carrier suitability tests of the new F/A-18 Super Hornet and was already a candidate for a shuttle slot at NASA.

Ten years in development, the Black Star was a secret known only to a dozen senior military and civilian officials and fewer than two hundred contract technicians. The initial proving flights were conducted from Groom Lake's five-mile-long runway under cover of darkness.

The test program was unlike anything Maxwell had seen. Because of the heavy veil of secrecy, each pilot was responsible for a specific area of testing. They didn't compare notes, and each was kept uninformed about the others' experiences.

Maxwell's job was to explore the air combat envelope—maximum rate turns, high and low speed buffet, accelerated stalls and departures from stable flight, sustained high angle-of-attack maneuvering.

By the end of the test series, he was impressed. The Black Star wasn't the best fighter he had ever flown—its airframe geometry and inherent instability made it a dog of a fighter—but it didn't matter. The Black Star traded agility for stealth. This stealth fighter was to air combat what the silent submarine was to naval warfare.

There was much he wasn't supposed to know about the fighter, but some of it he could deduce. By the radical design, it was obvious that the jet possessed new ways to elude enemy radar and attack targets undetected.

It wasn't until one dawn flight over Nevada that he observed the Black Star's most potent attribute. He was at 1,500 feet, flying down the length of Groom Lake's long runway, about to turn downwind and land. In the pale light, he had glimpsed the shape of the second test aircraft—Eaker's Black Star—lift from the runway and point its nose into the sky.

Maxwell rolled his jet into a turn, keeping his eye on Eaker's jet. Never before had he actually seen another Black Star in flight. As he brought his own jet abeam Eaker's, a thousand feet above him, it happened.

The Black Star disappeared.

Maxwell blinked, thinking he had lost it momentarily in the gloom of the Nevada sky. He peered again. Nothing. Eaker and the number two Black Star had vanished.

The truth dawned on him. He understood why the Black Star was more deadly than the most radar-elusive fighter.

It was invisible.

When Maxwell finished, Boyce asked, "How does it work?"

Maxwell shook his head. "I don't know exactly. They didn't tell us much about that. My understanding was that the composite skin had a plasma surface. An ionized gas with an electrical charge."

"Something they can turn on and off?"

"Probably. Now you see it, now you don't. That's why I could see Eaker as he took off. When he activated the skin masking, he became invisible."

Boyce nodded. "Like whatever it was that shot down Dynasty One."

"Like whatever it was that shot me down," said Catfish Bass. "And my wingman."

"Okay," said Boyce. "If such a thing exists, all it means is that we have it, not them. Somebody explain how a country like China, where they haven't figured out flush toilets, could have superstealth technology."

"Simple," said Ashby. "The same way they have cruise missiles and supercomputers."

"Which is?"

"They buy it. Or steal it."

Boyce made a face. "Or some elected asshole gives it to them."

"Either way. It's quicker and cheaper than developing it themselves."

"What about the Russians?" Maxwell said. "They've been working on their own stealth jets for years. Would they pass it to China?"

"Maybe in the old days, but probably not now," said Ashby. "But if so, we've got ways of making Ivan very sorry he did it. The fact is, Russia is just as worried about China as we are. It's pretty unlikely they would share their most valuable secrets."

"In the meantime," said Catfish Bass, "their invisible stealth jet is chewing up the Taiwanese air force. My Taiwanese F-16 pilots will get picked off like flies."

"It's not our fight," said Boyce. He held up a computer printout. "These are the Rules of Engagement. What they say, in essence, is that U.S. forces stay out of it. The *Reagan* battle group is supposed to keep a watchful presence out here to remind the ChiComs that we're friends of Taiwan. Fire only if fired upon, and avoid confrontations with the PLA air force. Washington thinks Taiwan can take care of itself if we just keep them armed."

"That was before Black Star," said Bass. "Now they're hosed."

Boyce didn't answer. A silence fell over the table. Boyce seemed to lapse into a trance. For a while he played with his cigar, rolling it around the table, while his eyes focused on some faraway object.

Finally, he looked up at the group. "I've got an idea."

It took six hours.

First he had to run it by the Battle Group Commander, Admiral Hightree, who gave it his own cautious endorsement. From the *Reagan*'s comm center, the proposal flew at the speed of light, via satellite, to CINCPAC in Hawaii, then up the ladder to CNO, the Joint Chiefs, and then to the White House, where it underwent the scrutiny of the National Security Council.

The tasking order came back the same route, only slightly watered down from Boyce's original plan.

"Here it is," he said, holding the document that Admiral Hightree had just given him in the flag intel compartment. "The go-ahead for the great Chinese stealth sucker play."

Maxwell noticed Hightree giving Boyce a curious stare. Hightree was new to the *Reagan* battle group, having taken command only a month ago. The Admiral had not yet been exposed to CAG Boyce when he was concocting one of his high-risk operations.

"What are the rules?" Maxwell asked. "I know they're not giving us carte blanche."

"Not bad, considering the old ladies on the National Security Council," said Boyce. He perused the tasking order for a moment. "No overflight of Chinese territorial waters, it says. Can't argue with that. No overtly hostile actions toward PLA aircraft. That's okay too, as long as we maintain a CAP between the battle group and the mainland. Here's the clincher. Use of the Chameleon decoy is authorized, but it mustn't overfly Chinese territory."

"Chameleon" was the working name of the new UAV-17, a single-engine, unmanned reconnaissance aircraft equipped with a configurable radar and IR signature. Using its own electronic emulation equipment, Chameleon could present itself on enemy radars and infrared sensors as a high-altitude bomber, fast-moving fighter, or a surveillance aircraft.

"Chameleon is an expensive piece of hardware," said Hightree. "Before I throw one of these away, you'd better tell me what you have in mind for it."

"What kind of intruder would get the Chinese most agitated?" said Boyce. "What would be the most likely thing to draw out the stealth jet?"

Hightree was giving Boyce the curious stare again. "Knock off the quiz game, Red. Just tell us."

"EA-6B Prowler." Boyce's voice was growing more intense as he warmed to his subject. The Prowler was a carrier-based, four–crew member jet with communications jamming, eavesdropping, and radar suppression capability. "The ChiComs are so goddamn paranoid, they'll assume the Prowler is either directing an attack or stealing all their secrets."

"Can the decoy really do that?" asked Maxwell. "Emulate a Prowler?"

"The electronic warfare geeks tell me it can emulate a seagull shitting on a beach ball."

Hightree made a sour face. "That's good enough, I guess." He rose and checked his watch. "You and group ops come up with an air plan by thirteen hundred. Run it by Captain Stickney, then send it to me. If it looks doable, I'll sign off on it."

When Hightree closed the door behind him, Boyce and Maxwell were alone in the compartment. Boyce settled himself back into the chair, pulled out a fresh cigar, and clipped off the tip. He had already figured out that Hightree detested cigars. "Well, here we go again."

Maxwell recognized the tone in Boyce's voice. "We?"

"I need a leader for the fighters."

"You've got twenty qualified strike leaders in the air wing."

"Only one of them has ever seen the Black Star."

Maxwell sighed. He should have expected it. "Yes, sir. What am I supposed to do if I encounter the thing?"

"You want the official order or the off-the-record version?"

"Both, please."

"If we succeed in drawing it out, we will use all our assets to get a make on it. We'll have every tool in our bag— IR, visual, radar, satellite imaging—to collect data and confirm the thing exists. That's the end of your mission, and Defense Intel takes it from there."

"Those are my official orders. What am I really supposed to do?"

Boyce pulled out his ancient Zippo and put a flame to his cigar. He took his time, squinting through the cloud of gray smoke, getting an ember going.

Finally he peered over at Maxwell. "You're supposed to kill the sonofabitch."

# CHAPTER EIGHT

# CHAMELEON

*Taiwan Strait*
*0820, Friday, 12 September*

"Runner One-one on station," Maxwell called.

His flight of fighters—four Super Hornets—had reached their CAP stations, orbiting at twenty thousand feet, one hundred miles from the coast of China. The second division was high, thirty-three thousand feet, twenty miles behind him. A hundred miles to the southeast, the *Reagan* battle group was cruising the southern Taiwan Strait.

"Alpha Whiskey copies, Runner One-one," answered a voice in his headset.

Maxwell nodded. CAG Boyce, the Air Warfare Commander whose call sign was Alpha Whiskey, was now ensconced in the climate-controlled, red-lighted space of CIC directing the action from his situational display.

To the east, Maxwell could make out the dark landmass of Asia. The sky was the color of slate, empty and yet filled with danger. *Is it out there? Will it take the bait?*

Boyce's voice broke the silence. "Runner One-one, Alpha Whiskey. Be advised Ironclaw is airborne."

"Runner One-one." The game was on, thought Maxwell. *Here comes the bait.*

*Ironclaw* was the usual call sign for an EA-6B Prowler. Today it meant something else. The Chameleon UAV—unmanned air vehicle—had just catapulted from the *Reagan*, cloaked in its electronic disguise.

On station also was an E-2C Hawkeye—the Navy's turboprop version of the Air Force AWACS with its own saucer-shaped radar dome mounted above the fuselage. The controllers in the Hawkeye were standing by to vector Maxwell's fighters toward any threat—and warn him of incoming bogeys.

*Those that they could see.*

With that thought, Maxwell gazed down at his radar display. Turning southward in his orbit, he picked up the returns of his high division, fanned out in combat spread. Led by Commander Rico Flores, skipper of the VFA-34 Blue Blasters, they were responsible for high-altitude threats. Maxwell's division would deal with any low intruders.

The space on the screen between his flight and the mainland was empty. So far the PLA was showing no curiosity about the American presence.

The pseudo-Prowler would fly a profile just like the one a real EA-6B might take, climbing to altitude, then descending on a track parallel to the coast. Then it would turn abruptly inbound, as if it intended to penetrate Chinese airspace. As if it were hostile.

"Ironclaw checks level, standing by for signal."

"Alpha Whiskey copies. Ironclaw, your signal is Oscar."

"Ironclaw, roger signal Oscar." As Maxwell listened to the exchange, he had to grin. It was bogus radio dialogue for the benefit of Chinese eavesdroppers. *Signal Oscar* was a fictional execute command. Though the transmissions were on a secure channel, it wasn't *too* secure. With only slightly sophisticated monitoring equipment, a skilled interpreter could intercept the communication. He would conclude that a Prowler was embarked on a mission toward China.

Maxwell forced himself to relax. For the moment, there was nothing he could do except sit back and watch the show. He and his fighters would maintain their CAP station until the Chameleon UAV had flown its first leg, paralleling the coastline. When it reversed course and turned inland, Maxwell's fighters would close in behind it, flying cover.

Would the deception work?

Maxwell could only guess how the Chameleon's electronic masking worked. Ship-based UAVs were something new, and the ability to emulate other aircraft was even newer. If the Chameleon's disguise was successful, Chinese air defense commanders would see what appeared to be an EA-6B Prowler entering their airspace. The Prowler—the *real* Prowler—was a derivative of the ancient A-6 Intruder attack aircraft. Crewed by a pilot and three ECMOs—electronic countermeasures officers—the twin-jet Prowler was the battle group's prime vehicle for radar and sensor jamming, targeting, and gathering of electronic intelligence.

Prowlers were the advance units of a deep air strike. Observing such a threat, the Chinese would *have* to react.

Or so Maxwell hoped.

"Ironclaw is checking in as fragged," said a voice on the radio.

"Sea Lord copies," replied the controller in the Hawkeye. "Picture clear."

More bogus dialogue. The controller was informing Ironclaw that no threat was showing on the display. Maxwell wondered if anyone was listening.

Boyce's voice came over the frequency. "Runner One-one, Alpha Whiskey. Ironclaw is on first base. Five minutes to second."

"Runner One-one, roger." Boyce was informing him that the decoy had completed its outbound leg and was flying back toward the Hornets' CAP station. Five more minutes. When the decoy was directly beneath the Hornets, it would turn again and point its nose toward China.

Maxwell tried to visualize the effect it would have on the mainland. Telephones would ring. Missile sites would be activated. Questions would fly like missiles through the ether. *Why is a Prowler invading our space? Are the Americans in the war?*

Fighters would be scrambled.

Maxwell punched a five minute countdown into his elapsed timer. It was vital that he fly the CAP orbit precisely so that his Hornets were on a northwesterly course when Ironclaw passed under them.

He glimpsed it, two thousand feet below. It looked nothing like a Prowler, which had a bulbous nose, spacious cockpit, and wide, swept wings. The Chameleon was a stubby-winged craft with a long nose unmarred by a crew enclosure. Its only protuberance was a pair of ECM pods attached to its underfuselage. The decoy had a V tail and, despite its ungainly appearance, was moving at a respectable 350 knots.

"Runner One-one tallies Ironclaw," Maxwell called, reporting that he had a visual on the decoy.

"Alpha Whiskey, roger. You're cleared to second base."

*The go-ahead.* He rolled out of his turn above and behind the Chameleon. Right on schedule, the pilotless aircraft banked to the right and slid its nose toward the looming coastline of Asia.

Fifty miles to the coastline. The game was on.

The Chinese had always insisted that their territorial boundary extended farther offshore than the twelve mile limit recognized by the United States. Over the years the disagreement over sovereign airspace had caused some incidents, including a collision between a Navy EP-3 surveillance plane and a reckless Chinese F-8 pilot.

That was then, Maxwell reflected, during a time of relative peace. This was now, and China was at war.

Forty miles.

"Ironclaw, you have multiple contacts near point alpha, one hundred miles from you."

"Ironclaw, roger." No surprise. Maxwell saw the same thing on his situation display. Over the mainland, near their bases. None was yet a threat.

Fifty miles. Only three minutes from the territorial boundary. If the Chinese were going to do something—

"Ironclaw, this is Sea Lord. Single group twenty miles southeast X-ray, hot on you."

"Ironclaw."

Maxwell saw them too. High and fast, and feet wet. *Hot* meant that their noses—and weapons—were pointed this way. Judging by their profile, they were Flankers.

*Damn!* That wasn't part of the game plan. He wasn't here to get into a furball with conventional Chinese fighters. Especially Flankers, which were fifth-generation, sophisticated interceptors.

Apparently Boyce had reached the same conclusion. "Ironclaw, Alpha Whiskey. Hotdog, hotdog. Scram east."

"Ironclaw, roger, hotdog."

*Hotdog* was the alert that they were approaching the international boundary. Maxwell saw the decoy turn to the east, on a course roughly perpendicular to the incoming bandits. He swung his flight of Hornets into position a few miles behind the decoy.

It was an old tactic. By turning perpendicular to the threat radars—beaming, it was called—you minimized the amount of Doppler shift the Flanker pilots could see, possibly denying them a radar lock. Sometimes it worked, especially if the fighters you were up against didn't have GCI or AWACS. Maxwell knew that multiple radars on the mainland were tracking them. In fact, he was counting on it. Ei-

ther way, it displayed a nonthreatening posture to the
Flanker pilots.

Forty miles to the merge. The Flankers were inside factor
bandit range—the distance at which Maxwell had to regard
them as a threat. He was paralleling the coastline. Did the
Flankers have orders to attack American aircraft in international airspace? If so, it meant China had just extended their
war to include the United States.

"Ironclaw, lean right twenty degrees," Maxwell ordered.
He was buying time. The slight offset would extend the
Flankers' time to intercept. These were not the trophies that
he wanted.

The Flankers were nose hot on the decoy. Maxwell
tensed, wondering if the Flankers had committed. Would
they attack the decoy or the Hornets? With their speed advantage—they were moving at about 1.8 Mach—the
Flankers would be in missile range within—

"Sea Lord shows all red fighters turning cold. They're
bugging out."

So they were. On his datalink situation display, Maxwell
saw the two blips moving back toward the mainland.

*Why?* They hadn't come close enough to the Chameleon
to get a visual ID. Were the two Flankers waiting for rein-
forcements before engaging four Hornets?

A new uneasiness passed over Maxwell. *Something was
happening.* He didn't believe in extrasensory perception, but
in twenty years of flying he had learned to trust his gut feelings. His gut was sending a persistent signal. Something was
happening. *What?*

In the next instant he knew.

B.J. Johnson's voice crackled on the radio. "Missile in the
air! Runner One-one, six o'clock low, hot on the Ironclaw."

A jolt of adrenaline surged through him. His RWR was
silent. "One's naked." Meaning he wasn't targeted by radar.

"Two's naked." No warning either.

Maxwell saw it. A tiny plume, ahead and below, between him and the Chameleon. Against the dull blue of the sea, it looked like a distant ember.

*It's targeting the decoy.*

With morbid fascination, Maxwell watched the plume close the distance to the Chameleon. *Where did it come from?* His eyes scanned the piece of sky where the plume had been when he first saw it. Then he scanned farther back to where it must have been when B.J. called it.

He did a rough calculation. If it was an AA-11 Archer, which moved at something better than Mach two, it would cover about—he scratched for an answer, then came up with it—1,500 feet every second. More or less.

His eyes went to the empty sky over his left shoulder. If the Archer was launched five seconds ago, it would have come from—

*There.* A glimmer, low, nearly abeam his port wing.

It was between him and B.J. Johnson's Hornet. He kept his eyes glued to that spot in the sky, unwilling to blink. Yes, for sure, there was *something.*

"Runner One-one is padlocked." Informing his wingmen his eyes were locked onto something. *What?*

As he watched, it faded from his vision.

Maxwell was still staring at the spot when, in his peripheral vision, he sensed an orange burst beyond the nose of his Hornet.

The missile had impacted the decoy.

"Runner One-two," came B.J.'s voice, "Ironclaw has taken a hit!"

Maxwell swung his gaze to where the decoy had been. It was gone. In its place was a roiling debris cloud, passing under the nose of Maxwell's Hornet. Well, he thought, that was a hostile act if he ever saw one.

He hauled the Hornet's nose toward the empty space

where he had last seen the glimmer. "Alpha Whiskey, Iron-claw is down. Runner One-one is engaged, neutral."

"Runner one-two, no joy, visual." B.J. didn't see the bandit, but she had visual contact with her flight leader.

"Runner One-two, cross-turn, I'm low, engaged." There was no time for explanations. He was having a hard enough time keeping sight of this bandit.

In the left break, he picked it up again. *The glimmer.* Coming toward him.

There was no shape to it, no definition. Only an ephemeral grayness, fading in and out of Maxwell's vision.

Again it vanished. Maxwell kept the Hornet's nose aimed at the spot where he had last seen the object.

The voice of B.J. Johnson came over his earphones. "Runner One-two's cross-turning high, visual, no joy, no joy. Where's the bandit?"

*Good question,* he thought. "Runner One-one, tally one, on my nose. Two, stay high and cover me. Three and Four, strip and bug east. Check six for spitters." He was ordering B.J. to stay and support him while the second element bugged out of the fight. *You can't fight what you can't see.*

Maxwell mashed down the weapons selector for AIM-9M. He turned to move the seeker circle over the place where he expected the stealth jet to be. To his surprise, he was getting an intermittent growl in his headset. He uncaged the seeker and it whistled a *shreeeeee* indicating a lock on the heat source.

Was the Sidewinder's heat-seeking head really tracking the invisible bandit?

Yes, definitely. He could see the gray shape again inside the HUD-displayed seeker circle. It was closing, head-on. The range was close for a head-on. It might be his only shot.

He squeezed the trigger.

*Whoom!* The two-hundred pound Sidewinder leaped from the left wingtip rail.

"Fox Two," Maxwell called, signaling the launch of a Sidewinder. With his eyes he followed the faint gray corkscrew trail of the missile. It would lead him to the bandit.

"Runner One, you're targeted!" called B.J. Johnson. "Missile in the air, on your nose."

*Shit!* The bandit had just taken his own shot. Now he was defensive. He could only hope his Sidewinder found its target.

He broke hard to the left, grunting against the G force. The missile had to be another heat-seeker. He was still getting no radar warning. He jabbed the flares dispenser, sending out a trail of incendiary decoys. Although he was belly-up to the missile coming at him he knew roughly where it had to be.

Maxwell tightened his rolling pull, continuing through inverted. Digging out the back side of the maximum-G barrel roll, the G force smashed him into the seat. The G suit squeezed his legs and abdomen like a hydraulic vise, keeping the blood in his head and not pooling in his lower extremities.

Still, his vision was tunneling down. He tightened his leg muscles, fighting to stay conscious against eight times the force of gravity. Sweat poured from under his helmet, stinging his eyes.

He rolled wings level, still pulling the jet to its computer-limited G load. The missile should be in terminal guidance. He *had* to see it. It should be—

There. Up and to the left. Passing aft of his wing line.

He relaxed his pull on the stick and gasped in relief. The missile had gone stupid. He was still alive.

He swung his attention back to the forward quarter. *Where was the bandit?* He had to be out there—

He was. Dead ahead and close. So close, he thought for a moment they would collide.

As the shimmering apparition flashed past on his left, Maxwell got his first good glimpse of the aircraft. He saw it clearly for less than a second, but it was enough. In that instant he felt as though he were peering through a window to his past. He was back in a place five years ago, in the high desert of Nevada. It was all there, as if in a dream.

The diamond shape. No vertical tail.

*The Black Star.*

Or a damned good knockoff. And it was trying to kill him.

"Runner One-two is still visual, no joy," called B.J. Johnson from directly overhead. "You got a tally on the bandit?"

"Affirmative. He just passed down my left side. I'm engaged, left hand turn." He hauled the Hornet's nose across the Black Star's tail, peering back over his shoulder to keep it in sight. It was gone. He kept his turn in, but relaxed his pull. He squinted, scanning the horizon for the telltale shimmer.

"Runner One-two, scan in front of me for that shimmer. I think we're in a single circle flow."

"Two's looking."

*Where the hell is it?* He felt like he was in a knife fight in a blackened room. The other guy could see him, but he was blind.

Maxwell felt a stab of fear. *It's out there somewhere.* It would fire another—

"Runner One, I see something. The shimmer is at your ten to eleven o'clock, maybe a mile, closing."

Okay, he knew where the bandit was, but he still didn't have a visual. The Black Star had made a level turn in a single circle flow. Turning inside of him.

"Skipper, he's pulling lead on you. Two's rolling in with guns."

Maxwell cursed and yanked on the stick. It had been a mistake, relaxing his turn after the head-on pass. He gave the bastard some turning room.

He glimpsed the grayish silhouette. Coming at him again. As he stared, the shimmering image faded from view.

A flash caught his eye. *Cannon!* Behind the strobing muzzle flash shimmered the amorphous shape of the Black Star.

"Tracers, tracers! Guns defense!" B.J. was screaming in to the radio.

Instinctively, Maxwell rolled out and pulled the nose of the Hornet up and away from the Black Star. Out of the enemy's turning plane. He hunched down in the cockpit, waiting for the cannon shells to shred his jet. It was a high deflection shot. At such an acute angle, the guy couldn't possibly hit him.

*Thunk. Thunk.* It felt like a giant hammer walloping the airframe of the Hornet.

The Chinese pilot, whoever he was, was no amateur. He was getting hits from a nearly ninety-degree angle. Maxwell turned harder, again grunting against the force of the Gs. The tracer arcs were falling behind him. The deflection angle and the Gs were too great for the Chinese pilot to keep tracking him.

The winking strobe of the cannon extinguished. The Black Star was again invisible.

Maxwell's Hornet was rocketing upward. He rolled right to see B.J.'s jet diving down toward the Black Star, cannon fire blazing from the nose.

B.J.'s voice crackled over the radio. "Runner One-two's lost sight."

That was it. Time to get of Dodge. Turn tail and run. It was an inglorious way to end a fight, but Maxwell knew they had no option. If they stayed, the Black Star would kill him and, probably, his wingman.

Their only hope was in the superior acceleration of the Hornet. Still in afterburner, he pointed the jet's nose toward the empty hole in space where he had last glimpsed the Black Star. With its two F-414 engines at full thrust, the Hornet was approaching supersonic speed.

"Roger. Bug out, bug out. One's visual. Come hard left to a one-thirty heading. I'm high at your ten o'clock."

"Two's visual."

"Runner One-two maintain that heading. One's shackling for position."

Maxwell pulled his jet across the top of his wingman in a hard S-turn for spacing. He rolled out into a tight combat spread position.

With their noses down, in full afterburner, they accelerated through Mach one, in the opposite direction the Black Star had been headed. It would be tough for the Chinese pilot to reverse his turn in time to catch them and get a missile off.

Maxwell knew it was luck that the guy hadn't killed him with the Archer. B.J.'s tally call had saved him. It was more luck that he hadn't killed him with the cannon. He had a feeling he'd used up his luck.

He craned his neck, peering around. No sign of the Black Star. No missile in the air.

He looked back inside, scanning the panel. He had taken at least two hits. What was the damage? No red lights, no warnings—

His fuel quantity. It was decreasing rapidly.

B.J. Johnson confirmed it. "Runner One-one, you're streaming fuel."

Maxwell shook his head. All in all, this was turning into a very shitty day. He was in a full afterburner dash to outrun an invisible enemy. And he would be out of gas in—he did a rough calculation—ten minutes. Maybe less.

"Stay with me, Runner One-two. We'll do a battle damage check after we've put some distance behind us. Alpha Whiskey, Runner One-one and One-two need the tanker, no delay."

"We copy all that, Runner. Oilcan is on station Bravo Lima. He bears zero-nine-zero degrees, eighty miles. Can you make it?"

"I don't know. I've got battle damage and a fuel leak."

"Alpha Whiskey roger. We're launching the SAR helo now."

He would have to come out of afterburner before the thirsty engines sucked his tanks dry. He could only pray that the Black Star wasn't still in hot pursuit.

It would be close. He knew Boyce wouldn't order the tanker to come any closer. If the Black Star was still out there, it could pick them all off.

Five minutes elapsed. No longer in afterburner, Maxwell's Hornet slowed back to subsonic speed.

The digital readout in the HUD indicated 410 knots.

While Maxwell flew a direct course for the tanker, B.J. Johnson flew a crisscross pattern behind him. The second section, Gordon and Miller, rejoined their flight leader. They remained high, off his starboard wing.

No missile alerts. No more wispy gray telltale trails of an incoming heat-seeker. The Black Star was gone, or he was setting them all up for a turkey shoot.

Maxwell's fuel totalizer was reading five hundred pounds when he acquired a visual ID on the tanker. Less than three minutes of fuel. At this low quantity, the gauges were inaccurate. It could be off by more than three hundred pounds.

"Oilcan, Runner One-one is closing. Start a left turn and give me the drogue."

"Oilcan is way ahead of you, Runner," said the tanker pilot. "Drogue's out, and here comes your turn."

The tanker was a three-engine KC-10, an Air Force version of the civilian DC-10 transport. Fifty feet behind the big jet streamed the drogue, the three-foot basket at the end of a flexible hose.

Maxwell ignored the persistent low fuel warning while he flew an intercept curve toward the turning tanker. He knew the indication had to be zero. At best, he'd get one shot at the drogue.

He extended the Hornet's in-flight refueling probe, affixed to the starboard fuselage. The gray mass of the big tanker swelled in his windshield.

*Hurry,* he told himself. No time for niceties like checking out the condition of the basket, like getting himself stabilized in position before easing the probe into the drogue. *Hurry.*

Fifty feet. *Don't overshoot.* He fanned the Hornet's speed brake.

He kept the jet moving, sliding into position behind the tanker. The drogue was dancing around in the slipstream of the turning tanker. The trick was *not* to chase the wiggling basket, but aim for the center of its movement. It was easy, when you had lots of gas for another try.

Twenty feet. Any second now the engines would gulp the last of the fuel. The whine of the turbines would go silent. The Hornet would be a glider.

Ten feet. The drogue was twitching around in the right quarter of his canopy. *Hurry.* If he missed—

The probe hit the rim of the basket, glanced off like a basketball on a hoop, then skittered into the opening.

*Klunk.* He felt the probe make solid mechanical contact with the refueling nozzle in the drogue. A ripple passed along the length of the hose as the probe shoved the drogue forward. Fuel began to flow down the hose, through the probe, into the Hornet's empty tanks.

Maxwell felt the pent-up tension peel away from him. The tanker could deliver fuel faster than he was losing it. He'd make it back to the *Reagan.*

"Good shot," said the tanker pilot. "No swimming for you today, Navy. The United States Air Force is taking you back to your boat. Tell you what. We're gonna have you sing the Air Force song on the way."

"No way," said Maxwell.

"Okay, we're flexible. You just hum the tune, and we'll sing."

# CHAPTER NINE

# DONG-JIN

*Taipei, Taiwan*
*0935, Friday, 12 September*

Incredible, thought Huang. Wireless technology. He still had trouble believing such a thing actually existed. The signal on the satellite phone was clear, no static, no interruptions. With such a device he could converse with anyone in mainland China—with whom Taiwan was at war—as easily as he could with a member of his staff in Taipei.

"What is the problem?" said the voice on the other end. "Who is in charge there?"

Huang bristled at the harsh tone. As the second-highest official in Taiwan's government, he was not pleased to be addressed in such disrespectful language.

He forced himself to keep his voice neutral. "Madame Soong continues to occupy the executive office, General. She has not yet resigned."

"That is preposterous. You assured us she would be gone within a day after Li was dead."

"So we expected. She seems determined to remain the head of state."

"And make war on the People's Republic of China. A

madwoman!" Tsin's voice was rising in a crescendo. "Have you and the other ministers lost your manhood? Why haven't you removed her?"

Huang held the earpiece of the satellite telephone away from him. He didn't want to tell General Tsin the truth—that the ministers were supporting Soong and not him, the Premier. "It is not a simple matter, General, deposing a President who refuses to step down."

"Why did you not warn us of such a development?"

He knew where this conversation was going. He had never met General Tsin in person, but he was well acquainted with the fiery officer's style. Tsin had risen to command of the PLA in the classic Chinese communist tradition. He overtook his competitors by eliminating them. Those he could not displace, he managed to label as traitors and had them, one at a time, arrested and tried.

One of the hallmarks of Tsin's long career was his abiding obsession to return Hong Kong and Taiwan to the sphere of the PRC. Hong Kong had come with relative ease, the result of long negotiation. Dealing with the dispirited Great Britain was like eroding a stone with dripping water. The former colony was returned to China in 1997.

Taiwan was another matter. Instead of clinging to the mantle of a decaying empire, it had thrived as a protectorate of the United States. Indeed, the status of Taiwan had been an ongoing source of tension between the PRC and the U.S. for half a century.

Five years ago General Tsin had cultivated Franklin Huang as a compliant negotiating partner. When Taiwan became a part of mother China, Huang was to be installed as the provincial governor.

At least, that had been the understanding. It hinged, of course, on his assuming the presidency after Li's untimely death in the Airbus. It should have been only a formality. He would replace the Vice President who would have the good

sense to step down when confronted with the gravity of Taiwan's situation.

She didn't step down. She declared war.

"It was a surprise to all of us," said Huang. "She gave no
indication that she would initiate military action."

"You have made a serious misjudgment, Huang. Now you
must correct your mistake. If you do not, I promise you that
you will end your career gathering shit in the worst of
China's collective pig farms."

Huang could feel his destiny slipping like an eel from his
grasp. "What would you have me do, General?"

"Get rid of the Soong woman."

"She has the support of several cabinet ministers, including old Ma. Most of the military general staff is backing
her."

"That is your problem. Do what has to be done."

"Do you mean that I—"

He heard the connection go dead.

Lowering the phone, he considered Tsin's words. *Do what
has to be done.* He knew what that meant.

*Chouzhou Air Base, People's Republic of China*

Colonel Zhang Yu couldn't believe it. *An easy kill.* And he
had missed.

Gazing back over his shoulder at the blue haze above the
strait, Zhang thought again about the encounter with the
American Hornet. The more he thought about it, the more he
was sure. It was a trap. And he had nearly been snared in it.

The damned Hornet pilot. Somehow he evaded the missiles Zhang fired at him, then he nearly killed him with a
shot of his own. It was luck—and the Dong-jin's miniscule
infrared presence—that allowed Zhang to defeat the missile.
Then the devil American had escaped even though Zhang

was sure he had put several rounds from his cannon into the
jet.

It all started with the idiots in Air Defense Command.
They had scrambled him to intercept what they said was an
American EA-6B Prowler. It was urgent that he shoot it
down, even though it was escorted by eight Hornet fighters.

The presence of a Prowler so close to the mainland could
mean only one thing. The Americans were entering the war.
They were coming to the aid of Taiwan.

"It wasn't a Prowler, was it?" Zhang said on the intercom.

"No, Colonel," answered Lieutenant Lo Shouyi from his
station in the backseat of the Dong-jin. Lo was Zhang's
weapons systems officer. His voice quavered.

"What was it, then?"

"A decoy of some kind. It was delivering a radar signature
like that of an EA-6B."

"That much was obvious. It was your task to determine
the difference. Why did you not recognize the false signature?" Zhang knew the young man was terrified. Flying such
a critical mission with the PLA air force's most eminent
squadron commander was a grave responsibility.

"I . . . had only the radar, Colonel. It was showing a precise image of an EA-6B."

Zhang wanted to shoot the incompetent fool. He had
fallen for the Americans' little hoax. Not until Zhang saw his
missile impact the target did the truth strike him. They had
been duped.

It still didn't make sense. For what purpose did they send
so many fighters to escort a worthless robot aircraft?

As the possibilities flitted like fireflies through Zhang's
mind, one thought kept inserting itself back into his consciousness. It was the only logical explanation. *They wanted
to draw you out.*

Which could mean only one thing. They knew—or
strongly suspected—the existence of the Dong-jin, the

stealth fighter the Americans called Black Star. They wanted to confirm its identity so that they could find a way to counter it. Or destroy it.

The secret of the Dong-jin was no longer a secret.

The brown-and-green patchwork of Fujian Province was slipping beneath them. Zhang eased the throttles back another increment, setting up for the approach to the base at Chouzhou. He would leave the plasma field of the Dong-jin energized until he'd landed and cleared the runway. The Taiwanese F-16 pilots would like nothing so much as to catch the strange-looking fighter when it was vulnerable, with its gear and flaps out.

Zhang broke radio silence to announce his arrival. "Chouzhou Tower, Dong-Jin One is ten kilometers on final."

"Dong-Jin One cleared to land on runway zero-two," answered the tower controller. "All surfaces reported satisfactory."

Zhang grunted his acknowledgment. The 3,000 meter northeast–southwest runway was cratered the night before by enemy bombs. Emergency crews had been working nonstop to patch the holes in the vital runway. Without the hard surface, Zhang's three Dong-jin stealth jets could not operate. Without the Dong-jin, they could not stop the Taiwanese air force from decimating their bases.

By the time they landed and cleared the runway, Zhang had gotten over his initial fury about the encounter with the Americans. Time was on his side, he reflected. Even if the Americans knew the secret of the Dong-jin and passed their knowledge to the Taiwanese, it was too late. Nothing would change the outcome of the war. The Dong-jin was still invincible.

But that didn't excuse the fools who had vectored the Dong-jin into the Americans' trap. Such incompetence must not go unpunished.

He rolled the jet down the ramp of the wide-doored revetment and brought it to a halt. The hangar doors closed behind him. He climbed down from the cockpit, not bothering to wait for Lo in the backseat.

He strode over to the squadron security officer, an unsmiling major who was armed with an automatic pistol. Zhang gazed back at the Dong-jin's cockpit. Lieutenant Lo was still unstrapping, watching them with wide, fearful eyes.

"Arrest him," said Zhang. "He is charged with dereliction of duty."

"Yes, Colonel. And then?"

"Execute him."

*Frigate* Kai Yang, *Taiwan Strait*

Watching the resupply ship pull away, Commander Lei breathed a sigh of relief. It had been necessary to rearm and reprovision at sea even though their home port, Keelung, was only 140 kilometers away. He had fired all the Harpoons and needed resupply. He had also expended half a dozen Mark 46 torpedoes, two of which had killed the Chinese Kilo boat.

Even if he had the time to cruise back into port, which he didn't, it was too dangerous. Keelung was only thirty kilometers north of Taipei, Taiwan's capitol, which was now under savage bombardment by PRC missiles.

The Chinese had nothing as good as the Harpoon, but they had something good enough—the C-801 Sardine. The short-range missile was armed with its own GPS guidance unit, courtesy of the U.S., and was now finding targets on the island of Taiwan with uncanny accuracy. Like the Taiwanese did with the Harpoon, the PLA had converted the C-801 to a land-attack missile and reconfigured the guidance system to a GPS tracking unit.

Taiwan's first line of defense against the PLA missiles was the Patriot. The trouble with the Patriot was that its typical intercept range put it perilously close to friendly soil. With a clean hit on the incoming target, the debris from both missiles sometimes did as much damage as an unintercepted missile.

Taipei was taking the brunt of it.

Being tied to a pier or even moored to a buoy in the harbor made Lei's frigate an easy target. Worse, he was sure enemy submarines were stationed at the entrance to every harbor and channel around Taiwan.

Win or lose, the *Kai Yang* would spend the war at sea.

*If we just had the Aegis system,* he thought bitterly. Aegis was the highly advanced American naval missile defense system. The heart of the Aegis system was the AN/SPY-1, a multifunction, phased-array radar that detected and tracked all incoming threats. A mix of onboard missiles protected the Aegis vessel, and weapons like the Tomahawk cruise missile gave it offensive clout.

The U.S. had decided *not* to sell the Aegis system to Taiwan.

Lei had to laugh when he thought of the so-called logic behind it. The U.S. had stopped recognizing Taiwan—the Republic of China—as a sovereign nation soon after it granted such recognition to mainland China—the People's Republic of China. That had been on Richard Nixon's watch, and every administration since then had gone a bit further to sweeten relations with China and to distance itself from Taiwan.

But America was still Taiwan's ally, at least in spirit. Whenever China huffed and puffed about forcibly absorbing Taiwan into the PRC, the U.S. had cast its heavy shadow over the strait—usually in the form of a carrier battle group.

So far it had worked. The U.S.'s policy toward Taiwan was maddeningly ambiguous. Taiwan was no longer a country. But Taiwan could not be taken over by China. Not yet, at least. Not as long as China's communist government continued its repressive ways against its own people.

Taiwan was a pawn in a power play between giants. It was neither independent nor subservient, and that was the way the American politicians wanted it. It made Lei snicker when he imagined how President Soong's preemptive war was upsetting those politicians' visions of a perpetual stalemate between the Chinas.

Lei's thoughts were interrupted by the OOD. "Course, Captain?"

"Steer two hundred sixty-five degrees. We're heading back into the strait." He turned to the executive officer. "Order the crew to battle stations."

*Chouzhou Air Base, People's Republic of China*

Colonel Zhang sipped at his tea as he reclined behind his desk. His hand still trembled from the closeness of the encounter with the Americans. *That damned Lo.*

It occurred to Zhang that he might have been too peremptory when he ordered the execution of Lieutenant Lo. Trained systems officers were in short supply. But this was war. Executing a bungler like Lo was necessary, not so much as a punishment but as an example. The other officers of the Dong-jin project had to understand the consequences of their blunders.

It was a task that Colonel Zhang understood well. His own rapid ascent through the ranks of the PLA he owed to his success in purifying the air force. He had been assigned the task of ferreting out the politically untrustworthy members of the PLA—dissidents, collaborators, rumormongers. His methods were harsh, meant to discourage others from breaking ranks.

As a reward for his diligence, his mentor and patron, General Tsin, Chief of Staff of the PLA, had given him command of the vital Dong-jin project.

Zhang set down his teacup. His hand had stopped shaking, and he felt once again in command of his emotions. He lifted the telephone that linked his office to that of his superior.

"This is Tsin," answered the General. "I've been waiting for your report."

"I am very sorry, General. I first had to deal with a matter of military incompetence."

Zhang told him about the encounter with the unmanned decoy and the Hornets.

"What is the disposition of this systems officer who mistook the decoy?" asked Tsin.

"He is dead."

Zhang heard a grunt of approval. Tsin said, "But this means the Americans know about the Dong-jin."

"So it would seem, General."

"And they know it was the Dong-jin that destroyed Li's aircraft?"

"Most probably."

"What else did they learn?"

"Not much, I think. Only that it exists."

A moment of silence passed. Zhang could imagine the grizzled general lighting another of his endless chain of aromatic cigarettes, eyes squinting against the smoke. Finally Tsin said, "It is of no importance. It will be a short war. What they know, or think they know, will have no effect. For the moment, the Dong-jin is invincible. Is that not what you have assured me, Zhang?"

To such a question there was only one answer. Zhang felt his hand tremble again. "Yes, General, you may be certain. The Dong-jin is invincible."

*Groom Lake, Nevada*

*That sonofabitch.*

Raymond Lutz felt a pounding in his temples as he stared at the photograph in the magazine. Even before he read the caption beneath the photograph, he recognized the smirking face in the picture, that cocky, glory-hound test-pilot posture.

Maxwell.

It was five in the evening at Groom Lake, and Lutz was alone in his research lab. He had just picked up the new issue of *The Hook*, the journal of Navy carrier aviation. He hated the magazine, but he always felt compelled to read it from cover to cover. In each issue he'd see the smiling cocky face of someone he knew from the old days. Commander Somebody bagging his thousandth carrier landing. Captain Somebody Else grinning from the cockpit of his Super Hornet like it was his personal sports car. Some other hotshot aviator taking command of his own fighter squadron.

This time it was Maxwell. The sonofabitch kept reappearing in Lutz's life like a bad dream.

An entire page of photos was devoted to the USS *Ronald Reagan*. In the center of the page was a pilot in a flight suit standing in front of a Super Hornet. Another officer wearing a flight jacket and two stars on his collar was handing him a plaque.

With his jaw muscles knotting, Lutz read the caption:

*Reagan Battle Group Commander RADM John Hightree presents VFA-36 skipper Brick Maxwell this year's Battle "E." Maxwell led his Roadrunners to a clean sweep over all Pacific Fleet strike fighter squadrons to capture the coveted award for battle efficiency.*

As he stared at the photo, the bad memories came flooding back like the pain of an old wound. *Maxwell.* How did the glory hound keep doing it?

He remembered exactly when his loathing for Maxwell began. They were in the same preflight class at Pensacola. Though Lutz finished number one in the class and Maxwell second, Lutz's 20/40 eyes disqualified him for a pilot's slot. Instead he went to naval flight officer training, which meant the backseat of a Navy jet. He was along for the ride.

Maxwell sailed through Navy flight training, graduating with a slot in F/A-18 Hornets. Meanwhile Lutz was denied his first choice—a radar intercept officer seat in the F-14 Tomcat—and became an electronic-warfare officer strapped into the back of a blunt-nosed, slow-moving EA-6B Prowler.

The next time he encountered Maxwell was at the U.S. Naval Test Pilot School at Patuxent River, Maryland. Maxwell was training to be a test pilot, while Lutz was at Pax River to become a flight test engineer.

Lutz was still finding it difficult to conceal his resentment of hotshots like Maxwell, but he knew his day was coming. He was on a fast track to NASA and a seat in the space shuttle.

He had all the right tickets—aero engineering degree from Cal Tech, a masters in astrophysics, summa cum laude, from Stanford. Number one class ranking in flight test school. Lutz was undeniably brilliant, and even NASA, populated though it was by Neanderthal hotshots, would *have* to select him as an astronaut.

One day, a couple of years after Lutz graduated from flight test school, he received the notice from the NASA selection board. The notice contained the list of selectees for the next space shuttle training class. Lutz knew most of them—test pilots from the Navy, Air Force, Marines, a few flight test engineering officers, and three civilians with advanced backgrounds in aviation medicine or physics.

Near the top of the list was a name that caused his jaw

muscles to clench uncontrollably: *Lieutenant Commander Samuel T. Maxwell, USN*. The glory hound was going to be an astronaut.

Lutz scanned the entire list. His name was not on it.

In the same envelope was a polite letter from the director of candidate screening, a woman named Fitch. She thanked Lutz for his interest in NASA and wished him success in his future endeavors.

Something snapped inside Lutz. He had never been a socializer, always preferring predictable bytes and digits and algorithms over the company of colleagues, but now he became a recluse. He stopped seeing his few acquaintances. He holed up for days at a time with his computer.

His wife, an attractive, brown-haired woman named Joanne, packed up and left, and that was fine with Lutz. To hell with her. Most of his former friends drifted away, and that was fine too. To hell with all of them. He didn't need a wife and he didn't need friends and he didn't need those overblown senior officers who kept calling him to say he ought to just kick back and lighten up or his military career might be affected.

It was too late, and he didn't care. When he was passed over for promotion to the rank of commander, Lutz resigned his commission. He took a position as a civilian research engineer on the secret Calypso Blue project at Groom Lake.

Groom Lake—and the fleshpots of Las Vegas—suited him just fine. Unlike the Navy, private industry didn't require Lutz to socialize with his colleagues. He could be a recluse. He could gamble in the casinos. He could pick up hookers.

He could be a spy.

Soon after he reached that conclusion, two years after he arrived at Groom Lake, he met the person who would make it possible. Someone named Tom.

# CHAPTER TEN

# MAI-LING

*Las Vegas, Nevada*
*1930, Friday, 12 September*

"Spy?" Tom took a drink of champagne and said, "That's passé, Ray. Find some other job description. One that's not so comic bookish."

"How about traitor?" said Lutz.

"A meaningless concept," said Tom. "At least to people like you and me. Traitor to what? That kind of Cold War sentimentality is reserved for all the simpleminded flag-wavers in the world."

Lutz tossed down his Scotch. It occurred to him that he knew very little about Tom, but he was always amazed at the agent's flippant attitude about the subject that could get them both snuffed out in a heartbeat. Though not Chinese, Tom had slender, almost delicate features. The agent had some kind of inner steel that Lutz could only imagine himself possessing.

Whenever they had this kind of dialogue in the casino, he did as Tom had taught him. He positioned himself next to one of the audio speakers so he could blend his voice into the din of the music. When he spoke, he shielded his lips with a glass, blocking any hidden surveillance cameras.

It was all part of being a spy—or whatever job description Tom wanted to use.

"How about purveyor of information?" said Tom. "That's a good one. Professional purveyor of vital information."

Lutz shrugged. The truth was, he didn't give a damn what they called him. Just so the money showed up in the account.

Sitting here in the bar, working on his third Scotch and still feeling the adrenaline rush of a successful transaction, he thought again how easy it had been to enter this business.

It started two months after he'd arrived at Groom Lake. That was when he realized that he had access to the most valuable military commodity in the world—the Black Star.

All he needed was a customer.

He wrote a page-long letter to the Consul General of the People's Republic of China in San Francisco. In the letter he explained the kind of work he performed at the research facility, and then he specified exactly how they should contact him.

Ten days later he was in the main casino of Caesar's Palace, sitting at the third slot machine from the end, sixth row, exactly where he had said in the letter. It was six minutes before nine o'clock. His pulse was racing.

The arrangement had looked foolproof on paper. Now Lutz was beset by doubts. What if the letter had been intercepted? What if the FBI showed up? What if—

"I've been looking forward to meeting you, Mr. Lutz." The voice belonged to the person next to him, playing the adjacent slot machine.

Lutz's heart rate accelerated another twenty beats. "I . . . I play this machine every Friday," he said, following the script in his letter.

"Fridays are better than Mondays."

The words were correct. Meaningless but correct, right out of the letter he had written. Lutz kept his eyes on his machine but now he was curious about the player next to him. "Who are you?"

"You can call me Tom."

He nodded. "My name is Raymond."

"Excellent," said Tom. "This is going extremely well. You see? We're already on a first-name basis."

They continued talking, and some of the trepidation slipped away from Lutz. In his worst fears he had imagined that the Chinese, for whatever reason, might have turned him in. A team of FBI agents might have been waiting for him. Instead, there was Tom.

Still playing the slot machine, Tom explained how Lutz was to make the data drops. The timing and locations would change, conforming to no predictable pattern. Tom was his handler and would be his only contact.

They haggled briefly over Lutz's compensation, then settled on a payment schedule. The total would amount to a hundred times more than Lutz had ever seen in his personal bank account.

Lutz began to feel giddy. He was beginning a whole new life. No longer was he wasting his finest skills on an undeserving client like the United States government. *He* was in control now. Master of his own destiny. He would extract justice for the disservice done him by his own country.

During the next months, Lutz learned that he had a taste for espionage. His engineer's brain came up with unique ways to transmit the ultrasecret data of the Black Star project. He devised a method of microencryption, fitting the secrets of Calypso Blue into the interior of a gaming chip.

The physical act of transferring the chip never failed to fill him with terror. But despite his gnawing fear, he discovered that he craved the heart-pounding, dry-mouthed danger of the game. There was something addictive about it.

And something else. After each drop, Lutz found to his astonishment that he was as sexually excited as a bull in rutting season. He was invariably drawn like a magnet to the casino bar where he knew he would find the special blonde in the leather skirt.

*USS* Ronald Reagan

"Gentlemen," said Admiral Hightree as he stepped into the compartment, "our guests from Taiwan."

The three Chinese had arrived aboard the *Reagan*'s C-2 COD—carrier onboard delivery—aircraft. Hightree had been there to meet them when they stepped onto the deck. He took them directly to the flag conference space.

Maxwell rose. So did CAG Boyce and Sticks Stickney, the *Reagan*'s skipper. Already standing at the end of the conference table were the two civilians—Ashby, the NSA analyst, and a bespectacled CIA officer named Salada, who was the assistant station chief in Taipei.

A moment of awkward silence passed as the Americans and the Chinese sized each other up.

"The senior military attaché in Taipei arranged this meeting," said Hightree. "He thought it was urgent enough that we have this group flown out to the *Reagan*."

Each wore a dark olive battle dress uniform. They still had their flotation vests from the ride in the *Reagan*'s COD. The senior officer, an unsmiling man with a lined, hard-eyed face, brought his heels together and said, "I am Colonel Chiu Yusheng, commander of the Special Operations Branch, Republic of China Army. This is my adjutant, Major Wei-jin, and this is"—he nodded toward the third person in his group—"Captain Chen Mai-ling, formerly of the People's Liberation Army."

Hightree and Boyce exchanged a quick glance. Boyce

looked at the woman again. "Excuse me, but I believe I heard that you—"

"You heard correctly," said the woman. "Mainland China. Fujian Province. I arrived in Taiwan two months ago."

Boyce nodded, still confused.

"Captain Chen is a defector," said Colonel Chiu in stilted English. "I brought her to this meeting because she has information that we think your government might wish to have."

From the end of the conference table, Maxwell studied the visitors. The woman was tall for a Chinese, about five-six. Even in the ill-fitting utilities, her figure was hard to conceal. There was something about her—long hair flowing beneath the black headband, the way she stood with one hip thrust outward—that didn't fit the mold of a military officer.

She caught him studying her. For an instant their gazes locked. Maxwell forced himself not to look at her.

Hightree motioned for them all to take seats at the conference table. "I'll remind everyone that everything discussed here is classified. No cellular devices or recorders will be permitted."

Colonel Chiu sat next to Boyce. Noting Boyce's gnawed cigar, he produced a pack of cigarettes. Without asking permission, he proffered the pack around, then lit up.

Boyce raised his eyebrows and looked over at Hightree. The Admiral just shrugged.

Chiu exhaled a cloud of smoke and said, "Captain Chen claims that she was a technician on a secret PLA project at Chouzhou Air Base."

"Not a technician," the young woman said, drawing a scowl from Chiu. "Research scientist. And I'm no longer a captain in the PLA air force. That life is finished. For your information, I have a bachelor's degree in thermodynamics, with graduate work in terahertz radiation."

Maxwell studied the woman as she explained how she escaped China aboard one of the fishing junks that regularly ferried refugees from the mainland. Chiu interrupted her several times to explain that portions of her story could not be verified.

Maxwell watched them. It was obvious they didn't hit it off. Her English was nearly perfect, which made him curious. "Miss Chen," he asked, "where did you do your graduate work?"

For a moment she gazed across the table at him. "In the United States. At Rensselaer Polytechnic, in Troy, New York. I studied there for two years."

Maxwell nodded, keeping his face impassive. "Who was your professor?"

She gave him a quizzical look. "I had several. Dr. Ormsby, in photoelectric theory. Dr. Thornblad was my academic counselor. He lectured in the graduate physics department."

"How about Professor Oglethorpe? Max Oglethorpe?"

"I don't recall the name."

"Where did you park your car when you entered Academy Hall?"

"Car?" Another quizzical look. "I didn't have a car. Academy Hall was for undergraduates. I never went there."

"How many columns are on the front of the engineering center?"

"Why are you asking these questions? Am I being interrogated?"

"Yes. How many columns?"

The almond eyes narrowed, watching him with wariness. "None. The Jonsson Engineering Center has a modern facade. No columns."

"Good answer."

"I take it you know something about Rensselaer," she said.

"Something. I'm an alumnus."

"Who is Professor Oglethorpe?"

"Nobody. I made him up."

"To see if I was lying?"

"More like an authenticity check."

"Does this mean I pass?" For another moment the eyes remained fixed on him.

"It means you went to Rensselaer. Or else you took the trouble to read a lot about the school."

Colonel Chiu was watching them both with a sour expression. He crushed out his cigarette in a coffee saucer. "Let's get to the reason we're here. Captain Chen claims that a secret stealth aircraft is based at the PLA field at Chouzhou."

"Not one," she said. "Two, and, by now, perhaps more."

"Have you seen these aircraft?" asked Boyce.

"Not in a finished state. I worked for two years on the development of the prototype. Six months ago, just as it was nearly ready to fly, I—"

"Defected," said Chiu. He spat the word out as if it were something vile.

"Why did you defect?" Maxwell asked.

"Political reasons." Again, the almond eyes. "My fiancé was a PLA air force major and a pilot. His name was Han Shaomin. He was arrested and accused of being a political dissident. He was sent to the *Laogai*—the PLA's concentration camps. I was informed that he was later executed."

"Was he a dissident?"

"He thought that the PLA was guilty of immoral conduct in suppressing the political minorities. If that made him a dissident, then I was one also."

"For which she was willing to betray her country," said Chiu. For a moment, the two exchanged another glowering look.

Boyce looked from one to the other. "It doesn't matter to us why she's here. What we want to know about is this stealth jet. If you will, Miss Chen, start from the beginning. Where did the technology come from?"

"Such information was not disclosed to me."

"But you have an idea."

"Of course. I presume it came from the United States."

Boyce nodded. "And how do you think it came from the United States?"

"In the usual manner. Bought. Or stolen."

"By whom?"

"That was never discussed. It was obvious that a great deal of secret information was flowing from the United States to China."

"Jesus," Boyce muttered and shook his head. "So tell us what you know about the—what do you call it?"

"Dong-jin. It translates roughly to something like Silent Wing."

She went on, in considerable detail, about her work on the stealth project. She told them about the electrochromatic plasma technology that, when energized, rendered the Dong-jin's shape nearly invisible in sunlight.

As she spoke, Maxwell followed her hands, watching her draw the invisible shape of the Dong-jin in the air. Again she caught him watching her. For a long moment the almond eyes locked on him.

When she was finished, a silence fell over the group. Maxwell looked around the table. He could sense each American thinking the same thing: An invisible killer—one they could neither see nor find—was hiding out there. And it belonged to China.

Finally Hightree pushed himself back from the table and stood. The other officers rose in unison. The meeting was over. The Americans shook hands with the Chinese, thanking them for the information.

Maxwell was the last. As he clasped the woman's hand, she held the handshake a few seconds longer than necessary.

"I enjoyed hearing about Rensselaer," he said.

"I liked it there," she said. "Maybe I'll go back someday." Still holding his hand, she said, "*Zaijian,* Commander Maxwell."

He looked at her quizzically. "Which means . . ."

"Good-bye," she said. "Until we meet again."

He smiled. "*Zaijian,* Miss Chen."

Chiu gave them both a scowl of disapproval. "Let's go," he said. "Our business here is finished."


"Was I imagining or what?" Boyce was tilted back in his desk chair, looking at Maxwell. "Did I observe some kind of basic hormonal chemistry bubbling between you and that Chinese girl?"

Maxwell shrugged. "We both went to RPI."

"Right. When old classmates get together, they always ogle each other like minks in heat."

"She's just glad to have someone to talk to. She has to deal with that hard-ass, Colonel Chiu."

"He seems to have a low opinion of defectors, even a foxy one like your classmate, Miss Chen." Boyce jammed his cigar back in his mouth and rose from the chair. "You heard her story. Never mind that you think she's got a cute butt. Is she telling the truth?"

"The part about Rensselaer was on the mark. It would be stupid of her to fake something like that because she knows we'll check it out. The stuff about the Black Star—the thing she calls Dong-jin—was spooky. Like she just came from Dreamland after working on the Calypso Blue project. She had too many details right. She couldn't know about that stuff unless she'd seen it."

Boyce seemed not to hear. He was on his feet, gnawing the cigar, staring at some object in infinite space.

Maxwell was getting a bad feeling. He'd seen that look before. Boyce was on to something, and it meant trouble.

*Groom Lake, Nevada*

The questions were stupid. And terrifying.

Lutz reclined in his desk chair and did his best to appear bored. He doodled on a notepad while the agents asked their questions. His heart was pumping like a steam engine.

"Who did you spend last weekend with?"

"Myself."

"Doing what, Dr. Lutz?"

"Gambling. Watching a show."

"Do you have a girlfriend?"

"That's my business. Am I accused of something?"

"We're just trying to establish your routine, how you spend your off time."

"My off time is my own affair."

"Do you ever hire a prostitute, Dr. Lutz?"

Lutz took a moment before he answered. They probably knew about his habits in the casino. If so, they would know about the hooker in the leather skirt. They wanted him to lie about it.

"I regard women as I do boats and airplanes," he said, trying to keep the tone light, "I prefer to rent."

The FBI agent's name was Swinford. He didn't smile. "Do you always rent the same one?"

"That's my business, not yours."

"Correct," said the agent. "You're not required to tell us anything. However, you should understand that it is our prerogative, if we feel you're concealing sensitive information, to place you under custody and continue this interrogation at our regional office in Las Vegas."

Lutz nodded. This jerk was used to getting his way, scaring the shit out of people with that stuff about placing them under custody and continuing the interrogation. Typical bullying tactics.

But it was working. Lutz *was* scared.

He forced himself to appear impassive. *Don't let them see that you're nervous. Don't talk too much.* "It might be helpful if you gentlemen would tell me the purpose of this interrogation."

Swinford said, "We're investigating possible . . . hypothetical breaches of security at the facility. This happens to be a high priority project, you know. We just like to run routine checks."

"What you mean is, there's been a leak."

The agents exchanged glances. "Why would you think that?"

"I've been here long enough. This isn't a routine check. You people are digging for something, these asinine questions about my sex life."

"What we want is for you to tell us about your routine. Talk us through your workday, how you secure the data you work with, what you do when you leave for the day or the weekend."

Lutz hesitated. "What I do here is classified top secret."

"We have top secret clearances."

"It doesn't matter what your clearance is. I'm not at liberty to talk about it."

Swinford produced a letter and laid it on Lutz's desk. "Notice the signature. That's the director of the research facility. The letter says that you will tell us everything we want to know about your job. If you have a problem with that, Doctor, pick up the phone and ask him yourself."

Lutz didn't bother reading the letter. He didn't need to call. The bastards had the keys to the kingdom.

He told them about his routine. He kept it loosely detailed, explaining how at the end of the day he deleted sensitive data from his hard disk, how the codes for access to the database were stored, how the software scrubbing program worked. In theory, nothing classified ever left his lab on paper or in digital form. Every byte of data was encrypted and maintained and stored in the facility's optical storage network.

As he explained the process, he watched Swinford's expression, trying to determine how much the man understood about the arcane technologies of data encryption and transmission. Not much, he judged. Swinford had that furrowed-brow look, like a man who was faking something he hadn't a clue about. Cops. They were like characters from comic books.

He finished the explanation. Swinford scribbled some notes, then said, "Okay, that's your routine. How about your colleagues? Have you ever noticed anything—you know, peculiar behavior, a habit pattern, a comment—that would suggest someone might be violating the security restrictions on the Calypso Blue project?"

Lutz nodded. There it was. They were telling him what they were looking for. Even the name of the stealth jet development project—Calypso Blue—was so secret no one knew it except those with the very highest clearance.

So they knew about the Black Star.

"You mean, have I ever suspected someone of leaking data?"

"Not suspected, necessarily. Just something that didn't quite fit. You know, someone whose behavior was a . . . little bit odd."

Lutz almost laughed. *A little bit odd.* That described half the research and development community. Research scientists were, by definition, a little bit odd. Some, more than a little.

But this was good. At least they were getting away from questions about him and the hooker in the leather skirt. He was beginning to relax now. And as he relaxed, he had the glimmering of an idea.

"Well, there was something . . ." He caught himself,

shook his head, then said, "No, never mind. It wouldn't mean anything to you."

Swinford perked up, like a dog seeing a bone. "What wouldn't mean anything?"

"Oh, it was just . . . no, it doesn't have any significance."

"Let us be the judge of that, Doctor. Tell us everything you've observed, and we'll sort out what's significant and what isn't."

Lutz put on a pained expression. "Well, I really don't think it means anything. But one of my colleagues, a fellow named Feingold—"

"Herbert Feingold?" Swinford was leafing through his notebook. "Works in the RAM lab of Calypso Blue?" The furrowed-brow look again. "What does RAM mean?"

"Radar absorbent material. Feingold is a physicist."

"Okay, fine. What about him?"

"Well, just that lately it seems that Herb—he's a bachelor too—seems to be spending a lot of money."

"On what?"

"Oh, the night life, I guess you'd call it. He's taken up heavy gambling, something he didn't do before. He always loses a bundle, thousands sometimes, which he never seems to mind."

Swinford was writing furiously in his notepad. "Where do you think he gets the money?"

"I wouldn't want to—"

"But you have an idea."

Lutz shook his head. "I know what you're suggesting, but it doesn't make sense. It's just too hard to believe that a guy like Herb Feingold would ever do anything, you know, disloyal." He looked at the three agents. "But there *were* those little hints. I guess you just never know about some people, do you?"

*USS* Ronald Reagan

Maxwell was right. Boyce was up to something.

They were alone in the air wing office. Boyce had sent Catfish Bass off to flag plot to retrieve the day's air plan. He was taking special pleasure in having the Air Force pilot run errands for him. Bass invariably got lost wandering the passageways, still bashing his shins into the knee-knockers. Boyce loved it.

Now Maxwell was seeing all the usual warning signals. Boyce was pacing the narrow compartment like a caged bear, gnawing on the cigar, hands jammed in his pockets.

He made one more circuit of the compartment, then stopped and removed his cigar. "Okay, now hear this. I've got an idea. We have to run it by the Admiral, of course, and after he cleans out his underwear he's gonna forward it up the chain. This one will go all the way to the Commander-in-Chief. But this President has a set of balls. I'll bet a case of twelve-year-old Scotch that he signs off on it."

"Signs off on what?"

"The Black Star, Chinese version."

Maxwell could hear the warning bells, loud and clear, going off in his head. "Ah, what exactly are we going to do, CAG?"

"Do?" He removed the cigar and looked at Maxwell as if he were a retarded sixth-grader. "What do you think? We're going to steal their little toy."

# CHAPTER ELEVEN

# THE VOLUNTEER

*USS* Ronald Reagan
*Taiwan Strait*
*1045, Saturday, 13 September*

It took eighteen hours.

When the Flash Priority message arrived on the *Reagan*—transmitted at the highest level of urgency via the carrier's Athena satellite connection—Boyce let out a war whoop. "Ha! I told you, didn't I? This is a President with *co-jones.*"

Boyce, Maxwell, Admiral Hightree, and the group operations officer, Captain Guido Vitale, stood around the long steel table in the SCIF—the Special Compartmentalized Intelligence Facility—located deep belowdecks in the ship's Surface Plot spaces. On the bulkhead next to them was an illuminated map of the Taiwan Strait, covering all of Taiwan and the coastal mainland of China.

Maxwell glanced at the tasking order. "How do we know this came via the President?"

"We know," said Hightree. "The spooks have an authentication system that verifies the origin of Flash Priorities."

Boyce said, "You can bet there's no way in hell CNO and

the Joint Chiefs would give this the go-ahead without the Commander-in-Chief signing off."

Hightree looked worried, like a man whose destiny was slipping out of his control. "Gentlemen, this operation has fallen into my lap, whether I wanted it or not. But listen to me. Every detail of the plan will be reviewed by me and my staff before your people lift a finger." He looked pointedly at Boyce. "Is that understood?"

Maxwell had to sympathize with Hightree. He was new to battle group command—less than three months—and he was not eager to take risks. Not as eager as Boyce.

"Yes, sir," said Boyce. "Understood."

"It's supposed to be a Taiwanese operation," said Hightree, "which means we get a sign-off from the ROC government before we go anywhere, do anything. They supply the logistics, the insertion team, all the firepower."

"So why do we have to be involved?" said Guido Vitale. He was a former patrol plane pilot who served as Hightree's group operations officer. Vitale and Boyce butted heads on a daily basis. "Why do they need us at all?"

"Because it's our problem too," said Boyce. "The Black Star poses an immediate threat to Taiwan, but in the long run it's a huge danger to the United States. It's our own stolen technology being turned against us. We're just gonna steal back what is rightfully ours."

Vitale had a sour look on his face. "And who did you have in mind to do the stealing?"

Boyce was studying the remains of his cigar. The end was gnawed into a wet sliver. "Well, obviously he has to be a pilot. But not an ordinary pilot. Someone capable of climbing into an exotic jet he's never seen before and flying the thing away."

Hightree and Vitale were nodding. Boyce was deliberately keeping his eyes on the map of the strait.

Maxwell was getting an old feeling. It was the same feeling he always got when he sensed something coming up with his name on it.

"Of course, he has to be a volunteer," Boyce went on. "We all understand that it's a high-risk operation. But if I know my man, he'll take the job." His gaze swung away from the map.

Maxwell felt all the eyes in the room on him. *That damned Boyce.* Some things never changed.


*Taipei, Taiwan*

*Don't let them see you cry.*

Charlotte Soong made a frozen mask of her face, trying her best to appear expressionless. She could feel the eyes of the general staff—senior officers of the air force, army, navy—all watching her, waiting for her reaction.

The news was devastating. Another frigate blown out of the water. A destroyer severely damaged. F-16s falling from the sky like shotgunned geese. Something—an invisible airplane—was killing Taiwanese jets.

Now it was killing ships. Her senior officers were divided about what to do next.

They were in the war room, a fortified chamber inside a bunker that extended for three hundred meters into the side of a hill. Connected by tunnels to the executive palace in Taipei, the bunker contained a military command center, an executive office and private quarters, and a communications post.

She had not yet told the general staff about the proposed raid on Chouzhou and the stealth fighters. The plan had been developed in secret and was known only to a handful of her aides and officers. General Wu had been involved with the planning, and he was not pleased. He considered an operation on Chinese soil to be too risky. If the mission failed—

and he predicted it would—it would only embolden China
to launch its own invasion force.

"What should I tell our flotilla commander?" said Admiral Weng-hei, the navy Chief of Staff.

"What do you mean?"

"Should I tell him to withdraw his forces from the strait?"

Charlotte still didn't understand. "You mean, turn over
control of the sea to the Chinese navy?"

"If we wish to preserve our surface forces, we have to
withdraw."

She tried to read Weng-hei's face. Nothing. She looked
then at General Wu, who was standing at the wall-sized
graphic display. Wu wore the same blank expression, giving
her no guidance.

A feeling of despair swept over her. The war was turning
against them, and the senior officers were making sure that
the responsibility—and blame—fell on her.

"I need time to consider the situation," she said, struggling to keep her face impassive. "I'll be in my quarters for
the next hour." She could feel her lower lip beginning to
tremble.

Not until she'd exited the briefing room, ignoring the hostile glares of the officers and closing the door of her private
quarters behind her, did she allow the mask to dissolve. She
slumped into the red satin chair next to the dresser. The tears
she'd been holding back sprang from a well deep inside her.

It was too much. She should never have accepted the position of President. They were right, Huang and Lo and the
others. She had no qualifications, no skills, no right to take
her country and all its people with her into an abyss of death
and misery.

She would resign.

Brave men were dying out there in the strait. Why? Because she was filled with the need to prove herself? Or was
it her own lust for revenge for her husband's assassination?

Through her tears she looked up at the framed photograph on the dresser.

*Kenneth, what would you do now?*

The handsome, bespectacled man in the photograph smiled back at her. Charlotte squeezed her eyes closed, feeling again the pain of her loneliness. How long had it been? Four years and a few months since the rainy April night they found him shot through the heart on the doorstep of his Taipei office.

They had been a team, Dr. Kenneth Soong and his vivacious wife, Charlotte. He, the scholarly, idealistic statesman who, everyone said, would someday lead Taiwan to its rightful sovereignty. She, the bright and dutiful helpmate who stood beside him, laughed at his convoluted jokes, edited his speeches, consoled him on his defeats.

*Helpmate.* The word had a bittersweet flavor as she dredged it up from her memory. The public perception of the Soongs was of a complementary pair—he the strong and resolute leader, she the supportive assistant.

It was a charade.

Gazing again at the smiling face, Charlotte forced herself to recall the truth. Despite Kenneth's undeniable brilliance, he was a man bedeviled by self doubt. She always knew that he lacked something—an inner strength, firmness of conviction, a sense of direction. He needed a compass. Charlotte supplied it.

It all came back to her now—the late-night sessions during which she bolstered his wavering confidence, coached him for the next day's confrontation in the legislative Yuan, instilled in him courage that he did not possess.

She was his compass. And his courage.

No one outside their little circle knew the truth. Together the Soongs climbed through the labyrinthine politics of Taiwan, battling both the factions that wanted war with China and those who preached capitulation. Kenneth Soong and his minority party were on the brink of winning leadership of Taiwan when his enemies decided to remove him. He had become too great a threat to their plans.

A feeling of utter hopelessness washed over Charlotte. Kenneth was gone, and with him her strength, her font of knowledge. Kenneth would know how to deal with this crisis. His analytical mind would sort out the false information from the true. He would know what to do.

*But he would be frightened to death.*

She nodded, looking at the smiling face in the photograph. Yes, sad but true. Kenneth would be wallowing in his own fear. His exterior manner would be firm, clear-eyed, focused on the objective. Inside, he would be screaming for help. Kenneth needed a compass.

*I am the compass.*

She wrestled with this thought for a while. She didn't believe in destiny, at least not in a metaphysical sense. It was pure happenstance that she occupied the office of President. She was an accident of history. Any of her cabinet ministers or officers on the general staff could manage the country better than she.

Yes, she would resign. She would turn the office over to Franklin Huang.

Something inside her instantly rebelled at the thought. *No.* She couldn't identify the source of her misgivings, but it was there. A strong voice was yelling at her. *I can't quit. Not now.*

Her thoughts returned to the war room. She could feel the gloom that pervaded the yellow-lighted room. Generals and admirals were quibbling over withdrawal, containment, retreat. They were good, well-intentioned officers, each with a different perspective. They needed direction.

*I am the compass.*

She felt the intelligent brown eyes of her husband gazing

at her. She could hear the words he would have for her. *Do it, Charlotte. You know what has to be done.*

She rose from the red chair. Peering into the mirror over the dresser, she dabbed at her eyes, freshened her makeup, gave her flowing black hair a once-over. She hooked her talisman, the umbrella, over her right arm.

On her way out she delivered a curt nod to the sentry, then strode back to the war room thirty meters down the hall.

They looked up as she entered.

"More bad news, Madame President," said Weng-hei. "The flotilla commander reports that two more of his ships have been sunk, a destroyer escort and a frigate."

"Sunk by what? A submarine?"

"He doesn't know. Possibly an aerial attacker that was undetected. They had no warning."

"The invisible enemy again?"

The Admiral nodded. "The commander has requested permission to withdraw his ships for rearming and repair."

She studied the Admiral's grave expression for a moment. He looked like a man who had resigned himself to defeat. "Withdraw? Is that what you recommend, Admiral?"

"If we wish to preserve what naval strength we have left, yes."

"Without control of the strait, we will have lost the war."

"Perhaps. But we still have aircraft overhead. We have submarines on station. We can—"

"Enough. There will be no further talk of withdrawal. Taiwan cannot afford such a luxury. Admiral, your task is to destroy the enemy's navy, not run from it."

Weng-hei looked as if he had been jolted with an electric current. "I did not mean that we should run. Only that—"

"I understand your meaning. Let me explain your duty in very simple terms. So long as you have one ship left afloat, you will use it to attack the enemy. Is that understood?"

The Admiral's face drained of color. "Yes, Madame President."

A hush fell over the briefing room. General Wu, who had been studying the wall-sized graphic display, turned and gave her a curious stare. At the duty desk, an army colonel's mouth dropped open as if he'd seen an apparition.

Her eyes swept the room, pausing to gaze at each of them. "Listen to me, each of you. The invisible weapon that the PLA is using against us has been identified. A plan has been proposed to deal with it."

She told them about Operation Raven Swoop, leaving out the specific details of time and force size. She also left out any mention that Americans would be involved.

When she was finished, she glanced at her watch. "General Wu will brief you on the mission and explain the support functions that the commandos will require. Wish them luck, gentlemen. Taiwan's fate rides with them."

Taking long, purposeful strides, she walked past them to the red-lighted exit. As she left, each of the officers, one after the other, snapped to attention.


*USS* Ronald Reagan

"Okay, assuming I took the assignment," said Maxwell, "who is the second pilot?"

Boyce looked up from the op plan. "Who says it has to be a pilot?"

"I do. I need somebody in the backseat who can run the Black Star's systems."

"How about a Taiwanese air force pilot? Some guy who speaks English and can talk you through the check lists and instruments."

Maxwell shook his head. "He ought to be an American. I don't want problems with chain of command if we have to do something innovative."

"That raises the ante, putting *two* Yanks on the ground in China. They'll have a field day if they catch you."

"You mean, losing me is okay, but two of us is another matter?"

Boyce shrugged. "Since you put it that way, yes."

"Whoever it is has to understand some Chinese."

"Why?"

"Even if they made this Dong-jin a carbon copy of the Black Star, everything will be in Chinese. I'll need help figuring out the instrumentation, the systems, the displays. I won't even know how to start the thing without a translator."

"Sounds like our choice is pretty clear, doesn't it?"

Before Maxwell could reply, a rapping sound came from the door. Boyce opened the door. "Come on in, Major Bass," he said. "We were just talking about you."

Bass waited until Boyce finished with his proposal. "No fucking way," he said. A second later he thought to add, "Sir."

Boyce just smiled. "But you're the right man for the job."

"I don't know shit about stealth jets, and that's the way I want to keep it. I'm a fighter jock, not a test pilot."

Boyce was perusing a manila file folder. "Your mother is Chinese, according to your records." He studied him for a moment. "You don't look Asian to me."

"My father was Irish. I take after him."

"But you speak Chinese fluently."

"Not anymore. I forgot it. Every word."

Boyce sighed. "I'm seriously disappointed in you, Major. Don't you Air Force people feel a sense of duty?"

"To the Air Force maybe. Not to the Navy. With all due respect, sir, you guys are crazy as loons. Can I leave now?"

"No." Boyce looked again at the folder. "According to this file from General Buckner, you have a career path that looks like a seismograph during an earthquake." Boyce made a show of leafing through the file. "I can't believe some of this stuff. Can this be true? You really got caught in the Langley O-club parking lot with a colonel's wife—"

"She assured me they were separated."

"By approximately fifty yards, according to this. That was until her husband found you in the backseat of your car. Which resulted in your transfer to Myrtle Beach, which was where you—"

"May I see that file, sir?"

"No." Boyce flipped a page. "It says here that you buzzed a sailboat off the coast at Myrtle Beach with an F-16. A boat that happened to belong to—"

"The base commander."

"Bass, you're a one-man train wreck. How did you ever make major?"

"By being the best fighter pilot in the Air Force, sir."

Boyce shook his head. "And the best fighter pilot in the Air Force will be court-martialed because he's too stupid to follow orders." He put down the file. "As I see it, Major, it's come down to this. You've got two career options left."

He left this thought hanging in the air while he unwrapped a fresh cigar and snipped a piece off with his cutter. Bass waited, watching him like a cat staring at a rottweiler.

Half a minute passed.

"Uh, I believe you said something about options, Captain?"

Boyce gave the cigar an appreciative look over, then wet the end of it. "Option one, I comply with the request of General Buckner, who—and I quote his exact words—now wants your sorry ass shipped back to Kadena so he can convene your court-martial. He figures you're good for five to ten in Leavenworth."

Bass's face was turning a shade of gray. "And the other option . . ."

"Volunteer for the mission to China with Commander Maxwell. If, by some rare happenstance, you actually live through the operation, I will intercede with the General and try to keep you from serving hard time."

Bass stared at him. "That's coercion."

"Correct. Do you know what the inside of a six-by-eight cell looks like?"

"I don't want to know."

"Then your decision is pretty easy."

For a long moment Bass stood there, wrestling with his choice. He could visualize the interior of a prison yard at Leavenworth. He could also visualize what it might be like to be caught as a spy in China. Neither choice filled him with joy. His shoulders slumped. He wished he had never arrived on that damned boat.

"Okay," he said in a low voice, "what do you want me to do?"

"You wanted to see me, Skipper?"

Maxwell looked up from his desk. Standing in the open door was Bullet Alexander, wearing a flight jacket over his khakis. Maxwell waved him in. "Close the door and take a seat."

Alexander sat opposite Maxwell. He glanced around the room, his eyes stopping at the photograph on the desk. It was a snapshot of Maxwell and Claire. They were sitting on a motorcyle. In the background was a boat dock and a body of water. "That the chick who makes you slam doors and beat up punching bags?"

Maxwell glanced at the snapshot and nodded. "You can knock off the counseling. I'm over all that."

Alexander kept looking at the photo. "Looks like a cool bike. A Harley?"

He nodded. "An old ninety-five Low Rider. I keep it in

my dad's garage in Fall's Church. Claire and I used to ride on the weekends along the river, down to the Chesapeake."

He lay the photo facedown on the desk. He looked at Alexander. "What would you say if I told you I was turning the squadron over to you for a while?"

"I'd say you had a lot of trust in your XO. Or else you're in some kind of deep trouble."

"Maybe both. I'm going off for a few days on a special assignment."

"One of those 'don't ask, don't tell' jobs?"

"Something like that." He watched Alexander for a reaction.

Alexander nodded, his expression not changing. "I see where this is going. You're worried about whether I'm ready to run the outfit, right?"

"Should I be?"

"Hell, Boss, with a possible war starting with the ChiComs, leaving your outfit in the hands of some dude who just checked in, yeah, I can see how you might be worried."

Maxwell gave it a second, choosing his words. "You may not realize it yet, Bullet, but not everyone in the squadron is crazy about you. There's at least one guy who'd like to see you blow it and get shipped back where you came from."

"My onboard warning system has already picked up hostile signals from Craze Manson."

"Then you ought to know he's telling all the junior officers that you're a carpetbagger who hasn't earned his credentials. He's going to do everything he can to make you look bad."

"That's nothing new. I've been dealing with assholes like Manson ever since I got my wings and went to my first squadron."

"You don't have to do this if you're not ready. CAG can

get someone to step in and run things. I'll make sure it doesn't reflect on your fitness report."

"Look, Brick, I don't give a damn about Craze Manson. Tell me what you think. Do you want me to stay?"

"I picked you for this job. I haven't changed my mind."

"Then you've got nothing to worry about."

"What about Manson?"

Alexander smiled his toothy smile. "Leave Manson to me."

Boyce caught up with him on the way to the flight deck. Maxwell carried a duffel bag with his flying equipment, extra clothing, and toilet gear. On the outside of his flight suit was his leather shoulder holster with the ancient Colt .45.

Boyce looked at the pistol. "Lot of good that'll do you."

"You never know. It saved me on the ground in Yemen, if you remember."

"I remember. With your sterling marksmanship, you almost blew away B.J. Johnson." Boyce paused, and his voice grew serious. "Look, Brick, this is a different kind of war. If it turns ugly, just get the hell out. I need you alive and back here on the *Reagan*."

Maxwell nodded. "Keep an eye on my squadron, CAG."

"Don't worry about your squadron. You've got Bullet Alexander."

He didn't know how much Boyce had heard about the new XO. They stepped onto the escalator that took them to the deck edge. "Bullet's still getting his feet wet," he said. "Some of the guys might try to give him a hard time."

"I know Bullet. He worked for me back in VFA-87 when I was XO and he was a lieutenant new to the squadron."

"You didn't you tell me you knew Bullet from before."

"You're his boss. I wanted you to form your own impression."

"So? How did he handle himself in your squadron?"

"Well, we had some young hotshots who thought Bullet was getting a free ride. You know, the old bullshit about the black guy getting special treatment. They figured that it would be great fun to humiliate him in one-vee-one ACM exercise."

ACM—air combat maneuvering—in its purest form was one-on-one dogfighting. It separated the amateurs from the pros. Maxwell said, "And did they humiliate him?"

"Bullet worked his way through the roster, flying against one pilot after the other. After he'd finished kicking each guy's ass, he'd present him with an eight-by-ten glossy from the HUD tape showing his tail superimposed in Bullet's gunsight. For extra measure, he'd autograph it for them."

Maxwell threw his head back and laughed. "Now *that's* ballsy."

"I think your squadron will be just fine."

They reached the top of the escalator. A short, red-lighted passageway led to the flight deck ladder. A C-2A COD was waiting to fly Maxwell and Bass to Taiwan.

The two men shook hands at the base of the ladder. Boyce clapped Maxwell on the shoulder and said, "Go get the Black Star, Brick. And come back alive. That's an order."

Maxwell picked up his bag. He knew that was as close as Boyce could come to being sentimental. "Yes, sir, I'll do my best."

He stepped up to the darkened flight deck.

# CHAPTER TWELVE

# CHINGCHUANKANG

*USS* Ronald Reagan
*Taiwan Strait*
*2015, Saturday, 13 September*

"Is this gonna hurt?" asked Bass.

Maxwell looked at him in the darkened cabin and nearly laughed. Strapped into the rearward-facing seat, wearing the float coat and cranial protector, Bass looked like an alien creature.

"Relax," said Maxwell. "When the catapult fires, just go with it."

In the dim light, Bass's eyes appeared as large as Frisbees. Maxwell knew the feeling. For a pilot, sitting backwards like a piece of cargo while being catapulted off a ship was the ultimate feeling of powerlessness.

He felt the rumble of the two turboprop engines going to full thrust. The airframe of the C-2A COD—carrier onboard delivery aircraft—was vibrating like a tuning fork.

"What's happening?" said Bass.

"You'll see."

"When is this thing going to—"

*Whoom.* Bass's head snapped forward as if he had been

tackled. He lurched into the straps that bound him to his seat. In three seconds the COD traveled the length of the catapult track, accelerating to 120 knots.

Maxwell felt the catapult stroke end. The nose of the COD lifted, and the landing gear clunked up into the wells.

Bass raised his head. "Are we dead?"

"That was nothing. Wait till you sit through a carrier landing."

"Screw the landing. That was the last boat I'm ever gonna be on."

Maxwell peered through the window on the opposite side of the cabin. He saw only blackness outside. No lights, no horizon, no sky. The COD was showing no navigation lights, droning northwest over the strait to Taiwan. They were bound for Chingchuankang, the air base nestled in the central mountains of the island.

The cabin was silent except for the metallic hum of the turbine engines. Bass settled into a contemplative mood, no longer his talkative self.

Maxwell had come to like the young Air Force officer. He guessed that beneath the flippant exterior, he was probably a competent fighter pilot. Over the years he had learned to spot the little nuances by which pilots revealed themselves—the way they talked with their hands, the way they described their own experiences. Boyce had seen it too, or he wouldn't be taking a chance on Bass.

Bass's voice broke the stillness. "You know how I got roped into this. But you seem like a pretty sane guy. Why the hell are you doing this?"

"I'm a tourist at heart. I've never been to China and this seemed like a good chance to have a look around."

"I take it back. You're not sane. In fact, you guys are all nuts."

"Now you know the truth."

"I should have let your boss send me to Leavenworth. At

least I'd get three meals a day, regular hours. They'd let me do crossword puzzles, maybe even shoot some pool. What's wrong with that?"

"Nothing, if you like bread and water."

"Do you know how the Chinese will treat us if they catch us? Fish heads once a day, bamboo under the fingernails, electrodes on the nuts to make us talk."

"Being a prisoner isn't our best option."

"Being dead sucks too."

Maxwell nodded. At least they were talking about it. It was healthy to vent their fear, to make jokes about that which terrified them. They were embarking on a trip into unthinkable danger. Maxwell didn't want to calculate how slim their chances really were.

Silence fell over the cabin again. Bass's question slipped back into Maxwell's mind. *Why are you doing this?*

He had given a flippant reply, carefully avoiding the truth. *Because I have nothing to lose.*

Everyone important to him was gone. No children, no wife, no family except an aging father. His astronaut wife, Debbie, had been taken from him in a fiery accident one sun-strewn day at Cape Canaveral. His own career as an astronaut had come to an abrupt end. He'd lost Claire Phillips once back in time, then she returned like a fresh wind to his life. Now he'd lost her again and—

He caught himself. *Knock it off, Maxwell. Stop feeling sorry for yourself.* He had been decorated for bravery in two wars. He had put his life on the line as a test pilot and astronaut. Had he done it for no higher reason than that he had nothing to lose? Was courage nothing more than an act of hopelessness?

Hell, no. There had always been more to it than that. It was a private set of beliefs, an ingrained code that was peculiar to the warrior class. Men like himself and Red Boyce—and, he hoped, Catfish Bass—followed a calling that transcended their own lives. They were patriots and warriors, in that order.

With that thought he told himself to quit thinking. Too much thinking before going into action dulled your senses.

*Let it go. Just do your job.*

He felt the drone of the turboprops change pitch. The nose of the COD tilted downward. In the darkness below lay Taiwan.

The clamshell door in the aft cabin swung open. A short, ramrod-straight figure stood in the darkness on the tarmac.

"Welcome to Chingchuankang."

Maxwell recognized the voice and his heart sank. *Oh, shit.*

"Colonel Chiu," he said. "Good to see you again."

Chiu didn't bother shaking hands. He gave Maxwell and Bass each a peremptory nod. "Follow me. Your bags will be brought to you."

The base was blacked out. There was no light spilling from windows, no illumination on the sprawling ramp, no taxiway lights. The COD had been nursed to its parking spot on the darkened tarmac by an unlighted follow-me jeep.

Chiu led them to his vehicle, a Suzuki four-wheeler in military drab. As Maxwell's eyes adjusted to the dim light of the ramp, he could see aircraft dispersed on the ramp— helicopters, C-130s, single-engine utility airplanes. Sandbagged gun emplacements were sited at regular intervals around the perimeter of the ramp. Taiwan's central base for special operations, Chingchuankang, was on high alert.

Driving the Suzuki himself, Chiu headed across the ramp. He made no conversation while he drove, speeding past sandbagged security posts with guards wearing black greasepaint and full combat gear, to a sprawling one-story complex. More sandbags, a machine gun post, and half a dozen grim-looking troops guarded the entrance.

Through a light-sealed inner door, Maxwell and Bass followed Chiu into an illuminated hallway. Squinting in the harsh fluorescent light, they entered a capacious room with charts covering three walls. At a row of computers sat half a dozen technicians. On one wall was a large flat-panel screen with blinking symbols that displayed, Maxwell presumed, a real-time military overview of Taiwan and coastal China.

In the center of the room, on an elevated platform, was a three-meter-square plaster-and-cardboard facsimile of an airfield. The miniature base contained runways, hangars, buildings, a water tower, revetments, gun emplacements, even missile batteries.

Chiu saw Maxwell studying the model base. "Do you know what you're looking at?"

Maxwell was impressed. "Chouzhou."

"The most accurate reproduction we could make, based on reconnaissance photos and the knowledge of defectors who worked there."

Maxwell noticed the disapproval in Chiu's voice. His opinion of defectors hadn't changed.

"When does the operation go?"

"Soon. Within forty-eight hours. It has been given the highest priority by our . . . current head of state." Maxwell caught the note of distaste. He wondered if Chiu had a dislike for the new President of Taiwan, or if he just hated women in general.

Bass was looking at the model, shaking his head. "Jesus, this looks like something from *Mission: Impossible*. How are we going to get in there and out again without getting our asses shot off? This place is more heavily defended than downtown Beijing."

Chiu gave him a cold look. "That is my concern, not yours. Your task will be to deal with the airplane, nothing more. It will be my responsibility to insert you into the base at Chouzhou."

"Your responsibility?" said Maxwell. "Does that mean that you—"

"I am in command of the raid," said Chiu. "This is a Tai-wanese operation, using our troops and equipment. Every-one"—he gave each man a glower—"will take orders from me. Without question. Is that understood?"

Maxwell felt himself bristle. No, it wasn't understood. Something had gotten lost in the mission description. Taking orders from a raving tyrant who hated women and Ameri-cans and all other living things wasn't part of the job.

For several seconds he kept his silence, weighing whether to tell Chiu to go stuff his model base and his mission and his orders—understood or otherwise—straight up his bung-hole.

Bass watched him, a curious expression on his face.

Maxwell took a deep breath. *The mission comes first. Humor this asshole.*

He gave Bass a barely perceptible nod, then he turned to Chiu. "Understood, Colonel."

Chiu wasn't finished. "If the United States had not aban-doned Taiwan, this operation would not be necessary. The war would be won already."

"You've not been abandoned, Colonel. The U.S. is sup-plying most of Taiwan's ships and aircraft and ordnance. We trained your pilots. The *Reagan* battle group is still on sta-tion in the strait."

"Will they deliver an attack on Chinese air defense sites?"

"Not without provocation."

"Will they engage the Chinese air force when we insert our team into Chouzhou?"

"You know the answer. The United States is not at war with China."

Chiu shook his head in disgust. "Talk. All empty talk. For fifty years the United States assured us they were our ally. In the final analysis, that's all it was. Talk."

Maxwell was getting a quick picture of Chiu. He was obviously a man with a mountain-sized chip on his shoulder. It was hard to figure whom he hated the most, China or the United States. It didn't matter. "Look, Colonel, we're here to do a job, not discuss foreign policy. If you don't wish to include us in the operation, that suits me. We'll return to the *Reagan* tonight."

Chiu's eyes narrowed. He was about to deliver another blast when he stopped and fixed his attention to something in the hallway behind them.

"Our team of foreigners is complete," he said. "Gentlemen, meet the defector who will take us to the Black Star."

Maxwell looked over his shoulder. He abruptly lost interest in the model air base, the charts on the wall, the tactical display. His eyes riveted on a rich tumble of black hair, flashing almond eyes, and a smile that erased all his anger.

She wasn't wearing the baggy fatigues and the clunky boots. They had been replaced by snug-fitting Levis, white sneakers, and a T-shirt that bore the likeness of, Maxwell presumed, some rock musician. Maybe a dead scientist. He couldn't tell.

Mai-ling looked like a kid on a college campus.

"I knew it," she said. "I knew I'd see you again."

*Frigate* Kai Yang, *Taiwan Strait*

*Sovremenny.*

Reading the urgent message on the bridge of the *Kai Yang*, Commander Lei Fu-sheng felt a surge of alarm pass through him. Everyone had presumed that the greatest threat would come from PLA navy submarines.

They were wrong. They hadn't counted on the Sovremenny destroyers.

Darkness had descended once again on the strait. The *Kai Yang* had lived through another twelve hours of daylight.

Lei could see only the silhouettes of his escort vessels cruising a parallel course.

After killing the first Kilo-class submarine, they had located another and hounded it into the jaws of a fast-moving destroyer squadron, who dispatched it with their own torpedoes. Elsewhere in the strait, another Kilo and a Ming-class Chinese submarine had been caught and killed. PLA navy submarines had accounted for the loss of only two Taiwanese warships—a frigate, the *Han Yang*, and a destroyer whose captain had been too complacent as he cruised out of his anchorage at Kaohsiung.

Until now, it had been a one-sided naval war. The PLA navy was overrated. They had decent equipment, but they were too inept at using it.

But the two Sovremenny-class destroyers were something else. They were crewed, according to intelligence briefs, by the cream of the PLA navy. Armed with supersonic 3M80E Moskit antiship missiles, the Sovremenny class could kill anything in its theater—surface, submerged, or airborne.

They weren't supposed to be a threat. Yesterday Lei and his fellow commanders received assurances that both Sovremenny destroyers—*Fan Tzu* and *Fan Tao*—had been caught in their berths at the naval yard at Xiamen when the war began. The first wave of Harpoon missiles had devastated the base. Neither destroyer made it to the open sea.

It was bad information.

The message arrived on Lei's bridge a few minutes after sunset. The two Sovremennys had appeared in the Xiamen channel, undamaged from the Harpoon barrages, steaming out of their concrete-sheltered berths. Dodging the flotsam in the harbor, they made for the Xiamen channel. They met no opposition as they steamed toward the safety of the strait.

Then they rounded Point Shima, the last promontory before the open sea. Lurking outside the channel entrance was the Taiwanese submarine *Hai Shih*, an old Guppy-class boat handed down by the U.S.

*Hai Shih*'s captain had been waiting for the Sovremennys. His first torpedo took the lead destroyer, *Fan Tzu*, amidships. The destroyer went into a sickening skid, a ball of flame belching from her midsection. Its stern buckled and broke away as the destroyer entered its death throes.

His second torpedo missed the stern of *Fan Tao* by thirty meters. Without slowing, *Fan Tao* raced past its dying sister ship. Before the submarine could pump another torpedo after it, the Sovremenny destroyer was launching antisubmarine missiles. Three of the high-speed missiles arced through the sky like killer hawks, plunging back to the surface and disappearing.

Seconds later, a geyser of foam and debris gushed to the surface. An ugly pool of black oil began to spread, marking the gravesite of the *Hai Shih*. The *Fan Tao* maintained speed, leaving in its wake the smoke and debris of the two shattered warships.

The Sovremenny destroyer was headed into the strait.

*Chingchuankang Air Base, Taiwan*

*Nice ass,* observed Catfish Bass.

Mai-ling was leading the way into the briefing room, the same one with the charts on the wall and the miniature air base in the center. Maxwell and Bass were following her. Bass noticed for the first time that she had a patch of an American flag sewn on the hip pocket of her jeans.

*Too bad she's a world-class bitch.* The snotty babe reminded him of the grad school women he used to know at UCLA. There was something about them. If they possessed the rare combination of good looks and exceptional brains, they usually had the disposition of a crazed mongoose.

Like this one. Hadn't missed a chance to sink her teeth

into his ankle. He wondered whether it had something to do
with his own ethnicity. The fact of his being half Chinese
seemed to trigger some kind of hate reflex in Chinese
women.

For reasons he hadn't figured out, Mai-ling had attached
herself to Maxwell. He was far too old for her—the guy had
to be pushing forty—and, anyway, he had other things to
think about. She probably had him sized up as her ticket to
the States. Or maybe something more than that.

Bass couldn't take his eyes off the little flag sewn on her
right hip pocket. It moved in a hypnotic rhythm as she
walked down the hallway. At the entrance to the briefing
room, Mai-ling stopped. She sensed something.

She whirled and gave him a fierce look.

"Nice flag," he said.

"Animal." She wheeled and marched on down the hallway.

*Predictable,* he thought. The type who couldn't handle a
compliment.

They entered the cavernous room with the model of the
Chouzhou air base in the center. Mai-ling, Maxwell, and
Bass took seats on one side. Opposite them sat a dozen Taiwanese army officers in their utilities. To a man, they were
compactly built, wearing the same intense expression, sitting in a row like coiled springs.

They refused to make eye contact. After an initial curious
look at the Americans, they kept their attention studiously
focused on some faraway object. Bass figured them to be officers of the commando unit that would insert them into
Chouzhou.

The thought of the coming operation sent a fresh chill
down Bass's spine.

He heard the clunk of boots on the wooden floor. All
heads turned to see Colonel Chiu, in battle dress uniform,

stride into the room. He looked like a drum major, arms swinging at his sides, heels hammering the floor.

Someone barked a command in Chinese. As if they were a single entity, the Taiwanese officers shot to their feet and stood quivering at rigid attention.

Not sure what to do, Bass glanced over at Maxwell. Slowly, without great precision, he unwound from the seat and rose to his feet, standing at a loose parade rest. Bass followed suit. Mai-ling made a sour face and stayed seated. "I'm not in their army," she whispered. "I don't have to do that."

*Cool,* thought Bass. The chick was finally showing a little class.

"Seats," Chiu barked out. In another single movement, the commandos slammed themselves back down in the seats.

*Joined at the hip.* Bass wondered if any of them was capable of thinking by himself. Maybe they weren't allowed to.

The colonel spoke in rapid Mandarin. Bass could follow only about half the content. Chiu told his audience that the raid on Chouzhou—now called Operation Raven Swoop—had been moved up. Taiwan's worsening military situation made it imperative that they execute their mission without delay. They would take off at 0300 local tomorrow morning. The colonel paused and looked at Bass. "Please translate for Commander Maxwell."

Bass nodded, then gave Maxwell an abbreviated version of Chiu's briefing. He saw Mai-ling shaking her head at his clumsy interpretations.

"Okay, tell him I've got it," said Maxwell.

Chiu continued in Chinese, pausing every couple of minutes for Bass to translate. Bass was having trouble following the quick, guttural speech. It was a country Mandarin dialect unfamiliar to him. Some of the peculiar nuances he had to guess at.

The commando force would total ninety troops, transported in four CH-47 Chinook helicopters and escorted by another four Cobra gunships. Diversionary attacks would be conducted on coastal targets, and a bogus amphibious force would be aimed at a site south of Chouzhou. Prior to the raid, the vicinity's air defense batteries would be raked by Harpoon missiles launched from offshore naval vessels.

The colonel walked up to the model of the air base. With a long pointer he indicated the landing sites of the helicopters, the locations of the base surface-defense units, and the routes taken by the elements of the commando force.

"These four hangars," Chiu said in English, "house the Black Star project." He pointed to a semicircle of fortified shelters. "According to our source"—he looked pointedly at Mai-ling—"we are supposed to find at least one flyable aircraft in Hangar Number One." He rapped on the first of the four shelters. "If there are more than one, as she claims, they should be in the adjoining hangar."

Listening to the briefing, Bass's sinking feeling returned. It was a desperate plan. Too damned desperate. The idea was to breach the tight ring of security the PLA had around the Black Star long enough to insert him and Maxwell into the hangar. What happened next depended on whether they found a flyable airplane. And whether they could fly it.

Bass was performing quick calculations. Ninety commandos versus the People's Liberation Army. How many PLA troops were in the vicinity of Chouzhou? A thousand? Ten thousand?

The sinking feeling was getting worse.

Chiu looked at Maxwell. "How much time do you require before you can move the airplane?"

"It depends on what we find," said Maxwell. "We need to

locate the specialized equipment—helmets with the correct radio connections, harnesses, oxygen masks."

"There will be no time for random searches. We will not be able to maintain a perimeter defense while you amuse yourselves looking at flight gear."

"If necessary we will use the generic equipment with standard fittings that we take with us."

"You haven't answered my question. How long before you will be prepared to fly the airplane?"

"At least half an hour. Perhaps longer. It depends on the complexity of the airplane."

Chiu looked disgusted. "I was informed that you were a test pilot. Why should the complexity of the airplane be a problem? You should be ready to leave without delay."

Bass could see the color rising in Maxwell's face. "My job is to fly the airplane—if I consider it feasible. Yours is to get me to it. I don't intend to tell you how to do your job, Colonel. Don't tell me how to do mine."

A thundercloud passed over Chiu's face. A heavy silence fell over the room, and for a long moment the two men locked gazes. Chiu was clearly not a man accustomed to taking rebukes, especially in front of his officers. He seemed to be weighing whether to remove Maxwell from the operation.

Abruptly he swung his attention back to the model of the base. "The purpose of this mission is to find the Black Star aircraft. If circumstances permit our foreign guests to capture one of the aircraft"—he shot a piercing look at Maxwell—"so be it. Otherwise, we will destroy the aircraft and all the production facilities. In any case, we will be in and out of Chouzhou in thirty minutes' time."

He went into detail about the disposition of the commando force—where they would disperse, which teams had responsibility for which shelters, where they would deploy their mortars and large-caliber weapons. The officers listened intently, nodding their heads.

When he was finished, Chiu said, "Questions?"

There were no questions.

He gave them all a curt nod. A command was barked in Chinese. Again the officers shot to their feet, standing at rigid attention.

Chiu marched to the exit. The briefing was over.

# CHAPTER THIRTEEN

# GWAI-LO

*Taipei, Taiwan*
*0935, Sunday, 14 September*

General Wu Hsin-chieh walked down the broad steps of the American Institute in Taiwan. He stopped in the courtyard between the main building and the perimeter wall and gazed around. Wu could remember when this place used to be called the United States Embassy, before Nixon embraced Mao and moved the embassy—and diplomatic recognition with it—to Beijing.

He blinked in the harsh light. The sun was streaming through a high veil of smoke. There was no wind. To the east, where the large industrial complexes nestled on the outskirts of the city, columns of black smoke rose straight into the sky.

War had come to Taipei.

In the first twenty-four hours of the conflict, a barrage of missiles had hurtled across the strait toward Taiwan. The Patriot antimissile batteries had performed better than anyone expected, intercepting over eighty percent of the incoming missiles. Still, the missiles were taking a toll. Entire blocks of Taipei's institutions were now heaps of smoking rubble.

The sounds of the city were replaced with the wail of sirens, the *whump* of exploding warheads, the screams of panicked citizens.

Wu saw his aide, Captain Lo Pin, and his driver waiting inside the guarded gate. A pair of guards in battle dress were stationed behind sandbagged emplacements on either side of the gate. Another contingent manned an observation post behind them.

The passenger door of the black government Lexus was open, waiting for him.

Wu was in no hurry. After the past two days inside the executive bunker, he wanted to taste the open air, the relative tranquility of the afternoon. Instead of climbing into the Lexus, he lit a cigarette and stood watching the traffic outside the gate.

He couldn't help noticing that this part of Taipei—the area around the American Institute—was untouched by the incoming cruise missiles. A coincidence? He doubted it. They already knew that China had retrofitted the guidance units of all their cruise missiles with GPS—global positioning system—technology furnished to the world by the United States. They could hit any target in Taiwan with a maximum error probability of thirty feet.

He guessed that it was a tacit protocol being observed by China and the United States. *Don't violate our space, and we won't touch yours*. Each side was scrupulously avoiding a confrontation with the other.

It was strangely quiet. At that time of day, mid-afternoon, Taipei should have been a maelstrom of gridlock and honking horns. Instead, an orderly parade of vehicles, mostly military cars and a few commercial vans, passed along Joping Street in front of the consulate. The light at the intersection was not working, and a uniformed policeman was directing traffic. No horns were honking.

He had often wondered how the Taiwanese would fare if

they actually experienced war. In normal times they were a noisy, quarrelsome, divided people. They fought over parking spaces, argued about food prices, insulted each other in public. Politicians in the legislative Yuan engaged in more brawls than debates.

A large faction in Taiwan had always clamored for total severance from China. Another faction, almost as large, preached reunification with their kinfolk across the strait—becoming one happy Chinese nation. Various splinter factions wanted a Marxist state, or a Buddhist state, or no state at all—a return to the feudal system of warlords and serfs.

Wu loved this country. It was flawed and feisty, filled with contradictions and pride and guts—but it was his homeland. As a young soldier nearly thirty years ago he had taken a vow to defend it. Nearing the end of his career, he had begun to think that it would never be necessary.

Until the day before yesterday. Until President Charlotte Soong.

He still didn't know whether he had admiration or contempt for her. Both, he guessed. He was too much of a loyal soldier to engage in an active conspiracy against her—but he didn't rule it out. If she proved herself to be disastrously inept, he would act. No President had the right to destroy Taiwan.

He saw Lo Pin signaling him from the staff car. "General, a call from the President."

Wu walked over to the Lexus and took the handset from Lo. It was the secure phone, a scrambled-signal satellite connection that linked him directly to Soong's office.

"Yes, Madame President."

"What was the outcome of your conversation with the director?"

Wu had long been acquainted with the senior American diplomat in Taiwan, Jennings Poynter, whose title was now Director of the American Institute. Poynter was a career foreign service officer who spoke Mandarin and liked to play poker with senior Taiwanese officers. He was also known to favor reunification of Taiwan with China.

"He is supportive, but, as we expected, he wants you to negotiate."

"Negotiate what? A surrender?"

"A truce," said Wu. "A cessation of hostilities."

A silence followed, and for a moment he thought he had lost the connection. Finally he heard Charlotte Soong's voice again. "Did you relay our concerns, General? About more weapons? About our need for U.S. support?"

"To the best of my ability. I am a military officer, not a diplomat."

"I understand. But I trust you, General Wu, more than my diplomats. I trust you to define our military position for the Americans."

Wu was about to reply when something on the western skyline caught his eye. A squiggly gray trail was pointing into the smoke-veiled atmosphere. As he followed the trail, it made a couple of corkscrew turns, then erupted in an oily black cloud. A shower of debris arced down toward the western suburbs of Taipei.

A Chinese missile, he realized. Intercepted by one of the Patriot air defense batteries. He guessed that it was another C-801 Sardine short range cruise missile. The bastards had an endless supply of them. Thank God for the Patriots. Without the Patriot antimissile batteries supplied by the U.S., Taiwan would now be a smoking ruin.

"Are you still there, General Wu?"

"Yes, Madame President. I am observing a demonstration that the PLA has not run out of cruise missiles."

"All the more reason that we need rearmament."

"Consul Poynter tells me that a resupply of the Patriot missile batteries has been authorized." Wu was watching the cloud of debris descend over Taipei. The sound of the explosion had not yet reached him. "To our request for more offensive weapons—land-attack missiles and more F-16s— he says Washington declines. There will be no rearmament of offensive equipment."

"I have a conference call scheduled in two hours with the U.S. President," said Madame Soong. "I will remind him that America is involved with Taiwan in this war. That we share a common interest in the outcome."

Wu knew she was being circumspect. Even though the telephone transmissions were scrambled, they had to assume that others would monitor the conversation. It was a fact of life that Taiwan—including the military and the executive branches of government—was riddled with PRC spies. Just as the PRC was well-infested with Taiwanese operatives.

He knew exactly what she meant. She was referring to an operation against a base on the mainland called Chouzhou. And a stealth jet called Black Star. It would commence in eight hours, and yes, the Americans were definitely involved.

*Chingchuankang Air Base, Taiwan*

*Smart-ass broad*, thought Bass.

It was the third time in a single conversation that she had corrected his imperfect Chinese. As if someone had appointed this Mai-ling chick to be his cultural supervisor. His nanny.

"Where did you say you went to undergrad school?"

"University of California," she said. "You may have heard of it."

"Which campus?"

"San Diego. Where'd you go?"

"UCLA. You probably never heard of it."

"I made it a point never to go there."

"I guess you learned all that California flake talk in San Diego?"

"Actually, I learned it from some Air Force ROTC guys. They weren't very bright."

Bass just shook his head. They had gone back and forth like this for most of the time he had known her. She had a comeback for everything.

"How does a student from China get into a university in the U.S.? Some kind of foreign assistance program?"

"By merit, mostly. China sends a thousand or so of the best and brightest students every year for studies in the U.S. Many go on to obtain advanced degrees. I was one of them."

"Are they all as modest and self-effacing as you?"

"Yes. They don't wish to embarrass their American male counterparts who are not as gifted."

"Then they go back to China to work on weapons to use against us."

"Of course. America educates its enemies and sells them its secrets. It's an old tradition."

Bass just nodded. He suspected that she was right. It didn't make sense, but a lot of things lately weren't making sense. His own situation, for example. He still hadn't figured out how he got into this mess.

"What will you do when this is over?" he asked. "Go to the United States?"

"I don't know." She seemed to drop some of the smart-ass posture, at least for the moment. "Maybe. Maybe not. It depends on what happens in the next few days."

Bass supposed that she meant the operation in Chouzhou. If it turned out badly, none of them had a future. Not him, not her, not Maxwell. China would win, and everyone else lost.

She was making no secret of her crush on Maxwell. Bass wondered if they were already sleeping together. Well, why the hell not? Life was short. For them, possibly very short.

He heard the sound of boots on the wooden floor. He glanced up to see Colonel Chiu striding into the room. As usual, he wore sharply creased battle dress fatigues with black, spit-shined boots.

Chiu glanced around, a look of disapproval on his face. He said to Mai-ling, "So? You have nothing better to do than spend your time talking with *gwai-los*?" *Gwai-lo* meant *foreign devil*, but was loosely applied to include all outsiders.

"I was helping him with his Mandarin."

"Why? So he can answer questions in Chinese when the PLA interrogates him?" Chiu's face creased into a humorless smile.

*Prick,* thought Bass. He noticed that Mai-ling wasn't giving Chiu any of the smart-ass treatment. Was she afraid of him?

Chiu glanced at his watch. "We have a briefing scheduled in ten minutes. I suggest you keep your thoughts directed on the mission."

"Yes, Colonel," said Mai-ling.

Bass just nodded.

*Taipei, Taiwan*

Something was happening.

Huang could sense it, like a change in the weather. In the executive bunker he had spotted General Wu skulking in and out of the President's private office. Staff officers— colonels and commanders—scurried back and forth clutching documents to their chests. Plainclothes agents walked the passageway of the bunker, mumbling hushed instructions into their pocket radios.

Outside the executive office he encountered Peter Weng, the President's administrative aide. He remembered Weng from the cabinet meetings. He was a prissy office type who followed Soong around like a pet poodle.

"Where is the President?" Huang demanded. "I need to speak to her."

"She's not in the office."

"I can see that, you idiot. Where is she?"

Weng looked like he'd been slapped. "I'm not authorized to divulge the President's whereabouts."

"Authorized? Do you know who you're speaking to? I'm the second-in-command of this government, and *you* are refusing to tell me the whereabouts of my only superior?"

"I—I'm not refusing, Premier. It's just—well, the President made it clear that—"

"This country is at war, you insignificant pest. You are interfering with the conduct of my official duties. Mr. Weng, I may have you arrested for obstructing the war effort and abetting the enemy. Do you know the penalty for such conduct?"

Weng knew. His face went white. He glanced up and down the hallway for help from someone. Anyone.

Huang knew he had overplayed his hand, but it was producing the desired effect. "Speak up, damn you. Or shall I call the chief of security and have you put in shackles?"

"If you give me a few minutes, I'll call her and have her get in touch with you."

"I'm the Premier, you pimple-headed moron. I don't require your permission to speak with the President. Where is she?"

Weng caved in. "She went to Chingchuankang."

Huang made a deliberate effort not to register his surprise. *Chingchuankang?* That was a secret facility where they staged commando operations. *Why is she there at this hour?* It was nearly nine o'clock in the evening. Something was definitely going on. Something she had kept from him.

"Of course, I know she went to Chingchuankang. I mean, where is she at this very moment? Has she left the base yet?"

"I'm not sure, Premier. I will find out."

"Do that. Be quick about it."

A look of relief covered the young man's face and he fled the area. Huang waited till he was gone, then he wheeled and went to the cubicle that served as his office in the underground bunker.

The rest was easy. Using his secure phone, he called the base commander at Chingchuankang. The commander, a colonel, was flattered by so much attention. First a visit by the President, then a personal call from the Premier. Yes, the President and her entourage were due to arrive in a pair of helicopters in not more than ten minutes.

Huang took a shot in the dark. "Of course, she expects to see the preparations for the commando raid?"

A pause, and Huang worried that the question maybe had aroused suspicion.

After a moment the colonel said, "Yes, Premier, we will review the plan with her. She wishes to emphasize to Colonel Chiu Yusheng and the two Americans how critical the raid is to Taiwan's survival."

Huang felt a ripple of alarm run through him. *Americans! A raid critical to Taiwan's survival.*

What was going on? Colonel Chiu Yusheng? He had heard of him. He was some kind of shadowy commando who was reputed to have carried out a number of audacious clandestine operations.

A dozen questions rushed to his mind, but he held them back. The base commander would be alerted if he realized that Huang had no real knowledge of an upcoming commando raid. Anyway, he had other sources.

"Thank you, Colonel. You are performing a valuable service."

"I am honored, Premier. Should I tell the President you wish to speak with her?"

"No, that isn't necessary. It's best not to distract her from her task at Chingchuankang. Our business can wait until she returns."

"Yes, Premier."

After he hung up, Huang sat alone in his office pondering this news. What sort of commando operation would merit a personal visit from the President? Why were Americans involved? There were two of them, the colonel said. Who were they? What sort of raid would be critical to Taiwan's survival?

He called Feng Pao, his aide in the central office of the Yuan. "Get me a brief on an officer based at Chingchuankang. A colonel named Chiu Yusheng. Everything about him. I need the information immediately."

"Yes, Premier. Right away."

*Chingchuankang Air Base, Taiwan*

Colonel Chiu was in the middle of his briefing, barking instructions to his squad leaders, giving directions to the helicopter pilots, stopping to growl orders to the two Americans and Chen Mai-ling.

"Here," he said, rapping a spot on the model Chouzhou base with his long pointer. "Helicopter One discharges First Platoon, who will secure the forward flight line. Helicopter Two then lands here"—another rap of the pointer—"with Second Platoon and the pilots who—"

He stopped in midsentence and gaped at something behind them. A noisy commotion burst from the back of the briefing room. Every head swiveled to follow Chiu's gaze.

Someone barked a command in Chinese. All the commandos jumped to their feet. Chiu slammed his heels together, bringing himself to rigid attention.

"What's going on?" Maxwell asked Bass.

"Something about the President. I think she's here on the base."

So she was. Escorted by half a dozen troops in full battle gear, Charlotte Soong and her party swept into the cavernous room.

Maxwell and Bass rose to their feet, and Mai-ling stood with them. The President of the Republic of China went directly to Colonel Chiu. Maxwell watched her shake the colonel's hand, exchange a few words with him, then gaze around the room. For a minute she studied the model of the Chouzhou base, asking questions of Chiu. Then she looked across the room at the Americans.

Maxwell knew little about her, only that Madame Soong had succeeded President Li after the shoot-down of the Airbus. He had presumed that she was a Chinese dowager, stout and formidable, whose authority was mostly ceremonial.

This was no dowager. Madame Soong was tall, with a slim waist and a long, graceful neck. Her hips swayed like a fashion model's as she walked toward them, taking strong, purposeful strides. She carried a flowered umbrella over her left arm.

"Holy shit," said Bass in a low voice. "That's the *President*?"

"Try not to be a pig," whispered Mai-ling.

Colonel Chiu was at the visitor's side. "Madame President, meet Commander Maxwell, of the United States Navy. And this is Major Bass, from the United States Air Force. They are the pilots who will accompany the mission to Chouzhou."

Mai-ling made a show of clearing her throat. She glowered at Chiu.

"Oh, yes," said Chiu. "And this is—"

"Chen Mai-ling." Mai-ling brought her heels together and bowed her head. "Formerly of the People's Liberation Army." She ignored the menacing look from Chiu.

Charlotte Soong shook hands around, bestowing a gracious smile on each. "I came here to personally thank each of you. The Republic of China will forever be in your debt for what you are doing for us." She turned to Bass. "You are already a hero in Taiwan, Major."

"I am?"

"You trained many of our excellent young fighter pilots. And then you led them into combat over the strait."

"Well, I, uh, I'm not supposed to . . ."

"Now you have volunteered for the raid on Chouzhou. You are a hero of the greatest magnitude, Major."

Bass mumbled thanks, his face reddening. Mai-ling was peering at him curiously.

Charlotte Soong turned her attention to Maxwell. "Commander Maxwell, may I ask you something?"

"Yes, of course, Madame President."

"I know you have a brilliant career in the U.S. Navy. Why have you volunteered for this mission?"

He felt her keen gaze on him, waiting for an answer. "I have some knowledge of the stealth fighter that no one else out here has. That made me the best candidate for the job."

A lame answer, he knew.

She shook her head. "No, it's more than that. I know something about you. I know that you were a test pilot and an astronaut, and that you have been decorated for bravery in several conflicts. You are a man who does not retreat from danger."

Maxwell didn't know what to say. Flattery embarrassed him, especially from a head of state, and a good-looking one at that. He looked over at Bass, then said, "We will do our best to accomplish the mission, Madame President."

She regarded him with interest for another moment. "Yes, I am sure you will."

She then chatted with Mai-ling. They spoke in Chinese, Mai-ling nodding her head, smiling, eagerly answering the President's questions. Madame Soong said something that gave them both a good laugh. Maxwell watched them, realizing that he had not seen Mai-ling this cheery or animated.

Colonel Chiu stood apart, listening to the two women, wearing a sour expression. He scowled, shuffled his feet, then made a show of studying his watch.

Finally Madame Soong said, "Our time is up. I must return to Taipei."

She shook hands again, wished them all success, then followed her escorts back to the darkened ramp outside where her helicopter waited.

"Wow," said Bass. "What did you think?"

"Impressive," Maxwell said. In his military career he had served under several good leaders and a few bad ones. Charlotte Soong, he had a gut feeling, was a good one.

Mai-ling was still staring at the door where Madame Soong had exited the room. A look of pure enchantment covered her face. "I think she's fantastic."

Colonel Chiu broke the spell. "It doesn't matter what you think. Quit wasting time and get to work."

# CHAPTER FOURTEEN

# FORTUNE TELLER

*Chingchuankang Air Base, Taiwan*
*1945, Sunday, 14 September*

He had been in his room only a few minutes.

A rap sounded on the door, and Colonel Chiu appeared in the doorway. "This came for you on the high-priority net. From the *Reagan*, I presume."

He handed the message to Maxwell, then didn't leave. Maxwell unfolded the printout. While Chiu watched him, he sat on the wooden chair and read the message.

*1205 UTC/16 Sep*
*To: Cdr S. Maxwell*
*From: Comairwingthree*

*Hope you're enjoying your holiday. The squadron running smoothly in your absence. Bishop advises he and all the monks send their blessings.*

*Kick some ass for the Gipper.*

*Love and kisses,*
*Battle-Ax*

It was typical Boyce, who liked to call himself Battle-Ax in cryptic communications. His standing orders were that Maxwell was not to proceed with the operation unless he got a final go-ahead.

Well, here was the go-ahead. Boyce's message reported that the President—the Bishop—and the chain of command—the monks—all the way down to the battle group command had given their go-ahead for the raid on Chouzhou.

Maxwell had to smile at the part about kicking ass for the Gipper—the nickname for the *Reagan*. More of Boyce's personal embellishment.

He put down the printed message. *Well, here we go.* Until the message arrived, he had nursed this secret expectation that at the last minute someone—CINCPAC, the Joint Chiefs, the National Security Council—would call it off. Too risky. Too interventional. Too explosive.

*Too damned crazy.*

Crazy or not, it was a go.

He was aware of the presence of Chiu, still watching him.

"You have received a personal message," said Chiu. "I presume that it pertains to your planned mission. As the commander of the operation, I must ask if you have received instructions that will affect my conduct of the mission."

Maxwell looked again at the message. "Yes, Colonel. We have received an additional task."

Chiu gave him a wary look. "An additional task?"

Maxwell held up the printed message. "We have to kick some ass for the Gipper."

"What are you thinking, Sam?"

Maxwell stopped walking and looked at her. The darkness outside the briefing building was almost total. Blackness covered the mountains around Chingchuankang. No exterior lights were showing on the base. No stars, no moon, no flashes of exploding warheads or incoming missiles broke the curtain of darkness.

"What did you call me?"

Mai-ling seemed startled by his tone. "I'm . . . sorry. I saw your name stenciled on your bag. I didn't mean to—"

"It's all right. It's just that no one has called me Sam for a long time. No one except my father and . . ."

"Your wife?"

"No wife."

"Girlfriend, then?"

"No girlfriend either." *Not anymore.*

The walk in the darkness had been her idea. To get some fresh air, she said, and he had agreed. They went as far as the flight line, where they could see the sandbagged sentry post.

"But you've been married."

"She died five years ago."

"I'm very sorry. Did she call you Sam?"

Maxwell hesitated, not comfortable with this conversation. *Yes, that's what Debbie called me. And Claire. The women I loved called me Sam.* "Yes," he heard himself say.

"It's a nice name, Sam. How did you become Brick?"

"A Navy thing. Instead of using our proper names, they give us call signs."

"An odd custom. Why Brick?"

Another flash of memory, this one back to his flight training days. One afternoon at Kingsville, the squadron skipper asked his instructor, Devo Davis, how his student was doing. *Maxwell? No problems, sir. He's solid as a brick.* The skipper nodded and scribbled something in his notepad, and that was it. Solid-as-a-brick Maxwell had a permanent call sign.

He didn't tell her the story. Instead, he pointed to his forehead. "Describes how I think. You know, like a brick."

"I don't believe it. You definitely are not like a brick."

"You don't know me."

"I'm learning."

He kept noticing her face. There was something about the animated expression, the way she seemed to probe his mind with her eyes. Something familiar.

Then it came to him. That rapt, curious look—it was how Claire used to peer at him. They were galaxies apart in looks and background and style, yet alike. In Mai-ling's intent brown eyes he was seeing that same eager intelligence.

It explained a lot. Like why he was here when it was half past eight and he had to get some sleep. He didn't want to leave.

He said, "This mission to Chouzhou isn't something you have to do. You could stay here."

She shook her head. "I'm the one who knows the ground. Only I can guide you to the right places, save Colonel Chiu's precious time."

"He doesn't like you, in case you haven't noticed."

"Nor you, in case you haven't noticed. He doesn't like anyone outside his own little clique. Chiu is like every senior Chinese military officer I've known, Taiwanese or PLA." She paused, looking off into space. "Like Zhang."

"Zhang?"

"Colonel Zhang Yu. Commander of the PLA air force's special operations squadron, the unit responsible for the Dong-jin—what you call Black Star. He is a very well connected political officer, said to be a protégé of the chief of the PLA air force, General Tsin." She paused, then said, "I hate him."

"Why do you hate him?"

"Zhang had the task of purging the PLA air force of political and religious dissidents. He was very good at his job. He arrested over a thousand, mostly officers, and sent them to the *Laogai*—the retraining camps."

"So you were a dissident?"

"More like an enlightened thinker. In the years after the

Tiananmen Square massacre and the persecution of the Falun Gong, many of us became enlightened thinkers. Some were more enlightened than others, and those were the ones Zhang arrested. One was my fiancé, Shaomin." At this, her voice caught and she fell silent for a moment.

Maxwell nodded, letting her collect her emotions.

She said, "He was a good man, very intelligent, perhaps too idealistic for his own good. I loved him for that."

"What happened to him?"

A cloud passed over her face. "He vanished. I knew that Zhang's thugs had come to the compound and taken him away to the camps. Then, a week later, I heard through our network that he was not in the *Laogai*. He had disappeared. We received a report that he had been summarily tried and executed. I knew by then that I was also in great danger because Shaomin and I had been—" her voice caught, then she went on. "We were lovers. It would be assumed that whatever he was involved in, so was I."

"That's when you defected?"

She nodded. "There was a network. Many who live in Fujian Province have contacts in Taiwan. When I indicated my willingness to leave China, they assigned someone to help me. We left one night from the port of Xiamen in a fishing boat. It was easy."

"It doesn't make sense. You're safe now. You have a terrific education, with a brilliant career ahead of you. Why do you want to risk it all by going back to Chouzhou?"

She chewed on a thumbnail for a moment. "Retribution, I suppose. A kind of quid pro quo. And redemption."

"Whose redemption?"

"Mine. And all the other dissidents who haven't yet been killed like Shaomin."

"How will that happen?"

"I haven't got that figured out yet. I just have this fantasy that I'll somehow encounter Colonel Zhang."

"And then what?"

"I want him to recognize me. When he realizes who I am, he'll know that I know he was responsible for the death of Shaomin. He will understand why I've come back."

Maxwell was getting the picture. "And then . . ."

She made a slashing motion with her finger across her throat.

In the shadows Maxwell detected a faint movement of something metallic. Something concealed. He stared into the darkness, then made out the dim outline.

A sentry behind a sandbagged security post.

"We'd better stop here," he said. "One of those guys will get nervous and shoot before he asks questions."

"I needed to get out of that building for a while. Away from Colonel Chiu."

"Chiu is a strange guy," said Maxwell. "Why is he so hostile to you?"

"He considers himself a patriot, and he thinks I'm not. As much as he hates the People's Republic, he hates people like me even more. He thinks I have no loyalty."

"Do you?"

"Yes. To science. To civilization." She smiled in the darkness. "To you, maybe."

"No feelings for the PRC? Or Taiwan?"

"Why should I? The PRC is a repressive government that persecutes its own people. They killed Shaomin. Taiwan? It's an island. That's all."

"What about the United States?"

"What about it?"

He gave up. The concept of patriotism was so ingrained in him that he couldn't imagine not having it. Mai-ling was a person without a country, and that seemed to suit her. Obviously, it didn't suit Colonel Chiu.

She fell silent for a while. Then, in the darkness, she said, "Brick, why don't you have a girlfriend?"

"I did. Now I don't."

"She left you? Or you left her?"

"It was more her idea."

She thought about that for a moment, then she took Brick's hands in hers. Her hands felt warm and dry.

"A woman who would leave a man like you must have very bad judgment. You are lucky to be free of such a woman."

"Well, that's putting a positive spin on it."

After a moment, she said, "You would have liked Shaomin."

"Your fiancé? Why?"

"He was much like you. Good looking. Very smart. He loved what he was doing—working on the Dong-jin project and flying fighters. But there was a secret part of his life that he didn't discuss with me. I think it was because he wanted to protect me."

"Protect you from . . . ?"

"The PLA security arm. Shaomin was afraid for my safety."

Maxwell watched her in the darkness, realizing again how very little he knew about her. He could understand, at least from a professional point of view, why Chiu distrusted her. How could you trust someone who had no loyalty to the traditional things—flag, country, homeland?

He didn't care. He could feel something in the touch of her fingers, like an electric field connecting them. Mai-ling Chen—he unconsciously made the switch from the Chinese usage to the Western practice of family name last—was a girl with whom he could be comfortable. He liked her quick brain, the dry humor, her irreverent worldview.

*That's not all, Maxwell.*

With a jolt, he realized he was smitten by the wide brown eyes, the lithe, curvaceous figure that even the baggy utilities couldn't conceal.

More than smitten, actually.

He felt himself wanting to draw her close to him. And it definitely wasn't her quick brain that he needed.

She sensed it too. She placed her hands on his forearms. "What if we don't come back?"

"I can't predict the future."

"I can. This is what I predict. You and I will come back and we will become lovers. It will be an intense and very physical relationship. After that, perhaps it will become something else."

"Like what?"

"Something more advanced. We will appreciate each other for what we really are."

"When did you become a fortune-teller?"

"When I was born. Chinese women have it in their genes."

*Be careful,* said a voice inside him. *You've got too much on your mind. This is no time to be thinking what you're thinking.*

Right.

With that thought, he felt himself filled with an even deeper longing. He told himself that what he sensed was just the chemistry of shared danger.

*Right.*

He felt her fingers sliding behind his neck. She was on her toes, her face six inches from his.

He gazed into her eyes for a full ten seconds, wrestling with his thoughts. *I'm on a mission that requires total concentration. My country trusts me. Stay focused.*

*Right.*

They weren't aboard ship. No nonfraternization rule here. What they did was no one's business except—

*Enough thinking.* He took her face in his hands and kissed her. Their lips barely touched, almost a social kiss, slow and tentative.

And then it became something else. She pressed herself to him, returning the kiss, her eyes wide open, hands entwined behind his neck. He could feel her heart beating against his chest.

He was aware that the sentry was watching them from his gun position. To hell with him. Nothing mattered at the moment. Nothing except the pressure of Mai-ling's body against him.

They held each other for what seemed like an hour but was, in fact, less than a minute. She tilted her head upward. Her hands were still clasped behind his neck. "You've done this before, Sam."

"I have? I don't remember."

"You want to make love to me, don't you?"

"Is that an invitation or an observation?"

"Neither. It's a question."

"The obvious answer is yes."

"Yes, but . . . ?"

"But we have a mission in five hours. And Colonel Chiu is spying on us."

"Have you always been so honorable?"

"No. I'm trying to impress you."

She laughed. "When we're finished with this mission, I'll let you really impress me."

Still holding her hand, he turned and started back toward the compound. Something made him stop. A sound, a low voice behind them.

He glanced back over his shoulder. The sentry was watching them, talking into a radio handset.

# CHAPTER FIFTEEN

# INGRESS

*Chingchuankang Air Base, Taiwan*
*0315, Monday, 15 September*

Sitting in the aft cabin, Maxwell could feel the vibration of the big turbine engines through his hard metal seat. The whopping noise of the twin rotor blades filled the cabin as the CH-47 "Super D" Chinook lifted from the tarmac at Chingchuankang.

Seated along either bulkhead and in rows to the front and back were thirty black-clad, black-faced troops of Colonel Chiu's special forces brigade.

Chiu sat next to him, on the side row of seats. He was peering at Maxwell's holstered pistol. "What is that thing?"

Maxwell pulled the weapon out of the holster. "Colt .45, model 1911."

"Why would anyone carry a relic like that?" Chiu said. "It belongs in a museum."

"Family tradition. My father wore it in Vietnam. I've had it with me on every combat mission."

"What for? To drive tent stakes?"

In the darkness of the cabin he couldn't tell if Chiu was

making a joke. With Chiu, you couldn't tell. He shrugged and replaced the heavy pistol.

Through the round cabin window of the Chinook he saw only the blackness of the tarmac, the faint silhouette of the high terrain surrounding Chingchuankang. Somewhere behind and in front of them were the other three "Super D" Chinooks carrying sixty more special ops commandos, led by their escort of four AH-1W Super Cobra gunships.

*With fewer than a hundred troops, we're invading China.*

This *was* a joke.

The throb of the rotors deepened further. Maxwell felt the big chopper tilt forward and accelerate. Like all fighter pilots, he held a deep-rooted mistrust of rotary-wing aircraft. There was something unnatural about helicopters, all those whirling parts, gears gnashing together like metallic demons.

He could tell that Catfish Bass felt the same way. The Air Force pilot looked like a man waiting for a hemorrhoidectomy. Bass sat with his arms folded tightly over his chest, his face frozen in a glum expression. Like the rest of the raiding party, he wore ninjalike black utilities and a Kevlar helmet with night vision goggles attached. His face was smeared with greasepaint. He wore a satchel over his shoulder containing a PRC-112 handheld communications unit and a flight helmet fitted with oxygen mask and PLA-standard connectors. In a shoulder holster he carried a 9 mm Beretta.

"Helicopters suck," said Bass.

"It beats swimming."

"Swimming sucks too."

"That's what I like about Air Force guys. You're so cheerful."

Bass nodded toward the front of the Chinook. "What about them? Do they have a clue what they're doing?"

Maxwell looked up at the darkened cockpit. He had been

wondering the same thing. Sneaking four troop-carrying helicopters and four noisy gunships across the Taiwan Strait into the most heavily defended air base in China was a trick of incredible audacity. What would happen when they triggered the alarm in the PLA's elaborate sensor net? What would happen when the air defense ring around the Chouzhou perimeter detected their unwelcome presence? The big twin-rotored Chinooks were the furthest thing imaginable from stealth aircraft.

He remembered Chiu's response when the question was raised in the final briefing. "Privileged information," was all he would say. "We have assets to deal with the base defenses. We will enter the Chouzhou perimeter without interference."

*Assets?* Maxwell decided not to press him. He assumed it meant they had operatives on the ground at Chouzhou. What kind of operatives? It made sense not to disclose details, in the event they were captured.

But what about the sensor net? How did they plan to suppress the surveillance radar that constantly probed the sky over the Taiwan Strait?

Did the Chinook pilots know what they were doing?

"It doesn't matter now," Maxwell said. "We're along for the ride until we get to Chouzhou and find the Black Star."

Bass nodded. His face became gloomier.

By the hum of the airframe Maxwell guessed that the Chinook was up to speed, something around a hundred forty knots. An occasional wink of light passed by the blackened cabin window. A hut in the mountains? A boat at sea? No way to tell.

They were in the second of the four Chinooks. Leading the column were the Super Cobras. If they ran into trouble, the rocket-firing gunships would be the first to engage.

He caught Mai-ling's eyes on him. She looked oddly subdued, dressed in the ninja costume, her face blackened.

Gone, at least for the moment, was the defiant attitude, the look of confidence in her eyes. For a moment Maxwell let himself remember. He could still sense the warm touch of her skin.

She seemed to be reading his thoughts. She nodded and gave him a tentative smile.

Chiu noticed. He looked at Mai-ling, then switched his gaze back to Maxwell, his eyes narrow and penetrating.

Chiu was a snoop, Maxwell thought. He had already learned from his sentries about the walk on the darkened ramp last night. So what? To hell with Chiu.

Chiu abruptly rose and went to the forward cabin. Along the way he stopped to clap several of his commandos on the shoulder, rapping his knuckles on their helmets, giving words of encouragement. Maxwell noticed how each of the young special forces soldiers looked at Chiu with reverence.

For all his personality deficiencies, Chiu had the total loyalty of his men. His troops would follow him into hell.

*Is that where we're headed?* With that question in his mind, Maxwell reached for his holster, checking that the clip was shoved all the way into the grip of the .45.

Chiu was carrying on an animated conversation with the two pilots on the elevated cockpit deck. Their heads were nodding, and they pointed to a display on the panel.

After several minutes Chiu returned to the cabin. He huddled for a moment with one of his platoon leaders, clapped him on the shoulder, then he came back to where Maxwell and Bass were seated.

Chiu glanced at his watch. "Halfway across the strait," he said to Maxwell. "Thirty-five minutes from Chouzhou."

Maxwell nodded. He glanced out the round window again. Nothing but blackness. He knew they were skimming the surface of the ocean, probably no higher than fifty feet.

Again he felt the impotence of a fighter pilot trapped in a clattering, low-flying helicopter.

Bass was right. *Helicopters suck.*

*Taipei, Taiwan*

It was eerily quiet in the bunker. Sitting at his desk inside his cubicle, Franklin Huang heard no explosions from the complex outside, no sirens, no clamor of fire trucks and ambulances. The war seemed to have entered a lull.

Huang considered again the faxed brief on his desk. Glaring at him from the black-and-white sheet was the visage of Colonel Chiu Yusheng. The colonel looked grim and unsmiling in the photo. His hard features glared at the camera as if he were ready for hand-to-hand combat.

So this was the legendary Chiu. Huang had heard of him.

According to the classified brief sheet, Chiu had participated in over a dozen clandestine operations inside mainland China. He had been inserted by raft, submarine, helicopter, and on one occasion, an ultralight aircraft. The sheet only alluded to Chiu's objectives, which Huang inferred to be intelligence gathering, rescue and retrieval of operatives, and a certain amount of discreet sabotage.

Huang nodded appreciatively. Colonel Chiu was a man of diverse talents.

Next to the briefing paper on Chiu was a report from the chief of the southern sector air traffic control center. Two nights ago, a U.S. Navy C-2 had been cleared into Taiwanese airspace. The American airplane had arrived at a low altitude from the southwest—the sector where the USS *Ronald Reagan* and its battle group were known to be stationed. The turboprop aircraft had landed at Chingchuankang Air Base, then departed forty-five minutes later. Nothing more had been reported.

Huang stared at the report. *What was the purpose of the*

*visit? To drop off the two Americans?* If so, it could mean that two U.S. Navy personnel were participating in a mission commanded by Colonel Chiu.

*What mission? To where?*

One more clue lay on Huang's desk. A series of reports that Taiwanese jets were being felled by some invisible weapon. Pilots were speculating that the Chinese possessed a phantom fighter that could attack without being detected. Even more oddly, one of the F-16s lost was flown by some overzealous U.S. Air Force pilot, an advisor to the Taiwanese air force.

Huang tilted back and considered the information. A picture was emerging, like the pieces of an intricate mosaic.

A commando raid against an unspecified target, presumably on the mainland.

An invisible Chinese fighter.

Involvement of Americans, probably pilots from an aircraft carrier.

As Huang's imagination ranged through the possibilities, he kept coming back to the same hypothesis. It was farfetched, but after all that had occurred in the last three days, nothing surprised him. Madame Soong had already demonstrated that she was willing to take insane risks.

Yes, this was something she would do.

He didn't have all the pieces yet, but he was close. It was time to issue a warning. He reached again for the satellite phone.

*Chouzhou Air Base, People's Republic of China*

Sirens. *Why?*

Colonel Zhang set his teacup down on the rosewood desk in his office. He stared for a moment at the blacked-out window. Why were the air defense sirens wailing again?

He thought again about the strange telephone call from

PLA headquarters in Beijing. General Tsin had received a vague warning from a highly placed source in Taipei that some kind of commando raid was in progress. The target was unknown. It was unlikely that the rebels would be brazen enough to attack Chouzhou, but—

He snatched up the direct phone to the sector air defense command post.

"It seems to be another missile attack, Colonel," answered the air defense commander. "Two, perhaps three cruise missiles were reported inbound, but they appear to be targeting the troop bivouac at Nanpo, not the Chouzhou Air Base."

"You're sure that is all? Missiles? No aircraft?"

"Nothing has been detected by the air defense net."

Zhang acknowledged and hung up the phone. As commander of the PLA air force's most precious commodity— the Dong-jin project—he lived in constant worry that the secret of Chouzhou had been discovered.

No, he decided. They wouldn't come to Chouzhou. Even if they somehow knew about the Dong-jin, they couldn't possibly breach the net of air defenses.

Based at Chouzhou were two squadrons of SU-27 fighter-interceptors and another squadron of F-7 attack aircraft. For close-in base defense, Chouzhou had a dedicated battery of SA-10 Grumble surface-to-air missiles, recently acquired from Russia and still maintained by Russian technicians. The presence of the deadly SA-10s had discouraged any ROC attempt to attack the base with F-16s. Their feeble cruise missiles, which were nothing but crudely reengineered antiship missiles, had caused some minor damage, potholing one of the runways and taking out two elderly F-7 fighters. A pinprick, nothing more.

If Chouzhou were in danger, it was not from exterior forces. Colonel Zhang knew that the greatest danger lay within.

The damned dissidents. They were a cancer in the PLA's flesh. They betrayed secrets, sabotaged infrastructure, destroyed the morale of the People's Liberation Army. Zhang hated them even more than he hated the decadent United States and its clients. He had built his career on ridding the PLA of these vermin.

Zhang finished his tea, then glanced at his watch. Twenty minutes before briefing. Another predawn sortie with the two flyable Dong-jins. Already they had established nearly total air superiority over the strait. Zhang himself had destroyed eleven F-16s, as well as one E-2C radome-equipped warning and control aircraft and an S-2 antisubmarine plane. It was like shooting geese from an invisible blind.

He removed his slippers and tugged on the high-topped flying boots. He was still lacing the left boot when the lights went out.

The power grid.

Captain Hu, the SA-10 battery commander, rushed outside the command shack. What was going on? Something had happened to the electrical power supply at Chouzhou. The base was plunged into total darkness.

He yelled inside to the technician seated at the control console. "Switch to batteries and generator. Quickly!"

"I'm doing it, Captain. It will take a minute to reset the systems."

Hu cursed the darkness. He had ordered the generators shut down and the power supply switched back to normal when the air raid alert had ended. It was routine, whenever a threat was detected, to transfer the SAM battery's power from the normal power supply to the backup system, which was independent of Chouzhou's power grid. Even if the base's large power grid were shut down, the air defense battery would continue to function.

Now it would take several minutes to restart the generators and reset the power supply to the standby system. Several minutes of vulnerability. Captain Hu didn't want to think of the repercussions when his superiors learned that he was responsible for crippling the air defense battery.

"Hurry! I want the generators on line."

"They're cranking now, Captain."

His eyes were still adjusting to the darkness outside. What happened to the power plant? Something strange was going on, and he was getting a bad feeling about it.

An eerie stillness had fallen over the base. In the far distance he heard the muffled sound of explosions. Missile strikes on the troop bivouac at Nanpo. *Better them than us.*

Hu turned to go back inside the command shack—then stopped. He cocked his head, listening. Something . . . a different sound . . . nearer than the distant explosions . . .

It was clearer now, more distinct. A pulsing, whopping noise, coming this way.

Helicopters.

Captain Hu was frozen, paralyzed with an unfathomable thought. Helicopters approaching Chouzhou!

*Who?*

There was only one explanation, and it had to be connected with the failure of the power grid.

"Standby power is coming back on line, Captain."

"Hurry, damn it!"

"Half a minute."

"Ready the target acquisition units. Prepare for an immediate launch as soon as you have power."

"Yes, sir."

The 3-D continuous-wave pulse Doppler acquisition radar was mounted on its own trailer thirty meters from the launch complex. Next to it was the I-band engagement radar on its own trailer. Both had powered down when the lights went out.

Hu couldn't bring himself to go back inside the command

post. He stood transfixed, studying the silhouette of the northern ridgeline. The whopping noise was intensifying.

*What is it?*

In the next moment he knew. The first helicopter broke over the ridge, clattering out of the darkness like an apparition. Hu could see only the ghostly shape, but he knew without doubt what it had to be.

A second helicopter appeared over the ridge. Close behind, a third. The staccato beat of the rotor blades split the silence at Chouzhou. Even as Hu whirled to dash back inside the command shack, he knew it was too late. The helicopters—they had to be gunships—were flying a direct course for the SAM battery.

A pair of orange flashes strobed from each side of the lead helicopter. Stunned, Hu saw the fiery trail of missiles sizzling down toward the battery. A surge of adrenaline strong enough to jolt an ox shot through his body. He reversed direction and launched himself in a hell-bent sprint for the drainage ditch a hundred meters away.

The first explosion caught him still running. Hu felt himself propelled through the air, over the ditch, tumbling end over end across the graveled surface. A second explosion split the air. He sensed the concussion of more blasts, one after the other. The SA-10s were exploding on their launchers.

Hu tried to roll into a ball, shielding himself from the rain of blazing debris. As though in a dream, he watched each of his six tractor-trailer launchers erupt in a cascade of fire.

One of the gunships was circling to fire again on the SAM complex. As Hu watched in morbid fascination, the acquisition radar unit took a direct hit. The battery command post Hu had just abandoned was a blazing inferno.

A deafening explosion nearly broke Hu's eardrums. He guessed that it was the cache of hundred-kilogram high-explosive warheads, stored a hundred meters away from the complex. Secondary explosions shook the earth beneath Hu.

Through a fog of disbelief, he tried to make sense of what was happening. Somehow they had shut down the power grid at Chouzhou. Was it the work of someone inside the base? Dissidents?

It had to be. If so, the timing was exquisite. The ROC helicopters had arrived to attack his SAM battery during the few minutes that he was unable to fire missiles. It was a co-ordinated assault on Chouzhou.

Why? he wondered, watching the flames leap from his destroyed missile battery. What were they after?

# CHAPTER SIXTEEN

# RAVEN SWOOP

*Chouzhou Air Base, People's Republic of China*
*0445, Monday, 15 September*

The Dong-jin.

Colonel Zhang stood on the darkened tarmac outside his office. Yes, that had to be it. It was his worst fear come true. *They know about the stealth jet, the one they call Black Star. They're coming for it.*

A hunched-over figure burst from the office door next to his, nearly running him over. Zhang seized the man's sleeve. He recognized the panting face of the base commander, Colonel Pao.

"What's going on?" Zhang said, holding Pao back. "How did those helicopters get inside the perimeter? What's happened to the electrical power?"

Pao yanked his arm free. "What do you think? The damned dissidents you claimed were all rounded up . . . well, there are more out there. They've sabotaged the power grid."

Officially, Pao and Zhang were equals in rank. As base commander, Pao's responsibility was the security and maintenance of Chouzhou, while Zhang confined himself to operational matters. But Pao understood the reality of the PLA. Zhang had powerful patrons. He could have Pao arrested and executed with a snap of his fingers.

"What happened to the air defense net?" demanded Zhang. "Why aren't the antiaircraft guns firing at those helicopters?"

"I don't know. I was on my way to the—"

Pao stopped in midsentence, his mouth frozen open. An orange glare illuminated his face, revealing wide-open, disbelieving eyes.

Zhang whirled to see what occupied Pao's attention. An orange pillar of flame was leaping a hundred meters into the night sky, lighting up the southwest corner of the base as if it were high noon.

Four seconds later, he heard the deep *whump* of the explosion.

"The fuel tanks," he said. "The bastards are attacking the fuel tanks."

In the orange light, they could make out the silhouette of the gunship skimming past the burning fuel depot. Two of the three huge fuel storage tanks were blazing fiercely.

"We have to save the last fuel tank," muttered Pao. "I need troops to fight the fire."

"Forget the tanks, you idiot," said Zhang. "Worry about the helicopters. They're inside your perimeter."

Pao seemed not to hear. "We have to save the fuel for the interceptors. I must order the troops to extinguish the fire." He yanked his arm free of Zhang's clutch and ran back inside his office.

Zhang shook his head in disgust. The enemy was wreaking havoc at Chouzhou, and all the base commander could think of was putting out fires. Pao had a thousand troops assigned to defend his base, and he wanted to use them as firemen.

The imbecile. When this night was over, he would see to it that Pao was reassigned to Tibet.

He climbed into his canvas-topped utility vehicle. Leaving the lights out, he drove along the semicircular taxiway that led to the number four Dong-jin shelter. With the base under attack, he would have to dispense with the long briefing and the preflight target assessment. This was a wartime emergency. They must get the Dong-jins airborne immediately.

Zhang passed groups of soldiers running in various directions, all seemingly without leadership. He was nearly past the flight line when he heard the throb of rotor blades. Instinctively, he swung off the taxiway. He jumped out and ducked for cover beside the corner of a concrete revetment.

Directly over his head swept a black shape—a helicopter gunship, he realized. As Zhang watched, a fiery hail of rockets erupted from each pylon on the gunship.

Zhang followed the path of the rockets. They were aimed at the flight line where the SU-27 and F-7 fighters were dispersed. The valuable SU-27s were parked inside revetments, while the more expendable F-7s were scattered on the open tarmac.

Zhang heard the sound of running feet. Coming down the taxiway were a dozen flight-suited pilots—the alert unit—running for their jets. As they jogged past, Zhang considered yelling at them, telling them to stay away. The parked fighters were prime targets for the gunships.

He let them go. Maybe some will make it into the air, he decided. A few might actually manage to shoot back at the enemy.

The rockets struck the flight line. An explosion and a column of bright flame marked the death spot of an F-7. Then another. Two more fighters exploded.

Zhang watched from his shelter, cursing the incompetent idiots that allowed this to happen.

The helicopter swept over the flight line, then turned to come back the opposite way, firing into the revetments. An SU-27 erupted in a ball of fire. The flight line was turning into an inferno.

By the flickering light of the blazes, Zhang could see the tiny figures of the pilots, still running toward the few undamaged jets. Give them credit, he thought. China produces brave pilots. Stupid, but brave.

The helicopter returned for another pass. This time Zhang noticed that it wasn't firing rockets. Were they out of ammunition? Did it mean the pilots could reach the jets and—

Something was spewing from the helicopter. It took Zhang a moment to realize what he was seeing. They looked like tiny trinkets, glistening in the orange light as they fell to the earth. Hundreds, clattering onto the concrete, bouncing off the wings of the parked jets, littering the flight line.

The pilots were just reaching the parked jets when the first of the objects detonated. Zhang heard the *whump* of an explosion, then the scream of the decapitated pilot.

Another explosion. More screams.

*Get back!* Zhang wanted to yell. The gunship had littered the flight line with antipersonnel mines—little round killers with hydraulic shock absorbers. They would spring up a meter from the ground and detonate at crotch level whenever a soft target approached.

As it was doing now.

Another muffled *whump*. More screams. Zhang cursed again. Chouzhou's fighter wing had been effectively neutralized until specialists could cleanse the area of the deadly little mines.

He climbed back into his vehicle. The helicopters were sweeping the perimeter of the base, firing at targets of opportunity. None of the heavy guns were firing back. No missiles were streaking into the sky.

Grudgingly, Zhang had to admire the professionalism of

the raid. The rebel pilots must be using night vision equipment. And they had to have human intelligence—spies inside Chouzhou—to inform them about the location of the missile batteries and antiaircraft guns. They had to have inside help to knock out the power grid.

With a growing sense of anxiety, he accelerated down the taxiway. Time was running out. The helicopters hadn't come all the way across the strait just to shoot up a SAM site and scatter some antipersonnel mines. There had to be more.

There was.

As Zhang listened, a deeper throb overrode the lighter beat of the gunships. He heard the heavy pulsing of multiple rotor blades.

More helicopters. Bigger, multiengine machines.

*Carrying what?*

Zhang glanced over his shoulder. In the flickering light, he could make out the silhouettes—four big, twin-rotored machines, alighting on the apron south of the shelters. It was the off-limits, close-hold area where no one at Chouzhou was allowed except those assigned to the ultrasecret Dongjin project. Clusters of tiny shapes were spewing out of each helicopter, quickly vanishing in the gloom of the darkened tarmac.

Zhang saw that no one was opposing the invaders. Not yet, at least. Colonel Pao had deployed most of his base defense troops to fight the fuel tank fires.

He shook his head in frustration. Tibet was too good for Pao. The idiot would face a firing squad.

He tore his attention away from the helicopters. He forced himself to think. Like an elusive solution to a puzzle, it was coming to him. The gunships had eliminated the SAM batteries and the perimeter air defenses. They had rocketed and neutralized the squadron of interceptors. They had torched the jet fuel tanks. But they hadn't attacked the prime target at Chouzhou—the two main assembly buildings and four reinforced shelters in the northeast quadrant. The Dong-jin project.

*Why?* Why didn't they just destroy it as they had the air defense system?

The answer came to him. *Because they want it intact.*

With that thought echoing in his mind, Zhang jammed his foot down hard on the accelerator.

Chiu hit the ground running. He didn't stop until he had put a hundred meters between himself and the CH-47. Then he dropped to one knee and looked back toward the helicopter.

*Good.* They were following, staying together as he had ordered. The two Americans and the Chinese woman, running pell-mell away from the helicopter to join him and the fire team of commandos.

With the PVS-7 night vision goggles pulled down over his eyes, Chiu scanned the quadrant in front of him. In the greenish light he had a clear view of the tarmac, the helicopters, the row of shelters to the northeast. All the helos were empty of commandos now. He watched the shapes of his commandos, joined in twelve-man units, sprinting across the tarmac toward their objectives.

Maxwell came jogging up, followed by Bass and the woman.

"Stay close to me," said Chiu. "Three meters, no farther."

They all nodded. Crouching in the darkness beside him was the team of six commandos, led by a grim-faced young lieutenant named Kee. Each wore helmet-mounted NVG, and one had the PRC-119 manpack radio by which Chiu would communicate with the helicopters and his dispersed squads.

The sound of automatic fire crackled nearby. Chiu turned his head and listened. It seemed to come from the shelters several hundred meters to the north. He recognized the distinctive burp of the commandos' H&K MP-5N submachine gun.

*Excellent.* On schedule, C squad was taking out the guard posts.

He nodded to the lieutenant. Without a sound, Kee and his team rose. Spread out ten yards apart, they trotted off toward the complex at the northeast quadrant.

"Follow them," Chiu said to the Americans. "Don't get separated."

Jogging along behind the commandos, he heard more bursts of automatic fire, this time from the right.

The northeastern security posts. There were posts every two hundred meters in the restricted area, and each had to be sanitized before the commandos could establish defensive positions.

It was going well, but Chiu knew their advantage was momentary. They had the cover of darkness and the NVG and, most important, the element of surprise. They enjoyed a numerical superiority only because the PLA forces—who outnumbered them twenty to one—were not yet positioned to oppose them.

Their advantage was dwindling with each passing minute. The blanket of darkness was diminished by the towering blaze of the fuel tank fires and the gathering dawn. In less than an hour, the new day would lighten the eastern horizon.

They had to find the Black Star, insert the Americans into the stealth jet, get them launched, then escape—all before the base defense brigade could organize a counterattack.

Chiu glanced over his shoulder. They were staying with him, as he had ordered. Even the woman, the Chinese defector, was trotting along in trail behind Bass and Maxwell.

As they neared the first of the two assembly buildings, he heard the sounds of the firefight from the nearest building in the complex. Staccato MP-5N bursts were mixed with the rattle of a Type 95 assault rifle—the Chinese derivative of

the venerable Kalashnikov AK-47. Lieutenant Kee, leading
the column, gave the signal to stop and crouch.

They huddled in the darkness, shielded from the flickering light of the burning fuel tanks by the wall of a revetment.
Sporadic sounds of battle spilled out of the buildings.

The radioman waddled back to Chiu. "Building One secure, Colonel. The second still contains a platoon of security
troops."

Chiu acknowledged. He signaled for Maxwell and the
other two to remain with him, huddled by the revetment
wall.

A minute later, the squad leader reported that the resist-
ance in Building Two had ended. Both assembly buildings
were secure.

"Tell the D squad leader I want snipers deployed to the
roofs of both buildings."

"Yes, sir."

He gave the signal for Kee to move out. In column behind
the commandos, Chiu and his group rose and headed toward
Building One, where the defector told them the Black Star
life support equipment shop was located.

Trotting across the open ground, Chiu glanced over his
shoulder to make sure the others were staying with him.
They were, Maxwell leading, with Bass and the Chinese
woman close behind. Even without using his NVG, he could
see their shadows flitting across the surface. The blazing
fuel fires were flooding the base in an orange glow.

The thought had already occurred to Chiu that the woman
defector, Chen, might be leading them into a trap. Even if
she were not a double agent, the accuracy of her information
could still be flawed. She was the one he had been most
worried about. Traitors by any other name or nationality
were still traitors. They were not to be trusted.

They had no time for a random search of the complex for
the Black Star and the equipment they needed to fly it.

*What then?*

About the woman, Chiu had reached a decision. It was possible that she had compromised the operation by seducing the American Maxwell. What information had she obtained from him?

He had already decided that her only remaining value was to point them to the Black Star. If she failed, Chiu intended to put a bullet in her head. No hesitation, no remorse. Defectors, even PLA defectors, had no claim to a long life.

The Americans were another matter. Taiwan's survival depended on getting them into the cockpit of the Black Star. The primary purpose of the mission was to insert these two into the stealth craft. For that reason, Chiu had not allowed himself to become friendly with them. The mission was too critical to be compromised by sentimentality.

If the mission failed, Chiu's duty was clear. The Americans must not be allowed to become prisoners of the PLA. He would kill them.


*Taiwan Strait*

From his bridge aboard the *Kai Yang*, Commander Lei peered into the gathering darkness.

He had a rendezvous scheduled with a tanker and a resupply ship. Only after nightfall would he undertake the risky operation of rearming and refueling. Returning to port, either to Keelung in the north or Kaohsiung in the south, was out of the question. If they weren't caught by missiles or PLA strike jets in the naval yard, they'd be picked off by one of the submarines that were parked outside every port in Taiwan.

Out of the murk the two provisioning ships appeared. No transmissions were exchanged as they took station, one on either side of *Kai Yang*. To the outboard side of the tanker, the pair of destroyer escorts were lined up, bow to stern, to take on their own fuel. Blinking lights from each vessel were the only communication.

Lei watched the reprovisioning with a vague uneasiness. It was an operation his crew had rehearsed a hundred times. To his port side, half a dozen lines drooped between the stores ship and *Kai Yang*. Containers filled with vital supplies—more Harpoons, more torpedoes, food and fresh water—wobbled across the narrow canyon between the ships, dangling from the lines.

They were headed into the wind on a southwesterly course. The four-foot swells were causing the dissimilar vessels to rise and fall in discordant rhythms. *Kai Yang*'s larger bow was lifting while the provisioning ship was dropping into a trough. The containers danced between the two ships like trinkets swaying on a chain.

On the starboard side, a single thick hose connected the *Kai Yang* to the fueling ship. In twenty minutes they would take on enough fuel to keep them at sea another five days. Lei knew he would cut his endurance by half if he were caught up in another flank speed duel with the PLA navy.

He glanced at the luminescent clock face on his console. Ten minutes into the reprovisioning. *Relax,* he commanded himself. There was nothing he could do except wait. He tried to focus on the dull pink void on the western horizon where the sun had set nearly an hour ago.

Commander Lei had fourteen years of service under his belt. With luck—and a favorable outcome of the war—he could expect another six years, perhaps command of a surface squadron. If all the circumstances of his career fell into supreme harmony, he might even be elevated to flag rank.

Admiral Lei Fu-sheng.

The prospect gave him no joy. The truth was, he no longer cared about the honor and trappings of high command. The events of the past two days had forced him to consider the harsh facts of his life. He had a wife whom he hadn't seen for more than a week of each month during their entire marriage. His two sons had grown to manhood in his absence. Neither was close to him, nor were they interested in military careers.

All because he had chosen a life of service to his country. A country that might not exist a week from now.

While this thought still played in his mind, he received the call from the surface watch officer, Lt. Fu Shing. "Radar contact, Captain."

He was instantly alert. "Range and distance?"

"Multiple returns bearing two-nine-zero, forty kilometers, constant bearing, decreasing range. They've already painted us on their radar."

Lei nodded. The hostile contacts had detected them first. No surprise, considering the archaic SPS-58 radar equipment installed on the *Kai Yang. Constant bearing, decreasing range.* It meant the contacts were on a direct course for *Kai Yang* and its two destroyer escorts.

"Does Dragon Boat have an ID?" Dragon Boat was the E-2C surveillance aircraft, overseeing the action in the strait.

"Nothing positive yet. The radar hits are definitely PLA navy, destroyer or frigate size."

Lei shook his head in frustration. Having a mini-AWACS like the E-2C on station was a nice idea, but its effectiveness against surface targets was minimal. The big revolving parasol radome atop the E-2C was intended for use against airborne targets. What they needed was a surveillance jet like the American RC-135 Rivet Joint. Or real-time satellite imagery, delivered by instant datalink. Instead, they had hand-me-down junk the Americans stopped using thirty years ago.

*It doesn't matter,* Lei reminded himself. *This is what you have. Fight the ship!*

The thought struck him that he and *Kai Yang* were about

to make history. *A surface naval battle.* No modern warships had engaged in a surface battle since World War II.

Of course, calling the *Kai Yang* a modern warship was stretching a point. If the old frigate were still in America, it would be a floating museum. Its surface search and fire control radars were inferior to the equipment on most private yachts. Originally delivered to the U.S. Navy as a destroyer in the 1940s, it had served a full career before being stricken from the list and transferred to the Taiwanese navy as a frigate.

Lei considered his situation. If he had any advantage over his Chinese adversary, it was his armament. He had Sea Sparrow air defense missiles for standoff protection. On either side he had twin turrets of five-inch, thirty-eight caliber guns. For extreme close-in defense, *Kai Yang* was outfitted with the Phalanx M-61A1 Gatling gun system. His two destroyer escorts, *Tai Yuan*, and *Wen Shan*, were each armed with Mark 46 torpedoes and twin turrets of five-inch thirty-eights.

For offense, Lei still carried Harpoon cruise missiles, reconfigured for antiship duty.

*Or did he?*

He tried to remember. Of the eight Harpoons originally stowed aboard *Kai Yang*, he had fired—how many? It came to him. Six, launched against targets on the mainland. The remaining two had been reserved for antiship attack.

"Have we loaded the Harpoons from the supply ship yet?"

"Don't know, Captain," The watch officer grabbed his sound-powered phone. "I'll find out."

"Forget it. Order the supply ships to break away. Suspend resupply and take us to General Quarters."

"Aye, Captain." While the watch officer barked the commands into the sound-powered phone, his hand hit a mushroom-shaped knob on the OOD console. One second later, a

Klaxon horn sounded and a recorded voice announced in Chinese, "General Quarters, General Quarters. All hands man battle stations."

Watching the crew below donning helmets and flotation jackets, scrambling to their stations, Lei nodded in approval. That was something they'd gotten good at. For most of the last two days, the crew of the *Kai Yang* had been running to battle stations.

"Captain, supply reports that we took three Harpoons aboard before breaking away."

"Have them fuzed and loaded immediately."

"Gunnery is already doing it, sir. They say they'll be ready in five minutes."

Lei felt a warm glow of pride for his crew. They knew they were in extreme danger. Never had he seen them perform with such cool efficiency.

"Conn, surface watch." It was Fu Shing, the watch officer again. "We're getting steady radar hits from the contact. He still bears two-nine-zero, range thirty kilometers, decreasing. Three distinct contacts, one emitting what we're sure is a Russian radar. We think it's a Sovremenny."

Lei felt a chill sweep over him. "What probability?"

"Perhaps seventy-five percent. Dragon Boat makes the same appraisal."

"Very well." Lei called fire control. "Obtain a Harpoon firing solution for the inbound target. The largest contact."

"Already done, Captain. He's well within Harpoon range."

Also well within Moskit supersonic missile range. The Sovremenny captain was taking his time. He knew his missiles could cover the distance between the ships in one third the time it took a Harpoon.

An old dictum from Lei's academy days came to him. *When you are outgunned, make sure you shoot first.* He didn't know who said it, but he believed it so much he had

had it etched in brass and mounted above his desk. He still believed it. The Taiwanese navy was always outgunned. *Make sure you shoot first.*

"Fire the first Harpoon."

"Aye, aye, sir."

Lei shielded his eyes as the orange glow erupted from the vertical launcher on the starboard bow. It was the same fire-tailed apparition he'd witnessed the first night of the war when they launched the Harpoons against mainland targets. Through the steel bulkhead of the bridge he felt the rumble of the booster rocket that would kick the Harpoon up to near-supersonic speed before the turbojet engine took over.

Lei watched the missile leap into the sky, then level off and pursue its sea-skimming course to the northwest.

"Fire the second Harpoon."

A moment's pause. "Sir, that will be our last until the new ones—"

"Fire, damn it!"

# CHAPTER SEVENTEEN

# DEFECTOR

*Chouzhou Air Base, People's Republic of China*
*0455, Monday, 15 September*

*The law of unintended consequences.*

It had not been repealed, thought Maxwell as he jogged over the soft ground toward the darkened Building One. You planned an operation down to the tiniest detail. You allowed for every contingency, looked for every glitch. Then something you didn't expect jumped up to bite you in the butt.

The fuel tank fire, for instance. The gunship crews had done a brilliant job of flaming the fuel tanks. The fire even had the effect of drawing off most of the security forces to fight the blaze. It also had the unintended consequence of bathing Chouzhou Air Base in an ethereal orange glow.

Now the damned place looked like a Fourth of July celebration. Bonfires, fireworks, crowds milling around without direction. Everything on the base was in view, illuminated by the fire.

The sounds of battle crackled from every direction. Chiu's commandos had occupied tactical positions—rooftops, security towers, revetments—from which they were firing on the PLA troops wherever they tried to organize themselves into cohesive units. So far it was working.

Even without his NVG, Maxwell could see running figures at the far end of the complex. Silhouetted in the soft glow of the fire, soldiers were racing across the open ground like shadow figures on a screen.

Another pair of muffled explosions came from the flight line, where the PLA fighters were dispersed. Maxwell winced as he thought about the carnage caused by the antipersonnel mines. They were nasty, inhumane little weapons—but highly suited to their purpose here.

The commandos had come to a halt. A hundred yards ahead lay the first objective. Building One housed the life support equipment shop. Not only did it contain the helmets, oxygen masks, and radio fittings specific to the Black Star, it had the special UV goggles that, according to Mai-ling, were supposed to penetrate the Black Star's cloak of invisibility. If it were true, it meant that the Chinese had developed a precious new item of technology.

Chiu was studying the buildings with his NVG. He motioned for Maxwell and Bass and Mai-ling to join him.

"Where is the door to the life support shop?"

Mai-ling gazed at the building. "I think it's the one at the right corner. Over there, maybe."

"Maybe?" He gave her a menacing look. "What do you mean, you don't know? I thought you worked there."

"I worked in the photonics shop. In the next building."

"If you have given us false information . . ." Chiu left the sentence unfinished. His hand went to the holstered pistol at his hip. Mai-ling's face was a frozen mask.

"We're wasting time," said Maxwell. "Let's find the shop."

Chiu's eyes blazed at Maxwell, then he swung back to Mai-ling. He snatched her sleeve. "You first, in front of us. Show us the door."

Bass stepped toward them, and Maxwell grabbed his arm. He said in a low voice, "Butt out. This isn't your show."

"What if he shoots her?"

"He won't."

"He's nuts. What if he does?"

"I won't let him."

Bass started to open his mouth again, but Maxwell shoved him in the direction of the commandos, who had already started off toward the building.

As they neared the building Maxwell could hear the deep-throated sound of large-caliber rifles. That was good. It meant Chiu's snipers were in position, finding targets back on the tarmac.

A dense cloud of black smoke from the fuel tank fire was drifting across the field, obscuring the landing zone where the Chinooks had dropped them off. Maxwell had lost sight of the helicopters. Even the gunships were out of view. He hoped the pilots had moved them into the smoke cloud to stay out of PLA gun sights.

They covered the last fifty yards in a dead run. The sound of the sniper rifles was continuous now. Not a good sign, thought Maxwell.

With Chiu shoving her from behind, Mai-ling reached the door at the right corner of the two-story, slab-sided building. She nearly stumbled over something—the crumpled body of a PLA soldier, still clutching his assault rifle. Another lay spread-eagled on the ground next to the door.

She stepped around the bodies, carefully avoiding looking at them. The commandos formed a defensive perimeter around the corner of the building while she tried the door.

It wouldn't move.

"Is this the door, or isn't it?" demanded Chiu.

"I don't know. It's locked."

A look of pure rage passed over Chiu's face. Keeping his

eyes on her, he snatched his automatic pistol from its holster and seemed to aim into her face. Mai-ling recoiled in shock.

"Don't!" yelled Bass, six feet away.

"Shut up." Chiu swung the muzzle of the pistol down to the lock mechanism. Shielding his eyes, he fired at the dead-bolt. The bullet twanged into the metal, creating a flash and a shower of fragments.

It still didn't open.

He fired again. Another flash, more sheared metal.

He stepped back and gave the door a kick. It swung open.

He shoved Mai-ling through the open door. "Take us to the equipment shop. No more excuses."

She hated him. She despised him with the cold, unthinking abhorrence one feels for a rabid animal.

Chiu was a madman, Mai-ling decided. She had been certain that he was going to kill her when he was forcing open the door of the equipment shop. If his second bullet hadn't shattered the lock, the next one probably would have gone into her skull.

Now she felt his hand between her shoulder blades, shoving her. "Move!"

*Where was the shop?* She prayed that it was in this building, somewhere on the bottom floor. She had never been in the crew life-support equipment shop. She only knew of its existence from Shaomin.

The door into Building One led them to a wide hallway with branches to separate bays on the ground floor. Chiu was holding a floor plan of the building in front of him, studying it under the red beam of his flashlight.

"Where is it? You said it would be at this end of the building."

She stared at the plan. Vaguely she remembered seeing the Dong-jin crews emerge from the building on the northern side, the side facing the shelters. If so, then the equipment shop would be to their right.

She saw the hostility in Chiu's face.

"There." She pointed to the place on the map. "Maybe."

Another flurry of gunfire from outside caused all their heads to swivel. Chiu listened for a moment, then stuffed the plan into his pocket. He seized her shoulder and steered her on down the hallway. "Be quick. We're out of time."

She moved down the darkened hallway, following the red beam of Chiu's gel-masked flashlight. Behind them Maxwell and Bass followed, keeping their silence.

They came to another door. It too was locked. Again Chiu produced his pistol, but this time he blew apart the lock with only one shot.

He swept the darkened room with his flashlight. From a row of pegs on one wall hung several hard-shelled flying helmets. A shelf contained oxygen masks and emergency equipment. Cabinets lined two walls, and another rack held torso harnesses with the fittings that secured the pilot to a jet's ejection seat.

The life-support equipment shop.

Mai-ling took a deep breath. Chiu would let her live, at least for five more minutes.

It took Maxwell and Bass less than a minute to find suitable helmets. Then oxygen masks. They attached them to the helmets with the peculiar Chinese bayonet fittings.

Mai-ling was conducting her own search, pulling out drawers, opening cabinets. At the far end of the room she yanked open a wall-length metal cabinet. It contained an array of peculiar-looking lenses, similar in appearance to the NVG they were wearing.

Chiu came up behind her. "Well?"

"This is it. Just like I said. The ultraviolet goggles."

He kept his face impassive. No acknowledgment, no sign

of approval. "Get what you need," he called to the two pilots. We're leaving."

He turned to Mai-ling. He was still holding the pistol at his side. "Now we see if you are a patriot or a traitor. Take us to the Black Star."

She nodded, feeling the confidence ooze from her. *Be calm. Your real objective is almost in reach.*

She gathered up two sets of the UV goggles and turned to leave. Almost as an afterthought, she reached back in the cabinet and snatched one more.

Stepping into the darkness, Maxwell pulled down his NVG. In the eerie green light of the NVG lens, he saw the four aircraft shelters arranged in a semicircle around a connecting taxiway. Each of the shelters had a large, folding door at the entrance. Just like the model back at Ching-chuankang.

Chiu was signaling for the group to gather around him. He turned to Mai-ling. "Which one contains the Black Star?"

"Number One, the shelter on the far right."

"You are certain?"

"Unless it has been moved."

He gave her a withering look. "Or unless you're leading us into a trap."

He gestured with his pistol for her to move out toward the shelter.

Maxwell could feel the heightened tension. The commandos advanced in a half-crouch, holding their submachine guns at the ready. Chiu moved like a hunting dog, stopping every several paces, scanning the terrain through his NVG.

When they were still fifty meters from the shelter, a figure emerged from the darkness. Behind him, another dark-clad figure. Each carried an assault rifle.

Sentries. They stood by the corner of the sprawling air-craft shelter, peering into the darkness.

The commandos froze. The sentries weren't wearing NVG. They hadn't yet spotted the intruders.

Chiu made a barely discernible gesture with his right hand. The two commandos on his right each fired a half-second burp of automatic fire from their MP-5Ns.

The first sentry toppled backward. The second spun around and fell. Wounded but still moving, he scuttled like a crab across the concrete for the cover of the shelter. The nearest commando ran to him, finishing him with a short burst before he reached the door.

"Move!" Chiu barked. "Get to the shelter."

In a fast jog they stormed across the remaining tarmac. Stealth was no longer a consideration. The distinctive sound of the submachine guns had been enough to give their presence away.

As Maxwell sprinted behind the commandos, he heard a chuffing noise behind him. He turned in time to see Mai-ling stumble and roll on the hard surface.

He stopped, ran back to help her. Her cheek was bleeding.

"I'm okay." The voice seemed tiny and uncharacteristically subdued. He felt her hand shaking as he hauled her to her feet. For an extra second she clung to him, then she continued jogging toward the shelter.

When the first commando was twenty meters from the side entrance, the door abruptly opened. Silhouetted in the doorway was another sentry, his assault rifle mounted to his shoulder.

He fired a quick burst, shooting the lead commando squarely in the chest. The commando tumbled onto the concrete. His SMG skidded across the surface and clattered against the wall of the shelter.

The sentry was swinging his weapon, picking his next target, when the hail of bullets tore into him. The rest of the fire team stormed out of the darkness, leaping over the bodies of the guards and the fallen commando. Kee and his team took positions on either side of the open door.

Maxwell knelt over the body of the commando.

"Leave him," said Chiu.

"He might still be alive."

"He's not. His job is finished and yours hasn't begun. Stay with me."

Maxwell hesitated, looking down at the commando's lifeless face. Chiu was right. The young man's chest was shredded. He had died instantly.

Maxwell rose and followed Chiu and three of the team inside the shelter.

A single yellow overhead light illuminated the cavernous space. While the commandos swept the shelter for more sentries, Maxwell gazed around in the subdued light.

Chiu's eyes were blazing like embers. Mai-ling's face was filled with despair.

The shelter was empty.

Colonel Zhang paused at the top of the boarding ladder. Even through the thick walls of the shelter, he could hear the sounds of automatic fire outside.

*They're looking for the Dong-jin. They haven't found it yet.*

He threw a leg over the cockpit rail and settled himself into the front seat. After he'd stowed his kneeboard and survival equipment, he allowed Chung, the crew chief, to assist him with the straps.

Chung was nervous, fumbling with the fasteners and connectors. He tried several times to connect the oxygen hose and radio jacks before he finally succeeded. "Why have they attacked Chouzhou, Colonel?"

"Because this is a military base and we are at war. Stop talking and hand me my helmet."

"Are they after the Dong-jin?"

"How do I know what they're after? Stop this useless talk and do your job. Hand me the helmet and UV goggles, then get Captain Yan strapped in." He nodded his head toward the back cockpit where Yan, the weapons systems officer, was hurriedly setting up his station.

"Yes, Colonel. I would just like to know if we were in danger from—"

"Shut up! These matters are not your concern."

Zhang was sure that the sergeant knew exactly why the enemy had come to Chouzhou. Chung had been with the Dong-jin project since its inception. Zhang made it a point never to discuss urgent matters with low-ranking subordinates, particularly ignorant sergeants like Chung. For all he knew, the sergeant had allied himself with the dissidents.

Zhang felt another wave of anger as he thought of the traitors who had betrayed the PLA and allowed the enemy to penetrate their defense network. When this war had been won—which would be in a matter of days—he would launch a purge of the PLA that would rid it once and forever of traitors.

It had been a close thing, getting to the shelter and into the cockpit of the Dong-jin. He had nearly run head-on into a unit of enemy commandos out there on the tarmac. Only at the last second did he see them. The bastards were wearing NVG—an item of equipment the idiot base commander at Chouzhou probably never thought to issue his own troops.

Zhang had swerved the Bei-jung—the Chinese-built, jeeplike utility vehicle—wildly off the taxiway, nearly rolling it over as he escaped the squad of black-suited commandos. One had fired several rounds into the Bei-jung, shattering glass and narrowly missing Zhang's head.

Now it was imperative that they get the Dong-jins airborne, not just to escape the invaders at Chouzhou, but to accomplish their mission over the Taiwan Strait. Victory was

within their grasp. Taiwan was about to be defeated and absorbed into the PRC.

In quiet moments, he liked to visualize the glorious moment. Col. Zhang Yu would be recognized as China's greatest modern hero. He would be awarded the military's
highest medal, presented by the President of the People's
Republic himself. He would be promoted to the rank of senior general. His portrait would hang in the Hall of Heroes
beside those of Mao and—

The voice of the weapons systems officer, Captain Yan,
crackled over the intercom. "Systems initialized and target
coordinates inserted. Byte check complete."

Zhang's thoughts returned to the cockpit. "Very well.
Begin your prestart checklist."

"Complete, Colonel. Ready for engine start."

"Ten seconds," Chiu said. He trained the muzzle of his
SIG Sauer automatic on her. "You have ten seconds to tell
us where the Black Star is."

His words echoed in the emptiness of the empty shelter.
For several seconds no one spoke. All eyes were on Mai-
ling.

"It was here. They have moved it."

"I have lost four soldiers to reach this shelter." He shoved
the muzzle of the semiautomatic pistol beneath the rim of
her helmet and pressed it against her ear. "Enough lies.
Where is it?"

"If they moved it"—she moved her lips in thought for a
moment—"it would have to be in one of the other shelters—
Number Two, probably. The one with the lift bays and the
overhead fork arm."

Chiu seemed to be weighing the decision whether to continue the search or kill her on the spot. His finger tightened
on the trigger.

"Listen to her," said Maxwell, trying to sound calm. "It

makes sense to search the next shelter. We've come too far to turn back."

Chiu whirled on him. "I give the orders, not you. You want to save the defector because you think you will have more sex with her. Don't you know her job was to seduce you?"

"It's not true," blurted Mai-ling.

Bass stared at Maxwell, then at Mai-ling.

Chiu still held the SIG Sauer to her head. "We are in this position because of your false information, and now the entire PLA knows we are here. If the Black Star is not in the next shelter, we return to the helicopters and withdraw. And I will put a bullet in your brain. Is that understood, Madame Defector?"

Mai-ling responded with a barely perceptible nod of the head.

"Move!" He gave her a hard shove toward the door.

Maxwell watched with a mounting sense of alarm. Chiu was a ticking bomb. He meant it. He *would* kill Mai-ling. He'd probably kill her even if she did take them to the Black Star.

*Shit.* His job description didn't include interfering with the mission commander. That much Chiu was right about. He *did* give the orders. He had his own reasons for distrusting Mai-ling, and maybe they were valid. Maybe she was a double agent, working both sides of the strait. Maybe she was leading them into a trap.

*Bullshit.*

Or was he blind to the truth? Not more than nine hours had passed since they had been together back on the darkened ramp at Chingchuankang. He no longer qualified as an objective judge.

What would he do if Chiu decided to terminate her? He didn't know. He pushed the matter out of his brain—for the moment. If she *was* leading them into a trap, it wouldn't matter who killed whom. It would all be over.

The Number Two shelter was a hundred meters nearer the still-raging petroleum blaze. Maxwell could see vehicles, hoses, dark figures moving around the flaming tanks.

In the dancing light of the fuel fire, he could make out the rounded top and the slab sides of the shelter. The entry door was in the same position as in the first shelter.

In front of them lay another fifty yards of open tarmac. Again they were exposed, vulnerable to snipers and guards and roving PLA security troops. Maxwell wondered whether the sentries were equipped with night vision goggles. Probably, he decided. NVG was nothing new. A prize as technically sophisticated as the Black Star would be protected with the most sophisticated devices they had.

Ahead, the orange glow of the blaze flickered over the dark outline of the shelter. The Black Star had to be there. It had to be.


On signal from Chung, standing in view beneath the cockpit, Zhang initiated the start cycle for engine number one. When the whine of the turbine had settled at idle power, he started number two. Chung scurried beneath the belly of the jet, disconnecting the umbilicals for electrical and pneumatic power. When he reappeared in front of the cockpit, he gave the signals for control surface checks and flap extension. Zhang cycled the controls, then extended the flaps to takeoff setting.

This hangar, like the other two specially constructed Dong-jin shelters, permitted the crew to start the engines inside the closed building, with the jet exhaust muffled and ducted to the outside. Not until the Dong-jin was fully ready for flight would he order the massive electrohydraulic bifold door raised. By this means the Dong-jin received minimum exposure to prying eyes before leaping into the air.

The Dong-jin was ready.

"Activate cloaking."

"Airframe cloaking coming on," answered Yan.

Yan was a competent WSO, more reliable than the blundering Lo Shouyi, whom Zhang had ordered terminated. Lo's removal had served as an excellent example to the rest of the Dong-jin unit. Fear was the most powerful of motivators.

Over the whine of the engines Zhang could no longer hear the outside chatter of machine guns. It didn't matter. He would make an abrupt departure and put his trust in the Dong-jin's cloaking technology. The second Dong-jin would trail him by a few minutes. By the time they returned from the mission, the raiders would be dead or captured.

He took a deep breath to steady his nerves. Then he gave the signal to open the door.

# CHAPTER EIGHTEEN

# KILLING MACHINE

*Chouzhou Air Base, People's Republic of China*
*0510, Monday, 15 September*

*Muzzle flashes.*

Chiu sensed bullets thudding into something close by. Then he heard the staccato rattle of another Chinese assault rifle. Ten meters away, a commando dropped to his knees and pitched forward.

"Down!" he barked over his shoulder, knowing it was too late. Rolling onto his side, he slipped the MP-5N off his shoulder.

Chiu cursed himself. More sentries. He should have anticipated that there would be more, probably equipped with their own NVG. Each shelter would have sentries posted in the same location. The PLA was predictable.

He peered into the shadows beneath the high slab side of the shelter, searching for the shooters. There were two, maybe more. He couldn't spot them in his own NVG, but he sensed movement where he had seen the muzzle flashes.

He glanced over his shoulder again. The two Americans were on their bellies, eyes fixed on him. Watching, waiting to see what he would do. The woman seemed to have attached herself to Maxwell. Why? Was she using him to betray the operation? Or was she—

Another burst of fire. This time Chiu got a fix on the shooter. He was crouched behind a low wall. From this angle, neither Chiu nor his troops could get a clear shot at him.

Chiu lay in the darkness, trying to assess the matter. They were pinned down, out in the open. He'd lost another commando and his ground time was running out.

He scuttled over to Kee, six meters away. "Over there," he ordered, pointing to the left. "Take two men with you, thirty meters away, draw their fire and give me cover."

Kee gave him a quick nod and crawled into the darkness.

Chiu waited until they were in position. More muzzle flashes appeared from the low wall. When Kee's SMGs opened up, returning the sentry's fire, Chiu was on his feet. Sprinting toward the concealed sentry position, he kept an oblique angle to the low wall.

Not until he was nearly perpendicular to the wall did they spot him. The two startled sentries whirled, swinging their assault rifles. Too late.

Chiu fired from the waist. The spray of his 9 mm bullets ricocheted off the butt end of the wall. Sparks showered against the concrete side of the shelter.

The first sentry spun like a top and flipped over the wall. The second got off several wild rounds before Chiu's bullets hit him in the upper chest, driving him backward into the wall of the shelter.

Silence.

Chiu dropped to one knee. Keeping his MP-5N at the ready, he swept the perimeter with his NVG. No more sentries, at least that he could spot.

He signaled Kee to bring the team to the shelter while Chiu covered them from the corner. Kee stopped, kneeling to check the fallen commando. He rose, shaking his head negatively.

Chiu felt the fury rising like lava inside him. *Another fatality*. The losses they were taking, all in order to find a—

Through his boots he felt a vibration. A rumble came up through the concrete. Then another sound—a high-pitched metallic whine, swelling in volume like the wail of a banshee.

Perplexed, Chiu gazed around. In the greenish twilight of the NVG, he could see his commandos stopped on the tarmac. They were staring at the front of the shelter.

It came to him. The shelter door. It was opening. The rumble he felt through his boots—it was some kind of high-energy hydraulic device.

The other noise—the wailing metallic sound—was reaching a crescendo, bringing real pain to his ears. In the next moment, the advancing commandos broke and scattered across the sprawling concrete apron.

Even before the apparition burst onto the darkened tarmac, Chiu knew what it was. And he was too late.

Stunned, he stared at the specter. He saw only an amorphous shape, shimmering in the darkness like a winged wraith. Its engines were bellowing at full thrust.

As Chiu stared, the craft became invisible, blending into the night.

*The Black Star*. Chiu could tell by the changing roar that it was accelerating toward the runway.

He shouldered his MP-5N and fired a long burst. Not until the submachine gun had stopped firing for several seconds did he realize he was still holding the trigger down. He'd fired the entire thirty-round magazine.

At nothing.

The Black Star was gone.

Another burst of gunfire, this time from inside the shelter.

Chiu recognized the brittle sound of a Type 95. *Another damned sentry?*

One of the commandos yelped and dropped to the tarmac. The others dived for cover and opened fire on the shooter.

It was over in seconds. Chiu ran to the cavernous opening of the shelter. He saw the shooter—a man in coveralls, some sort of ground crewman. He was sprawled on the hangar floor, his body riddled with bullets. His assault rifle lay beside him.

A feeling of rage swept over Chiu. He had come this far to find the stealth jet—only to lose it in a single blinding moment. And he had lost another commando, killed by a grease monkey in coveralls.

He was still staring out into the darkness when Maxwell and Bass and the fire team came trotting up. The woman was with them.

"It was the Dong-jin," she said in a flat voice.

He stared at her. For once she had been correct. The shelter contained the Black Star. But it didn't matter now.

Chiu shook his head in frustration. "So what? It's gone."

"There might be another."

He was too overcome with rage and frustration to listen. It had been so close. One minute sooner. In his mind's eye he could still see the shimmering ghost of the Black Star vanishing in the night.

"I've lost too many men because of you. Our time is up. We will withdraw."

"Listen to her," said Maxwell. "She was right about this shelter. We have to look in the next one."

"If she hadn't led us to the wrong shelter, we would have stopped the Black Star."

Maxwell inserted himself between Chiu and the others. In a low voice he said, "Listen Colonel, get over your problem with the woman. If there's another Black Star out there, we have to find it."

"Do not presume to tell me what I have to do. The woman cannot be trusted and neither can you. You have been sleeping with a traitor."

"Damn it, use your brain. Don't you understand that this is your last chance to stop China from winning this war?"

A long silent moment passed between them. He desperately wanted to kill the woman defector who had led him to this impasse. But despite the cloud of anger that enveloped him, he sensed that the American might be right.

"Our objective is to find the Black Star," said Maxwell. "If we abort the mission now, the war will be lost."

Chiu didn't answer. It seemed that nothing that had occurred in his life up to this moment mattered. What he did in the next few minutes would define his existence.

And that of Taiwan.

Maxwell was standing there, looking at him. So were the others, waiting for his decision.

*You are a warrior. Let them see how a warrior leads.*

He released the empty clip from his MP-5N and shoved in a fresh magazine, letting them hear the hard, metallic click of the lower receiver.

He turned to his fire team. "Reload your weapons. Check flash suppressors."

Only four of this squad remained, including the corporal who had been wounded by the crew chief in the shelter. He looked at the commando next to him. "Get the wounded man back to the helicopters. Kee and Lam, you stay with me."

Chiu took the wounded commando's MP-5N and handed it to Maxwell. He walked over to the dead Black Star crew chief and picked up his assault rifle. He tossed it to Catfish Bass. "You two are now commandos. Check that your weapons are loaded and ready, then follow me."

Bass looked uncertainly at the Chinese rifle. "Where are we going?"

"To find the Black Star. Isn't that what you came for?"

He didn't hear Bass's answer. From the distant runway, the roar of two jet engines reverberated across the open space, filling the night sky. Each pair of eyes swung to look for the departing fighter.

They saw nothing. The sky was empty.

*I failed, Shaomin. I should have killed him, but I failed.*

The words replayed in Mai-ling's head like a mantra. For the rest of her life—measured now perhaps in minutes—she would wonder if the face staring down at her from the cockpit of the Black Star belonged to Colonel Zhang Yu.

She was sure he recognized her. They both wore night vision equipment. His oxygen mask had been hanging unfastened from the side of his helmet. Their gazes had met for only a couple of seconds, but it was enough. If it was Zhang, he would have understood in that compressed instant why she had come to Chouzhou.

It didn't matter now. Whoever it was, he had escaped. Free to kill again, just as he had killed her beloved Shaomin. It meant that she had failed.

She carried the Beretta in the pocket of her utilities. She was not supposed to be armed—Chiu was emphatic about that—but she had conveniently recovered the pistol from the body of the fallen commando back at Shelter Number One.

But then came the time to use it—when the Dong-jin roared past her like a dragon from hell. With the shape of the fighter still shimmering in the darkness, she had glimpsed the face of the pilot sitting in the cockpit. She might have avenged the death of her beloved Shaomin.

She didn't shoot.

At the last instant, she had been distracted by the gunfire—the crew chief, as it turned out—from inside the shelter. She stood there like a lump of clay. Then it was too late.

Was it Zhang?

The uncertainty hung over her like a leaden weight.

*Maybe it wasn't him. Maybe he was still here.*

She decided to cling to that hope. It was the only way she could go on. With that thought planted in her head, she turned and trudged along in the darkness behind Chiu and his team.

Perhaps they would find another Black Star in the shelter. She no longer cared. She had already decided that she would surely die whether she found Zhang or not. If the PLA didn't kill her, Chiu would. She would not be allowed to leave Chouzhou, and that was all right too. It meant that she would be joining Shaomin in eternity.

They were thirty meters from Shelter Number Three, still in the shadow of the second shelter, when Chiu signaled for them to take cover. The petroleum fire was casting a greater flood of orange light over the shelters. Even without NVG, Mai-ling could see details and objects around the third shelter.

"I'm not wasting any more time looking for sentries," Chiu said.

While the others watched, wondering what he meant, he pulled a grenade from his belt. Motioning for them to remain in place, he crawled on his belly another ten meters toward the corner door of the shelter—the location where the sentries at the other two shelters had concealed themselves. A low wall jutted from the door, just as it had in the other shelters.

Chiu stopped and rose to a kneeling position. He pulled the pin and tossed the grenade. It skipped off the concrete and slid to the edge of the wall.

Chiu rose to his feet. He turned on a flashlight and waved it like a wand. He yelled in Chinese. "Ho! Soldiers of the PLA sleep with pigs. Look over here, you pig fuckers!"

A head appeared over the wall. Then another. The sentries rose, swinging their weapons toward Chiu—

The grenade exploded.

In the flash and shower of debris, the sentries were flung back behind the wall. Even before the dust had cleared, Chiu covered the distance in a dead run. The muffled burp of his muzzle-suppressed MP-5N echoed from the shelter wall as he finished the sentries.

He waved to the fire team. "What are you waiting for? Move! We have work to do."

Rising to their feet, Bass and Maxwell looked at each other.

"Is that guy the meanest sonofabitch in the world," said Bass, "or is he just crazy?"

"Both," said Maxwell.

Following Chiu's hand signals, Maxwell stationed himself at the left of the shelter door. He kept the MP-5N submachine gun at the ready. On the opposite side, Bass was hunkered down with his assault rifle.

When Chiu gave the nod, Lieutenant Kee flung the door open. Chiu tossed an IR Chemlite flare through the opening, then pulled the pin on another and tossed it inside. With the NVG tilted down and SMGs mounted at the shoulder, he and the two commandos charged inside, followed by Maxwell and Bass.

As Chiu had instructed him, Maxwell broke to the left and ran toward the front of the hangar, aiming the barrel of his SMG like an extended antenna. The two Chemlites cast a flickering infrared glow through the hangar, giving it the appearance of a witch's cave.

Not until he reached the front of the hangar, finding no armed PLA troops, did Maxwell stop. He allowed himself to stare at the object that filled the center of the hangar.

He had gotten only a brief glimpse of the first jet that nearly ran over them when it burst from Shelter Number Three. The crew had already activated cloaking, and he couldn't make out the details of the airframe. He hadn't even seen the shape of the fighter before it was gone.

Over five years had passed since he flew the original Black Star at Groom Lake. He had already forgotten some of the exotic nuances in the jet's design, the peculiar geometry of its airframe that absorbed and distorted and shed radar emissions and made it invisible on air defense displays. Now it came back to him.

Its wings were flat, not dihedral, sharp as a knife along its leading edges, swept back in a delta plan form. The two jet exhausts were embedded in the aft, triangular tail section. No vertical surfaces protruded to interrupt the flatness of its shape.

*Beautiful.*

*No,* he corrected himself. *Not beautiful.* The Black Star didn't possess the slick, streamlined shape of a supersonic fighter. It was all angles, thick and flat, swept back like a manta ray.

*Exotic.* That was it. An exotic killing machine.

He heard a commotion in the back of the hangar where Chiu and one of the commandos had gone. He swung the submachine gun around and squinted through the night vision goggles.

A sentry? Another gun-wielding crew chief?

Holding the MP-5N extended in front of him, Maxwell slipped beneath the wing of the Black Star and moved toward the rear of the hangar. Next to a long workbench and a row of cabinets, Chiu and the two commandos had seized a man in coveralls. His wrists were already strapped with a plastic tie-wrap. The man was nearly blind in the infrared-lighted hangar.

Chiu looked at Maxwell. "He says he's the crew chief. He was preparing the jet for a mission."

"Where are the pilot and weapons officer?"

Chiu prodded the man with the muzzle of his MP-5N and

said something in Mandarin. The crew chief blinked in the dim light, keeping his eyes locked on the submachine gun. He stammered an answer.

"Gone," said Chiu. "He says they ran away when they heard the grenade explode outside."

"Is it fueled and ready to fly?" Maxwell asked.

Chiu repeated the question for the crew chief. The man answered in Mandarin, his eyes firmly fixed on the MP-5N.

"Yes," said Chiu. "The plane—he calls it Dong-jin—has full tanks and had been preflighted. It's ready."

Maxwell looked around for Bass. The Air Force pilot was standing beneath the cockpit, staring at the black mass of the fighter. His mouth was agape. "Holy shit," he said. "That thing doesn't look like any airplane I ever flew."

"It's not supposed to," said Maxwell.

"How does it fly without any tail surfaces?"

"Same way the B-2 does it. Computerized flight control system, no aerodynamic stability of its own."

"Like a big airborne video game."

"Yeah. Just made for a guy like you."

Chiu walked up to them. "What are you standing around for? You should be getting ready to fly."

"I need Mai-ling to help with the cockpit setup," said Maxwell. "She knows the switch logic and the display functions. And we need the crew chief to cooperate. He can work the access ladder and open the hangar bay door when we're ready to launch."

"He will cooperate," said Chiu, hefting the MP-5N. "So will the woman." He peered around the big hangar. A deep frown passed over his face. "Where is she?"

They counted heads. There were five of them—Maxwell, Bass, Chiu, and the two remaining commandos. They scanned the cavernous space of the shelter.

Mai-ling was missing.

An ominous silence fell over the group.

"I knew she was a traitor," snapped Chiu. He whirled and headed for the side door, slipping his pistol from its holster. "I will deal with her."

*Let him be there,* she silently implored. *Let Zhang be there. For Shaomin's sake.*

Mai-ling slipped across the tarmac behind the shelter as quickly as she could without making undue noise. The towering petroleum fire was casting an orange glow over the entire expanse of concrete. She knew she made an easy target for an alert sentry. Caution was no longer an option.

The crew briefing room, if she remembered correctly, was in the row of spaces in back of Hangar Number Four, the next shelter across the tarmac. She hadn't told Chiu about the briefing room. He would want to go there first. And ruin her plan.

She wanted Colonel Zhang. She wanted to see him, face to face, to watch him cringe and beg. She would make him tell her what he had done with Shaomin.

Then she would kill him.

Could she do it? A few months ago such an act would have been unthinkable. Though she held the rank of captain in the PLA, she was a scientist, not a soldier. She had never killed anyone. But that was before the hate had built up in her like a raging fever. Now every fiber in her body was urging her to put a bullet in the brain of Col. Zhang Yu.

She hesitated before starting across the open expanse between Shelters Three and Four. She decided to walk openly, as if she were on official business. If a sentry challenged her, she would bluff, throw some names out that he would recognize, then shoot him at close quarters.

Keeping a hand around the grip of the Beretta in her pocket, she started across the tarmac.

Forty meters to go. No challenge from a sentry.

Twenty meters. Perhaps there was no sentry—

She saw him.

Mai-ling froze, not sure whether he had spotted her yet. She could see the sentry at his post, slouched on the ground beside the side entrance. He was motionless, staring in her direction. Not until she had studied his features for several seconds through the NVG did she understand why the sentry had not challenged her.

He would never challenge anyone. A single, oozing hole glistened in the center of his forehead. Chiu, or one his commandos, had already taken care of the sentry. It meant, probably, that they were inside the shelter now looking for the remaining Black Star.

*Go!* she ordered herself. Run for the briefing room. Get there before it's too late.

She darted to the right, toward the warren of spaces and offices built into the back of Shelter Four. The rooms were not accessible from inside the hangar without a special key—or so she remembered—which meant that Chiu would not stumble onto Zhang's briefing room.

Not before she had concluded her mission.

In the darkened walkway behind the shelter, she had to peer carefully at each recess, each crevice in the wall. There were several metal doors, all alike. Which one? Which was Zhang's briefing room? Nothing looked familiar in the darkness.

She tried the first door, applying a gentle pressure to the lever handle. It didn't move. Should she rap on the door, try to bluff again? If she entered the wrong room, encountered someone besides Zhang, she was finished.

If only she could remember which door. She had been there on a couple of occasions, invited by Shaomin for an audience with the high and mighty Zhang. The same Zhang who turned on them and sent Shaomin to his death in the camps.

The recollection of his cruel, smirking face served to jog

her memory. It was coming back to her. She remembered that they had arrived at the shelter in Shaomin's Bei-jung—his army utility vehicle. He had parked directly beside Zhang's entrance door.

*There.* Just as before. Ten meters away, in the deep shadow of the high rear wall—a drab-painted Bei-jung with a canvas top, just like the one Shaomin once drove.

The thought reinforced her sense of purpose. The fear and anxiety slipped away from her like an unwelcome burden. She slid the Beretta from her pocket and approached the door, taking small, determined steps.

No light was leaking around the doorjamb. She pressed her ear to the door. She could hear a rustling sound, the noise of scuffing feet on the concrete floor.

Someone was inside. How many? It didn't matter. She would kill whoever was there with Zhang. He would be the last.

She hesitated at the door, gathering her resolve. She took a long, deep breath, then yanked the lever. The door swung inward, and she stepped inside.

A dim red light illuminated the room. She saw a desk, someone sitting behind it, watching her with intense interest. She held the Beretta in both hands, keeping it trained on him.

Even before she discerned his features in the thin light, she recognized the familiar presence. He wore flight gear—a torso harness and G suit—and leaned with one elbow on the desk, peering at her with that casual, bemused expression.

Just as she remembered.

"Come in," said Major Han Shaomin. "I've been waiting for you."

# CHAPTER NINETEEN

# GHOST

*Groom Lake, Nevada*
*1815, Monday, 15 September*

Feingold had vanished.

Lutz waited at the terminal gate to observe each load of passengers board the nightly flight. Feingold was not among them. He hadn't answered his phone at the lab, nor had he shown up as he usually did for a beer in the club lounge.

They'd grabbed him. That had to be it. Lutz could picture the physicist's terrified denials as he was being grilled by the FBI stooges. It made him laugh. Feingold, with his compulsive blabbiness and taste for the Vegas fleshpots, was the perfect fit for the FBI's stereotyped spy. The case against him would build until the lack of evidence became so apparent that even the feds would figure it out. Then they'd resume the hunt for the real spy.

At least he had bought time.

Lutz boarded the last of the 737s bound for Las Vegas. His gut was empty tonight, no data capsule residing in his intestine to be deposited in a slot machine tray. It was too dangerous. He had to assume everyone associated with Calypso Blue was under intense scrutiny.

He heard the engines spin up, then felt the lurch as the brakes released and the jet accelerated down the runway. Yielding to his ingrained ritual, he hit the timer button on his chronometer. As the nose of the 737 lifted, he hit the button again.

Twenty-eight seconds. Same as always, give or take a few seconds. One more reason to be glad Feingold was gone. He would be sitting there, making one of his typically banal comments about the length of the takeoff roll and how things never changed. For the rest of the flight he would pester Lutz with that insipid crap about how many kilowatts Las Vegas uses or how many tons of sewage are treated annually in Nevada.

Good riddance.

Watching the blackness of Groom Lake drop away beneath him, Lutz thought about the future. The end game was near. The danger level had become unacceptable. The time was near when he would either be snared by the FBI, or the Chinese would throw him to the wolves.

But not quite. There were still secrets that the Chinese needed to keep their own Black Star invulnerable to new detection technology.

Already stored in Lutz's accounts was a fair sum of money, nearly half a million, deposited by his Chinese employers. But it was still not enough. He needed to milk it longer, collect the final large sum they still owed him.

Then one fine Nevada day they would come looking for Raymond Lutz in his lab at Groom Lake, and they would find him gone. The man who had enabled the People's Republic of China to acquire twenty years of stealth technology in less than three years would be as invisible as the Black Star.

Gone where?

The matter of where Lutz—or whoever he'd decide to become—would live the rest of his life had occupied much of his conscious thought this past year. Anywhere in the U.S. was out of the question. The war against terrorists had generated rapid advances in personal identification technology. It had become nearly impossible to change one's identity.

No, it would have to be a third-world country, but one with a culture and climate that suited the needs of a polymath like Raymond Lutz. A place where, if the danger of his being discovered became a concern, he could slip away to the sanctuary of China.

Sri Lanka. It was a richly endowed country, located on the rump of the Indian subcontinent, filled with ancient art and culture but beset by civil war and turmoil. He could settle there, live well but not conspicuously so, and indulge himself in all the comforts and stimuli that he needed.

These days, whenever Lutz suffered from one of his increasingly frequent anxiety attacks, he forced himself to think about the new life. In Sri Lanka he would have servants, women, spacious gardens, a security system that would protect him from all his enemies.

The lurch and *thunk* of the 737's landing gear extending returned his thoughts to the present. The lights of Las Vegas were illuminating the desert like a field of fire.

Catfish Bass was getting a bad feeling.

Mai-ling was missing, and since he couldn't remember any woman, Chinese or Caucasian, being more of a world-class pain in the ass, he ought to be having a celebration. But now Chiu had gone missing too. It could mean only one thing.

He had gone to put a bullet in Mai-ling's brains.

So good riddance. Who cared?

Certainly not him, he told himself as he tried to make sense of the rear cockpit displays in the Black Star. Why should he care? He didn't know, except that whenever he got a feeling like this, it usually meant that he was about to do something stupid.

*Okay, Bass, get it over with.*

He threw a leg over the cockpit rail and climbed down from the Black Star. Maxwell was still in the front seat, trying to decipher his own panel. One of the commandos stood watch at the entrance to the shelter. The other had gone off with Chiu.

"We need pneumatic power to crank the engines," said Bass.

"Use your Chinese on the crew chief," said Maxwell. "Get him to cooperate."

"I'll tell him Chiu will cut his balls off."

"Good idea. That'll win his heart and mind."

Bass went to the workshop area in the back of the shelter where the crew chief was tie-wrapped to the leg of a sturdy bench. A section of duct tape covered his mouth.

Bass lifted one end of the duct tape from the prisoner's mouth. "Where is the rear exit door?" he said in halting Mandarin.

Gazing at him with wide, terrified eyes, the crew chief blurted an answer.

"*No comprende,* pal," said Bass. He hadn't understood a single syllable. He explained to the crew chief that he was talking to a Santa Monica Chinese, not the real thing. "Try it again, ve-ry slo-wly this time."

The crew chief nodded, then told him in deliberate, schoolchild Mandarin that Bass would find the exit door in the rear corner of the shelter between the air compressor and the oxygen storage tank. And be careful not to trip over the hoses on the floor.

"Thanks, chum." Bass replaced the tape over the man's mouth. "I'll see to it you get a bonus for this." He ignored the worried look of the commando, observing them from the front of the shelter.

The rear exit door opened to a darkened driveway that connected the backs of all four shelters. The area behind each hangar was cast in darkness, shielded from the light of the petroleum fires. Even with the NVG, Bass had difficulty picking out details.

He wished he had brought his pistol. It still lay in the satchel that he left in the rear cockpit. Maxwell would have asked him what the hell he was doing. Instead, he took the assault rifle—the knockoff AK-47 that Chiu had thrust on him. He wondered if the thing would actually fire. The crude ammo magazine didn't seem to fit. It was loose, rattling ominously inside the lower receiver.

Reverse engineering. He remembered hearing the Taiwanese pilots joke about it. It was the core of China's research and development program—steal someone's shitty product, then make it shittier.

He adjusted the NVG, peering in each direction along the darkened pathway. He had no idea where to look, nor what he expected to find. Where would she go? Back the way they came, or to the left, in the direction of Shelter Four?

Left, he decided. That was her most logical escape route. He had no idea why Mai-ling had flown the coop, but he doubted that she was a double. Maybe she was looking for another Black Star. Or, more likely, she concluded that Chiu was going to kill her and she saw a chance to slip out of the noose. Give the chick credit. She wasn't dumb.

Five minutes, he told himself. That was all. Do a quick sweep, just in case she was in real trouble, then get back to the Black Star and help Maxwell.

Holding the clunky assault rifle in front of him, he headed for the darkened area behind Shelter Four. He moved quickly across the open tarmac between the shelters, aware that the flickering tank fires made him a target.

He made it to the deep shadow behind Shelter Four without drawing fire. For several seconds he remained motionless, listening for movement, studying the darkened pathway behind the shelter.

Gradually the details emerged from the darkness. There were doors in the wall. He saw an object . . . what the hell was it? Some kind of vehicle in the pathway.

Bass worked his way along the back wall, stopping every few meters to check for signs of activity. He saw nothing. No sentry, no sign of life.

He reached the vehicle, a square-shaped thing that looked like an ugly jeep. More Chinese reverse engineering. It was parked next to a metal door in the wall of the shelter.

From inside the door Bass could hear the faint buzz of voices. Someone inside was speaking in Mandarin.

He cupped his ear to the door. He heard a man's voice. And then a woman's.

It happened so quickly. While she stared in disbelief, he reached over and snatched the Beretta from her hand, and she was disarmed.

She was seeing a ghost.

Mai-ling knew she had to be dreaming. None of this was making sense. Nothing in the room came close to reality. She stood there like a sleepwalker, listening to the smiling apparition say unspeakable things.

"Stupid whore." It was Shaomin's voice, that much she had to admit. But it couldn't be Shaomin because he was gone, and even from another world he would never call her such a thing. Not her beloved Shaomin.

"Why did you come back?" he said. "Did you think I would sleep with you again?"

"You're not Shaomin," she heard herself say. "Shaomin is dead."

This brought a laugh, that old familiar dry rasp—just like Shaomin's. The sound sent a tingle like an electric current through her. It was *his* laugh. She had lain awake these countless nights yearning to hear it again.

"The Shaomin you knew is dead," he said, "because he never existed. I let you think I was a dissident so that I could penetrate the circle of traitors in the PLA." He smiled again. "For which I thank you."

It couldn't be Shaomin. She stared at the man's face, looking for the telltale evidence that it was someone else. This man, whoever he was, had Shaomin's same handsome features, the high cheekbones and fine, chiseled nose. He laughed like Shaomin, even possessed the same mannerisms, leaning his elbow on the desk as Shaomin liked to do while he talked.

"You loved me," she blurted. "I know you did. What we had was real."

"Love." He spat the word out as if it were something vile in his mouth. "I endured your pathetic fantasies, that's all. Don't you realize that I can have any woman—any real woman—I want in China? Why would I willingly make love to a slut like you?"

The words pelted her like hammer blows. Tears filled her eyes. She wanted this nightmare to be over. Living in loneliness for the rest of her life, even death, was preferable to this pain.

Through the blur of tears she glimpsed the Beretta on the desk beside him. She lunged for the gun, not caring whether he killed her or not.

He caught her by the shoulder, yanked her upright, then brought the back of his hand in a smack across her face. The blow stunned her, rendering her nearly senseless. She felt a warm trickle of blood from the corner of her mouth. His hand grasped her shoulder, squeezing like a vise.

The backhanded slap had brought clarity to her thinking. She gazed at him again. Yes, she made herself admit, it was Shaomin. She had been deceived. She was a gullible fool.

He spun her around, then seized the back of her neck. She remembered how Shaomin had always prided himself on the strength of his hands. His daily martial arts drills included smashing through layers of fiberboard with the edges of his hands.

"The enemy has come here to destroy the Dong-jin," he said. She could feel the powerful fingers burrowing into her flesh through the collar of the black utilities. "And it was you who brought them, wasn't it?"

She didn't answer.

The fingers tightened. "Answer me. It was you, wasn't it?"

She tried to close her mind to the pain. She kept her silence.

"Bitch! The interrogators will make you answer. They will peel away so much of your flesh you'll look like a skinned rat."

Keeping one hand clamped on her neck, he shoved her toward the door. On the way out, he flipped the light switch, extinguishing the red overhead lamp. The room was plunged into darkness.

In the pathway outside the briefing room door, she was still blind. She stumbled on the hard surface, nearly suspended by the viselike hand on her neck. She knew she was being taken to the *Laogai*—the dreaded place she had never seen but everyone in the PLA knew about. People who went there never came out.

She was dimly aware of the box-shaped Bei-jung parked in the pathway—the vehicle she thought looked like Shaomin's old car. The truth struck her. *Because it* was *Shaomin's vehicle, you idiot. How many clues did you need?*

He was holding her at arm's length, shoving her head down so that he could stuff her into the right seat of the Bei-jung, when she caught something—a dark blur of movement in her peripheral vision.

Shaomin saw it too. He whirled, almost in time, but not quite.

An object—she saw that it was the barrel of some kind of weapon—struck him a glancing blow on the shoulder, dropping him to his knee. Mai-ling felt the grip release on her neck as Shaomin spun to confront his attacker.

She glimpsed a figure in ninjalike utilities, black-faced, wearing NVG. *One of the commandos? Chiu?*

No. She saw that he was swinging the assault rifle like a baseball bat. Mai-ling's heart sank. Only an American klutz would do something like that. "Shoot, you idiot! Shaomin will—"

Too late. Shaomin aimed a kick at him, hitting him in the chest and knocking him backward. The assault rifle spun out of his grip, clattering on the concrete.

Hearing the breath whoosh out of him, seeing the awkward way he fought Shaomin—she knew who it was.

Shaomin launched another kick. The man dodged, seizing Shaomin's ankle. With the intruder clinging to his leg, Shaomin danced on one foot, yanking him around, while he drew an automatic pistol from his shoulder holster.

Mai-ling leaped on him. The three went down in a heap, writhing on the concrete, Shaomin atop the man in black, Mai-ling on Shaomin's back, clawing and flailing at him.

The man on the bottom—she knew now it was Catfish Bass—had both hands fastened on Shaomin's gun hand, trying to wrest the pistol from him.

With a violent lurch, Shaomin flung Mai-ling loose. Using his left hand, he swung a roundhouse blow that caught her on the side of the head, sending her rolling across the concrete.

The two men rolled over each other, still grappling for possession of the pistol. Reeling from the blow to her head, Mai-ling rose to her knees, trying to see in the darkness. Six feet away she saw the dark shape of Bass's assault rifle.

Scuttling like a crab across the concrete, she snatched up the weapon. She jumped to her feet, training the gun on the bodies grappling on the ground. Without the NVG it was hard to see who was on top. She had to be careful. She might shoot through one and hit the other.

In the dim light she picked out the drab flight suit of Shaomin. He was the one on top, at least for the moment. They were still fighting for the pistol.

She aimed the rifle. Was it on automatic or single fire? She couldn't tell. It didn't matter. *Shoot the damned thing. See what happens.*

She squeezed the trigger.

Nothing happened. *Damn it.*

She squeezed the trigger harder. Nothing.

Was the safety on? No. She stared at the receiver mechanism, at the trigger guard, ran her hand around the barrel. It was some kind of PLA weapon that she vaguely recognized but had never fired. The magazine rattled inside the receiver as if something didn't fit.

*Why doesn't the damned thing shoot?*

She had no idea except that it was some piece-of-shit Chinese knockoff assault rifle that didn't work. Period. Which was why Catfish Bass, the klutz, had been swinging the thing like a bat.

She heard the pistol fire.

Horrified, Mai-ling froze, still clutching the useless rifle. For a moment, neither man on the ground moved.

She saw Bass start to sit up. He stared at her for a moment with an intense, serious expression. He gasped, closed his eyes, and dropped back to the concrete.

Shaomin rose to his feet. In his eyes was something she hadn't seen before—a gleaming that sent a chill through her. He looked at the useless rifle in her hands. Then he glanced at the body of Catfish Bass.

"Incompetent bitch. You and your *gwai-lo* lover would

have killed me if you weren't so stupid." His eyes fixed on her like lasers as he raised the pistol.

Mai-ling didn't try to escape. Better a bullet than the interrogation chamber of the *Laogai*. Get it over with.

She flinched as a gunshot split the air.

# CHAPTER TWENTY

# PREFLIGHT

*Chouzhou Air Base, People's Republic of China*
*0525, Monday, 15 September*

He missed.

*Damn,* thought Maxwell. He was always shocked by the ferocity of the Colt .45. The muzzle flash and deep-throated boom felt like a Howitzer going off in his hand. Sparks and shattered plaster erupted from the shelter wall next to the man's head.

From thirty feet away Maxwell fired again. Another flash, another shower of concrete and sparks from the wall behind the man.

He was a pilot or crew member, Maxwell guessed. He was wearing a PLA flight suit and some kind of torso harness. The man had released his grip on Mai-ling. He whirled and got off a snap shot with his own pistol. Maxwell felt the bullet whiz past his ear. After the heavy boom of the Colt, the Chinese pistol sounded like a popgun.

The man was scooting backward toward the cover of the parked vehicle. Maxwell fired again. And missed.

*Why didn't you practice with this damn thing?* He got off

two more fast shots. *Damn!* Both went wild, spraying more concrete and sparks.

The man was backing up to the vehicle, aiming the 7.62 with both hands—when he stumbled over the body of Catfish Bass. Off balance, he lurched backward, firing another round into space.

Maxwell followed him with the muzzle of the .45. He fired again. Sparks and a metallic twang came from the vehicle as the Glazer bullet ripped into the car's frame.

He took a deep breath and leveled the sight of the .45. The Chinese pilot was regaining his balance, taking aim with his pistol. *Squeeze. Don't flinch. It's your last chance.*

The .45 boomed in the darkness. Instead of feeding the next round, the Colt's slide remained open. The chamber was empty, all seven rounds expended from the magazine.

For what seemed like an eternity, Maxwell and the Chinese pilot held eye contact. Maxwell kept the empty weapon trained on him. Neither man moved.

In slow motion the Chinese pilot lowered the pistol to his side. He tilted back against the vehicle and slid to a sitting position on the concrete.

Maxwell walked up to him and removed the pistol from his hand. He was motionless, eyes staring into the night sky. The small hole in his chest was matched by a gaping exit wound in the back of his flight suit. A dark swath of blood glistened on the side of the vehicle. The last .45 slug had taken out the man's heart.

"Is he dead?" The tiny voice came from Mai-ling, huddled against the shelter wall.

Maxwell nudged the Chinese pilot with his foot. He fell over onto the concrete. "Very."

She walked over to the man's body. For a long moment she stood over him, looking into the dead man's face. A look of sadness covered her face.

"Is that who I think it is?" said Maxwell.

She nodded. "Shaomin."

"I'm sorry. I had to—"

"I'm glad he's dead."

A groan came from Catfish Bass, lying with his knees drawn up to his chest.

Mai-ling swung away from the dead man and knelt over Bass. Maxwell helped her open the top of his utility coveralls, checking his wound.

As he knelt over Bass, Maxwell sensed another presence looming out of the darkness. He snatched Shaomin's 7.62 pistol and jumped to his feet.

Colonel Chiu—dark-clad, black-faced—materialized in the gloom of the pathway. "I told you that ancient gun was useless."

"I hit him, didn't I?"

"One hit, six misses."

"How do you know?"

"I was standing over there." He pointed across the pathway. "Watching your superb display of marksmanship. I've seen blind men shoot better than that."

"Why the hell didn't *you* shoot him?"

"I could see that you needed the practice."

Maxwell felt a rush of anger. He could still hear the Chinese pilot's bullet whizzing past his ear. He fought back the impulse to punch Chiu's lights out. *Later,* he told himself. "Listen, Colonel, we've got a big problem. Catfish is badly wounded. He can't fly in the Black Star."

At this, Bass tried to sit up. "The hell I can't." His voice was a low croak. "Just get me in the cockpit and—"

"He can't fly anything," said Mai-ling. She was applying a compress to his wound. "He's got a bullet in his chest and he's lost too much blood."

Chiu looked at Maxwell. "You'll have to fly it by yourself."

"No way. It's a two-man jet. I can't even decipher the instruments without a Chinese-speaking systems officer."

A flurry of automatic fire a few hundred yards away drew Chiu's attention. From just beyond the perimeter of the field came the sound of armored vehicles. To the east, on the opposite horizon from the fuel fire, the sky was beginning to show pink. "Our time is up," he said. "We have to get out of Chouzhou. If you don't fly the Black Star, then I'll destroy it." He patted his belt on which half a dozen grenades were hooked. "I'll blow up the jet and the equipment—"

"I can fly the Black Star."

They stared at Mai-ling. Chiu shook his head. "No. Not you."

"I helped build the airplane, and I know the systems. I can interpret the instruments for him."

"You're a defector and a security risk. I won't permit it."

Maxwell's anger peaked again. Chiu was a pigheaded idiot. "It was your job to get me to the airplane. It's my call how and with whom I fly it."

Chiu's face hardened. "I can't permit her to jeopardize the rest of the unit."

"You're already jeopardized. Do you want to report to your superiors in Taiwan that you failed?"

A moment of tense silence passed. Maxwell knew he had touched a nerve. The muscles in Chiu's jaw were knotting.

"Why should I trust any of you? It's not your country at war."

"We've just put our lives on the line for your country," said Maxwell. "Bass and I, and Mai-ling too. Doesn't that mean anything?"

Another silence. Chiu glanced at his watch, then glowered at Maxwell. "So quit wasting time. Go. Get in your damned airplane."

*Frigate* Kai Yang, *Taiwan Strait*

Another flood of orange blazed from the starboard vertical launcher. A plume of fire trailed the second Harpoon into the night sky, a mile behind the first.

As his eyes readapted to the darkness, Commander Lei could see the ghostly shapes of the ordnance men on the forward deck. They were scrambling to load the three fresh Harpoons.

The umbilicals from the two provisioning ships—the great wallowing 20,000-ton supply vessel and the tanker—had been disconnected and both ships were dropping astern. For mutual protection they would remain with *Kai Yang*'s group. Each carried its own single turret of twin five-inch thirty-eights.

*If we only had the Aegis,* Lei thought. Then he ordered himself to stop wishing for the impossible. *Fight the ship.*

His eyes went to the clock face again. He calculated the missiles would take three minutes to reach their target. A lot could happen in three minutes.

"Are you tracking the Harpoons, fire control?"

"Yes, sir. Both missiles locked on and tracking. We've got . . . stand by. It looks like another contact . . . it's separating from the first—it's a missile! They've got a missile in the air."

"What is it? What speed?"

A few seconds passed. The fire control officer's voice was hoarse. "Fast. Supersonic now. Inbound time is one minute, twenty seconds."

Lei took a deep breath. *Supersonic.* It had to be a Moskit antiship missile. It was the deadliest ship-to-ship weapon in the world. It was coming at them at over twice the speed of sound.

"Fire control, ready the SMS battery."

"Aye, Sparrows ready to fly."

The RIM-7 Sea Sparrow was a medium range surface-to-air missile adapted from the AIM-7 Sparrow carried on air force and navy fighters. It was radar guided and was effective against attacking aircraft and incoming subsonic missiles.

Against a low-flying, supersonic Moskit, the Sparrow was outmatched. "Second missile in the air, Captain. Two Moskits inbound, one minute and one-and-a-half minutes to impact."

Lei could imagine the sea-skimming missiles hurtling through the night faster than a rifle bullet. Dodging them with a surface vessel was hopeless.

But he didn't have to give them an easy target. "Hard to port, steady on two hundred ninety degrees."

"Aye, port to two hundred ninety degrees."

The turn would point *Kai Yang*'s bow directly into the oncoming missiles. It presented the smallest possible target, but more important, it gave his five-inch guns and the Phalanx CIWS—Close-in Weapons System—the ability to fire from both port and starboard turrets. The Phalanx was a last-ditch weapon—a radar-directed six-barrel 20 mm cannon with a rate of fire of 4,000 rounds per minute.

Lei hung on to the brass rail on the bulkhead, steadying himself against the heel of the ship as it turned hard to port.

"Third missile in the air, Captain. Another Moskit, one minute, forty-five seconds out."

"Activate the EWS," Lei ordered, though he was sure it had already been done. The SLQ-32 electronic warning system was intended to jam the radars of enemy fire control and guidance systems. Lei was also sure the Moskit 3M80 missiles had guidance units that could counter the jammers.

"Launch RBOC," he ordered. Seconds later, he heard the boom of the chaff canisters being launched. The Super RBOC—Rapid Bloom Onboard Chaff—threw up a cloud of fine aluminum foil intended to decoy and confuse the radar homing unit of the antiship missiles.

Lei wasn't optimistic. The Moskit was a smart missile with a guidance unit that wasn't fooled by decoys.

"Fire control, stand by the five-inchers. Commence firing as soon as you have a radar solution. I want a wall of shrapnel out there, proximity fuses."

"Standing by, Captain."

Shooting supersonic missiles with five-inch guns was more an act of defiance than anything else. Like swatting flies with a sledgehammer. Lei would use every weapon he had. If these were the final minutes of his career, he wanted the record to show that *Kai Yang* went down shooting.

It occurred to him that none of his crew—not the officers on the bridge or in fire control or surface watch, nor any of the enlisted signalmen or gunners or loaders—were exhibiting signs of panic. They were going about their duties with poise. Their voices were calm. No matter how the battle turned out, Lei told himself, he would always savor this moment.

He wished he had been able to close with the Sovremenny before the missile fight began. At closer range—thirteen to sixteen kilometers—perhaps the Moskits would have more difficulty locking on. Even with the Sovremenny's superior firepower, he was certain that his gunners could direct their fire with more accuracy than the PLA crew. It would be sweet to pound the Russian devil ship with a barrage of five-inch shells—

"First missile, thirty seconds out," called the watch officer.

"Do we have SMS acquisition?"

"Not yet, sir, still trying—there! There it is, the first missile, six miles. Sparrow away."

As the fire control officer spoke, a blaze of light from the starboard side signaled the launch of the Sea Sparrow missile.

Then another flash. "Second Sparrow away."

More flashes. A steady thunder erupted from the five-inch gun turrets. In his peripheral vision Lei caught similar flashes from behind and off the starboard aft quarter. The supply ship and the tanker were opening up with their own guns. So were the two destroyer escorts.

A wall of fire was going up against the Moskits. It was everything they had.

"Forward battery reports the new Harpoons loaded and ready, Captain."

Lei could barely hear him over the roar of the guns. He had three more Harpoons. *Fire them or save them?* If the incoming Moskits struck *Kai Yang*, it wouldn't matter. The unfired Harpoons would be useless. But if he somehow evaded the first volley of Moskits, he would need them.

"Fire Harpoon One."

"Aye, Captain."

This time the flash of light from the Harpoon launch was almost undetectable. The bow of the *Kai Yang* was already ablaze with the muzzle flashes of the five-inch guns. The night sky looked like a pyrotechnics display, shells bursting in a mile-wide pattern.

Lei was peering intently toward the west. The horizon was a yellow pencil line, illuminated by the glare of the exploding shells.

Something, a reddish pinpoint of light, was emerging from the curtain of fire.

"First Sparrow is a miss!" called fire control.

The Moskit was already through the wall of five-inch fire. Lei could see it now, sizzling over the ocean at only a hundred feet altitude.

Coming at them.

Through the steady thunder of the guns, he heard a new sound. A deep-throated, staccato hammering noise.

The Phalanx Gatling guns. They were on automated fire, locked on the incoming Moskit. The combined moan of the two Phalanx turrets, spitting a hail of depleted-uranium penetrator shells, sent a high-frequency vibration up through the deck of the *Kai Yang*. Lei could feel it in the soles of his shoes.

The red pinpoint of light was zigzagging in a crazy mosquitolike path. No doubt about it, thought Lei. Definitely a Moskit. Its autopilot was programmed to deliver violent evasive maneuvers during its final flight path.

"Fifteen seconds to missile impact," called out fire control.

*Where will it hit?* Without taking his eyes off the western horizon, Lei removed his battle helmet from its hook on the bulkhead and set it on his head. Instinctively, his hand checked the buckle on his life vest.

As he watched, the zigzagging Moskit steadied its course, aiming straight for *Kai Yang*.

"CIWS hits!" called out fire control. "The Phalanx is getting hits on the missile."

Lei stared, fascinated, at the incoming Moskit. It was low, trailing fire like a comet.

Four hundred meters short, the missile exploded. Flaming chunks soared like meteors in a shower toward *Kai Yang*.

Fragments rained into the sea in front of the bow. Pieces skipped off the water and clanged into *Kai Yang*'s hull. Larger pieces arced through the sky, descending toward the frigate and her escorts.

Lei saw a cluster of flaming debris hurtling directly for the bridge. He ducked as a piece impacted the deck at the base of the superstructure. Another blazing chunk struck the gun turret on the starboard side. More shrapnel ricocheted off the deck, slicing through antennae and stowed equipment and ventilator shafts.

He raised his head and peered through the window. The forward deck was ablaze. The starboard five-inch turret was a mess of smoking steel.

"Twenty seconds to second missile impact."

The remaining five-inch guns were still hammering. Another Sparrow leaped from its launcher and blazed off toward the wall of gunfire. The Phalanx cannons were moaning like demons from hell.

Another red pinpoint of light appeared, zigzagging through the shell bursts.

The pinpoint erupted in a brilliant flash. Like an exploding star, the pieces radiated out in a shower of burning fragments, plunging into the ocean a mile short of *Kai Yang*.

"A Sea Sparrow kill," announced the fire control officer.

Before Lei could acknowledge, he heard the surface watch officer's cold voice. "Our first Harpoon is gone. Looks like they killed it."

Lei wasn't surprised. The Sovremenny had defensive weaponry every bit as good as *Kai Yang*. The slow-flying Harpoon was not a difficult target. Nothing like a Moskit.

"Third Moskit, thirty seconds to impact."

Okay, thought Lei, they'd been lucky. Two out three misses with a Moskit was as good as they could hope for. *Here comes number three.*

As he waited, he saw the damage control party in asbestos suits scurrying across the forward deck, extinguishing the blaze, checking for survivors. He wondered how many were killed in the gun turret. The ship had only taken fragments from the destroyed Moskit. What kind of hell would they experience with a direct hit?

*You'll know in fifteen seconds.*

As he strained to pick up the telltale red point of light

through the shellfire, he heard the watch officer call out, "Harpoon strike! We've got impact on the target ship."

Lei wanted to know more. Which Harpoon, the second or the third? What was the Sovremenny doing? Was it slowing, turning, sinking? Launching more missiles?

He couldn't tear his eyes away from the red point of light zigzagging through the turbulent sky toward them.

*Number three.* By its frenetic close-in zigzagging, Lei could tell that the missile had not been touched by the Phalanx, nor by a Sea Sparrow. With every undulation it returned to its relentless inbound course to *Kai Yang.*

The missile burst through the curtain of five-inch fire, flying a corkscrew pattern. The Phalanx Gatling guns on either side of *Kai Yang* were moaning in a ghostly death rattle. The missile continued inbound. Still untouched.

From his bridge, Lei watched in morbid fascination as the fire-tailed Moskit took one last swerve, then aimed for the bow of *Kai Yang. Here it comes.* He clenched the brass handrail with both hands and kept his eyes on the incoming missile.

Lei saw a flash in the flight path of the missile. *The Phalanx,* he realized. *The Gatling gun was hitting the Moskit.* Another flash. The red plume behind the missile sputtered and diverged from its previous angle.

Lei ducked as the missile skimmed over the bridge of *Kai Yang.* He braced himself for the explosion.

Nothing.

He swung to follow the track of the low-flying Moskit. His eyes located the red plume in time to see it transform into a billowing orange ball of flame. Lei watched in horror as the ball of flame expanded, exploding outward like a newborn star.

The sky became bright as high noon. He could see the surface of the ocean, his escort ships, the faces of the sailors in their gun turrets.

*Chi Chuan*, the fueling ship, had taken the Moskit missile amidships. Twelve thousand tons of fuel oil erupted in a thousand-foot-high inferno. The blaze was lighting up the Taiwan Strait for a hundred square miles.

It took eight seconds for the blast to reach *Kai Yang*. A dull rumble of thunder, then a wave of superheated wind swept over the frigate. Lei saw the men in the gun turrets duck behind their armor, shielding their faces from the heat. The orange light danced on the skin of the ship like a rising sun.

"Captain," Lei heard the surface watch officer report, "we show a second Harpoon strike on the target. Looks like the Sovremenny has taken heavy damage. He's slowed to five knots."

"Is he firing more missiles?"

"No, sir. No more radar separations. Looks like we shut his missile batteries down."

Lei's eyes were still on the blazing tanker a mile astern. A hundred fifty sailors had just been incinerated by the blast that his Phalanx guns had diverted from *Kai Yang*.

A seething anger was taking a grip on him. "Give me a bearing and distance on the Sovremenny."

"Three-one-five degrees, eighteen kilometers, Captain. He's reversing course. Looks like he's making for the coast."

Lei turned to the OOD. "Steer three-one-five, full speed ahead." Then he barked into the sound-powered phone. "Fire control, reload and stand by all guns, ready torpedo tubes one and two."

"Aye, sir." A pause, then, "What are our intentions, Captain?"

"Intentions?" Lei glowered out into the darkness. "We're going to blow him to hell."

*Chouzhou Air Base, People's Republic of China*

*Time to kill the beast.*

Chiu took one last look at the ominous shape of the remaining Black Star. In the dim red light of Shelter Four, it looked like a living object—a great, bat-winged bird of prey. Killing this thing would give him pleasure.

Lieutenant Kee was watching him, waiting for his signal. Chiu gave him a nod, and Kee headed for the door.

Chiu unhooked two grenades from his belt. With slow, deliberate movements, he pulled the pins, one after the other. He tossed one into each jet intake atop the wings of the Black Star. Then he turned and hurried out of the shelter, following Kee.

They were twenty yards away when the grenades exploded, half a second apart. It felt like a subterranean tremor, shaking the ground under Chiu's feet. He saw the walls of the Shelter bulge outward. The bifold door ripped free at one hinge, and black smoke billowed out the gap.

*The beast is dead.* Chiu turned his back on the destroyed building and headed for Shelter Three.

Maxwell and the woman were already inside the tandem cockpit. "How much longer?" Chiu called from the floor of the shelter.

"One minute," said Maxwell. "The auxiliary power unit is starting now." Chiu could hear an ascending whine as the auxiliary power unit inside the jet's belly cranked up.

He heard a series of explosions outside, three in a row, not more than two or three kilometers away. Mortars, probably fired from just outside the perimeter. If the PLA units managed to take out the helicopters, it was all over. Their only allies were the dissidents who shut down the power station and took out the air defense net. They had long ago run for safety.

He glanced at his watch. Forty-six minutes since they

landed at Chouzhou. Already sixteen minutes over his al-
lowance. In twenty minutes, dawn would come. If they
hadn't left Chouzhou by then, they'd be dead.

In the cockpit, Maxwell and the woman were wearing
their helmets with the strange goggles. She was talking to
him on the intercom, giving instructions, reading the instrument markings, explaining what the displays meant.

Chiu reflected again on what would have happened if he
had found her before Bass and Maxwell. He would have put
a bullet in her without hesitation. He still had the nagging
thought that perhaps he should have done that anyway.

Why had she sneaked away? According to her story, she
had gone to find the Black Star squadron commander—
someone she called Zhang—in order to kill him. Instead,
she had found the other pilot, Major Han, a former colleague
whom she thought was dead.

And so he was, thanks to Maxwell and that ancient blun-
derbuss, the .45 caliber pistol.

Which made a nice bit of irony. In accordance with Chinese tradition, it meant that Maxwell, having saved the troublesome woman's life, was responsible for her.

The notion almost—but not quite—made Chiu smile.

"Ready for engine start," Maxwell called out. "Stand
clear when she energizes the skin-cloaking field. There may
be a static discharge."

Chiu wasn't sure what that meant, but he nodded and
moved to the side door.

"When I give the thumbs-up, raise the bifold door. Then
run like hell."

*About time*. This had turned into the longest night of
Chiu's life. If he lived beyond dawn, it would be a miracle.

Waiting in the commandeered Bei-jung vehicle was Kee
and the wounded American. As soon as the door to the shelter opened, Chiu would join them and they would race for
the waiting number three helicopter.

More explosions pounded the apron outside.

"Colonel," said the commando on the manpack radio, "helo two reports that the armored column is breaching the perimeter at the southwest corner."

"Order the Cobras to engage them."

"They're already engaged, sir. They're taking fire from the APCs, and they can see mobile missile launchers approaching."

*Hurry*, Chiu urged the American in the Black Star. Their lives could now be measured in minutes.

The whine of a jet engine filled the expanse of the shelter. Then another. The second engine was still accelerating when Maxwell flashed a thumbs-up.

Chiu understood. *Raise the door*.

While the door was raising, Chiu climbed into the waiting Bei-jung. Kee was in the driver's seat, with the unconscious Bass in the backseat.

He saw Maxwell watching from the cockpit, waiting for the shelter door to fully open.

"Go," he ordered Kee, sitting in the driver's seat. "We've done all we can for them."

As the vehicle pulled away into the darkness, Chiu looked back and gave the pilot of the Black Star a salute.

# CHAPTER TWENTY-ONE

# EGRESS

*Chouzhou Air Base, People's Republic of China*
*0538, Monday, 15 September*

At least the stick and throttles were in the right place. But that was all. Not much else about the Black Star's cockpit—the four display screens, the enunciator panels with script that looked like chicken scratchings, the enumerated gauges indicating mysterious values—made much sense.

He had located the airspeed and altitude readouts—all in metric, of course. The rest was hieroglyphics to him. Like one of those movies, Maxwell thought, where the hero climbs into an alien spaceship and flies it away.

*Not that far from the truth.* The Black Star—*this* Black Star, anyway—was about as alien as it got.

Another hour. Sixty more minutes—that's how much he needed—to familiarize himself with the cockpit layout. Mai-ling could have educated him about the unintelligible Chinese instrument symbology. He would have had time to match up the layout with what he remembered from the Black Star back in Dreamland.

Now he'd do it the hard way. Cold.

"Canopy coming closed," said Mai-ling over the intercom.

He heard the electric whine of the big Plexiglas canopy, then a *clunk* as it locked shut. They were enveloped in near silence, closed off from the howl of the Black Star's two jet engines, from the *whump* and clatter of the firefight taking place on the base perimeter.

"APU shut down."

"APU shutting down," Mai-ling replied, confirming that the auxiliary power unit was no longer online. She sounded excited, thought Maxwell. It occurred to him that although she knew the Black Star's systems, she wasn't a flight crew member. The hard part—flying the jet—lay ahead of them.

"Confirm nav system initialized."

"That's a problem," she said. "I put in the base coordinates, but I can't tell whether the nav computer accepted it."

Maxwell couldn't tell either. The situational display looked okay to him. It would have to do.

"Fuel quantity check."

"Eighty-three hundred kilos," she replied. Then she did the math for him. "If it helps, that's 18,000 pounds, plus a little."

"Thanks." Maxwell didn't know the fuel burn rate of the Black Star's engines. Somewhere around five thousand pounds per hour, he estimated. Figuring extra for takeoff and climb, it gave them around three hours' endurance.

Through the expanding cavity in the shelter opening, Maxwell could see the expanse of Chouzhou Air Base sprawled out before him. The taxiway from the shelter veered forty-five degrees to the right, then joined the approach end of runway one-six. It was the closest runway— but the shortest. At the far end of the field was the east–west runway, zero-nine and two-seven. It was ten thousand feet long.

"What runway did the Black Star use when they took off at Chouzhou?"

"The long one," she said.

"They never used one-six?"

"No. Too short. Why?"

He didn't answer. He tried to remember how long runway one-six was. He pulled the diagram of the Chouzhou runway complex from his cargo pocket. Runway one-six was 1,980 meters in length. He did a rapid calculation and came up with a rough runway length. About 6,500 feet.

That was short, very short for a fully-loaded jet. Was it too short?

As a test pilot, he always calculated to the foot how much runway distance his jet required to lift off. Lacking data about the Chinese Black Star's performance, he didn't have a clue. The original Black Star, he remembered, had been sluggish in takeoff performance. But that was at Dreamland, some 4,000 feet above sea level, where the hot, thin air took a slice out of a jet's performance. Chouzhou was nearly at sea level. Maybe this version would do better.

The big electro-hydraulic bifold door was nearly open, and through the chasm he could see flashes and eruptions of flame in the southeast quadrant, where the commando landing zone had been.

Forget the long runway. It would be runway one-six, too short or not.

"Time to leave town." He advanced the throttles. The Black Star lurched forward, trundling along on its tall, spindly landing gear.

They rolled out of the red-lighted shelter, onto the darkness of the apron. Maxwell lowered his night vision goggles and peered into the greenish landscape ahead. He could see the curving taxiway, the distant runway, the perimeter fence beyond.

He tested the nose wheel steering, making gentle turns

left and right. He tried out the brakes, tapping the pedals with his feet. The jet skittered almost to a halt, its nose bobbing downward. He had to jam hard on the right pedal to keep from slewing off the taxiway into the dirt.

"What are you doing?" said Mai-ling.

"Testing."

"You're supposed to steal this thing, not test it."

"Be quiet. You're a systems officer, not a check pilot."

"I'm a concerned crew member."

"Then be concerned and shut up."

"But I—"

She shut up. Something ahead caught her attention. Maxwell saw it too—a massive dark shape—rumbling toward them.

An armored personnel carrier. It was charging through an opening in the perimeter fence, just beyond the petroleum farm.

Illuminated in the glare of the burning fuel fires, the APC was on an intercept course. Its turret gun was swiveling toward the Black Star.

Kee was driving too damned slow. Chiu could feel the time slipping like sand through his fingers. "Faster. Move this vehicle!"

"It's too dangerous, Colonel. We mined this route. I have to watch for the explosive units."

Chiu just grunted, sorry for his outburst. He didn't believe in yelling at his troops. Kee was a good officer.

The bad news kept pouring in. Over the manpack PRC-119 radio he heard the number one helicopter pilot report a column of armored personnel carriers three kilometers from the field perimeter. Two PLA assault helicopters had already blundered inside the base perimeter, probing for the invading party. Each had been shot down by a missile-firing Cobra gunship.

It was only a matter of minutes before the PLA overran them.

Ahead he could see the landing zone, three hundred meters away. The first two Chinooks had already lifted, carrying half the commando unit. The rest were maintaining a perimeter around the zone.

The Cobra gunships were doing their best to keep the armored column at bay, but they were taking heavy fire now. The other two Chinooks were ready to lift, waiting for Chiu and Kee and the wounded American.

Chiu could see that Bass was in bad shape. His eyes were closed, and he slipped in and out of consciousness. Before they reached Taiwan—*if* they reached Taiwan, Chiu corrected himself—he'd probably be administering last rites to the dying American.

Chiu had the man-pack radio in the backseat of the Beijung, staying in contact with the helicopters. The Cobras had done a good job of suppressing the oncoming PLA armor, but time was against them. Already the APCs had breached the perimeter, breaking through the fence south of the fuel farm.

A mortar exploded a hundred feet ahead of them, setting off two more secondary explosions from the mines.

Another mortar, this time closer to the number three helicopter. Where were they coming from? Were the PLA troops inside the fence already?

He snatched up the transceiver from the manpack. "Whiskey One, this is Reaper," he said, calling the lead Cobra gunship. "We've got incoming mortars. Can you spot them?"

After a lapse of several seconds, "Whiskey One is looking, Reaper. Troops are concentrating in Zone Two, coming out of the APCs. They're probably setting up mortars."

"Try to suppress them. They're getting the range on the helos. We'll have to—"

The next mortar exploded fifteen feet from the Bei-jung. The blast rocked the vehicle up onto its side. Chiu heard the scrape of metal against earth, of glass shattering from the windshield.

The Bei-jung lay still. Dirt and broken glass settled onto the wreck.

It took him a moment to orient himself. He realized he was lying against the right door. Kee was atop him, writhing in pain. From the back, Bass emitted a low moan.

He untangled himself from Kee and pulled out his knife. As he tried to slash the canvas cover of the vehicle, he felt a sharp pain in his right shoulder. His collar bone. He switched hands and finished ripping away the canvas. He helped Kee climb out of the damaged Bei-jung.

Kee's face was bleeding. He was blinded from the shattered glass of the windshield, and his left arm seemed to be broken.

With his left arm, Chiu pulled Bass out of the Bei-jung. His chest wound was bleeding again. Chiu made another compress with a piece of the slashed canvas and applied it to the wound.

For a moment he gazed around in the darkness, assessing his situation. Things had rapidly gone to hell. The Bei-jung was totaled. The left front tire was blown and steam was gushing from under the hood.

Waves of pain were radiating from his shoulder down through his left arm. Kee was ambulatory, but he couldn't see well enough to make it to the helicopters without assistance. Bass would have to be dragged.

He heard more mortars, closer to the two Chinooks. The landing zone was still a hundred meters away.

From inside the vehicle came the crackle of the radio. "Reaper, Reaper, this is Whiskey Two. Come in Reaper. Do you read?"

Chiu retrieved the transceiver. "All teams, this is Reaper.

Pull back to Charlie Three." Charlie Three was the first of the two Chinooks still at Chouzhou. "Launch Charlie Three as soon as you have everyone aboard."

"Copy that, Reaper. Where are you? Are you boarding Charlie Four?"

"We're on our way. Be prepared to launch immediately if we don't make it. If your position becomes threatened, go without delay. Acknowledge?"

"Charlie Three copies."

"Charlie Four copies, but Reaper, we'll come to—"

"I just gave you orders! Stand by to launch. Reaper out." Chiu released the transmit switch and hooked the transceiver to his belt.

"Lieutenant Kee, you will follow me. Keep a hand on my shoulder so you won't get lost." He bent over and seized the collar of Bass's utilities with his good hand. He began to drag him across the ground.

Bass cried out in pain. He shook his head. "You guys won't make it if you try to drag me along. Go on, Colonel, haul ass for the helicopters. Get out of here."

"I won't leave you behind," said Chiu.

"I'll be a prisoner. That's my problem."

"No, it's my problem."

Bass gave him a wary look. "What does that mean?"

"No prisoners." Chiu unholstered his Beretta. "I have to kill you." He aimed the pistol at Bass's forehead. "Is that your choice?"

With wide, unblinking eyes, Bass peered into the muzzle of the pistol. "You've got a point, Colonel. Maybe I'll just come along for the ride."

"Good decision." Chiu holstered the pistol and seized Bass's collar again. He ignored the frequent moans as Bass bumped along on the uneven ground. Kee plodded along behind, hanging on to Chiu's sleeve.

The mortar shells were landing with greater accuracy.

Chiu saw Charlie Two, the second Chinook, kicking up a storm of dirt and blown debris. The big chopper lifted and tilted its nose toward the southeast fence.

From thirty meters away, Chiu saw Charlie Four's twin rotor blades whopping the air. From the open cargo door, the crew chief saw them coming out of the darkness. He jumped out and came running to help with Bass. The American was unconscious again, limp as a bag of laundry.

Probably dead, thought Chiu. It didn't change the problem. He still had to take the body. He couldn't leave evidence that Americans were involved in the raid.

While the crew chief took over the burden of dragging the pilot's body, Chiu took one last look around.

Then he looked again.

*Damn!* An armored personnel carrier was roaring across the field, aimed like a leviathan toward the end of the runway.

He grabbed the transceiver off his belt hook. "Whiskey One, Whiskey One, you've got a target, Zone Two, an APC."

"That's the opposite side of the field from us, Reaper," said the Cobra pilot. "Too far away. We're engaged with the armor column."

"I don't care what you're engaged with. Kill the APC." *Before it kills the Black Star.*

"We'll try, Reaper, but the action is getting very hot at the LZ. The Chinooks need cover."

Chiu wanted to scream in rage and frustration. After all this! The lost lives, the immense risk, to lose the Black Star now, when they were so close . . .

Another mortar shell exploded thirty feet behind them, showering them with dirt and fragments. Then another, closer than the first. A trail of eruptions was walking across the field, tracing a route toward Charlie Four.

Chiu felt the crew chief grab him, spin him around, shove

him toward the waiting Chinook. He half ran, half stumbled, sensing with each new explosion that it was already too late.

*Uh-oh.*

Through his NVG, Maxwell stared at the apparition. In the next instant he saw a flash from the APC's gun turret—and braced himself.

The round hit twenty yards to the left of the taxiing jet. Maxwell could feel the concussion through the airframe of the Black Star.

"How the hell can they see us?" he asked over the intercom. "Didn't you activate cloaking? I thought this thing was supposed to be zero-viz."

"The skin cloaking doesn't work so well on the ground. Too much IR reflection, or some kind of photonic resonance problem."

Maxwell had no idea what she was talking about. It didn't matter. All that mattered now was that the gomers in the APC could see them and they were drawing a bead on the Black Star.

The next round hit closer, only ten feet from the left wingtip.

*What now?* For a fleeting moment it occurred to Maxwell that he could shoot back. If he knew how. By the time they figured out how to activate the Black Star's own weapons system—the Gatling gun or the internally stored missiles—it would be over.

The APC was angling across the field, headed for the runway. It was clear what the driver had in mind.

He was going to block the runway.

Another round, this one just behind the right wing. The gunner was getting the range.

"How do I arm the cannon?" Maxwell yelled on the intercom.

"You have to select it on the weapons display."

"I've got four screens. Which one is it?"

"Bottom right. There should be an icon for each armament store."

Maxwell looked at the display screen. He hated taking his
eyes off the apparition out there that was trying to kill them.
The screen was covered with icons, all with indecipherable
hieroglyphics. *Shit!* He didn't see anything that looked like
a gun selector.

The APC had almost reached the edge of the runway.
Maxwell was out of ideas. They were an easy, slow-moving,
non-invisible target. He couldn't shoot back because he
couldn't arm the damned gun! In ten more seconds they
might as well abandon the jet because they wouldn't have a
runway to—

A rain of fire appeared from behind the APC. A flurry of
small explosions danced around the vehicle.

*Rockets.* In the night sky they looked like sparklers rain-
ing down on the APC. Maxwell guessed that they were 2.75-
inch air-to-ground rockets. An entire pod of them—*fired
from what?*

Then he saw it. Descending like a specter out of the darkness, the dim shape of a helicopter—a Cobra gunship. From
the gunship came another flash, this one larger and brighter
than the 2.75 pod. A pulse of fire beamed like a laser toward
the APC.

The armored vehicle erupted in an orange ball of flame. *A
Hellfire missile,* Maxwell guessed. Only a Hellfire armor-
piercing antitank missile could take out an APC like that. He
didn't know where the gunship came from, or how he got
there in time, but Maxwell uttered a silent thanks to the
pilot.

The fast-moving Cobra swept over the burning APC,
passing directly in front of the Black Star, then skimmed low
across the field to the LZ where the Chinooks were lifting
off.

Maxwell followed the dark silhouette of the gunship. Two hundred yards in the distance, the last Chinook was kicking up a storm of dirt, its blades biting into the air as it lifted from Chouzhou.

*Good*. That had to be Charlie Three, the last chopper. Col. Chiu and Catfish Bass and Lt. Kee were aboard.

He saw mortar rounds landing around the Chinook. The big cargo helicopter lumbered into the air. Its nose tilted down as it gathered forward speed.

A mortar round exploded directly behind the aft rotor. One of the blades separated and whirled like a rapier across the darkened field.

As Maxwell watched, the chopper began a slow rotation to the left, rolling onto its side. A front rotor blade caught the earth, kicking up a geyser of dirt and debris.

Slowly, majestically, the Chinook rose up on its nose, then over onto its tail. In a macabre death dance, the helicopter flopped end over end for a hundred yards, shedding parts, spitting smoke and tortured metal.

Abruptly, the Chinook exploded. Magnesium and ammunition and jet fuel combined to send a billowing fireball a hundred feet into the sky.

"Oh, God," muttered Mai-ling in the backseat. "They didn't make it."

Maxwell kept his eyes riveted on the inferno. He didn't see anyone escaping, no figures emerging from the wreckage. The Cobra gunship was circling the burning hulk, firing with its twenty millimeter cannon at something in the near darkness.

He banged his fist against the front console. Goddamnit! They almost made it. Another ten seconds. Chiu, Catfish, Kee—they would have been on their way to Taiwan.

"It was my fault," said Mai-ling. "If they hadn't taken the time to look for me—"

"It wasn't anyone's fault," he snapped. "This is war. This

is what happens. I know it's hard, but we have to stop thinking about it. You and I have a job to do."

Silence from the backseat. Maxwell hoped she hadn't gone catatonic on him.

He saw the end of the runway coming up. He steered the Black Star onto the runway and aligned it with the center stripe.

He peered down the length of the darkened runway. No lights marked the edges or the end. Only the blaze of the still-burning APC illuminated the eastern edge of the concrete.

As a test pilot he had made many first flights with experimental aircraft. Every new airplane had surprises, unexpected tendencies, but he had always been ready. It was what he was trained to do.

This time was different. Never had he felt so ill-equipped to fly a new machine.

Across the field the PLA armored column had broken through the fence line and was heading at full speed for the runway. To his right, in the flood of orange light from the petroleum fires, another cluster of APCs was storming across the open field.

The destroyed Chinook was still burning like a funeral pyre.

"What are you waiting for?" said Mai-ling. "Isn't it time to leave?"

*Frigate* Kai Yang, *Taiwan Strait*

"Range seven thousand meters," called out the fire control officer.

Close enough, decided Commander Lei. Seven kilometers was well within the kill range of the Mark 46 torpedoes. The enemy Sovremenny destroyer was limping along at five knots, making for the Chinese coast. His search radar was still emitting, which meant he knew he was being stalked by the *Kai Yang*. If he could fire more Moskit supersonic missiles, he would have done so already.

*Kill him. Get it over before someone comes to his rescue.*

They were in dangerous waters. *Kai Yang* and her two destroyer escorts were within thirty miles of the mainland. Dawn was arriving. Already the sun was cracking the horizon in the direction of the Asian continent. The PLA would come to aid of the stricken destroyer with more destroyers, submarines—aircraft, perhaps.

It was time to kill the damned thing and run for the western side of the strait.

But something—an inner voice—was warning him. *Be careful. Perhaps they no longer care about the Sovremenny.* Maybe it was a trap. Maybe they wanted the *Kai Yang*.

"Ready tubes one and two."

"Aye, ready one and two."

Lei heard the gurgling sound of water filling the launching tubes. He could use his remaining Harpoons to dispatch the wounded destroyer, but the inner voice was coming in louder now. *You're deep inside enemy waters. Save your missiles.*

"Forward tubes ready to fire, sir."

Lei peered into the gray murk ahead of the *Kai Yang*. He knew now why he had waited this long to deliver the coup de grace to the Sovremenny.

He wanted to see it die.

Lei had dreamed of such a moment for his entire career. In this, perhaps the first surface naval engagement since World War II, he wanted to experience close-up the din and thunder of battle. To see the Sovremenny destroyer blow apart like the fueling ship it had destroyed with its Moskit missile.

"Fire one and two."

"Aye, Captain, fire tubes one and two."

He heard the familiar, satisfying rumble of the Mark 46 torpedoes, three seconds apart, leaping into the sea like greyhounds after a hare.

Four minutes.

While he waited, Lei paced his bridge, growing more uncomfortable with the quickly approaching dawn. They'd been lucky. He and the crew of the *Kai Yang* had survived three days of war. How many enemy warships had they sunk? Five? Or was it six?

Had the PLA navy figured out that one obsolescent frigate, the *Kai Yang*, was methodically destroying their mighty fleet? If so, they would be coming after him with all their knives drawn.

"Both torpedoes on active guidance now, Captain."

He nodded, forcing himself not to stare at the situational display on his console. The torpedoes were autonomous now. They would find the target or—

"Impact!" called out the sonar man. "Torpedo one has struck the target."

Three seconds later, "Torpedo two impact. I'm getting secondaries—the Sovremenny is breaking up. I've got separating returns."

For a fleeting moment Lei wished he had waited, pressed the attack to visual range. It would be an exquisite pleasure to see the enemy destroyer blowing herself into pieces.

No. It was time to run for the safety of the eastern strait. At the moment his crew was flushed with their splendid victory over the Sovremenny, but that would wear off soon. They were tired, drained from the unrelenting pressure of combat.

"Steer one-seven-zero degrees, maintain speed. Remain on battle stations until—"

"Radar contact! Incoming, low altitude, low speed."

*Low speed? What could it be?* "Do you have an electronic ID?"

"I'm checking with the Hawkeye. It must be a—" The technician's voice cracked. "Another contact! Two-five-zero, range a thousand meters. The track looks nearly vertical."

Lei snapped his attention to the situational display. What the hell was going on? A slow-moving contact, low on the water. A helicopter? And then something else—inbound and nearly vertical.

Vertical? It could only be one thing. But that didn't make sense.

Three seconds later, he heard the technician's voice again. "Incoming weapon," said the technician. "A missile or a bomb."

"From where? That's impossible. Is there an aircraft up there?"

The technician shook his head. "No, sir. Nothing."

Lei tried to make sense of the situation. What kind of bomb? Radar guided? No, they'd have picked up the emissions from the guidance unit. It had to be infrared or GPS.

"Hard to starboard!" he commanded. "Flank speed. Ready the Phalanx batteries."

He knew it was futile, trying to evade a precision-guided bomb, trying at the same time to get a snap lock on a vertical target with the CIWS—Close-in Weapons System. But he had to try.

How could a bomb suddenly appear from an empty sky? It had to have been released by an aircraft. Why hadn't they gotten an alert from the multitude of air defense radars scanning the area?

By now, each head on the bridge was tilted up, peering toward the southwest. From both Phalanx turrets came the deep moan of the Gatling guns putting up a hail of penetrator shells.

Lei knew it was a gesture of defiance. A feeling of inevitability had settled over him. They had been luckier than they had any right to expect. Now their luck had run out.

He gripped the handrail and waited for the bomb to hit his ship.

# CHAPTER TWENTY-TWO

# ONE-VEE-ONE

*Chouzhou Air Base, People's Republic of China*
*0610, Monday, 15 September*

Maxwell took a deep breath, then advanced the throttles. The dull hum of the two turbofans deepened to a throaty rumble. A quick check of the gauges—the indications meant nothing, but at least he could see that the two engines were making the same numbers—and he released the brakes.

The sudden acceleration surprised him. The nose bobbed up once on its long slender strut, and he felt himself shoved back in the seat.

The Black Star surged down the runway.

*Thunk, thunk, thunk, thunk.* The runway felt as rough as a logging road. As the Black Star sped down the strip of concrete, the nose wheel clunked over the grooves in the uneven surface. The jet was accelerating faster than Maxwell expected.

"A hundred kilometers per hour," Mai-ling called out, giving him the airspeed.

He had to make quick conversions from metric. A hundred kilometers per hour equated to fifty-four knots—nautical miles per hour. If this jet flew like the Black Star at

Dreamland, he should keep the nose wheel on the concrete until he had 140 knots. That was—how much? Almost 260 kilometers per hour.

Unless he ran out of runway. Then he was in no-man's-land. He'd do what he had to do.

"A hundred fifty."

*Eighty-one knots.* They had gobbled up half the available runway. *Come on, baby, accelerate.*

"Two hundred."

*A hundred eight knots.* The thunking of the nose wheel on the rough concrete had become a steady rumble. The vibration from the rough runway resonated through the airframe, into Maxwell's cockpit, making it difficult to read the instruments.

In the greenish twilight, he could see the end of the runway rushing toward them.

"Two-twenty." Mai-ling's voice was rising in pitch.

*A hundred eighteen knots. Not enough.*

"Two-forty." Her voice cracked.

The end of the runway was disappearing beneath the Black Star's nose. *The moment of truth.* He nudged the stick back. The Black Star would either fly or it would become a smoking hulk at the end of runway one-six.

The nose of the jet lifted. The main gear stayed rooted to the concrete.

*Come on, fly!* He pulled the stick back further.

Still on the ground.

The end of the runway was under him, gone from sight. The digital readout, blurred from the intense vibration, read 238 knots. He felt a violent clunking as the main gear rolled into the rough overrun.

Maxwell hauled the stick back in his lap. The jet's nose rotated to a steep upward angle.

*Come on, damn it . . .*

*Taiwan Strait*

Zhang could see it clearly, a dark shape against the slate gray sea.

The IR tracker had already locked on to its surface target. Hot stacks over hot boilers against the cool ocean background. No challenge at all.

The laser designator would illuminate the centroid of the heat source for the final fifteen seconds of the bomb's fall time. Only then would the frigate have any hint that it was targeted. Their radar might pick up the descending laser-guided bomb, but it wouldn't matter. They would receive no return from the Dong-jin, not even in the second and a half that the bomb bay doors were open and the five-hundred-kilogram laser-guided bomb kicked out.

Colonel Zhang was eager to destroy the Taiwanese frigate. It was a devil ship, according to the preflight intelligence briefing. If the report was to be believed, this vessel had inflicted unbelievable losses on the PLA navy—at least two submarines, an amphibious landing craft, and three destroyers, and was trying to sink one of the PLA navy's prized Sovremenny-class destroyers. All in three days.

The Dong-jin would balance the score. Already it had changed air warfare, and now it would revolutionize sea warfare. With this weapon, he would shift the balance of power in Asia. He would be recognized as a great national hero. Zhang Yu's place in history was assured.

But he was running out of time. An urgent matter required his attention. His squadron of supersecret stealth jets had been detected and attacked by an enemy commando unit even as he took off. Because of the base commander's stupidity the commandos had apparently destroyed one Dong-jin. Much worse, they had *captured* the remaining Dong-jin. Stolen it from under their noses. He wondered what other havoc the rebel commandos had wreaked at Chouzhou. He had warned them about this very possibility. *Idiots!*

"Twenty-five seconds to impact."

On the cockpit IR screen Zhang could see the frigate in a hard right turn. They had detected the incoming bomb. It would make no difference.

"Ten seconds, laser on."

A bright flash blanked Zhang's screen. When the picture returned, he saw that the entire aft end of the ship was engulfed in fire and black smoke.

"A good hit." He shoved the throttles up and hauled the nose of the jet up in a climbing turn to the left. "Now we hunt for the thieves."

*Chouzhou Air Base, People's Republic of China*

The clunking from the main gear abruptly ceased. Maxwell sensed a blur of earth and trees and buildings beneath them. Finding air beneath its wings, the Black Star lifted into the morning sky.

He raised the landing gear. The airspeed indicator was slowly ticking upward. Two-fifty. Three hundred. The altitude readout—also metric—had left zero and was slowly increasing. Carefully he raised the flaps.

With the airspeed accelerating through 320 kilometers per hour, altitude a thousand meters and climbing, he gave the stick a gentle nudge to the left. The jet rolled into a crisp left bank.

He was pleasantly surprised. The airplane had a solid, responsive feel to it. The controls were balanced and harmonized. Just like the original model he remembered at Dreamland. The Chinese might be copycats, but they got this part right.

The bright rim of the sun was breaking the eastern horizon. In the gathering dawn, the shoreline of China stood out like a dark paint stroke against the grayness of the Taiwan Strait.

"Are we okay?" Mai-ling's voice sounded weak and far-away. It was the first time she had spoken since the takeoff.

"We're okay. You were right, by the way."

After a couple of seconds, "What was I right about?"

"The runway. It wasn't long enough."

"Next time you will believe me."

"Yes, ma'am."

He put the jet through a series of quick turns, then a rapid 360 degree roll to the left.

*Not bad.* As fighters went, the Black Star was definitely not a hotrod, but it had good subsonic performance. The turbofan engines lacked afterburners for augmented thrust. The radical, kitelike shape was designed for stealth, not speed.

Nonetheless, he was surprised. The Chinese Black Star seemed to be stable in all axes, even though it didn't have vertical fins. The elevons—surfaces in the trailing edge of each wing—provided pitch and roll control and extended downward to act as lift flaps for takeoff and landing. For directional stability, the tailless fighter was fitted with computer-driven control tabs—two on the top wing surface and two on the bottom.

He pulled the nose up, then rolled to the right.

"You're making me sick."

"Sorry. I need to know how this thing flies."

"Why? All you have to do is land it."

Maxwell didn't reply. Maybe that was all he had to do. Maybe more than that.

With that thought he lowered the UV goggles—the Chinese-developed helmet device that penetrated the Black Star's skin cloaking. They were over the strait now, flying what seemed to be a very flyable airplane. In the distance he could see the dark hump of Taiwan jutting from the horizon like the spine of a dinosaur.

The sky was empty. No other aircraft, friend or foe. Either one would kill them in an instant if they could see them. But they couldn't. The Black Star was invisible to all of them.

All except one.

"At what altitude did they report the target?"

"Unknown," said Yan from the backseat. "Central Command reports that they took off a little over ten minutes ago. They would be level at cruise altitude by now."

Zhang shook his head in frustration. It meant the stolen Dong-jin could be at any altitude from the surface to over fifteen thousand meters. It complicated the task, but did not render it impossible.

He was certain that the enemy pilot was surely heading for an air base in southern Taiwan. Probably Chai-Ei, which had lengthy runways.

But first they had to cross the Taiwan Strait.

Yan's voice came over the intercom. "Colonel, a course of two-three-five degrees should place us directly in their flight path. We can position ourselves in midstrait and set up a barrier orbit."

Zhang grunted his acknowledgment. He swung the Dong-jin's nose to the southwest, toward the middle of the strait. He and Yan would have to acquire the Dong-jin visually. The only way was using the special ultraviolet goggles developed in Zhang's lab at Chouzhou.

The Dong-jin's stealth masking technology used visual-spectrum light to mimic background scenes of varying intensities. It rendered the jet virtually invisible to the naked eye. But the masking did not extend into the ultraviolet spectrum, where it dramatically *increased* the radiance. Seen through the UV goggles, the Dong-jin stood out against the flat sea like a neon sign.

As he climbed into the dawn sky, Zhang considered how he would initiate his attack. When they were developing tactics for the new stealth fighter, they had not considered such a scenario. One Dong-jin engaging another in air-to-air combat had been unthinkable.

In such a fight, the Dong-jin's own onboard radar was useless. Even the deadly Archer missiles were of limited use, and in the rear quarter only. The Dong-jin was an awkward dogfighter, having traded agility for stealth. The absence of a vertical tail made it increasingly unstable at higher angles of attack.

The UV goggles were his ultimate advantage. With them he could see through the Dong-jin's veil.

A thought inserted itself into his brain. Had the thieves also taken the UV goggles? Probably not, he decided. The goggles were kept in a locked container in a separate, guarded room in the operations building, apart from the normal flight gear. Even if the commandos had broken into that particular room, it was unlikely that the foot soldiers would recognize the goggles for what they were.

He would attack from behind with the Archer missile, then follow up with a gun attack using the Dong-jin's 30 mm cannon. So far it had worked with astonishing success.

As he climbed into the morning sky, Zhang wondered again about the pilot of the stolen jet. Who was he? The Dong-jin was one of the most technologically complex aircraft ever built. How did he know enough to climb into it and fly it away?

Was he Taiwanese? Zhang doubted it. Chinese? Not likely. His pilots were all hand-picked for their ability and for their loyalty. Each knew with a certainty that his family would be tortured to death if they ever contemplated such a betrayal.

Who then? American?

Possibly. Only someone with knowledge of their own stealth jet technology would possess the skill to steal the

Dong-jin. Shooting down an American would be an even sweeter pleasure.

"Attach UV goggles," Zhang ordered.

"Already fixed and functioning, Colonel."

Zhang pulled his own goggles from the compartment in the side console. He had to fumble for half a minute before he could get them fixed to the attachment on the front of his helmet, then he activated the tiny battery pack.

Peering around, he saw that nothing much changed—except the view of his own jet. The Dong-jin's wings—the leading edge portion on either side, which was all he could see from the cockpit—were shimmering with a brilliant ghostlike radiance.

The goggles were working.

They were still climbing, going through ten thousand meters. In air-to-air combat, higher was better. Altitude translated to energy, which was life itself to a fighter pilot. And in the thin light of early morning, the stolen Dong-jin would contrast better with the gray-green surface of the sea below.

On his passive sensor display, Zhang detected a flight of four F-16s headed west. He ignored them. Down low he saw the silhouette of something, an old S-2 Tracker, he guessed. Probably hunting submarines. He ignored him, too. He had a more urgent target.

Five minutes elapsed. They were at the calculated intercept point.

No sign of the Dong-jin. Zhang's frustration was mounting. The whole war might hinge on finding the stolen stealth jet. The thought that he could miss the intercept crept into his mind. It was a hateful thought. He could already imagine the report he would have to make to General Tsin. *We were defeated, General, because we lost our Dong-jins. One destroyed by commandos, one stolen by—*

Yan saw it first. "Two o'clock low, Colonel. About ten kilometers."

Zhang swiveled his head. He had to squint, blink several times, refocus his eyes. Then he saw it too, ahead and to the right. A thousand meters beneath them, flying straight and level. A diamond-shaped object, shimmering like a wraith.

"How do I arm the weapons systems?"

"It depends," she answered. "What do you want to arm?"

"Everything. Heat seekers, the cannon, flare dispenser."

It occurred to him again how maddening this arrangement was—using the systems officer in the back to handle armament selection. Especially an untrained systems officer like Mai-ling.

"I handle the flares from my console back here. You can select the air-to-air missile stations and the cannon on your number three display, the one on the right. I have my own armament display back here."

But this time, without the pressure of an armored personnel carrier bearing down on him, the display was making more sense. Yes, there it was. An icon in the shape of a gun. Not much doubt about that one.

He touched it. The icon blinked twice, then changed color.

Two other icons were in the shape of missiles. One, he guessed, would be a heat-seeker, probably an AA-11 Archer. The other appeared to be radar guided. Probably an AA-10. He selected the heater.

Mai-ling explained how to uncage the Archer missile's heat-seeking head and cause it to track a target. She was just getting into the radar-guided launch sequence when she abruptly stopped. "Oh, shit."

"Oh shit what?"

"Are you wearing your goggles?"

"Yes." He didn't tell her he had been wearing them since shortly after takeoff.

"We have company. High, angling in from the left toward our tail."

Maxwell peered through the goggles, looking for the incoming fighter. "I don't have him. Where is he?"

"Coming toward us, curving in from the left."

He rolled the Black Star into a hard left turn.

"It's the Dong-jin, Brick!" Mai-ling's voice had gained an octave.

"The what?"

"The other Black Star. It's Colonel Zhang, and he sees us."

He was still having trouble with the goggles. *Damn these things.* It was like peering through binoculars. When he moved his head, he would lose focus in one or the other eye.

Ninety degrees into the turn, he saw it. In the purplish glow of the UV goggles, it looked like a kite. A glistening, diamond-shaped kite. The kite was in a classic pursuit curve, arcing toward their tail.

Setting up for a—*what?*

Mai-ling's excited call told him. "Missile in the air!"

Maxwell saw it track and pull lead. It had to be a heat-seeker. Their Black Star was invisible to radar.

He broke left, into the missile. "Flares. Dispense flares now!"

This was nuts, depending on someone in the backseat to actuate the infrared decoys that would save their lives.

"They're out. Flares are dispensing." Her words spewed over the intercom like a sped-up audiotape.

Maxwell didn't know how tightly he could turn the Black Star. How many Gs would the jet take before it stalled? Did the flight control computer limit the G pull to prevent a stall?

He pulled harder, tightening the turn into the oncoming missile. At seven Gs he felt the jet shudder, and eased off on the stick. *Okay, now you know.* The flight control computer didn't care whether he stalled or not. But he couldn't turn tightly enough to defeat an Archer missile.

He wondered vaguely what sort of seeker head the missile had. How could it be tracking a stealth jet that emitted almost no IR signature? He remembered taking a Sidewinder shot at the Black Star that came after the Chameleon decoy. The Sidewinder lost its lock because it couldn't find enough IR signal.

A second later, he had an answer. "The missile's lost tracking," said Mai-ling. "It's going ballistic."

*Their missiles don't track stealth jets any better than ours.*

Maxwell saw that his break turn had also spoiled the other Black Star's pursuit curve. The ChiCom pilot was going wide to the right, in a flight path overshoot. Now they were even.

Good. He pulled the nose up, further aggravating his opponent's overshoot. *Fight's on, Colonel.*

# CHAPTER TWENTY-THREE

# THE MOST
# PRIMITIVE WEAPON

*Taiwan Strait*
*0648, Monday, 15 September*

Zhang was getting an uneasy feeling. Instead of a quick kill, a missile shot backed up by a guns pass, he was now neutral in a one-versus-one turning fight.

As if the pilot of the other Dong-jin had been expecting him. Waiting for him.

"He's reversing, Colonel. He's in a right—"

"Shut up," snapped Zhang. "I see him."

It had to be a *gwai-lo*—a Caucasian foreigner. An American *gwai-lo*, probably. *Wearing my UV goggles.* The *gwai-lo*'s use of vertical tactics was eerily reminiscent of the F/A-18 pilot who had tricked him into shooting the decoy drone. The one who nearly killed him.

He saw the enemy Dong-jin's nose come up, reversing the turn hard to the right.

He kept his own left turn in, and pulled harder, underneath the opposing Dong-jin. Toward the *gwai-lo*'s six o'clock. As the enemy crossed over the top, Zhang rolled wings-level and pulled up, trying to gain angular advantage behind him. He continued to roll, racking the Dong-jin into a hard right turn.

The enemy countered, going up and making a hard left turn back into him.

*Gwai-lo bastard.* They were now in a flat scissors, a level turning fight, crossing nose-to-nose, then reversing to cross again, each trying to work himself inside the other's turn. From such an engagement, there was no escape. If either combatant tried to turn and run, the other would have an easy shot.

Zhang cursed himself for losing his initial advantage. The enemy pilot had surprised him with his initial break turn. He hadn't counted on their having the UV goggles. Firing the Archer missile had been a mistake. It would only have scored a kill if the American—he was now sure that it *was* an American—had continued on his course. The Archer's heat-seeker head was unable to track the faint IR signal of the Dong-jin in a maximum-performance turn.

He should have used the cannon. Zhang's favorite killing tool was the cannon. It was the most primitive, most visceral of aerial weapons. And the surest. The nose-mounted 30 mm gun in the Dong-jin gave no warning, required no special technology. Deadly and efficient. All he had to do was position himself behind the enemy fighter.

Which was proving to be more of a problem than he anticipated.

Another reversal. Zhang still held a slight angular advantage, but the enemy was gaining an advantage in altitude. Impossible! The *gwai-lo* was outflying him.

Again the enemy Dong-jin passed over his nose. Zhang rolled with him, nudging the nose upward, trying to get the *gwai-lo* centered in his HUD.

For an instant, barely a heartbeat, he had a shot. He

squeezed the trigger, felt the gut-pleasing, staccato machine gun chatter resonate through the airframe of the Dong-jin. He saw the tracers arc through the void between him and the enemy jet.

And miss. The tracers were falling behind and beneath the enemy.

A split-second later, Zhang felt his jet buffeting, trying to stall and drop from beneath him. He relaxed pressure on the stick, lowering the nose, letting the diamond-shaped wing regain stable flight. *Another mistake.*

Again the two fighters swept past each other. They were so close Zhang could see the enemy pilot peering at him through the top of the canopy. *Who was he?* Zhang wondered again. *Where did he learn to fly the Dong-jin?* Zhang could almost feel a grudging admiration for his boldness. Almost.

The missed shot and the near stall had cost him more advantage. Now they were even in the scissors, crossing nearly canopy to canopy. He resisted the urge to yank the stick again, try for another shot—and stall out in the process. The *gwai-lo* had maintained his altitude advantage.

*Be patient,* Zhang ordered himself. *Wait for him make a mistake. He doesn't know this airplane. You do.*

He reminded himself that he had already scored thirteen air-to-air kills with the Dong-jin. Fourteen, if he counted the lumbering Airbus carrying the Taiwanese President. That made him, Col. Zhang Yu, the top scoring fighter ace in the world at the moment.

The thought made him almost giddy. It was appropriate— no, *inevitable*—that the pilot of the stolen Dong-jin be added to Zhang's list of victories. Kill number fifteen. He would be a triple ace.

The scissors fight had depleted the airspeed of both jets. With each turn now, they were bleeding off altitude. The duel was taking them southward, down the middle of the strait. Away from the coast of Taiwan. Away from the coast of China.

"We will be fuel critical in a few minutes, Colonel," said Yan in the backseat. "We have to turn back to Chouzhou."

Zhang glanced at the fuel counter. Yan was correct. The lower altitude and the need for maximum thrust were depleting their fuel at a horrific rate.

But turning back was not an option.

"Colonel, I repeat. Our fuel is low. We have to—"

"I heard you. We have to destroy the other Dong-jin first. We will choose a field on the coast that is nearer our position. Keep a continuous radius of action for our fuel state."

"Yes, sir."

The two fighters were in a stalemate. Zhang knew that in the end it would be fuel—and the distance to a safe landing—that would determine the outcome. He was not willing to forfeit the last flyable Dong-jin because he exhausted his fuel in a fight with a damned *gwai-lo* bandit. The Dong-jin was too precious to lose.

But the worst of all outcomes would be if the *gwai-lo* got away in the stolen Dong-jin. That could not be permitted.

Zhang would have to gamble.

"This looks bad, Brick. We're getting farther and farther away from Taiwan."

"Tell me something I don't know."

"We're running out of fuel. Eleven hundred kilos."

"I know that too. I've got a fuel counter."

"What are you going to do?"

"I'm open to suggestions."

She didn't have any. Maxwell returned his attention to the fight with the Black Star.

As a fighter pilot, he hated this—sloshing through descending scissors turns, trading off energy and altitude in order to maintain turning speed. For all its effectiveness as a stealth aircraft, the Black Star was not intended to be an air combat maneuvering fighter. If he were in a Super Hornet, he'd be in full afterburner, going vertical on this guy. This reminded him of fighting in the old A-4 Skyhawk.

They were consuming fuel at a greater rate than he expected. In a matter of minutes he would be too low on fuel to make Chingchuankang or Chai-Ei or even Kaohsiung, near the southern tip of Taiwan. They would be forced to eject over the water—a prospect that filled him with gloom.

He shoved the thought from his mind. The middle of a one-vee-one was the wrong time to worry about ejecting. *Think, Maxwell. Beat this guy before he runs you out of gas.*

The basic rule in a turning fight was to get inside your opponent's turn. When you had an angle on him, you had a shot. If you and your opponent were evenly matched, neither gaining angles, you turned with him, waiting for him to make a mistake.

The ChiCom pilot—Colonel Zhang, according to Mailing—hadn't made any more mistakes since he'd taken the gun shot after the first turn. But he had been airborne longer than Maxwell, and that was working against him. He had to be sweating his own fuel.

Their noses crossed again, passing within a hundred yards. Maxwell saw Zhang's uptilted helmet, peering at him through his own UV goggles. Maxwell had a slight advantage in altitude. It might be decisive. It all depended on how he played it.

*Put yourself in Zhang's cockpit. What is he thinking now? He's low on fuel. He knows he can't bug out without being killed. He'll make another mistake. He's going to do something desperate.*

*What?*

"Colonel, we have to disengage." Yan's voice was emphatic. "We barely have enough fuel to make land."

Zhang was silent for a moment. They had fought long enough that the *gwai-lo* would also be fuel critical. "How much fuel does the enemy have?"

"Not enough to land in Taiwan. He has to go almost twice the distance that we have. We have forced him to lose the Dong-jin, Colonel. Now we must disengage."

Zhang didn't bother telling Yan that they *couldn't* disengage—not without giving the *gwai-lo* bastard a shot at them.

Still turning in the scissors, he glanced inside the cockpit to see the altimeter unwind through three thousand meters. He looked out again as the enemy scissored back across. The *gwai-lo* was gaining altitude, gaining advantage. If this continued, Zhang would be the first to run out of altitude as well as fuel.

He had to break the stalemate and run for it. He needed an opening.

*He's getting desperate,* thought Maxwell. *Throw him some bait.*

In a few minutes they would be at sea level. No more turning fight. They would either both go into the water or one would get a shot at the other.

*Give him an out. See if he goes for it.*

They approached again, nose to nose, Maxwell on the high side. Instead of reversing his turn, Maxwell rolled into a steep right bank, as if he were trying to ram Zhang's Black Star.

But he didn't pull hard. He rocked the wings, making it appear as though the jet were buffeting under the excessive G load. *Would he go for it?*

Zhang rolled into a steep left bank and pulled hard to escape the collision. Then he kept pulling, nose down, diving for airspeed.

Headed for China.

*He's going for it.*

Maxwell continued the right-hand roll, following the Black Star around and underneath. He rolled out directly behind, his nose buried low. Too low for a gun shot. But he'd have a missile shot in a couple of seconds.

He pulled hard on the stick. His eyes were locked on the fleeing Black Star. "Select heat missiles," he ordered.

"What?" Mai-ling answered.

"Heat missiles. I'm in guns right now."

"I thought you were trying to shoot him with the gun."

"We're out of range. I need heat missiles."

"I don't understand. He's right there. Why don't you shoot him?"

*Damn.* He longed for the *HOTAS*—hands on throttles and stick—design of American fighters. That was one thing the Chinese hadn't figured out how to copy. He also wished he had a real systems officer in the backseat.

He took his eyes off the Black Star long enough to find the icon on the armament screen. He touched it, saw it blink obediently and change color. He felt a slight rumble in the airframe as the bay door opened. The Archer missile was exposed, ready to fire.

*Finally.*

Peering through the HUD, he superimposed the seeker circle over Zhang's jet and uncaged it. The missile chirped in his headset, signaling target acquisition.

He squeezed the trigger.

*Whoom!* The missile was noisier than the American-built Sidewinder, he noted, watching the heat-seeker roar ahead of the jet. And a hell of a lot faster.

Zhang sensed the danger and broke right. A trail of decoying flares spewed in his wake. The Archer missile lost its lock on the stealth jet and exploded harmlessly into the trailing flares.

Zhang continued pulling hard in a right turn, trying to force Maxwell into an overshoot.

Instead of following, Maxwell rolled out, taking his nose off the Black Star, lagging the turning stealth fighter, opening up the angle between them. The changed geometry would quickly put him in position to fire another Archer. Unless Zhang—

*Went up.*

Yes, damn it, that's what he was doing. The Black Star's nose was pitching upward, going vertical. Maxwell had to give the guy credit. It was a desperate move, but a smart one.

Maxwell had no choice except to match the vertical pull. He hauled the nose of his Black Star up, grunting against the G load, countering Zhang's move. He had both an airspeed and an angular advantage, but he knew Zhang was betting that he would overshoot the top of the vertical cross.

*Guns.* He needed the cannon for a raking gun shot when they merged at the top.

"Switch to guns on the armament panel," he ordered on the intercom. He almost said please, but caught himself.

There was no argument this time. A second later, he saw a gun sight appear in his HUD. The cannon was armed, ready to fire. "Thank you," he said.

The airspeed was diminishing rapidly. The Black Star was definitely *not* an optimum air-to-air fighter. It turned and climbed like a pig.

Opposite him, on the other side of the vertical circle, Zhang was pulling toward him, trying to cut him off, trading airspeed for angles, going for the first guns shot.

Approaching the apogee of the vertical maneuver, Maxwell pulled, eking the last bit of energy from the nearly stalled jet. He felt a shudder—*there it is*—and eased off on the stick pressure. He didn't know how slow the Black Star could fly before it departed from controlled flight, but he was close.

Through the top of the canopy he saw the diamond profile of Zhang's jet. He was cranking hard toward him, pulling for his own firing solution. Zhang's nose was almost in the firing cone, almost pointed at Maxwell's fighter.

Maxwell saw a pulsing strobe from the enemy Black Star. He felt a stab of fear. *The cannon.* Tracers streamed upward, arcing wide.

Missing, arcing below him. Zhang didn't yet have the angle.

Another mistake.

*Turn,* Maxwell implored his own sluggish fighter. *Get inside his turn.* He was already pulling maximum Gs, willing the nose of his own Black Star to knife inside Zhang's turn. Both jets were nearly stalled, about to drop out of the sky like flightless birds.

Almost. Another ten degrees of deflection.

*Now.*

The image of Zhang's Black Star appeared in his HUD. It would be a snap shot, nothing more. He squeezed the trigger.

The hammering of the single-barrel cannon rattled the airframe, coming up through his seat, through the stick in his hand.

He kept the trigger depressed. The tracers arced forward, streaming thirty feet in front of the Black Star.

He nudged the right rudder pedal, walking the tracers toward Zhang's jet.

He felt the Black Star shudder, trying to drop from beneath him. *Don't stall, don't lose it.* If he let the Black Star depart—stall and go out of control—Zhang would pounce like a hunting animal. The fight would be over in seconds.

He nudged the right rudder pedal some more, working his stream of cannon fire toward the center of the diamond-shaped jet. The tracers had a slow, lazy appearance, like the stream of a squirt gun.

They found the top of Zhang's wing. Black puffs of debris—shattered metal, composite material, fuel—streamed behind the jet.

The range was less than five hundred yards and closing. Maxwell could see two helmeted, goggled figures in the cockpit staring back at him as the tracers ate into them. The image lasted less than a second.

Zhang's Black Star exploded.

Maxwell kicked in left rudder to avoid the fireball.

"You got him!" yelped Mai-ling. "He's going down—*Oh, damn!*"

The Black Star pivoted on its left wingtip and cartwheeled out of control. The gray surface of the Taiwan Strait blurred across Maxwell's windshield, then the pink and blue morning sky. The jet's nose rose level while it rotated around the horizon, then plunged again.

A classic departure. The Black Star's nose yawed to the left, bobbing down, then back up in a flat spin. Maxwell fought the jet, trying to regain stability. He pulled the throttles back and shoved the stick forward.

His test pilot training kicked in. *Abrupt departure with adverse stall characteristics. Apply recovery inputs. Unload the wing.*

It wasn't working. The jet continued to spin.

*Counter the yaw. Regain stable flight.* He shoved in the right rudder pedal, trying to stop the hard left rotation of the nose.

That didn't work either. The Black Star was still out of control. Pitching up and down like a deranged mule. *Highly oscillatory departure characteristics. Another undesirable attribute.*

"Stop it, Brick. I don't like this."

"I'm working on it."

He glimpsed the altimeter readout clicking through two thousand meters. *Now what, smart guy?* It was crunch time.

Recover or eject. He had done all the right things. How the hell did you stop autorotation in a jet without a tail?

An old test pilot's technique came to mind. *When everything else fails, turn loose.*

He released his tight grip on the stick, putting it in a neutral position. He removed his feet from the rudder pedals.

The whirling fighter continued to spin. One more violent revolution. Another. *Time to go.* Maxwell reached for the mike button to order Mai-ling to eject.

Abruptly, the jet stopped spinning. In a forty-five degree nose-down attitude, the fighter's wings were level. Flying again.

The altimeter readout was winding through a thousand meters—about three thousand feet. The airspeed indication was increasing, going through 250 kilometers per hour.

Gently, so as not to initiate another departure, Maxwell nudged the stick back and advanced the throttles. The Black Star's nose lifted back to level flight. The altimeter bottomed out at 200 meters. He could see the white streaks on the wave tops.

"What was that all about?" Mai-ling asked. Her voice sounded tiny.

"Just a spin." *A loss of control that nearly dumped us in the ocean.*

"I'm going to barf."

"Not allowed. No barfing on this jet."

Over his shoulder Maxwell saw the debris field of the destroyed Black Star. Pieces were falling like black confetti toward the sea. The oily gray cloud was already dissipating in the atmosphere.

"Is Zhang dead?" she asked.

"I didn't see any chutes."

A moment of silence. "I'm glad."

Maxwell didn't need to ask why she was glad. The coldness in her voice told him.

He had a more urgent concern. The fuel quantity indicator was showing less than 700 kilos. For the Black Star's two thirsty engines, that translated to twenty minutes' flying time.

"What's our distance to Chingchuankang?"

She studied her navigation display for several seconds. "Over four hundred kilometers."

"No good. How about Kaohsiung?" Kaohsiung was a base on the southwestern coast of Taiwan.

"Still too far, more than three hundred."

"Chai-Ei?"

"We won't make it to any field on Taiwan."

He watched the descending debris from the destroyed Black Star. Against all odds they had stolen a stealth jet from China. If they hadn't been engaged in the fight with Zhang, they would have made it.

She seemed to be reading his thoughts. "Where are we going to land, Brick?"

He didn't answer. Manila was too far. So were Hanoi and Camranh Bay. Landing anywhere in China and handing the Black Star back to its former owners was out of the question.

There were no available landing sites anywhere within their range. Except one.

# CHAPTER TWENTY-FOUR

# BARRICADE

*USS* Ronald Reagan
*South China Sea*
*0705, Monday, 15 September*

Boyce must have heard wrong. He *had* to have heard wrong.

He removed the cigar from his mouth and said, "Excuse me, but I'll swear I heard you say 'No way.'"

"You heard right," said Sticks Stickney, skipper of the *Reagan*. "No way is that thing coming aboard my ship. Not without a tailhook and a direct order from the Battle Group Commander."

Boyce's eyes bulged. He fought back the urge to seize Stickney by the collar and shake him till his beady little eyes crossed. Stickney was a good carrier skipper, but he was also a hardnosed, head-up-his-ass military bureaucrat.

They were standing on the flag bridge. They'd just gotten radio contact with Maxwell in the captured stealth jet. He was nearly out of fuel and he needed a ready deck. He'd be overhead the *Reagan* in five minutes.

To hell with Stickney. Boyce swung his attention to Admiral Hightree, sitting in his padded leather chair. "Sir,

Sticks is missing the point here. We can't afford to lose this jet. Not to mention my best squadron skipper when he punches out with that rinky-dink Chinese ejection seat."

Hightree looked uncomfortable. Both Stickney, as the carrier captain, and Boyce, who commanded the carrier's air wing, reported to him. The two officers were equal in rank and responsibility. "It's Sticks's ship," said Hightree. "If he thinks it too great a risk to—"

"Risk?" Boyce said. He knew was exceeding the limits of protocol, but—damn it!—these two weren't getting it. "With all due respect, Admiral, we just took the mother of all risks when we sent Maxwell in there to grab that thing. Now he's sitting on the biggest intelligence coup of the decade, and Sticks here wants to dump it in the ocean."

"Knock it off, Red," said Stickney. "What I want is to *not* blow up everything on my flight deck with that flying bomb. We'd have to rig the barricade, and there's no data, no way of knowing what will happen when it engages the net. It could slice right on through. It could explode on my deck. It could swerve up forward and take out airplanes and people."

Hightree frowned, seeming to agree with Stickney. Boyce had to admit that Stickney had a valid argument. The barricade—a wall of nylon webbing that could be stretched across the landing deck—was intended to snag carrier-based jets that couldn't trap in the arresting wires with their tailhooks. No one knew what would happen when the Black Star slammed down on the *Reagan*'s deck. It might stop. Or it might slice through the nylon like a sword through butter.

*What the hell,* thought Boyce. This was war—or the next thing to it. You had to take chances.

He glanced from one to the other, gnawing on his cigar, trying to hold down his anger. Jack Hightree was a competent flag officer, but he was new to battle group command. He wasn't a risk taker. He had earned his two stars by taking a cautious, noncontroversial career path.

Stickney, who had his sights on a star of his own, was following Hightree's example.

"All right, gentlemen," said Boyce. He made a show of glancing at his watch. "Five minutes. That's what we've got. Then Maxwell and his systems officer punch out. After that, we can start writing the reports."

"What reports?" said Stickney, narrowing his eyes.

"About why we let the weapon that was winning the war for China wind up on the bottom of the ocean. About why we were so concerned with saving our asses that we sacrificed the lives of the two heroes in that jet. Right or wrong, we're going to be judged by what we decide in the next five minutes."

Stickney wasn't buying it. "Don't pull that crap on me, Red. I'm willing to answer for my decisions. You know Admiral Hightree is, too."

Boyce nodded. He could tell he'd touched a nerve.

He pressed harder. "Look, gentlemen, the Black Star is the most critical piece of technology to come out of China. We need to know how they got it, what they're doing with it, how they've improved on it. That's priceless intelligence that we'll lose if we give up on that jet."

Hightree was giving him a dubious look, like a gambler eyeing a card shark. "That's easy for you to say, Red. It's not your ship."

"It's my pilot, and I'm the guy who sent him on this mission. If he gets out of this alive, I want to look him in the eye and tell him I did everything I could to back him up."

Hightree kept his eyes riveted on Boyce for several more seconds. Abruptly, he rose and walked to the bulkhead. He stood there for half a minute, peering through the thick glass. Down below, tugs were hauling jets across the sprawling flight deck. In the distance, spread out in formation, were the ships of Hightree's battle group.

He turned back to the two officers. His face had taken a hard, determined set. "How long to rig the barricade?"

Stickney looked surprised. "How long? Uh, the last drill, the deck crew put it up in less than ten minutes."

"Tell them they've got five," said Hightree. "Let's move, Sticks. We're gonna recover that thing."

"Now what are you doing?" she asked from the backseat.

"Seeing how slow we can fly." Maxwell shoved the throttles up and lowered the nose, recovering from the Black Star's low speed buffet. "Okay, that's minimum. No slower."

The digital airspeed readout indicated 324 kilometers per hour—175 knots. That was as slow as he could fly the Black Star without stalling. Over forty knots faster than a Super Hornet's carrier landing speed.

Too damned fast to be coming aboard ship.

*So what? What's your alternative?*

Only one, and he didn't want to think about it. Ejecting from the Black Star was a lousy option.

"We're almost out of fuel, Brick. Four hundred kilos remaining."

"I know." He had already done the math. Four hundred kilos equaled eight hundred eighty pounds. Ten minutes flying time. Maybe more, maybe less. He had no faith in Chinese quantity-measurement technology.

A familiar voice crackled over the radio. "Runner One-one, do you read Battle-Ax?"

"Battle-Ax" was CAG Boyce's radio call sign. Maxwell, as skipper of the VFA-36 Roadrunners, was "Runner One-one."

"Loud and clear, Battle-Ax. Nice to hear your voice."

"You too. Here's the deal. Mother is rigging the barricade as we speak. You've got four minutes to a ready deck. What's your fuel state?"

"Ten minutes. Maybe less."

Several seconds passed. He knew that Boyce was conferring with the captain or the air boss. "That ain't good," said Boyce. "You only get one shot at the deck."

"Okay. Who's waving?"

Another voice broke onto the frequency. "The best damn LSO in the fleet, Skipper. It's me, Pearly."

Maxwell had to smile. Pearly Gates was one of his squadron pilots. In Maxwell's opinion, Pearly was probably correct: He *was* the best damn landing signal officer in the game.

He had his work cut out for him today. *One shot at the deck*. It was a joke. How did you land on a carrier in a jet that you've never landed before? In a jet that wasn't designed to land aboard a carrier?

The answer was . . . *Very carefully*.

He could visualize the flurry of activity on the *Reagan*'s deck. Crewmen were working like ants to erect the wall of nylon webbing across the landing deck.

The barricade was, by definition, a dangerous and undesirable way to land jets aboard ship. The landing signal officer would monitor the jet's approach to the deck, just as he did with every normal pass. But as the jet neared the ramp— the blunt, unforgiving back end of the ship—he would order the pilot to cut the throttle. What happened after that was irrevocable. No turn back, no go around. The jet would plop onto the deck and plunge into the barricade.

The nylon straps of the barricade, as Maxwell knew, were intended to grab the protruding surfaces of a conventional fighter—external fuel tanks, probes, racks, empennage— wrapping around the jet like a spiderweb.

The Black Star didn't have protruding surfaces. The fighter's airframe was as slick as a razor blade.

Maxwell disabled the Black Star's airframe cloaking.

"Runner One-one, this is CATCC, we've got you on radar

now, fifteen miles, three thousand feet." CATCC was the *Reagan*'s carrier air traffic control center. "Take heading one-nine-five degrees, descend to twelve hundred feet. Acknowledge."

"Runner is turning to one-nine-five, down to twelve hundred."

"Runner One-one, we show you doing one hundred eighty knots. Is that your best approach speed?"

"I'll give you one seventy-five. That's as slow as it gets."

Several seconds of silence. Maxwell knew that another worried conference was going on between the senior officers on the *Reagan*. *How are we going to trap something going that goddamn fast?*

"Roger, Runner One-one. Here are your instructions. If you wave off, climb straight ahead to at least three miles past mother. Five thousand feet if you can, then you will eject. Do you copy that?"

"Runner copies."

Not much doubt about that one. One pass, that's all. They didn't want him taking it around and then flaming out on short final to the boat.

"Runner One-one, turn one-zero-five degrees. You're on a ten mile final."

Maxwell turned to the new heading. As he rolled out, he saw the dark shape ahead—the craggy, irregular shape of the carrier. Behind it glistened a wake, trailing the ship like a white trace marker.

"Two hundred kilos remaining," said Mai-ling. "Are we going to make it?"

"I don't know. If we flame out, don't wait for instructions. Grab the handle and eject."

"What about you?"

"I'll be right behind you." Maxwell didn't know how good the Chinese ejection seats were. He didn't know if the canopy departed first, or they punched through it.

He forced his thoughts back to the approach. *Compartmentalize*. It was what naval aviators were taught to do. Think about the problem at hand.

"Runner One-one, this is Paddles," Pearly radioed from the LSO platform. "Call the ball."

Maxwell acknowledged. The ship was swelling in his windscreen. At 1,200 feet altitude, he was supposed to pick up the *ball*—the optical glide path indicator mounted at the left deck edge—about half a mile from the ship.

The deck of the *Reagan* was coming into view. He adjusted the Black Star's heading to line up with the landing deck center line.

He saw a glimmering, a yellow pinpoint of light at the left deck edge.

The ball.

"Runner One-one, ball."

"Roger ball," answered Pearly Gates. "I've got you, Runner."

He nudged the throttles back, starting the Black Star down the glide path to the deck. The trick was to keep the ball in the center of the Fresnel lens—the optical signboard mounted on the deck. On either side of the lens was a row of green datum lights, marking the center, or optimum glide path. The idea was to fly the jet so as to keep the ball between the two rows of green lights.

The ball was going above the datums.

"*Do-on't* go high," said Pearly, using his best LSO sugar talk.

Maxwell squeezed off a touch of power. The ball settled back between the datums.

His hand felt moist, and he made himself relax the death grip he had on the stick. At approach speed, the Black Star's controls felt sloppy, not crisp and responsive like the Super Hornet. It felt as if he was wallowing around on a high sea.

The ball was going low.

"*Pow-werrrr,*" called Pearly in a soothing voice.

Maxwell nudged the throttles forward. He could feel his pulse racing. *Settle down. Be smooth.*

The ball wouldn't stay in the center. As the ship swelled in the windshield, Maxwell wrestled with the Black Star, willing it onto the glide path. Sweat trickled from beneath his helmet. *Easy with it.* If he went low, he risked crashing into the ramp. High and he'd catch the top of the barricade with his landing gear.

*Fly the ball.* The ramp of the carrier was rushing toward him, sweeping beneath the Black Star's long pointed nose. The ball was still moving, up, down, Maxwell's hands stroking the throttle, nudging the stick, adjusting the jet's flight path. More sweat streamed from his helmet, stinging his eyes.

He blinked, focusing on the moving ball.

He was fast. Too fast. The great gray mass of the ship was swelling in his windshield at a faster rate than he'd ever seen.

"Cut, Cut, Cut!" called Pearly Gates. It was the command to chop the throttles. Pearly's job was finished.

Maxwell snatched both throttles back to idle. He felt the Black Star drop toward the steel deck of the USS *Ronald Reagan*.

*Holy shit.*

Boyce was astonished. How the hell could a shape as weird as that fly? Even with its cloaking sheath deactivated, the Black Star looked like something out of *Star Wars*.

Stickney, standing beside him on the bridge, must have had the same impression. Boyce heard him suck in a lungful of air, then hold it.

The deck was nearly empty of personnel. Every nonessential crewman on the flight deck and in the tiers of the carrier's superstructure had been ordered belowdecks.

The few who would see the mysterious jet descending toward the *Reagan*—the LSO, a handful of watch personnel on the bridge, even Sticks Stickney, the ship's captain—would be sworn to secrecy.

They watched the Black Star sweep over the ramp.

Stretched across the landing deck, the barricade was fluttering like a ribbon in the thirty-knot wind. Boyce was suddenly filled with doubt. The Black Star was moving at an impossibly fast speed.

It looked like a hatchet blade. *It's not going to stop.*

The diamond-shaped jet slammed down on the deck. Something black—Boyce guessed it was rubber from one of the main tires—shot out from under the wings. The nose gear came down hard, compressing the long, skinny strut. Boyce winced. He expected to see the strut snap, the jet collapsing and breaking apart.

It didn't. It continued hurtling down the short deck, trailing hunks of rubber, traveling faster than Boyce had ever seen an airplane move on a carrier deck.

The jet plunged into the nylon webbing. And kept plunging straight ahead.

"Oh, shit," Boyce heard someone say. The wedge-shaped nose of the jet was knifing through the webbing like a scimitar.

Through the thick glass on the bridge, he couldn't hear the sound of the straps snapping and flailing the air. They were slicing backward along the sharp leading edges, breaking away like rubber bands.

"There it goes," muttered Stickney. The nylon net was near its limit, stretching in a tight V-shape toward the end of the angled deck.

The jet was still careening ahead. Involuntarily Boyce glanced at the end of the deck. Beyond it waited a sixty-foot drop to the sea.

A strap grabbed the nose gear strut. More straps wrapped around the main gear.

The Black Star lurched like a tethered beast. Its nose protruded through the webbing, clawing its way to the open sea beyond. The jet was slowing . . . slower . . . not slow enough.

The nose gear rolled over the edge of the deck.

And stopped.

With its long nose and cockpit extending out over the open sea, the Black Star hovered like a praying mantis over the deck edge. Behind it trailed a web of torn and stretched and snapped nylon.

Stickney sucked in his first breath since the Black Star appeared behind the *Reagan*'s ramp. Boyce jabbed him with an elbow. "You see that, Sticks? I told you it was a piece of cake."

# CHAPTER TWENTY-FIVE

# ZAIJIAN

*USS* Ronald Reagan
*Taiwan Strait*
*1035, Monday, 15 September*

Alone, finally.

The two-hour debriefing was over. There would be more later, but Boyce had intervened by declaring a temporary moratorium on stupid intelligence officer questions.

The Black Star had been wrapped in a shroud and hustled down an elevator to a sealed compartment off the hangar deck. The few personnel who had seen the mysterious jet land aboard the *Reagan* had been ordered down to the SCIF—Special Compartmentalized Intelligence Facility—where an intelligence officer gave them dire warnings about the penalties of disclosure and had each crewman sign a declaration of understanding.

Maxwell walked Mai-ling to her assigned stateroom. Neither spoke as they navigated the labyrinthine passageways, down the ladder to the O-3 deck, through a score of knee-knockers.

As he stepped over the knee-knockers, he recognized the old familiar numbness that clung to him. It was the product of a nonstop adrenaline rush, the sweet satisfaction of a mission accomplished, a bone-deep fatigue from lack of sleep.

They located Mai-ling's stateroom, on the forward deck. She let them in and closed the door. It was a junior officer's room, with two bunk beds and two steel desk-cabinets.

She peered up at him. "You may kiss me now."

"Excuse me?"

"I saw the way you were looking at me. Go on, admit it. You've been wanting to do it for the past two hours."

"Okay, I admit it." He did exactly as she ordered. He tilted her chin up and kissed her.

It was just like the first time back at Chingchuankang—tentative, polite, barely touching her lips. Then she pressed herself to him. Her arms went around his neck, kissing him back with an energy and passion that took him by surprise.

A wave of conflicting emotions washed over him. Chen Mai-ling clearly possessed every essential quality a woman ought to have. Even through the coarse ninja suit he could feel the tight, slender body and firm breasts pressed against his chest. She had loosened her tied-back black hair, letting it flow in a cascade over her collar.

There was more. She possessed a keen, high-spirited intelligence. She was undeniably brave. Mai-ling would be easy to love.

*Why not?*

Good question. Why was he even asking the question? What was holding him back?

Fatigue, for one thing. And something else. Something from another part of his life that he hadn't let go. Not yet, anyway.

He looked at her. "We're getting very close to a breach of Navy discipline."

"What kind of breach is that?"

"Intimate relations while aboard a naval vessel."

"I'm not in the Navy."

"Good point. But I am, at least for the moment. As a squadron skipper I'm supposed to discourage this sort of activity."

"Does that mean we shouldn't make love?"

"It means another place, another time."

She was quiet for a moment. "Another life, you mean?"

He didn't answer. In the silence that passed between them, he sensed a chasm opening. He continued holding her. Nearly a minute passed while neither spoke.

He knew he couldn't trust his feelings now. The past twelve hours had produced a special intimacy between them. More than intimacy. Passion for sure. Was it more than that?

She seemed to be reading his thoughts. Without lifting her head from his chest, she said, "What will happen to us, Brick?"

"What do you want to happen?"

"The usual things. I want us to be happy."

"What would it take to make you happy?"

She thought for a moment. "To find a place where I belong. With someone I love and trust." She took his hands in hers. "I don't know where that is. Or with whom. But my Chinese woman's intuition is talking to me."

"What is it telling you?"

"That you, Sam Maxwell, are not truly free. That your heart belongs to someone else." She looked up at him. "Am I close?"

He nodded. Maybe it was true about Chinese women. He had never told her about Claire or any of the secret things that had dwelled in his heart.

She lapsed into a silence. Finally she said, "What will they do with me?"

"Swear you to secrecy. What happened never really happened. The jet will go to the United States somewhere, and they'll take it apart to see how much the PLA has learned about stealth technology."

"And you?"

"I'll resume my job as commanding officer of VFA-36, here aboard the *Reagan*."

She thought for a moment. "Then I will return to Taiwan. It's a place where I'm needed, at least until the war is ended. Then maybe I can go to the United States. I'm still a scientist. Perhaps I can be useful."

He nodded. "You're brilliant—as well as gorgeous."

She looked at him. "You're my hero. I will always love you because you saved my life."

There it was. They both knew it. Another place, other circumstances, another life—it would be easy. But, not here, not now. They were ships on different courses, to different destinations.

They stood with their arms around each other. She looked up at him with large, somber eyes. He saw tears forming.

"*Zaijian,* Brick." She kissed her finger, touched it to his lips. "Live well."

"*Zaijian,* Mai-ling. You too."

A laundered set of khakis was hanging inside the door. Fresh towels lay on the steel cabinet. His stateroom had been unoccupied for the past three days while he was chasing the Black Star.

He dropped into the chair at the desk and powered up the notebook computer. While he waited, his eyes wandered to the photograph on his desk.

He and Claire on the Harley. They were smiling for all the world as if they were a couple in love. Which, once upon a time, they had been.

The computer booted up. The Mail Waiting icon was flashing.

He retrieved his backlog of mail—thirty-two messages,

mostly junk mail, jokes forwarded to mailing lists, newsletters he never intended to read. There were several notes from old buddies in the fleet. A couple from his father wondering how he was doing.

Nothing else.

A feeling of gloom settled over him.

*Well,* he thought, *what did you expect?* Nearly a week had gone by since he'd jammed down on the SEND button and told the woman he loved to have a happy life. Stupidity was seldom rewarded with a second chance.

He shut down the computer.

Sitting in the desk chair, overwhelmed with fatigue, he felt the loneliness sweep over him like a winter chill. God, he was tired of this shit. Tired of flying home to an empty steel cell aboard a cold-blooded, hundred-thousand-ton barge.

He thought again about the reality of this life. You put your life on the line flying off the deck of these massive ships, and when it was over and you were still alive you went back down to the same steel room and confronted your loneliness. You lived without a real home, a family, even the comforts of cocktail hour, walks on the beach, nights at the movies with your girl. Hell, even the Air Force lived better than this, as Catfish Bass would remind him if he were still alive.

*Get a grip, Maxwell. You knew all this when you took the job.*

True. Nobody was kidding him when, as a young nugget naval aviator, he checked into his first squadron and found himself flung into the first war against Iraq. He knew what he was getting into.

That was a decade and a half ago, and not a hell of a lot had changed. Not the loneliness, not the danger.

He looked again at the photograph. He remembered that

day. It was one of those spring afternoons that sparkled like a field of jewels. He'd picked her up on his old Harley.

"Where are we going?" she had asked.

"Somewhere romantic." That was all he'd tell her.

They went for a ride along the Potomac, then stopped at a riverside restaurant. They'd had their picture taken by the waiter.

The couple in the photo smiled back at him. In the background was the water, a riverboat, a sky dotted with puffs of cumulus.

He lay the photograph facedown on the desk. He was tired. Too much had happened that he couldn't control. He could feel a gaping hole in his heart where the presence of Claire Phillips used to be.

All he knew was that he missed his girl and his home country and afternoon rides along the Potomac. He missed living a normal life. Hell, sometimes he even missed the motorcycle.

He slept for five hours. That was enough. He was back aboard the *Reagan*, and he had a strike fighter squadron to command.

Walking down the passageway to the ready room, he wondered what he'd find. He'd been gone from the squadron—how long? Only three days? It seemed like a month.

He opened the door to the ready room—and nearly ran into the banner draped over the entrance.

Cheers and applause spilled out of the room. Across the banner was the message: SIERRA HOTEL, SKIPPER. WELCOME HOME.

*Sierra Hotel*—phonetic code for *Shit hot*—was the highest unofficial accolade a fighter pilot could receive.

They were all there, almost every officer in the squadron. Bullet Alexander stood in the front row, wearing a grin that looked like a piano keyboard. Next to him was Sticks Stickney, applauding with the rest of them. CAG Boyce was gnawing a cigar, flashing a thumbs-up.

Maxwell was too stunned to speak.

Boyce grabbed his arm and dragged him into the room. A linen-covered table was set up in the front of the room with a large cake and a coffee urn from the wardroom. "If we were ashore,"said Boyce, "we'd be having a proper celebration with booze for all the troops." He glanced at Stickney. "On his tab, of course."

Maxwell accepted handshakes and back-claps and high-fives from the assembled airmen. He felt as if he were dreaming. A few hours ago he had thought he might spend the rest of his life as a prisoner in China. Or be killed in the Black Star. Or be adrift in the South China Sea.

Instead, he was where he belonged—aboard USS *Reagan*, in the ready room of his own squadron. Somewhere in the depths of the ship, under a shroud and guarded by marines, was the Black Star. It would soon be on its way to the place of its conception—Groom Lake.

Boyce steered him toward the back of the ready room, away from the tumult around the coffee urn and the cake, now being devoured by the pilots.

"The good news is that I put you in for a decoration," said Boyce.

"What's the bad news?"

"You won't get it. What you did never happened. CINC-PAC says that we will all erase our memories about invisible Chinese airplanes."

"I don't want a medal. I just want to get back to running my squadron."

"That might take a while. They want you back in the states for extensive debriefing."

Maxwell groaned. "CAG, my squadron needs—"

Boyce held his hands up. "It's not me who's calling the

shots. Those orders come all way from the top of the mountain. I'm just the messenger."

*Damn it,* thought Maxwell. Just when he thought he was returning to his real job. He glanced toward the front of the room. Bullet Alexander was talking to some of the junior officers, gesturing with his hands in the way fighter pilots were prone to do.

"How about Bullet?" he said, nodding toward the XO. "Did Manson give him a hard time?"

Boyce let out a snort. "Take a look at this."

He walked over to the big corkboard mounted on the bulkhead next to the LSO's carrier landing records. Thumbtacked to the board was a grainy black-and-white photograph.

Maxwell peered at the photo. It was an enlarged shot taken from a HUD videotape. Superimposed in the reticules of the gunfight were the twin canted vertical stabilizers of an F/A-18 Hornet. It was a classic rear-quarter gun kill.

Then he saw the handwritten message at the bottom of the photo.

> *For Craze,*
> *A little memento, so you won't forget.*
> *Fondly, Bullet*

"He scheduled himself for a one-vee-one against Manson," said Boyce. "Of course, everyone in the air wing wanted to watch, positive that Manson was going to carve him a new bunghole. As soon as they merged, Bullet was all over Manson like a cheap suit. Craze hasn't shown his face in the ready room since. Look over there. All the JOs think Bullet Alexander walks on water."

Maxwell glanced up at the front of the room. It was true. The junior pilots were clustered around Bullet Alexander, hanging on his every word.

He smiled, remembering the way it had been when he was new to the squadron. They'd given him the same reception. The carpetbagger treatment.

It wasn't fair, but that was the way the system worked. They wouldn't let up until you'd proved yourself. They'd wouldn't quit until you'd gone out there and kicked some ass.

# CHAPTER TWENTY-SIX

# ARMISTICE

*Taipei, Taiwan*
*1645, Tuesday, 16 September*

Something was different.

As she walked down the underground passageway to the cabinet room, Charlotte Soong tried to put her finger on it. What was it? Something had changed.

With her was General Wu, carrying a stack of briefs. She carried only the umbrella, hooked as usual over her right arm.

Not until they reached the big double door, held open by a staff officer, did it come to her. "Do you hear it, General?"

He looked perplexed. "Hear what, Madame President?"

"The silence. Taipei is quiet. No explosions, no bombs, no sirens."

She smiled at the realization. Not since noon had any missiles or bombs rained down on Taiwan. Nor, for that matter, had any weapons been launched against the mainland of China.

The stillness lay over Taipei like a soft blanket.

The ministers rose in unison as she entered the chamber. In a spontaneous gesture, they broke into applause. All except Franklin Huang, who wore his standard sullen expression of disapproval.

"Thank you, gentlemen." She took her place at the head of the massive teak conference table. She hung the umbrella in its usual place over the arm of her chair. "Please be seated."

The ministers already knew, at least in principle, about the armistice. In the briefs that General Wu placed before her on the table were the transcriptions of the discussions with the President of the United States, who had brokered the agreement. These she intended to read to the ministers, then she would explain how the President had extracted the necessary concessions from Beijing.

Looking at the faces around the table, Charlotte knew that not all would be pleased with her handling of the armistice. Least of all, the Premier, Franklin Huang. But Huang would not approve of anything she did.

"As most of you know, the terms of the armistice were verbally agreed to by the President of the PRC and me. A formal treaty will be signed by our emissaries in two days' time in Hong Kong." She nodded to Ma Wang, the Foreign Minister. "That, Minister Ma, will be your task."

"That is a violation of the constitution," declared Franklin Huang. "Any such treaty must be approved by the legislative Yuan. And if anyone is to be a signatory to the armistice, it should be me, the Premier and head of the Yuan."

"I have consulted our supreme court justices," said Charlotte. "They assure me that in the case of war, no such approval is required. And it is entirely the President's prerogative who is designated as my emissary. In this instance, I have my own reasons for assigning Foreign Minister Ma."

"May I ask what those reasons might be?" Huang demanded.

"No." She didn't bother looking up from the brief. "You'll learn in due time."

Huang looked as if he were about to choke.

She ignored him and went on. "This cabinet should know that a very special operation—and certain special heroics—were required to create the conditions for the armistice."

"Are you referring to Operation Raven Swoop, Madame President?" asked Ma Wang. "The effort to remove the invisible fighter aircraft that was plaguing us?"

"I am. Unfortunately, much of the story must remain secret. But I can tell you this much. The PLA's ability to use their secret weapon was neutralized by our special operations forces—with, uh, some outside help."

At this, several ministers nodded. They were guessing, she assumed, about the United States's role in Operation Raven Swoop.

"These are the basic terms of the armistice." She picked up the top sheet from the stack. "All units of the PLA and of the Taiwanese self-defense forces will cease hostile actions. No military aircraft will be flown over the other country's landmass, including the island group of Qemoy and Matsu. All naval vessels, submarines included, will withdraw from the other country's territorial waters.

"In a mostly carefully worded statement, the People's Republic of China acknowledges the right of Taiwan to govern itself. For our part, we will forgo any public declarations of independence from the PRC."

"You mean a return to the status quo?" asked Feng Weishan, the Minister of Finance. "You have renounced President Li's declaration of independence?"

Charlotte nodded. "That was the President of the United States's stipulation. The PRC, for its part, is to publicly declare that Taiwan will not be forced to join the communist republic of mainland China. The door will remain open for Taiwan at a future date, and only after a democratic vote, to become a province of the People's Republic of China. It will be our choice and not theirs."

She watched the reaction around the table. As she expected, the hard-liners like Feng and Lo were not pleased. None, however, wanted a continuation of the debilitating war with the PRC. Each minister knew in his heart that Taiwan would not survive a protracted war with China.

Charlotte was pleased with the outcome. She had achieved the best of all possibilities. Taiwan would continue to prosper as a free country without the threat of a military takeover by China. She knew that if she did nothing else in her tenure as President, she would be remembered for this accomplishment.

"Perhaps you could elaborate on some of the circumstances of this armistice," Minister Feng said. "Has China acknowledged starting the war by murdering President Li?"

Charlotte and General Wu exchanged a silent glance. "No," she said. "In fact, the President of the PRC denies any connection with the shoot down of President Li's jet."

"That's a lie, of course," said Feng. "We are certain that the Airbus was shot down by China's secret stealth jet."

"Yes, Minister, we have convincing evidence to that effect. What the President of the PRC means is, *he* didn't issue the order. In fact, if he is to be believed, he was as surprised as we were when it happened."

Feng scoffed at this. "That is ridiculous. You don't believe him, of course."

"In fact, I do."

Around the long table she saw only open mouths, astonished stares.

Feng asked the question on all their minds. "Who, then?"

Charlotte nodded to General Wu, who was standing at a projector across the room. He flicked the switch, and an image flashed onto the wall-length white screen.

It was blurry, taken through a high-powered telephoto

lens, but the faces were recognizable. Two men stood on the terrace of a country lodge.

Around the table, a collective sucking-in of breath took place.

"The man in the foreground, for those of you aren't familiar with him, is General Tsin Shouyi, Chief of Staff of the PLA. The other some of you know."

They did. A murmur swept over the room.

"His name is Robert Liu, and he is the senior aide to the Premier of Taiwan."

By now all the eyes in the cabinet room were trained on Franklin Huang.

Huang slapped his hand down on the table. "Preposterous," he said in a derisive voice. "Just another pitiful attempt by our temporary President to discredit me. I have no idea how or when that photo was taken, or for what reason. If Robert Liu is guilty of collaborating, then we will deal with him."

"We have already dealt with him. And he is cooperating fully. He readily admits that he was acting as your emissary in his meeting with General Tsin. That photo was taken exactly two days before President Li's flight to Kuala Lumpur, which was the subject of their meeting." She turned her gaze directly on Franklin Huang. "Is that not true, Premier?"

"Nonsense! If Robert Liu is a spy, which has not been proven, he would try to implicate whoever he could, especially a senior statesman. His word means nothing. You have no proof."

Charlotte nodded again to General Wu, who pushed the play button on a digital recorder. The distinctive, high-pitched voice of Franklin Huang crackled over the two speakers on the wall.

*". . . plane will depart Kuala Lumpur at 2:30 this afternoon. The route of flight will be via the*

*commercial airway, along the Vietnamese coast, then over the South China Sea."*

*Another voice, speaking in a heavy Mandarin dialect, asked, "The type of aircraft?"*

*"An Airbus A-300. His radio designation will be Dynasty One. There is a problem, General. Li has requested that the United States Navy provide fighter escort for his aircraft."*

*After a moment's silence: "That is not a problem. The problem is the woman . . ."*

*"Soong."*

*"Yes, Soong . . . if she does not relinquish the office to you."*

*"She will relinquish the office. If she refuses, she will be removed. The silly woman has no interest or ability to be—"*

At this Huang leaped to his feet. "Stop this charade!" He pointed a finger at Charlotte Soong. "This woman has produced a falsified recording in order to discredit me. It's absurd."

"Is it? Then why did you inform President Li only an hour before his departure that you would not accompany him on the flight."

"Because I . . . I was ill."

"And during your illness you made the call to General Tsin, which we have just heard. It was recorded by the monitoring device implanted in your satellite telephone that we recovered only yesterday."

"You are such a fool," said Huang. "Do you really think that the Chief of Staff of the PLA would carry out such a plan without the knowledge of his own superiors in Beijing?"

"I'm glad you mentioned that, Franklin," said Charlotte. "It may interest you to know that we transmitted a copy of this tape to the President of the PRC." She held up a printed message. "This came from one of our operatives in Beijing this afternoon. General Tsin was removed from his quarters this afternoon by armed troops. He has vanished, and we have an unverified report that he has already been tried and executed."

A silence fell over the room. Huang's chest was heaving. He stared at Charlotte Soong as if he were seeing her for the first time.

"You conniving bitch! We should have killed you with the same bullets that removed your husband."

Charlotte Soong felt a jolt like an electric shock passing through her. "My husband? It was you who . . ."

"Kenneth Soong was a pathetic weakling. An insignificant politician who would have dragged the country into the sewer."

Charlotte felt as if she were awakening from a drugged sleep. *It was Huang. He was the one who killed Kenneth.*

Everything seemed to be happening in slow motion. Huang was yelling incoherently. "You and your useless husband—you have ruined this country . . ."

She was dimly aware that he had a gun, though she hadn't noticed where it came from. Beneath his jacket? Or was it in his briefcase? He seemed to have come unhinged. He was waving the pistol, looking for a target. Each of the ministers was diving for cover beneath the table.

"Traitors!" Huang yelled. "Every one of you! I'll kill all of you!"

General Wu was unarmed. He was edging his way toward the raving man when Huang noticed him. He aimed the pistol and shot Wu through the forehead.

The General spun around and toppled over two chairs as he crashed to the floor.

The loud report of the pistol crystallized Charlotte's thoughts. She knew what she had to do.

Charlotte lifted the umbrella from around the arm of the chair. Years ago, Kenneth had gotten it for her. He insisted that she carry it, even though he refused to have such a thing himself. All these years she had hauled it around out of respect for Kenneth's memory. She had never actually used it, even in practice. She often wondered if she could bring herself to do it.

With her right thumb she slid the safety off. She aimed the shaft of the umbrella—a 9 mm gun barrel—and fired. The sharp crack of the shot and the recoil of the umbrella barrel shocked her.

Franklin Huang stared at her in disbelief. He looked down at the red-stained hole in the front of his shirt.

He lifted the pistol.

She fired again. The bullet hit him in the chest.

The pistol slipped from his hand. Clutching his chest, he toppled backward into the chair behind him.

Charlotte lay the smoking umbrella on the table.

One by one the heads of the cabinet ministers were reappearing from beneath the long conference table. They peered around the room, taking in the carnage.

General Wu lay on the floor, killed instantly by Huang's bullet. Huang was slumped over the armrest of his chair, his sightless eyes staring at the ceiling.

A strange sense of calm settled over Charlotte. Kenneth would be proud, she thought. Using the umbrella had not been difficult at all. Killing Franklin Huang had come to her as naturally as launching the war against China.

*Groom Lake, Nevada*

Raymond Lutz stared as the technicians slid the shroud off the buff-colored airframe. The overhead halogen lights flooded the hangar in a harsh yellow light.

Incredible, he thought. Even though he had been the principal source of the technology that went into its development, he had never actually seen the Chinese product.

Lutz couldn't help but be impressed. The Chinese had faithfully reproduced the geometry of the diamond-shaped airframe, even the intricate vaning that guided inlet air to the engines in the front and obscured the exhaust signature in the aft section. Except for the color and the slightly different landing gear design, it could be the same Black Star he had worked on here at Groom Lake these past eight years.

They had brought the captured Chinese jet here to Hangar 501 in the north complex. Only a handful of senior engineers and technicians had been invited to watch as they unwrapped it. Now they stood in a silent cluster, no one speaking, studying the object that had somehow, incomprehensibly, been copied from *their* design, built in secret half a world away. Now the technology had come full circle and found its way back to Groom Lake.

Unbelievable. The engineers were staring at the foreign object, their mouths half open, shaking their heads and muttering expressions of wonder under their breath. Each seemed captivated by this manifestation of his handiwork.

Each except Lutz.

He was no longer staring at the captured stealth jet. His eyes were fixed on the small group of men across the hangar floor. He recognized the director of the Calypso Blue project, a man named Ratchford, with whom Lutz had only a nodding acquaintance. Ratchford was talking to a taller man in khaki slacks and an open-collared sport shirt. He had a brown mustache and a straight, military bearing. There was something familiar about him.

The man seemed to sense Lutz watching him. He peered across the hangar floor, scanning the group clustered around the Black Star. Then his eyes fixed on Lutz. For a long moment the two men locked gazes.

In a single blinding flash of clarity, Lutz understood. It all came together in his mind like a complicated mosaic. He knew how the Chinese Black Star had been captured. And he knew who had done it.

*Maxwell.*

Lutz felt the rage sweep over him like a sheet of lava. *That damned Maxwell.* Of course. Maxwell had been in the South China Sea aboard a carrier. It would have been he, of all people, who would have ferreted out the secret of the Chinese stealth jet.

It was always Maxwell. At every crucial juncture in Lutz's life, there was Maxwell, showing up like the spoiler from hell.

Maxwell was saying something to the director, his eyes still on Lutz. Then he started walking toward Lutz.

Lutz didn't wait. He didn't want to talk to Maxwell. A hatred more intense than anything he had ever felt had taken hold of him. Trembling with rage, he turned his back and walked briskly toward the exit, back toward his lab.

It was already past four in the afternoon, and most of the lab technicians had gone home. As Lutz rounded the corner of the long hallway that led to his office, he saw someone coming out. The man's back was still to him as he turned a key in the door. Lutz recognized the man's shape, the shapeless dark wrinkle-free trousers and white shirt.

The FBI agent. What the hell was his name?

It came to him. *Swinford.*

*Swinford has a key to the lab.*

Lutz ducked back around the corner, his pulse racing. What was Swinford looking for? Had they figured out that Feingold wasn't the leak?

Time was running out. Lutz could sense his world collapsing around him. It was time to conclude this chapter in his life, leave Groom Lake, collect his money, and exit the United States.

First, though, he had business to negotiate. He had to see Tom.

Maxwell watched the man walk away, past the security gate at the exit and out of the hangar.

It had to be Lutz. He was sure of it—that hunched, thick-shouldered shape, the way he walked with a shuffling, bear-like gait.

And he was sure that Lutz had recognized him. So why did he whirl like that and leave?

It was strange, but he remembered now that Raymond Lutz had always been strange. Even when they were at Pensacola together, years ago, Lutz carried a giant-sized chip on his shoulder. He could never hide his resentment of the officers like Maxwell who were lucky enough to possess good vision and thus were handed a ticket to fly fighters. Lutz thought he had been cheated.

It didn't stop there. Later, when he didn't make the cut for NASA, he became hostile and bitter. Soon after that, Maxwell recalled, he had left the Navy and come to work here at Groom Lake.

On the Black Star.

For a while Maxwell stood there gazing out at the shimmering desert. Something was scratching at the back of his subconscious—some connection he couldn't quite make.

Maxwell and the Chinese Black Star had stayed together. He rode aboard the CH-53 that hauled the shrouded stealth jet from the *Reagan* to a waiting C-5 in Taiwan. He managed to sleep for most of the seventeen-hour, nonstop flight to Nevada, which included three in-flight refuelings.

His orders had come directly from the Joint Chiefs: Report to the director, Groom Lake Test and Research Facility, for extensive debriefing regarding Operation Raven Swoop.

Dreamland hadn't changed much, he thought. Still barren and brown, grim as the moon. The runway was even longer than when he had been assigned there several years ago. It was now 27,000 feet, nearly twice as long as the space shuttle runway he'd used at Cape Canaveral.

Gazing out the window of Hangar 501, Maxwell could see Bald Mountain and the hills of the Groom Range. To the south was Freedom Ridge, where the UFO zealots used to gather to get glimpses of the facility before the Air Force chased them away.

Dreamland had always attracted strange people, he thought. Both inside and outside the fence. He thought again about Raymond Lutz.

*Las Vegas, Nevada*

"I'm sorry," said Tom. "No more deposits. The payments have stopped. Those are my orders."

"Orders?" Lutz was on his feet, pacing like a tethered animal. He could feel the anger bubbling up inside him. "Orders from whom? You know the terms of our agreement. Five million dollars. It's supposed to be on deposit in six accounts."

Tom sat on the edge of the bed. On the table was an ice bucket with an unopened bottle of Moet Chandon. Twelve floors beneath was the main floor of the casino. "It's time to be realistic, Ray. Five million was a hypothetical amount. That much would have accumulated only if your services continued to be in demand. The situation has changed. As you know, the project has been . . . ah, interrupted."

Lutz struggled to control his temper. *Interrupted*. That was a bullshit way of saying that some sonofabitch had gotten into China and *stolen* the stealth jet that he risked his life to develop. And Lutz already had a very good idea who the sonofabitch was.

"I don't care what's changed. I delivered what you

wanted, and now I expect to be compensated. Five million, just as we agreed."

"You have received half a million, Ray. Five hundred thousand dollars is still a great deal of money. I think it would be in your best interest to be satisfied with that amount. Remember the source of these funds, and then consider . . . the consequences of a misunderstanding."

Lutz recognized the not-so-subtle threat. Tom's lilting voice had taken a nasty edge. Lutz had never met any of his Chinese employers. Just Tom.

Lutz was too furious to reply. He turned and gazed out the window that overlooked the street. The Las Vegas strip was ablaze with glittering light. Feingold's favorite banality came to him. *Did you know Las Vegas burns more kilowatts than the rest of Nevada combined?*

He still didn't give a damn. What he wanted was to get out of Las Vegas. Out of the espionage business and out of the United States, and he needed money to do it. A lot more than five hundred fucking thousand dollars.

He could feel Tom's eyes on him. As he stood peering down at the blazing lights, he considered his options. He could gather his funds from the half dozen accounts, then go make another life for himself. But it wouldn't be the life he had dreamed about. Not on half a million.

An ominous silence had fallen over the room. Tom's normal patter was missing. Lutz could feel that something had changed.

He wondered if it was just his paranoia taking off again. He and Tom had disagreed about money before. It was nothing new, just part of the normal bargaining process. But this was different. *Consider the consequences of a misunderstanding.*

It wasn't just paranoia. Tom had threatened him.

Always before he had been afraid of the FBI and the CIA and the Defense Intelligence goons who snooped into his activities at Groom Lake. Now his warning system was sending a different alert. He could sense immediate danger.

Something alerted him—a rustling noise, a miniscule movement of air. He turned from the window.

Tom had slid across the bed and was reaching into a leather satchel on the nightstand.

In a flash of understanding, Lutz understood.

He bolted across the three feet of space that separated them just as Tom's hand emerged from the satchel. The muzzle of the .38 caliber revolver was just coming up.

Lutz glimpsed the surprise on Tom's face. No one could ever believe that someone the size of Raymond Lutz—six three and a solid 260 pounds—could move with such agility.

His hand caught Tom's narrow wrist, snapping it back with such force that he heard the *crack*. Tom shrieked and kicked out at him.

With a backhanded slap, Lutz smashed Tom across the face, cutting short the piercing shriek. Tom reeled back from the blow, toppling to the floor beneath the oncoming rush of Lutz's weight. The pistol dropped to the carpet.

Lutz clamped his hands on the slender throat.

"Ray . . . don't! Please, Ray . . ."

He cut off the protest, pressing his thumbs into Tom's larynx. He let all the animal rage spill out of him. A low noise swelled from his chest. He could feel the fragile bones and gristle and capillaries crackling like matchsticks beneath his fingers.

Tom fought back, flailing with frantic but ineffective blows. With Lutz's full weight atop his victim, it was no contest. His powerful hands clamped down like a vise on Tom's neck.

For nearly a minute Tom's hands fluttered in the air like moths, then they relaxed and went limp. Lutz maintained his grip, squeezing hard, the animal growl rising from some dark place within him. Spittle bubbled from his lips.

Finally he released his grasp and rose to his feet. He was breathing in a hoarse rasp. He could feel his heart pounding like a jackhammer, not from exertion but from the excitement.

Everything, of course, had changed. The game—this one, anyway—was over. He couldn't go back to Groom Lake. He was certain that Swinford and his FBI goons were looking for him. The money he'd been promised by the Chinese— five million dollars—would never be paid. He had just murdered his handler, and he sensed that the Chinese would not forgive him for that.

He was a fugitive.

For a long moment he gazed down into Tom's contorted face. The unblinking green eyes still stared at him in fear and panic.

Tom. It occurred to him that he knew almost nothing about the agent. Throughout their relationship, Tom had remained an enigma, able to change roles like a chameleon, one moment a spymaster, handler of secrets, operative of a foreign power. In the next moment—the one Lutz remembered now—Tom was something else.

Tom was his lover.

Her professional name was Thomasina Maitland, and it never bothered Lutz that she was a hooker. She was a professional and so was he. The fact that she received money for her service was irrelevant. It was the quality of the service that counted.

Of course, she never charged Lutz. That was supposed to be part of the carefully constructed cover—Lutz and his predilection for hookers. Tom wasn't the wholesome, girl-next-door that mothers and government agencies favored, but at least it didn't raise undue flags with the FBI. It made you less a security risk than being homosexual or alcoholic or drug dependent.

It was a good cover, but for Lutz it became more than just

a professional cover. He and Tom shared a common danger. And then, after the thrill of the transaction, came the exquisite, high-voltage sex. They had something special.

Or so he had believed.

The truth hit him like a hammer blow. *It was an act.* Nothing more. It was her way of handling him—keeping him from becoming too difficult, too contentious. Tom made him think that maybe, just maybe, she was doing it for love.

The oldest trick of the world's oldest profession.

He gazed down at the lovely dead face. A wave of rage consumed him, and he delivered a kick to the inert, tanned figure in the short leather skirt. *Bitch.* He'd been used again.

*Groom Lake, Nevada*

Maxwell's debriefing went on for a week.

In an underground, sound-and-emission-proof chamber, he underwent questioning by specialists from all the intelligence communities, some he had never heard of. They wanted to know not just the details of the raid on Chouzhou, but his recollection of flying the Black Star, of the engagement with Colonel Zhang, and how he managed a carrier landing with a hookless stealth fighter.

"And what makes you think it was this Colonel . . ."

"Zhang."

"How did you know he was flying the Black Star you shot down?"

"From my wizzo, Captain Chen, a PLA defector who had worked in the Black Star unit."

The questioner just nodded.

When the debriefing was complete, Maxwell's orders and airline tickets were waiting for him. That night he took the facility's 737 to Las Vegas. The next morning he boarded a Delta jet to Los Angeles, connecting to a China Airlines flight to Taipei.

No one had told him why he was going to Taipei, nor why he wasn't returning to the *Reagan*, which he knew was making a port call in Manila.

Not until he walked through the jetway into the Chiang Kai-Shek International Airport in Taipei did he begin to understand. At the arrival gate stood a familiar figure. He wore running shoes, wrinkled chinos, and a beat-up old leather flight jacket. He was gnawing the stub of an unlit cigar.

# CHAPTER TWENTY-SEVEN

# MAI TAIS AND
# A GUITAR

*Taipei, Taiwan*
*1430, Friday, 26 September*

"Where are we going?"

"To the American Institute in Taiwan," said Boyce, climbing into the taxi with Maxwell. "Formerly known as the United States Embassy before they moved it to China and gave this one a bullshit name. It still operates like an embassy, with all the stuff—a visa section and military attachés and intelligence specialists and a visitors' quarters, which is where we're staying tonight."

Maxwell was feeling the effects of jet lag and dehydration and, most of all, the endless questioning by teams of unsmiling intelligence specialists.

To hell with intelligence specialists. "If I'm here for another debriefing, they can get stuffed."

"No debriefing. You're here because the President of Taiwan wants to thank you and some other guys."

"I don't want any thanks. I want a Scotch and a steak and some sleep. In that order."

"Tough shit. Nobody said being a hero was going to be easy."

They drove down a street that had been devastated by incoming missiles. Debris from shattered buildings was bulldozed onto the side of the road, forming a continuous wall of rubble on either side.

A commercial district had taken a direct hit. Along a row of storefronts a destroyed building left a jagged gap like a missing tooth. Broken windows were taped over. Hulks of ruined automobiles were shoved up on the curb.

Maxwell stared at the destruction. He shook his head. "I had no idea they were hit this bad."

"War sucks," said Boyce.

The rubble abruptly disappeared. They drove along a tree-lined street that looked like a scene from a postcard.

"Tsin Yi Road," said Boyce, "and that's the American Institute up there on the left. No bomb craters, no destroyed buildings, no burned-out hulks. Says something about the politics of war."

After an ID check by the guards at the main gate, they climbed the broad steps and entered the compound. Boyce led him to the front desk of the visitors' quarters. "All you have to do is sign in, then we head for the bar. I've already put your stuff in your room."

"Stuff?"

"You needed a fresh uniform for the ceremony with the President, so I took the liberty of bringing it from your stateroom on the ship. Also warm civvies because Taipei gets chilly at night."

Maxwell looked at Boyce. He had known the CAG long enough to recognize the clues. He was up to something. *What?*

In the next moment, he found out.

"About time you got here," said a booming voice behind him. "Leave it to you Navy pukes to show up late."

Maxwell turned to see a barrel-chested man walking toward them. He had short-cropped brownish hair and very large teeth. He was wearing an Air Force uniform with two stars and a name tag that read BUCKNER.

The General paused, martini glass halfway to his mouth, and said, "You've gotta be shitting me, Maxwell."

"No, sir. I'll put it in writing. I think Major Bass deserves a posthumous silver star. Or even higher."

Buckner looked at Boyce, who seemed to be studying a spot on the ceiling. "Did you put him up to this, Boyce?"

"I told him Bass was his problem. He was the guy in charge, and if he thinks Bass deserves a medal, that's his call."

"Commander Maxwell, are you implying that the Air Force doesn't take care of its own people?"

"No, sir. It's just that after we picked up Major Bass after his . . . ah, ejection over the strait, I gathered that you weren't exactly pleased with his actions."

"Pleased? What I said was that I intended to kick his insubordinate ass up between his shoulder blades. Then send him to Leavenworth for ten to twenty."

"Yes, sir, and having known Catfish, I understand your feelings. But as you know, he was assigned to me during a . . . very sensitive operation."

"I know all about Raven Swoop. I received a top secret briefing."

"Then you also know that Catfish distinguished himself in combat. I can attest that without his bravery, the operation would not have succeeded. That's why I'm recommending him for a posthumous decoration."

Maxwell saw Buckner and Boyce exchange a quick glance. Buckner seemed to be enjoying himself. He said,

"What's this world coming to? A Navy commander recommending a medal for an Air Force officer? Have you guys been at sea too long?"

"General, you said something to the effect that you didn't want Bass back. I took that to mean Bass's official record was my responsibility. I intend to see that he gets the honor he deserves."

At this Buckner grinned, displaying a row of very large teeth. "What I said, if I remember correctly, was that you guys could keep the dumb bastard until hell freezes over or the war is finished, whichever took longer."

Maxwell took a deep breath, trying to suppress his anger. General or not, this Buckner was a jerk. "Well, sir, the war *is* finished. And since Catfish is no longer with us, I want to set the record straight."

"The record *is* straight. Whether or not he deserves a medal, he also deserves a kick in the ass. He's a goldbricking, showboating goof-off who should have been court-martialed."

Maxwell had heard enough. Catfish Bass, for all his faults, didn't deserve bad-mouthing from some blue-suit windbag.

"General, with all due respect, you're full of crap." In the corner of his eye, he saw Boyce's eyeballs roll. "Major Bass lost his life trying—"

"Commander, how long have you been away from your carrier?"

"A week, nearly two."

Buckner looked at Boyce, who had resumed his study of a spot on the ceiling. "You haven't enlightened him about recent events, have you, Red?"

"No, sir."

"What recent events?" asked Maxwell.

"You'll see." The General polished off his martini and rose to his feet. "Follow me."

They followed him through the main hall of the visitors' quarters, up the stairs to the second floor, down another hall. The General said nothing as he marched down the aisle. His leather heels hammered like drumbeats on the marble floor.

Maxwell heard a sound wafting from the end of the hall. It sounded like guitar music. Or some variety of stringed instrument played off key. To his ear, it sounded like bungee cords being tortured.

Buckner stopped at an unmarked door. Without knocking, he marched inside. Maxwell followed—then stopped in his tracks. He stared at the apparition in the bed. His guess had been correct—it was a guitar.

Played by Catfish Bass.

Maxwell's gaze shifted to the figure in the chair next to the bed. He recognized the black hair, the high cheekbones, the slender shape—but it didn't compute. Nothing computed anymore.

"Hey, shipmate," said Bass. "You're a long way from the boat, aren't you?"

Maxwell stared, unable to speak.

"Hello, Sam," said Mai-ling. "The General said you'd be surprised." She handed drinks to the newcomers. "I made mai tais. Catfish loves them."

"General," said Bass, "this is the guy I told you about. Brick Maxwell, coolest Tac-Air jock outside the Air Force. Saved all our butts, even though he couldn't hit a bull in the ass with a pistol."

He was wearing a white hospital robe, and an IV unit was parked next to his bed. But he didn't have the appearance of a man who had been shot in the chest and then incinerated in a horrific helicopter crash. Catfish Bass looked more alive than Maxwell had ever seen him.

He sipped at the drink, not trusting himself to speak. It was possible, he thought, that he was hallucinating. None of this was making sense. The guy in the bed looked exactly like Catfish Bass. And the black-haired Chinese girl in the tight jeans and T-shirt looked just like the girl he'd seen in her stateroom on the *Reagan* two weeks ago.

"Excuse me for asking," said Maxwell. "But why aren't you dead?"

"Good question," said Buckner. He closed the door behind them. "Major, I'll remind you one more time, this information is classified. Go ahead and tell your tale, and this time leave out the extraneous bullshit."

"Yes, sir." Bass set the guitar aside. "You have to take some of this on hearsay, Brick. As you know, I took a bullet back there at Chouzhou. I was pretty much out of it by the time Colonel Chiu hauled me aboard the Chinook. Just after the chopper lifted off, a mortar round took out one of the aft rotor blades and we did some kind of gyration that trashed the helicopter. The bullet was still in my lung, and I wasn't doing so good."

Maxwell nodded. "I saw it. I was still on the ground."

"So was I," said Mai-ling. She was sitting next to Catfish again, stroking his hand.

"I don't know exactly what happened next, but while the chopper was tearing itself to pieces, Chiu and one of his commandos managed to jump clear, and they dragged me with them. With his tac radio, he was able to call the Chinook that had already left. He came swooping back and snatched us out of there just before the ChiComs overran the LZ."

Listening to the story, Maxwell thought again of the taciturn Colonel Chiu, who disliked Americans and then risked his life to save them. He had been wrong about Chiu. He had been wrong about several things.

"We weren't out of the woods yet," Bass went on. "The Chinook that rescued us also took some hits. We barely made it past the coast before things started getting ugly. The sun was just coming up when one of the engines crapped out. The pilot told us we were going to ditch, and I knew then that it just wasn't my day. The only thing I hate worse than getting shot is getting dumped in the ocean."

"Another reason to be in the Air Force," muttered Buckner.

"Yes, sir, my thoughts exactly. The damned chopper started losing power and—*plop!*—there I was in the drink again."

Maxwell frowned, listening to the story. Catfish Bass's life was becoming more and more bizarre.

"Now this is the really weird part. The chopper pilot must have had contact with his central command, because he was heading for a Taiwanese warship—a destroyer or frigate or whatever you guys call those boats. Before we ever reached the ship—you're not gonna believe this, Brick—a bomb had already come from absolutely nowhere and hit the ass end of the ship."

"What do you mean, from nowhere?"

"The captain of the ship—a really cool guy named Lei Fu-sheng—said he had nothing on the radar, no aircraft overhead, no enemy activity. And then, boom, the *Kai Yang*—that's the name of the ship—took a hit."

Maxwell nodded. "And you knew where the bomb came from?"

"Sure I knew, and so did Colonel Chiu, but we didn't say anything. By the way, I heard that you gave that Chinese stealth pilot some serious payback."

Maxwell and Mai-ling made eye contact. She gave him an imperceptible nod.

"Anyway," Bass went on, "my world was turning into shit city. While the crew of the destroyer was still fighting this fire, we ditched alongside. As you can imagine, the captain was very happy to have a bunch of shot-up grunts to add to his problems. But he had his ship's doctor do emergency surgery on me in their sick bay. He removed the bullet from my chest and got me stabilized. Just in time, they tell me, or I'd have been room temperature."

"What happened to the ship?"

"Dead in the water, a sitting duck for another bomb or a sub attack. But one of their escort destroyers shows up and takes us all aboard, shoots a couple torpedoes into the *Kai Yang* to sink her, and off we go again. I woke up in the military hospital here in Taipei."

"You'll meet Colonel Chiu and Commander Lei tomorrow," said Boyce. "Madame Soong wants to pin medals on all of you. She thinks you guys saved Taiwan."

At the mention of Chiu's name, Maxwell saw Mai-ling's nose wrinkle. He wondered if Colonel Chiu would be pleased to see the Americans again. Probably not. He'd be even less pleased to see Mai-ling.

"That's not the end of it," said Buckner. "In a few days Maxwell here will be flying back to Washington for a very discreet ceremony in the Pentagon. Someone wants to give him a Navy Cross."

"Me?" Maxwell said. "What about Catfish? Why doesn't he get—"

"You've been out of the loop," said Buckner. "It seems that someone in the Navy"—he shot Boyce a look—"has already made an end run and convinced my boss that the Navy shouldn't have the only hero in this caper. I had no choice except to put Bass in for an Air Force Cross. It was either that or court-martial him."

"Good choice, General," offered Bass.

"Don't be too smug," said Buckner. "It's a symbolic medal only. No photos, no public record, nothing in your file. The medals and the citations that go with them will be sealed for fifty years. You get to wear them in your next lifetime."

"Beats Leavenworth," said Bass.

Mai-ling nodded her agreement while she stroked Bass's hand.

Watching the two, Maxwell had the distinct feeling that he was still missing part of the story. There was something more. Had to be.

"Another mai tai, General?" said Mai-ling, smiling sweetly.

"Why not?" Buckner allowed her to refill his glass, then he raised it. "A toast, ladies and gentlemen. Out of this dangerous episode, our Major Bass has not only covered himself with glory, he has acquired something more significant than a medal."

"A sucking chest wound?" said Boyce.

"That was nothing. Something much more significant."

Maxwell nodded. Here it comes, he thought. There was more.

Boyce asked the question. "What is it that he has acquired, General?"

"What do you think? A gorgeous girlfriend."

"More than a girlfriend, General," said Bass. "A lot more than that."

Mai-ling was smiling. Maxwell thought he even detected a blush on her high, regal cheeks.

Bass turned to Maxwell. "Remember when she said she hated those smart-ass Air Force ROTC guys?" He squeezed Mai-ling's hand. "Guess what? She got over that."

Boyce walked Maxwell to his room.

"Your dress blues are in the closet," he said. "And I brought you this." He handed Maxwell a packet of letters bound with a rubber band. "Your mail from the ship. It came while you were goofing off in Nevada."

He watched while Maxwell unwrapped the packet. "The one you're looking for is on top."

Maxwell opened the letter. He recognized the handwriting.

*Washington, D.C., 19 September*

*My dear Sam,*
*Still nothing further from you—no e-mail, no*
*letter—which can mean only one thing. You've made*
*a decision about our relationship. It also means that I*
*was wrong about you. I thought you loved me.*
*Somehow I thought that you would understand my*
*dilemma and wait for me.*
*I didn't want to believe that Sam Maxwell would*
*just walk away. You are a fighter pilot. I thought I was*
*worth fighting for.*

*As always,*
*Claire*

Boyce waited until Maxwell finished. "Judging by your face, it must be a Dear John."

"No. I got that a couple of weeks ago."

"Too bad. Did she meet someone else?"

"Yeah. Her husband."

Boyce looked at him. "Baghdad Ben? I thought that Iraqi-sympathizing asshole was dead."

"Not dead enough. He's back, and it turns out he was CIA, and now Claire thinks that maybe he wasn't such an asshole."

Boyce gnawed on his cigar for a moment. "Look, it's none of my business, but what does she say in Dear John, Part Two? That it's *really* over?"

Maxwell considered telling him he was right, it was none of his business. But he knew Boyce. He wouldn't leave it alone until he'd gotten the story. "She said that I was a fighter pilot and . . . that she thought she was worth fighting for."

"Yeah?" Boyce removed the cigar and looked at him. "So what seems to be the problem?"

# CHAPTER TWENTY-EIGHT

# RED ROSES

*Washington, D.C.*
*1445, Monday, 29 September*

It was midafternoon and the traffic in downtown Washington was already gridlocked at the intersections. Horns blared, and pedestrians scuttled between rows of stopped automobiles.

He knew he should have telephoned, but something prevented him. If what they had to say was finished in only a few minutes, he wanted it to be face to face, not over the phone.

Half a block before G Street, he spotted what he was looking for. Ten minutes later, carrying a dozen red roses with their stems held upward, he strode into the Media One Building lobby. He took the elevator to the eighteenth floor, then entered the front office of Mutual Studios.

"Whom did you wish to see, sir?" asked the receptionist, a prim, middle-aged woman with round glasses.

"Miss Phillips. Claire Phillips."

She looked him over, noting the Navy uniform, the motorcycle helmet under his arm. Then her gaze fixed on the roses. "Who may I say is here?"

"Sam Maxwell."

Her face broke into a smile. "Commander Sam Maxwell? The one we've heard so much about?"

He nodded.

"Is Claire expecting you, Commander?"

"No."

"Hmm." She peered into her computer monitor. "She's supposed to be doing an interview down at the Mall this afternoon. Shooting at"—she poked at the keyboard—"let's see . . . four-fifteen to four twenty-five. Traffic is terrible right now, but if you have a fast way to get there, you might catch her before she's finished."

"I have a fast way." He turned to leave. "Thank you. You're very kind."

"Excuse me, Commander, but are those roses for Claire?"

"Yes, ma'am."

"You want a tip from a lady? Just give her one. Trust me, it works."

He dropped the Harley into first gear and drove the bike up on the sidewalk. The staccato bark of the twin pipes cleared the pedestrians out of his way. Dodging a pair of Roller-bladers, he veered onto the grass and motored over to where the crowd was gathered.

Ahead he could see the equipment vans and the people clustered around the cameras. On the ground were coils of cable and boxes and audio equipment. A man had a large dolly-rigged camera trained on the tall woman standing inside the ring of spectators.

She had just finished interviewing someone. He looked like a Beltway type—a congressman or some administration official in a gray suit. He was walking away from the set. Behind them the Washington Monument rose like a monolith against the pale blue sky.

Maxwell recognized her outfit. It was her standard choice

for outdoor shoots—silk scarf, sleeveless blouse, long skirt rustling around her legs. Her chestnut hair ruffled in the breeze that blew in from the Potomac.

His heart skipped a beat.

She was speaking to the camera when she spotted him. She continued talking, but her eyes kept darting to the apparition coming toward her—a Harley-Davidson ridden by a man in a Navy dress blue uniform. The deep-throated, blatting exhaust sound was feeding into the audio.

Heads in the crowd turned. Maxwell heard a voice boom into his ear. "What the hell do you think you're doing? You can't ride that thing in here."

The voice belonged to a cop. He was a heavyset, African-American man with a mass of wiry gray hair jutting from beneath his uniform cap.

Maxwell stopped the bike. "I'm here to see Claire Phillips." He held up the single rose. "And to give her this."

"Yeah, right. Get outta here or I'll have you and the noisy damn bike hauled away to the station."

Still watching the commotion off the set, Claire finished her remarks for the camera. She removed the clip-on microphone and walked over to the cop.

"Miss Phillips, this guy says he's here to see you. Do you know him?"

"No. Who is he?"

He turned to Maxwell. "That's it, pal. You're outta here."

"She's saying that because she's in love with me."

The cop's eyes narrowed. He looked Maxwell over, taking in the uniform, the three gold stripes on the sleeves, the rows of campaign ribbons. He turned to Claire. "This guy thinks you're in love with him. That true?"

"Not anymore. He's an idiot."

The cop nodded and turned to Maxwell. "Sounds like you blew it, buddy."

"Yes, I know. I came to apologize."

"Ah." He turned to Claire. "Does it help if he apologizes, ma'am?"

"No. Why didn't he answer my mail?"

He looked at Maxwell. "You got an answer for that?"

"I was away on an assignment."

Claire said, "What kind of assignment?"

"I can't tell you."

The cop said, "Ma'am, this might be a misunderstanding. Maybe you oughta give the guy another chance."

"Why? So he can tell me to have a happy life again?"

"He probably needs a little help. Some guys aren't real good at expressing feelings, you know."

"Probably why they call him Brick."

The cop shook his head. He said to Maxwell, "Sounds like you messed up big-time, buddy. You better think of something good to say."

"How about if I tell her I love her?"

"Yeah, that might work." He took the single rose from Maxwell and handed it to Claire. "He says he loves you, ma'am."

She studied the rose. "How do I know he means it?"

He looked at Maxwell.

"She knows I love her. I always have, always will."

The cop shrugged and said to Claire, "Okay, the guy's not real smooth, but I think he means it."

"What's he going to do about it?"

He looked at Maxwell. "Well?"

"I'm taking her to dinner."

"Where?"

"Somewhere romantic. A place on the river."

"Good call. Maybe one of the waterfront joints in Alexandria? Go for an outside table."

They both looked at Claire. She wasn't buying it. She stood there twirling the rose in her fingers, her hazel eyes regarding the two men.

A crowd had gathered around them. She twirled the rose, saying nothing. Seconds ticked by. In the distance hummed the traffic of the city. Time stood still.

She reached a decision. She hiked her skirt up over her knees, showing a length of tanned, freckled legs. She climbed onto the backseat of the motorcycle and put on the spare helmet.

The crowd burst into applause.

She clasped her arms around Maxwell's waist. "Okay, sailor, this is your lucky day. You get one last chance."

"Yes, ma'am."

He buckled his helmet, then gunned the Harley's engine and kicked it into first gear. As he pulled away, he looked back over his shoulder and waved to the cop.

Standing with his hands on his hips, Sergeant Grover watched them motor back down the slope, over the sidewalk and onto the street. A nice couple, he thought. The guy was a klutz with women, but he was okay. He'd get it right sooner or later.

Then he noticed something else. An automobile creeping out into traffic behind the motorcycle. It was a plain white something, one of those bland-looking Japanese rental cars. A Virginia tag. Nothing out of the ordinary except—

Grover had been a D.C. cop for twenty-one years. During that time he had learned to listen to his instincts. Now his instincts were gnawing at the edge of his awareness, whispering some kind of subliminal signal. Something he wasn't getting. What the hell was it?

The driver of the white car. For just an instant the cop had glimpsed the face of the driver, and the image was still stuck in his mind's eye. It was not an ordinary face. The man's eyes were burning like embers. The face of a man filled with rage.

Grover removed his cap and scratched his head, watching

the white car disappear in traffic. What did it mean? He
didn't know. Nothing, probably. Nothing at all.

Maxwell toed the shift lever into third and accelerated
down the two-lane state road. They had left the commuter-
clogged metropolitan area and were entering the suburbs on
the southeast shore of the Potomac. Along both sides of the
road, stands of ash and maple were glowing in the soft light
of early autumn. Long rays of evening sun slanted through
the trees, casting shadows on the gray surface of the road.

He could feel her arms clasped around him. Her chin was
resting on his shoulder.

"Where are we going?" she asked.

"Anywhere you'd like."

"I like this, wherever we are. Can we just ride for a
while?"

He nodded. Conversation was tough on the bike. The
deep-throated rumble of the two-cylinder engine reverberated from the pavement, drowning out their words. There
were a hundred things he wanted to tell her. Questions he
wanted to ask. Later.

Traffic had thinned to a trickle. They were in a wooded
section, between bedroom communities in the flatlands of
northern Virginia. The Harley was purring like a well-fed
lion. He passed a slow-moving panel truck, then crested a
small hill and saw open road ahead.

A car was overtaking them. He saw it in the rearview mirror and slowed back to fifty, thinking it might be a police
car. It was moving up fast, doing well over seventy. He
moved over to the outer half of the right lane.

It wasn't a police car, and it didn't pass. It was a white
car—a Toyota, he guessed. It slowed down and stayed behind him, two car lengths back. There was no oncoming
traffic.

Maxwell slowed to forty and signaled for the car to pass.

The white car didn't pass. He stayed behind, following them around a gradual turn.

Maxwell watched the car in the mirror. There was a man behind the wheel, no passengers. He signaled again for him to pass. The car still didn't move.

Angling toward the road from the right was a railroad track on an elevated mound. Ahead Maxwell could see a tunnel where the high bed of the railroad track crossed the road. A brick wall covered the outer face of the tunnel.

When they were still two hundred yards from the tunnel, Maxwell saw the white car swerve out into the passing lane. This guy was a nutcase, or drunk, he thought. It wasn't possible to see any oncoming traffic coming at them through the tunnel.

The car vanished from Maxwell's mirror. Where did he—

*There.* In the left lane, close, pulling alongside them. Too damned close. Close enough for Maxwell to reach out and touch. The side mirror was only inches from his elbow.

Claire's fingers were digging into his sides. "What's he doing? Why is he so close?"

Maxwell didn't know. He only knew that some crazy bastard was shoving his car into their lane. He looked through the open window on the Toyota's passenger side, directly into the driver's face. For a second that seemed to drag on for a minute, Maxwell and the driver locked gazes.

In an instant of comprehension, it came to him. It was the same face he had seen back at Groom Lake.

*Lutz.*

He knew now why Lutz had whirled away and walked out of the hangar. And he knew exactly why Lutz was here now.

The car swerved toward them. Ahead, the brickface of the tunnel entrance swelled like an oncoming apparition.

The car thumped against the left handlebar of the motorcycle, sending it into a violent oscillation. Maxwell heard Claire scream, and he fought to maintain control.

He clamped on the brakes, trying to slow down and drop behind the car. Lutz slowed with him, still swerving, again banging into the bike. Maxwell jammed on full throttle to accelerate ahead.

It didn't work. Lutz sped up, turning to cut him off. The Toyota swerved into the bike again, veering it toward the ditch.

The brick wall was on them. Maxwell turned the bike hard to the right, off the road and through the shallow ditch. The bike hit the slope of the embankment, missing the brick tunnel face by three feet.

*Whump.* The Harley bounced off the incline of the embankment, the front wheel kicking high in the air.

The bike was airborne, sailing over the embankment. He heard a piercing wail from behind him. Claire's fingers were gouging like daggers into his ribs. In his peripheral vision Maxwell saw the white car vanish into the tunnel.

The railroad track skimmed beneath them. The bike cleared the crest of the embankment, still airborne, descending rear-wheel first, plummeting toward the hard Virginia soil like a stone.

Maxwell's last impression before impact was the long, loud wail from the girl on the seat behind him.

*Darkness.*

It happened so quickly. Lutz's head was turned to the right, watching the bike disappear, when he entered the tunnel at over fifty miles per hour. Then the blackness inside the tunnel. It was if a switch had been thrown.

Fifty yards ahead he saw an expanding light at the end of the tunnel. It was like peering through a telescope.

*The motorcycle?* His last glimpse was as it veered off to the right. Then it hit something. The wall? The embankment?

He would stop beyond the tunnel and go back on foot.

He'd find the wreckage of the motorcycle, and if they were somehow still alive he'd finish them.

Squinting in the darkness of the tunnel, he could see trees and foliage ahead. Then he saw the diamond-shaped sign just beyond the exit. A left-turn arrow.

And something else.

Lutz was momentarily blinded as the car flashed back into the sunlight.

Too late, he saw it. The orange construction barricade, blocking the right lane. He was going too fast, still over fifty. He slammed on the brakes and snatched the wheel hard to the left. The Toyota went into a tire-screeching skid.

The car smashed broadside through the wooden barrier. Skidding through the depression of the freshly excavated asphalt, the Toyota spun around, sliding backward, and left the road in a sickening skid.

When the Toyota hit the ditch, it flipped onto its side, then slid through the brush and low saplings until it impacted a solid stand of maple trees.

A cloud of dust and leaves settled over the wreck. No sound came from the Toyota except the tinkle of glass and settling debris and the hiss of steam.

A hell of a ride.

Wobbling to his feet, Maxwell removed his helmet and did a damage assessment. The helmet had an ugly scrape where it had contacted something solid. His uniform coat was torn, one sleeve hanging like a pennant. The knee was gone from one trouser leg.

For some reason he couldn't explain, he seemed to be alive. Leaping a railroad embankment at fifty miles an hour on a motorcycle was a feat he had never expected to survive. He should have broken every bone in his body.

He stood there, his thinking still muddled, trying to reconstruct what happened. They had landed in a hedge, which had probably—

*Claire. Oh, hell, where is Claire?*

He had a vague memory of flying over the embankment, plunging into the hedge, being vaulted over the handlebars. He'd landed on his side, rolling in a ball down the slope into a waist-high thicket of vines and saplings.

*Where is Claire?*

He clambered back up the slope. The Harley was protruding from the hedge like an abstract sculpture. The front wheel was skewed back at a grotesque angle, and the handlebars were bent like a pretzel.

No sign of Claire. She wasn't in the hedge. Nor was she on the embankment where he had landed after departing the bike.

Then he saw her. She was in a thicket of briars and vines, thirty yards away. The foliage was so thick he hadn't seen her right away. She appeared to be okay except—

She wasn't moving. She was sitting in the weeds, motionless, as if she were paralyzed. Or badly hurt. Or worse.

Maxwell stumbled down through the weeds to her. "Claire! Are you—"

"Sssshhh." She held her finger to her lips. She wasn't paralyzed. She was kneeling, pointing at an object fifty yards away. It was the hulk of what used to be a white Toyota, crunched up against a stand of trees. A wisp of steam was coming from the crumpled hood.

"Are you okay?" he whispered.

"I think so. Where you'd learn to ride like that?"

"Like what?"

"Like Evel Knievel."

"I didn't. That's why we crashed."

She made a face, then turned back to the wrecked Toyota. "That's the car that almost killed us. I think he hit something coming out of the tunnel."

Maxwell looked at the car. There was no sign of life. If Lutz was still in it, he was unconscious. Or dead, which was even better.

He started toward the car.

Claire grabbed his sleeve. "Where are you going?"

"To have a chat with the driver. He needs some remedial training."

"Don't, Sam. Did you see his face? He's a killer."

*Worse than that,* thought Maxwell. If he was right about Lutz, he was the one who gave the Black Star to the Chinese.

"He's probably unconscious. Don't worry, I'll be careful." He gave her a quick kiss and a smile that conveyed more conviction than he really felt.

Watching for movement, he crossed the low thicket between them and the smashed Toyota. The car lay on its side, driver's side up. The roof was crunched up against the trunk of a large tree. As he approached, he saw no sign of life.

Maxwell knelt and peered through the broken back window. He couldn't see the driver. Maybe he was slumped on the floor.

He walked around to the front. Steam was hissing from beneath the wrinkled hood. The windshield was shattered, the spiderweb of cracks making it difficult to see inside. He had to stand on the bumper, raising himself up to peer through the broken glass.

He was still standing on the bumper when Claire's voice reached him from across the thicket. *"Sam! Behind you!"*

Maxwell whirled, and there was Lutz. His face was twisted into a snarling mask. Behind his glasses, the bulging orbs looked like the eyes of an undersea creature.

Lutz was on him before he could react. From three feet away he lunged, grabbing Maxwell around the torso. They hit the ground in a heap, Lutz on top, ramming the breath from Maxwell.

Lutz had a hand clamped on his throat. His other hand was clawing at Maxwell's face, gouging at his eyes. Lutz glowered down into Maxwell's face. "Hello, glory hound," he said. "Remember me?"

Maxwell was shocked at the man's agility. Lutz was big, at least two inches taller and a good sixty pounds heavier, but he had moved with surprising speed.

Lutz's fingers were probing for his eyes, clawing his face. The hand on his throat was squeezing the life from him. Maxwell's vision was fading into a dark field of tiny twinkling lights. He felt the life draining from him.

He summoned all his remaining strength and rammed a knee hard into Lutz's crotch. He felt the grip loosen on his throat. He swung a wild, wide haymaker that caught Lutz in the side of head and rolled him onto the ground.

Maxwell rolled away from him, gasping for air. The two men rose, facing each other. Lutz's nostrils were flared, his features contorted into a feral snarl.

Maxwell remembered seeing that face. It was in the martial arts course in the Navy's preflight school at Pensacola. He'd been matched against an opponent heavier and stronger than he. The man came at him like a bear, all mass and fury and brute strength.

It was Lutz, and he hadn't changed his style.

Lutz lunged at him, thick arms slicing the air, groping for Maxwell's throat. A low guttural noise swelled from inside him.

Maxwell took a step back, ducked the flailing arms, and drove a hard left jab into Lutz's face. Lutz recoiled from the blow. He blinked and shook his head, spraying blood from his nose.

Then he charged again.

Maxwell hit him again with the left jab, then followed with a hard right cross that thudded into his cheek bone.

Lutz reeled backward, somehow staying on his feet. He spat blood from his mouth and glowered at Maxwell.

He charged again.

Maxwell backed up, moving on the balls of his feet, looking for an opening. As Lutz's big arms came for him, Maxwell saw it. He stepped in with a left jab, all his weight behind it, straight into Lutz's face. It sounded like an ax thudding into a log.

Lutz wobbled on his feet, glasses askew, blinded by pain and fury. Maxwell moved in, driving a hard right into the broad belly. Lutz whooshed air like a spouting whale and his knees buckled. He dropped in a heap, his head thumping up against the wrecked Toyota.

Maxwell rubbed the knuckles of his left hand. It felt like he'd broken a bone. His chest ached, and he was sure he had some broken ribs from Lutz's first charge.

Lutz was spurting blood from his nose, breathing with a noise that sounded like a sputtering engine. His eyeglass frames were twisted, slanting across his forehead.

Lutz replaced his glasses and spat a wad of blood on the ground. For a long moment the two men held eye contact. Maxwell watched him, sure that Lutz was defeated, no longer a threat. But Lutz was a crazed animal. He'd try it again, and when he did—

There was something about Lutz's expression. He didn't look defeated. He was leaning back against the car, his chest heaving. His face was twisted in a smirk.

From the pocket of his jacket he produced a pistol.

Maxwell cursed himself for being so careless. He should have expected it. Of course Lutz would have a gun. That was his style—to inflict maximum pain and suffering, go for the eyes and throat. If that didn't work, then he'd go for the gun.

It was a semiautomatic, a Beretta, Maxwell guessed,

probably 9 mm. Lutz's eyes stayed fixed on him as he raised the pistol.

Only three feet away. No place to hide, no way to escape.

"You . . . fucking . . . prima donna." Lutz's breath came in hoarse rasps. "I've been waiting fifteen years . . . to do this."

Maxwell flinched at the sharp crack of the pistol shot. In the same instant he felt the hot flash of pain through his upper right arm. He clutched his left hand over the wound, feeling a warm trickle of blood through a half-inch gash in his arm.

Lutz was smiling through his battered lips. "Just like old times . . . isn't it, glory hound?"

Maxwell saw the pistol rise again, aimed at his abdomen. He could make a run for it, but he dismissed the idea. It would just get him a bullet in the back instead of the front. He hoped Claire was already running, getting the hell away.

Maxwell tensed himself. He'd rush him. Maybe cause him to shoot wild. It was useless, but—

Another shot cracked the still air. He flinched, waiting for the inevitable pain. It didn't come. Dimly he was aware that the gunshot had a different sound, a more deep-throated bark. From a different direction.

He stood there, frozen, staring at Lutz. Something had changed. Lutz was still leaning against the car, but the pistol was lowered to his side.

His glasses. The left lens of Lutz's round spectacles had a starburst pattern with a neat hole in the center. Behind the shattered lens was a purplish cavity where Lutz's eyeball had been.

A crashing noise came from the brush behind Maxwell. He whirled to see a burly man in a police uniform charging through the thicket. He held a heavy revolver in his outstretched hands, keeping it pointed at Lutz.

It was the cop who had tried to chase him away from

Claire's interview back at the Mall. He stood over Lutz for a moment, keeping the pistol trained on him.

"I heard the shot and I—" He noticed Maxwell clutching his arm. "Uh, oh. How bad is it?"

"Could have been worse," said Maxwell. "I don't suppose you could have arrived a minute sooner?"

"No. You criticizing my marksmanship?"

"No, sir. Excellent shooting."

"Thank you." The cop holstered his pistol. "Are you sure you're okay?"

"I'll live." He looked at Lutz. His remaining eye was staring blindly into the evening sky. "Which is more than I can say for him."

"Who is he?"

"His name is Lutz." Maxwell hesitated, not sure how much to say, not sure if he knew the truth himself. "He's an engineer on a classified defense project."

"So why was he trying to whack you?"

"He was, ah, selling military secrets. I got in his way."

The cop's eyes narrowed. "Uh-huh. So who are you? Some kind of spy catcher?"

Before Maxwell could come up with an answer, they heard a commotion in the thicket behind them. They turned to see Claire wading through the high weeds, making her way down to them. Her elbow was bleeding, and she had grass stains on her skirt.

She went straight to Maxwell and hugged him so tightly it made his injured ribs ache. Then she saw his wounded arm.

"Oh, Sam, are you—"

"It's okay."

"I was so frightened, Sam. I thought you were—" She broke down sobbing, shaking uncontrollably. For nearly a minute no one spoke while Maxwell held her, stroking her hair, letting her cry.

Claire sniffed, wiped her eyes, then composed herself. She took a cautious look at Lutz's body, shuddered and immediately looked away. "Is he . . . somebody you know?"

He nodded, telling her with his eyes to leave it alone. She nodded back, but he knew Claire. She was a reporter. The questions would come later. Lots of them.

She turned to the cop and said, "I never heard your name, officer."

"It's Grover, ma'am. Sergeant Earl Grover."

"How did you happen to be here?"

"That guy." The cop nodded toward Lutz's corpse. "I've seen some mean-looking dudes in my time, but he took the prize. When I saw him back at the Mall, I could tell by his face that he meant to do you folks some harm. So I decided to follow him in the patrol car."

"You saved our lives." Claire reached out and took his hand. "How can we ever repay you?"

The cop looked embarrassed. He removed his cap and wiped his brow with his sleeve. He scuffed his shoe on the ground, then replanted the cap on his mat of wiry gray hair. "Well, Miss Phillips, uh, there is one small favor . . ."

"Yes?" She looked at him expectantly.

"Me and my wife, we both just love your TV show. Would it be possible, do you think, to get your autograph?" He produced a pad of paper and a ballpoint. "She'd just be tickled to death if . . ."

"It would be an honor, Sergeant."

Maxwell stood to the side while she wrote in the cop's notebook. Claire was a mess, he observed. Her hair was disheveled, hanging in sweaty strands over her forehead. Grass stains covered the backside of her skirt. A streak of dirt ran down the length of her fine, tapered nose.

He almost laughed, but the ache in his ribs cut it short. This was not the cool and composed Claire Phillips seen by millions on nightly television. She looked as if she'd been flung through a hedge at fifty miles an hour, rolled like a bowling pin down a hillside, then dumped in a briar patch.

Which, as he thought about it, was pretty much what had happened.

She caught him watching her and flashed a smile. Despite the stinging in his arm and the ache in his ribs, he felt a warm glow settle over him.

So much had happened these past weeks, some of it good, much of it bad. Seeing Claire Phillips smile at him, dirty face and all, made it okay. He had the sure sense that life was about to get better. Much better.

# CLASSIFIED MATERIAL—TOP SECRET

*Note: The enclosed evidence was recovered from the*
*personal effects of Dr. Raymond Lutz, suspect in*
*Groom Lake Research Facility security breach.*
*Access restricted to FBI Director, Deputy Director,*
*and designated members (list attached) of Counter-*
*Espionage Section, Las Vegas Field Office.*
                         */s/ Special Agent Frederic R. Swinford,*
                                           *Chief of Section.*

## Specifications: YF-27 Black Star

Contractors: Lockheed Martin/Northrop-Grumman
Power Plant: Two General Electric F-404-GE-F1D2
  engines
Wingspan: 41.7 (12.7 meters)
Length: 36.2 (11.0 meters)
Heigght: 9.15 feet (2.8 meters)
Speed: High subsonic
Ceiling: 50,000 feet (15,152 meters)
Take-off Weight (Typical): 46,000 pounds (15,263
  kilograms)
Range: 750 nautical miles (1390 kilometers)
Armament: Cannon, air-to-air missiles, internal bomb
  bay
Payload: 5,200 pounds (2359 kilograms)
Crew: Two
Unit Cost: Approximately $1.157 billion (2003 constant
  dollars)

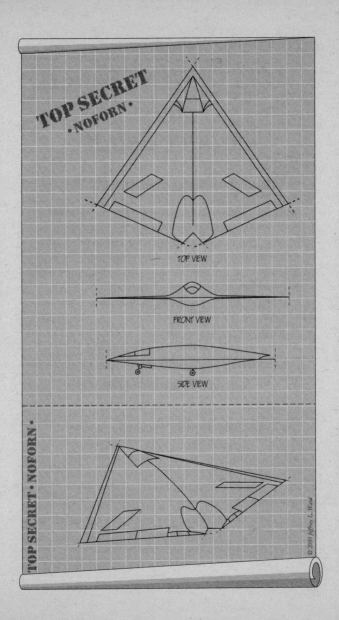

TOP SECRET
· NOFORN ·

TOP VIEW

FRONT VIEW

SIDE VIEW

TOP SECRET · NOFORN ·

© 2001 Jeffrey L. Ward

Brick Maxwell is back in

# *ACTS OF VENGEANCE*
## *by*
# *Robert Gandt*

When a motor launch carrying the *USS Ronald Reagan*'s top brass is attacked, the U.S. vows a swift reprisal. Enter skipper Brick Maxwell and his roadrunners—the jocks who fly the F/A-18 Super Hornets. Their mission: a deep air strike in northern Yemen. But their target—the commander who masterminded the attack—has laid a deadly trap for Maxwell and his fellow warriors...

0-451-20718-1

## A MILITARY WRITER WHO
## "TRANSPORTS READERS INTO THE COCKPIT."
### —*San Diego Union-Tribune*

Available wherever books are sold, or
to order call: 1-800-788-6262

# WITH HOSTILE INTENT
## by
## Robert Gandt

*The Gulf War has been over for ten years. It's up to pilots like Brick Maxwell and his glory-seeking commander Killer Delancey to keep the peace by a narrow margin—a margin called the No-Fly Zone. The Iraqi pilots like to buzz the borders—just close enough to shake up the U.S. Hornets' nest. And everyone knows these Hornets can't sting unless the Iraqis show hostile intent.*

"Aerial flight scenes more thrilling than a back-to-back showing of *Top Gun* and *Iron Eagle*, this red-hot piece of military fiction is certain to keep readers riveted."
**—Publishers Weekly**

0-451-20486-7

Available wherever books are sold, or
to order call: 1-800-788-6262